the Final Sacrament

JAMES FORRESTER

sourcebooks
landmark

Published by Sourcebooks Landmark, an imprint of Sourcebooks, Inc.
P.O. Box 4410, Naperville, Illinois 60567-4410
(630) 961-3900
Fax: (630) 961-2168
www.sourcebooks.com

Originally published in 2012 in the UK by Headline Review, an imprint of
Headline Publishing Group.

Library of Congress Cataloging-in-Publication Data

Forrester, James
  The final sacrament / James Forrester.
      p. cm.
  "Originally published in 2012 in the UK by Headline Review, an imprint of
Headline Publishing Group."
  (pbk. : alk. paper) 1. Great Britain—History—Elizabeth, 1558-1603—Fic-
tion. I. Title.
  PR6106.O7755F56 2013
  823'.92—dc23
                              2013017035

              Printed and bound in the United States of America.
                    VG 10 9 8 7 6 5 4 3 2 1

Also by James Forrester
Sacred Treason
The Roots of Betrayal

This book is dedicated to my uncle Gerald Harvey
with great respect and much love.

And the Lord said unto Satan, "Hast thou considered my servant Job, that there is none like him in the earth, a perfect and an upright man, one that feareth God, and escheweth evil?"

Then Satan answered the Lord, "Doth Job fear God for nought? Hast not Thou made an hedge about him, and about his house, and about all that he hath on every side? Thou hast blessed the work of his hands, and his substance is increased in the land. But put forth Thine hand now, and touch all that he hath, and he will curse Thee to thy face."

Job, Chapter I, verses 8–11

Prologue

~

Wednesday, February 19, 1567

The boy's shoulders were tense with cold as he stood on duty near the King's Gate. Although it was almost dark he could still see the high wall running along the left-hand side of the street. The flickering glow of a torch lit the nearest stretch of brickwork. On his right, the palace rooftops loomed black against the frozen sky. Two servants came out of the shadows, walking into the palace. One caught his eye but did not acknowledge him. Three weeks had passed since he had come to court, supposedly to finish his education, and already he was regretting his father's decision.

He rubbed his hands together, and blew on them. Tucking his fingers under his arms for warmth, he ran the toe of his shoe over the smooth surface of a small patch of ice. The air smelled of frozen earth, with traces of burning pitch from the torch. He felt hungry as well as cold. When he was older he would buy himself some gloves, he vowed, and never have to stand with such chilled fingers again.

He started to walk across the width of the gatehouse, whistling snatches of a tune he remembered his mother singing. He wondered if his parents were well. He thought of them talking about him back home in the village—about how proud they were that he was in the queen's service at Whitehall. That image sweetened him and saddened him at the same time, for he knew how shocked they would be if they could see the way he was treated. Dick Venner regularly shouted at him as if he were his master, even though Dick was only a year older. It was Dick who was responsible for teaching him the ways of the court, and it was Dick who had beaten him with a wooden rod when he did not bow low enough to a Polish nobleman.

The sound of horses approaching at speed broke into his reverie. A moment later he saw their shapes come out of the darkness. There were four of them, their eyes great black beads in the torchlight, their heads glistening with sweat. Two men dismounted, both out of breath; one took the reins of his own horse and those of the other man. The latter was short and thin. The boy noticed the fine cut of his clothes; but even by torchlight he could see that the riding cloak was splattered with mud, the black silk doublet beneath it similarly besmottered. The man had a crease between his eyes so that it seemed like he was permanently frowning. His head was covered by a black skull cap—but he was not that old, only in his midthirties. He seemed distant from his companions. The two who remained mounted bade him farewell and departed; his companion led the two horses away to the stables.

"Boy, take me to Sir William," the man said between short breaths.

Sir William. One of the first things that Dick Venner had taught him was that there was only one "Sir William." Other men might be called "Sir William this" or "Sir William that"—but there was only one plain "Sir William." He was Sir William Cecil, the queen's Principal Secretary, and the most powerful man in the government: in fact, the most powerful man in the whole *kingdom.* He was also reputed to be the most intelligent. Normally the boy would not have known where Sir William was, but on this occasion he did. Sir William had rushed to court two days ago, when terrible news had arrived from Scotland. The rumor among the other boys was that Lord Henry Stewart was dead. Many messages had been delivered since then—one almost every hour. Sir William had barely left the queen's side in all that time.

The boy bowed politely. "With all respect for your lordship, Sir William has given instructions that he is not to be disturbed, except for messengers coming from Sir William Drury."

The small man with the skull cap looked directly at him. "Do you not know who I am?"

The boy stood firm, though inside he was quaking. "No, my lord."

"My name is Francis Walsingham. Sir William is my patron. I have news for him that will turn his hair gray. Now..." Walsingham reached forward and grabbed the boy's ear in his right hand and twisted it. "Take me to him, without delay."

"Mr. Walsingham, sir, he has already received the news about the Scottish—"

"TAKE ME TO HIM!" shouted Walsingham, pushing him toward the side door that led through into the privy palace.

Tears came to the boy's eyes, but he blinked them back as he led the way along the covered corridor behind the Lord Chamberlain's house. The route took them into a whitewashed corridor, through another door, out into the cold night again, and along a path between the mass of irregular buildings that formed part of the old palace. They passed the busy figures of servants, gentlemen, cooks, and clerks in the near darkness. In some places torches lit the route. Where it was dark, he felt his way, running his hand along the wall. He led Walsingham through to the great court and along one side of it, and under an arch into the stone gallery that ran between the privy palace and the privy garden. Finally, after hearing the heels of Walsingham's nailed boots ringing out behind him against the flagstones of the gallery for about fifty yards, he came to the entrance, lit by a wall-mounted metal lantern. He took the ring of the door handle, turned it, and entered, and after closing it again behind the visitor, went up a flight of stairs to the first of a series of antechambers.

He had expected to see two guards here, men who should have been on duty outside the closed door to the privy palace. But there was no one. He turned to Walsingham to explain that he was not allowed beyond this door.

"Open it," snapped Walsingham before he could speak. The boy turned the handle and pushed the door open.

The chamber had large gilded beams in the high ceiling, with red and blue painted decoration between them. The colors were clearly visible in the light of six burning candles that hung in the center of the room. There were warming tapestries too, the figures on them like mysterious onlookers from the shadows. A fire was burning on a hearth—but there was no one to be seen.

"Lead on," ordered Walsingham, his boots thudding on the floorboards.

At that moment the door at the far end of the chamber opened and a man in purple ecclesiastical vestments entered. He looked surprised to see them.

"Your Grace," said Walsingham, bowing. The boy also bowed low.

"Walsingham, you cannot go in," said the bishop in a deep voice. "The queen and Sir William will not be disturbed. Besides..." He looked down at Walsingham's mud-spattered clothes and filthy shirt, "her majesty will not approve of your apparel."

"I am not looking for her approval. Sir William will not forgive me if I delay."

"But will the queen?" The bishop looked Walsingham in the eye. "Never mind. If it concerns Lord Henry Stewart, you're too late. They've already heard it. Drury has been sending letters at regular intervals, and others have hastened here directly from the north."

"My news is of quite another order. But what is this about Lord Henry? I have been away."

"A sorry tale, but one that I fear was inevitable. He has been murdered—killed in the grounds of his house at Edinburgh. No one knows who is guilty and it seems the Scots queen has not arrested anyone, which leaves the finger of blame pointing at the lady herself."

The boy looked at Walsingham. The crease between his eyes seemed even deeper.

"Then I have all the more reason to speak to Sir William immediately," he said.

"I have already told you—"

"Lead on," commanded Walsingham, putting his hand on the boy's shoulder. "Thank you for your information, my Lord Bishop; thank you."

He pushed the boy toward the oak door, and went through to the next antechamber. This was better lit. More tapestries, another hearth, a servant piling fresh logs on the embers. The beams were similarly gilded, with deep blue azurite decoration and stars in the depicted firmament. Two gentlemen ushers were at the far end. One was doing the rounds, lighting candles; the other was listening at the door. The one at the door turned, alarmed, when he heard Walsingham enter.

"Do you have nothing else to do?" asked Walsingham, his voice self-consciously loud. "Get you hence!"

The usher, astonished at Walsingham's arrogance, moved and Walsingham boldly marched up to the door and opened it. The boy stood back, nervous about intruding on the royal presence. He wanted to return to his cold station at the gate but Walsingham grabbed the scruff of his doublet and steered him through into the queen's great chamber.

It was a huge room, with a high, gilded ceiling and wide, gilded walls, as large as any room the boy had ever seen: as big as the largest great hall known to him. He wanted to look up and gaze at the spectacle, for the whole room seemed to be encased in gold, but his attention was commanded by the sudden lack of noise. More than thirty men were here, standing or sitting, and the talk had died abruptly. They all looked at Walsingham. Some were gentlemen and knights of the royal household; others were lords and courtiers identifiable as such by their lavish silk and satin doublets, fine ruffs, and embroidered hosen. Two or three men were wearing gowns, being men of the law or of the Church.

Walsingham did not stop but kept walking, still pushing the reluctant boy before him. Two men-at-arms looked startled, uncertain whether to stop them.

"Announce me," he said loudly. To a man-at-arms he ordered, "Open the door."

"Do you realize what you are doing?" called a man's voice nearby. Another shouted, "Show some respect!" A third man stepped in front of Walsingham and told him, "You cannot do this, Walsingham. We are all waiting our turn." A fourth man added, "The queen is with Sir William; she does not want to be disturbed."

A tall, exquisitely dressed lord approached; he was wearing a black velvet cape embroidered with gold and silver thread. "Look at the state of you, Walsingham," he chided. "For your own good, I suggest—"

"For your own good, my Lord Chamberlain, be out of my way," retorted Walsingham, pushing past those who stood between him and the next door.

"For *your* own good, you are still wearing your sword," snapped back the Lord Chamberlain, his eyes meeting Walsingham's.

Walsingham stopped, unbuckled his sword, and without a word, thrust it at the boy. Then, staring at the Lord Chamberlain, he spoke to the boy. "Go through that door and announce me. *Now!*" Again he ordered the guards, "Open those doors."

The guards looked at one another. One nodded. Together they opened the doors. The boy, scarcely able to control his nervousness, handed Walsingham's sword to one of them, who accepted it without a word. Then he tiptoed into the queen's chamber, with Walsingham hard behind him.

The room was dark and vast, almost as large as the great chamber, with just two points of light in the far corner. The boy found himself moving as if in a dream, entranced by the strange riches around him and the sense of being in a forbidden place, as if he were in Heaven or the Underworld. He wondered whether it was treason to enter the queen's presence without permission. He feared it was. Maybe he would be sent away in disgrace. A chamber clock chimed the sixth hour and he stopped outside; a great bell also chimed six times.

The two lights were a pair of candles on a standing iron frame beside the glowing fire. He could see two figures: a seated woman in a scarlet-colored gown, and a slightly portly gentleman who moved uneasily across the line of light. The boy was halted in his tracks by the man's voice.

"Who the devil comes here at this time? Who are you who dares come in here?"

The echo of the voice died away.

"Announce me," hissed Walsingham.

"My lord, your Royal Majesty," said the boy, who had never been allowed anywhere near the queen before, and had never been told how to address her or her Secretary. His courage failed him. He faltered, and fell silent. Dick Venner had advised him that, "If you see the queen, bury your forehead in the ground." He now followed that advice, and went down on both knees, and spoke to the floor. "Your Grace," he began, not knowing how to address a man more important than a bishop, "this is Mr. Walsingham, who…who comes on urgent business."

Walsingham stepped forward. "I would speak with you alone, Sir William."

The boy could not believe what he had just heard. Even though he knew little about etiquette, he understood that Walsingham had just shown huge disrespect to the queen. He heard a rustle of silk skirts and slow footsteps. He dared not move but remained pressed to the floor.

"What did you say?" said the queen. Her voice was that of a young woman but more clipped, controlled. The boy sensed Walsingham slowly go down on his knees.

"Your Majesty."

"Tell me, Mr. Walsingham, what business brings you here to speak to our Secretary who is with us in a private audience? We are conscious of your lack of tact, which is sadly habitual. We are all too well aware of your rudeness and your clumsiness of manner, but no matter what you think you are doing, we still expect you to act like a gentleman. Speak, or we will have you whipped out of this room."

The boy did not dare to move. He hoped the queen would overlook his presence. Maybe he could slide away when Walsingham left without her even noticing him?

"Your Majesty," said Walsingham, "given that I must speak, and urgently, would you permit me to tell Sir William the grave news—that Clarenceux is dead."

The queen turned to Cecil. "Clarenceux King of Arms? Is that news sufficient to disturb us?" She turned back to Walsingham. "Do you not realize the gravity of the situation? A prince of the royal blood has been murdered. Lord Henry Stewart might have been a drinker and a philanderer, not to mention a stupid young man, but he was of the royal blood, and now he is dead, killed by whom we know not. What is the death of a herald in comparison? Are you going to interrupt my privy meeting to tell me one of my cooks has died?"

She glared at him. Walsingham met her gaze, then bowed his head. "Ask Sir William, Your Majesty."

Cecil had regained his seat and was sitting, leaning forward, looking down at the infinite space before his mind's eye.

"Sir William?"

Cecil took his time. "Your Majesty, I have something to tell you. Something of even greater gravity than we have been discussing. But the boy should not hear it."

"What disrespect is this?" demanded Elizabeth. "Walsingham blasts in here—a man who is not even a peer of the realm and therefore has no right to demand access to my presence—he marches in here, without so much as a dignified word of greeting and *demands* to speak in private with *you*. His excuse, if you can call it that…" She did not finish the sentence but addressed Walsingham directly. "The heralds are members of my household, as well you know. If the death of one of them concerns anyone, it concerns me. Now speak quickly. You will explain this fully, here and now."

"The boy," repeated Sir William.

The boy was staring at the floor, not daring to look up. He heard the queen walk closer to him until the hem of her skirt was in front of him. "Do you have a face?" she asked.

He looked up and saw her bright red skirts trimmed with cloth-of-gold fanning out from her narrow waist in a wide circle around her ankles. "I am sorry, your Royal Majesty, I heartily beg you—"

"Shhh, enough," she said. "Get to your feet."

He rose as quickly as he could. He saw a very white cheek lit by the distant light of the candle, the rest of her face in silhouette. He noted the reddish-brown of her hair and the string of pearls around her neck. Her sleeves were close fitting to her arms.

"Let us walk to the door," she said.

He walked unsteadily, too conscious of himself. "Stop," she said gently. She came up close behind him, put her hands on his shoulders, and whispered in his ear, "You have done the right thing. It was wise to let Mr. Walsingham through. We know he has our best interests at heart. What is your name?"

"Cleaver," he said, not daring to turn around. "Ralph."

"We will remember you, clever Ralph. We will ask Mr. Edwards to give you a gift in the morning. Now go, and close the door behind you. Tell those outside we are not to be disturbed again."

Ralph turned awkwardly, keeping his head down, and bowed to the queen. He left the chamber.

Elizabeth waited until the door had closed. Then she took a deep breath and walked back to the glow of candlelight where Sir William was seated. Walsingham was now standing beside him, leaning over the gout-stricken man, whispering to him.

"Do not whisper, Mr. Walsingham," she said. "It is bad manners. Worse—you are likely to arouse our suspicions." She paused. "We are owed an explanation at the very least. We would also like to know what you are discussing so quietly. What news do you have for our Secretary—and therefore for us?"

"Your Majesty," said Walsingham, straightening himself, "I have to tell you that there was a fire at Thame Abbey on Monday, two days ago, which engulfed part of the monastic buildings. Mr. Clarenceux was inside. I watched, I waited, and I prayed—but he did not leave. My men and I attended the building all afternoon and all night, fighting the fire and preventing it from spreading, but no one inside was able to escape the flames. The heat was too intense. Yesterday morning the refectory was a mass of charred and smoking ruins. We searched the underground drains from the monastery and found a girl there, sheltering from the blaze, and she confirmed that Clarenceux had not left the building."

"You are sure?" asked Cecil. "Absolutely sure?"

Walsingham nodded. "There was no way out of it—no way anyone could have survived it. I had the place surrounded and my men could not get within thirty feet of the walls because of the heat."

The queen took her seat beside the fire. "We know that you and Mr. Clarenceux were not close. You and your men let our herald die. Is that not nearer the truth?"

"No, Your Majesty."

"You were there, guarding the abbey, by your own admission. You stopped Mr. Clarenceux escaping. It suits you well that he is dead, does it not?"

Walsingham stiffened. "No, Your Majesty, I most earnestly assure you that that is an unfounded accusation. It is true that Mr. Clarenceux and I had our differences, but in the manner of his death, he showed himself to be most loyal, and utterly undeserving of any criticism I have laid at his door over the years. I can explain my past view of him. In serving you, Your Majesty, I must presume some individuals are guilty until I know otherwise. I must sometimes be suspicious even where there is apparent loyalty. In trying a man in court we may presume him innocent, but in investigating a crime we must hold everyone potentially guilty. Mr. Clarenceux was a maverick, and came close to treason on more than one occasion, but ultimately he proved himself innocent."

"It is easy to apologize to the dead, Mr. Walsingham. And to see one of our servants do so is distasteful to us. We tend to wonder why the apologizer did not prove as apologetic in life." She addressed Sir William, seated in his red fur-trimmed robe. "Does your gout permit you to tell me whether we should trust Mr. Walsingham? You use it as an excuse to sit in our presence, but we will not let you keep treason from us."

Sir William chose his words carefully. "Your Majesty, Mr. Walsingham has my utmost trust, as you know from the number of his reports that I have laid before you. He is a man who loves nothing more than to uphold your security."

"In that case you will understand why we are most concerned that, when we asked him to explain the meaning of this herald's death, he said that we should ask you. What secrets are you keeping from us, Sir William? If he is trustworthy, what does he mean by telling us to ask you?"

Cecil sighed. He was used to laying traps for other people, and not used to being caught in one himself, especially not one set by a woman—and a younger woman at that, for Elizabeth was not yet thirty-four. But he was wise enough not to let it show and not to let himself be hastened into saying something he would later regret. He had not survived the calamitous accession of the late Catholic queen, Mary, and made his peace with her, witnessing the execution of his friend the duke of Northumberland and the duke's daughter, Lady Jane Grey, only to stumble now.

"Your Majesty, I must crave your indulgence, and your forbearance. I must speak about the succession."

"You know that we have forbidden that. To any of our subjects."

"I have not forgotten. I also know that you would rather face an unpalatable truth than have it kept from you."

"You know us well, Sir William. Speak truly."

"William Harley, the late Clarenceux King of Arms, was a man of the old religion. Like most people whose business harks back to the past, to heraldic achievements and rituals of ancestral respect, he did not wish to break with Rome. Nor did he wish to see the churches desecrated and their monuments defaced, the tombs uprooted and the monasteries and chantries demolished, their ancient manuscripts burned—"

"Sir William, we must caution you. We are the Supreme Governor of the Church and we intend to exercise our rights in that capacity as freely as our father did. We will stand by those Acts by which corrupt monastic houses were abolished. They were passed for the good of the soul of the kingdom."

"Your Majesty, I was merely illustrating what Mr. Clarenceux felt in his heart. I was not moralizing. You need to understand that even a royal officer might be nostalgic, and loyal to other things as well as your royal person. And please, if I may, let me speak without another warning as to the succession. There are no other men in this realm of yours who have worked so assiduously for your safety as the two of us here now. Mr. Clarenceux has long been the subject of our attentions in this regard—for more than three years, in fact."

The queen looked at the figure of Walsingham in his filthy clothes, standing not far from Cecil's chair, then back at Cecil. "Very well, go on."

"Thank you, Your Majesty. The date to which I refer was in December in the sixth year of your reign, 1563. An old man called Henry Machyn, a merchant taylor living in the parish of Little Trinity, gave Mr. Clarenceux a chronicle. That chronicle contained the key to finding a document which touched upon the matter of your succession. To be specific, the document in question relates to the circumstances of your birth. It is a marriage agreement between your mother, the late Queen Anne, and Lord Henry Percy, earl of Northumberland—"

The queen could not contain herself but spoke with passion. "My mother *never* married Lord Percy!" She rose to her feet. "What you are describing is nothing more than a rumor which came to my father's ears. Do not presume to tell me I should believe such lies."

Cecil was alarmed by her sudden use of the first person. "Your Majesty," he said gently, "I suspect you have never been told the full circumstances of your mother's death."

Elizabeth stared at him. She saw the beard, the expression of warmth in his eyes, and recognized the integrity of a loyal subject. She resumed her seat.

"Thank you, Your Majesty. You need to understand this. Originally your father decided to divorce your mother, not to have her tried for treason. I myself have copies of the letters sent home by the Ambassador of the Holy Roman Emperor at the time, Eustace Chapuys, who was very well informed. I also heard this from those who were at court at the time. Some of them are still alive—it was only a little more than thirty years ago. The grounds that your father chose for the divorce were that your mother had previously agreed a marriage with Lord Percy."

"No!" exclaimed the queen, but her protest was one of unwilling belief, not disbelief.

Cecil went on. "The information came from your father himself. There is independent verification too. In 1527, when your father arranged his marriage to your mother, the permission from the Roman pontiff carried a special provision. It stated that the marriage would be valid even if she had previously conducted a betrothal with another man. The reason for that provision was that she had confessed to your father that that was exactly the case. She had been betrothed to another man. Therefore the pontiff agreed to sanction your parents' marriage with just one condition."

"One condition?" repeated Elizabeth. "Tell me."

"That the earlier marriage had not been consummated."

Elizabeth sat motionless, thinking. Both men watched her intently. She rose to her feet and walked toward the fire. "You are now going to tell me that my father discovered that the earlier marriage had been consummated."

"He found many people ready to attest that it had been. But you also need to know what happened next. When your father declared that he would divorce your mother on the grounds that she had been previously married—which would, in law, have been a valid reason for divorce—he made a terrible mistake. For no one had considered you, Your Majesty. The law as widely understood and articulated in an Act of 1484, *Titulis Regis*, rendered the situation thus: because your parents had both been married before to other partners, and because they had subsequently married in *secret*, you would be—well, you do not need me to speak the word."

"Say it, Sir William. Say it as cruelly as you can. 'Your parents' marriage was void.' Tell me I am a bastard. Commit that treason—if you dare! Remind me that my father killed my mother for incest and adultery. My father severed my mother's head from her body. Do you not see that I will burn with the memory of that fact every day of my life? It is as if my father cut me in two as well. I will never be whole."

Cecil took his time. "I am deeply sorry, Your Majesty, but I have to—"

"And another thing," said the queen. "*Titulis Regis* was repealed. It has been cut from the statute books. No trace of it exists any longer, except in certain old chronicles that we have yet to destroy. It does not apply."

"Your Majesty," replied Cecil, "it is not the Act of Parliament itself that is crucial but the law that that Act clarified. Edward the Fifth was deposed because of illegitimacy even before the Act was passed. But you have not understood my main point. When it became apparent that the king was making public the prior matrimonial alliance of your mother, together with the consummation, lawyers hastened to give him advice. They told him that he should not do this. By that course of action, they informed him, he would render you illegitimate and incapable of occupying the throne. That would leave your Catholic sister, Mary, as the sole potential heir to the throne. They advised him to find another way to end the marriage, namely those charges for which your mother was eventually tried. The king, your father, was given a simple choice: to let your mother live in a divorced state and have you declared the child of an illegal union; or to concoct heinous and false charges against your mother and execute her for treason, thereby allowing you to remain a lawfully conceived daughter of the king."

"Lies!" shouted Elizabeth. "Though it pains me to recall the fact, my father had me declared a bastard anyway, at the time of my mother's death. If he contrived to have her executed to save me, why then kill my mother *and* bastardize me?"

Cecil looked at Walsingham. He took a deep breath. "Your Majesty, I am bound to speak the truth to you. There were those at court who wanted your mother disposed of and who wanted the king to recognize your Catholic sister as your father's only legitimate offspring. Thomas Cromwell in particular hoped that, by making your parents' marriage null and void, he would force your father to re-legitimize your sister Mary, and make her his heir. Cromwell cited certain just and lawful impediments at the time of your parents' marriage. He meant, of course, the marriage of Lord Percy and your mother. It makes no sense, but your mother was killed for adultery which, according to Cromwell, she could not have committed, not being properly married to your father."

Elizabeth brooded. Neither Cecil nor Walsingham could see her face. They heard her slow footsteps as she moved away, and heard the rustling of her dress.

They waited.

When she spoke, tears were heard in her voice. "I never believed the lies they said about my mother. I always believed my father was misled, and that he killed my mother as a result of his fear, his gullibility. You cannot know what it is like—to fear all the time, *all* the time—never to know who is plotting against you until it is too late. My father's offense was one of ignorance, I believed, not malice to my mother. But I often wondered why she forgave him on her deathbed, for everyone tells me that she did. At her trial she denied every charge laid against her and then, just three days afterward, as she faced death, she prayed for my father—her killer—and called him a gentle prince, and forgave him, and urged no one to speak against her fate. She said her death was lawful—even though she knew that the charges against her were lies and contrary to her plea." Elizabeth paused and wiped her face again. "And he betrayed her anyway." She made the sign of the cross. "Now I can see. She was told, wasn't she? She did it for me. She reconciled herself to my father at her execution, for my sake. She pretended that all those accusations were true—to save me."

"That is my understanding, Your Majesty," answered Cecil quietly. "Your mother's sacrifice was the last thing left to her. Through her death, she saw she could save you. And even though Cromwell betrayed her, she did save you. Everything would have turned out as she hoped, had it not been for one problem. Despite her final speech and confession, there was documentary proof of her previous marriage. It passed from Lord Percy at his death to the man who conducted his funeral, Henry Machyn, an ordinary man. Machyn gave the document to Mr. Clarenceux. That is the problem we face now. At the time of his death, Mr. Clarenceux had possession of that proof."

Elizabeth's mood shifted instantly from one of regret and sadness for her mother to one of cold alarm. "Then where is it now?"

Cecil looked at Walsingham. "I too would very much like to know."

Walsingham looked reluctant to speak. But he had no choice.

"Mr. Clarenceux went to Thame Abbey two days ago supposedly to hand the document over to a Catholic conspirator. As Sir William is aware, he gave us prior warning. I was greatly alarmed and had a large number of men standing guard. But as I watched, the building burst into flames—with Clarenceux and his Catholic contacts inside. There was nothing we could do. There were explosions. We formed a chain to bring water from the fishponds to fight the blaze, but the refectory and everything inside it was lost in the intense heat. It was when I heard the explosions that I knew that the fire was not accidental. Clarenceux had led his contacts there to destroy them. The girl whom we found confirmed these things."

Elizabeth was silent. "And the document? The supposed proof?"

"Mr. Clarenceux certainly took it into the abbey. But there were two other people with him, besides the girl: a gentleman by the name of John Greystoke and a woman, whom the girl informed me was called Joan Hellier. Both must have perished in the flames. I presume the document was destroyed with them."

"Presumption is not enough, Mr. Walsingham."

Sir William broke the uneasy silence that followed, shifting in his chair and wincing with the pain in his foot. "I can say nothing about the document but I can say something about the late Mr. Clarenceux. He may have been a supporter of the old religion, but he was not a revolutionary. He did not want to use that document to further the Catholic cause. If that had been his plan, he could certainly have done so to good effect. But he refused. He came to me recently; he was distraught. Seeing the danger, I insisted that he surrender the document to me rather than risk it falling into his enemies' hands. He would not. I told him he had no other option but to bring the business to a final conclusion. It now appears that he has done exactly that. That is why I too presume he took the document into the fire with him."

Walsingham spoke. "A message was taken to Clarenceux in the abbey by the girl just before the fire. It was a date, the thirtieth of June last year—but what it signifies, I do not know."

The logs on the hearth crackled. "We need to know," Elizabeth said, walking around the back of Cecil's seat. "We want to know everything—what happened, whether this man was loyal or a traitor. We must know if that document has been destroyed. Interrogate anyone who had dealings with him—anyone to whom he might have slipped it before he climbed onto his heretical pyre."

"Your Majesty, it will be done," said Walsingham, looking at Cecil. "To that end I shall now take my leave of you, with Your Majesty's permission."

"You have it."

Walsingham bowed and left the chamber.

The sound of the door closing echoed away. Elizabeth walked back to the fire. "We see that he remembers his manners when taking his leave." She resumed her seat and sat in thought. "Sir William, it is not just the document we need to know about. It is the truth—the whole truth. We feel naked. No matter what clothes we use to adorn this royal body, the truth makes us feel that we are open to the view of all our subjects. 'The queen is this, the queen is that.' We cannot escape their suspicions, their name-calling, their disrespect. We can pretend that lies do not touch the woman inside us, but the truth— the truth strips us of all defenses and leaves us exposed. If this document is indeed reflective of what happened all those years ago, and we are illegitimate, then we have no right to rule. The truth in time will overwhelm us, and we will be destroyed, clinging to our crown for the sake of our own personal safety. But we do not believe it. We believe we have a right to rule, and we believe that our rule—though it be sometimes affected by our weaknesses—is that of God, and that people trust us to rule in the eyes of God. You must find out whether our self-belief is justified or not."

"You are England's ordained queen; no one can doubt that," Sir William replied carefully. "Moreover, you are your father's only surviving child. No one can doubt your right to rule—neither for dynastic reasons nor in the name of God."

"Every Catholic in England doubts it. Our cousin Mary doubts it. Her late husband Lord Henry Stewart doubted it."

"Ah, yes. Lord Henry. We will need to send someone to the Tower to tell his mother. My wife knows her. I will ask her to perform that duty."

Elizabeth approached Cecil. "You are avoiding our question, Sir William. Perhaps we did not express it sufficiently clearly. Tell us, in truth, did our mother marry Lord Percy?"

Sir William felt as if he had been struck in the chest. Words failed him. He tried to force himself to tell the queen what she yearned to hear, but then he looked up at her and could not bring himself to lie.

"I believe so."

Elizabeth was silent for some seconds. "It exposes our humanity, does it not?"

"I do not know what you mean."

Elizabeth closed her eyes. "It reveals our fears and anxieties so clearly, and so fully. A political life is one of an intensified conscience, in which all the worries of the painful day and the tumult of the soul are thrown together, and we have to exist between them, from moment to moment. We despair, Sir William. A man can be a king in every way but a woman who is expected to perform the functions of a king…no. She has to bear the twin weights of her womanhood and the crown which she is not physically capable of bearing. She has to be ruthless where a man would be ruthless, strong-minded where a king would be stern—and yet she has to be a woman too. A king can have children and remarry if his wife dies in childbed, but can a queen make that same reckless decision? We think not. That is why we despair."

"Your Majesty, do not despair. On your shoulders England's salvation rests. If you despair, then England despairs. In churches they will despair of the righteousness of their faith. At sea, mariners will despair of the safety of their vessels. Merchants will despair of the fairness of their trade. I cannot counsel you as to what passed between your mother and Lord Percy. However, I do know this. Your reign is founded on hope, not despair. You are the hope of the kingdom—and without you and your faith in yourself as well as in God, England will lose its way."

"Then let us hope that that part of the past which suddenly causes us so much grief and doubt was consumed in the flames with Mr. Clarenceux. For, as we surmise, if it still exists, it is no longer in his hands, but in those of a Catholic rebel. And then our private doubts will become public fears, and we will be called an impostor queen—without just right or divine grace. And then…" She paused and looked at Cecil in the candlelight. "Then our father's destruction of our mother will have been nothing but selfishness—the cruel machinations of his ministers—and her self-sacrifice will have been in vain."

"Your Majesty…" Cecil began, instinctively trying to reassure her. But he had nothing more to say. She had just said it all.

1

Two months earlier
Thursday, December 19, 1566

William Harley, Clarenceux King of Arms, sat at the table in his second-floor chamber, carefully cutting a goose quill. He fumbled as he tried to hold the feather steady, his fingers stiff with cold. Every so often, he looked out the window at the house on the other side of Fleet Street, watching for movement. The uneven quarrels of glass slightly distorted his view, but by shifting his position he could recognize the men coming and going. That house was a three-story, timber-framed building, not unlike his own, but in the middle of a row rather than at the end of one, and southfacing. It had a window in the gable facing the street—very similar to the window he was looking out of, except that it was unglazed. Even though it was sunny today, the shutters were not wholly open. They never were. They seemed never to be wholly closed either. If you compared it with the houses to the left and right, both of which were occupied by couples, there was a marked difference in the pattern of their opening and closing. This was what had alerted Clarenceux four months ago.

Since then he had kept a record of the people who came and

went from the house. They were almost all men. A woman brought two pails of water once a week on a yoke over her shoulders and stayed for about two hours each time. No other woman ever entered the building—not even as the companion of one of the men who lived there. Once he had seen his own stable boy, Nick, go into the house. That had greatly alarmed him. On being questioned, Nick had pleaded innocence—saying that he went there simply to borrow a hand saw. Clarenceux had banished him from the house, forcing him to sleep above the stables, and had prohibited him from speaking to the men again. He had no doubt that they were watching him, and that they were working for Francis Walsingham.

Despite there being a small fire in the hearth, he could still see the clouds his breath made in the cold air. He breathed on his fingers to warm them, then pulled out a sheet of paper hidden under a heavy leather-bound volume on the corner of the table. He dipped the newly cut quill into an open inkwell and marked two short downward strokes on the paper, one under a column marked "GrB" for "Greybeard" and the other under a column marked "ShF" representing the shortest of the men who came and went regularly and who had fair hair. He put the date in the right-hand column and waited. A few minutes later, the unpleasant old man who called himself Tom Green, and whom he had once encountered, left the building and started walking back east toward the city gate. Clarenceux turned the previous day's line for "Tom Green" into a cross. He watched. No one else left. That meant there were three of Walsingham's men in the house for the moment.

Clarenceux set down his quill. For four months it had been just one man changing stations on an irregular basis; for the last three weeks it had been two, every day. Something had happened. If the windows revealed that these men were watching him, their new pattern of attendance revealed that Walsingham was employing a different strategy, and that meant a different objective or different circumstances.

The door of the house just to the right opened and Mistress Knott stepped out. Her maidservant came with her, holding a wooden pail. While the maidservant started to clean the two steps up to the front door, Mistress Knott walked to the city with a scarf around her head and a basket under her arm. The Knotts were a Dutch couple originally called Annoot; they had come to London as refugees the previous year, fleeing the Spanish persecution of Protestants under the duke of Alva. Her husband was a physician of some fame. At first he had had great difficulty finding work, due to his lack of a license to practice in England, but things were better for them now. Mr. Knott had treated enough prominent people with sufficient success that his business and status were assured. Clarenceux had helped, finding out for himself how efficacious the Dutch physician's remedies and cures could be and recommending "Mr. Knott" to his friends and acquaintances.

In the city, the bell of St. Martin le Grand began to ring nine o'clock. Then another chimed. A moment later, all the city churches began to ring the hour. Nearby, the great bell of St. Bride's Church also clanged out. Clarenceux went back to studying the manuscript volume he was reading: the chronicle of Henry of Abingdon, which had been lent to him by Sir Richard Wenman. This was, as far as Sir Richard knew, the sole surviving manuscript. Clarenceux was sure Sir Richard was right; he had never heard of another copy. That it was unique was not surprising: Henry was a tedious writer, more concerned with ecclesiastical doctrine than people's lives. Nothing gave him greater pleasure, it seemed, than recording at length the proceedings of the church council at Constance, which he had attended from 1415 to 1417. However, the chronicle also contained a wealth of information about the Lollard knights—the ardent gentlemen supporters of the church reformer, John Wyclif. Many Lollards had been imprisoned for heresy and some had been burned at the stake. Clarenceux could not help but reflect on the comparison with his own time, having seen, heard, and smelled the terrifying burnings of Protestant Christians under Queen Mary, just ten years ago.

Clarenceux was not reading Henry of Abingdon for the history of Lollardy, however. It was because he had been forced by his superior, Sir Gilbert Dethick, Garter King of Arms, to undertake a visitation of Oxfordshire after Christmas. This would entail an inspection of the rights of all the gentlemen in that country who claimed to be esquires: to determine whether or not they truly were entitled to bear a coat of arms. To establish that right, they needed to be able to demonstrate that they were descended from a knight. Henry of Abingdon had been a Warden of Merton College in Oxford; hence many of his Lollard knights came from Oxfordshire, presumably inspired by followers of Wyclif, who had been a teacher at the university.

Out of the corner of his eye, he saw the door to the spies' house open. A tall, thin man with long hair left. Clarenceux marked the "ThLH" column of his paper accordingly, and returned to his chronicle.

Until the ringing of the next hour he made himself read the neat lines of Latin, his eyes skipping past justifications for the Church claiming certain revenues and fees, and the responsibilities of absent rectors and vicars to their parishioners; he was looking for names of prominent men. He had already found references to two marriages of Lollard knights, by which he could determine the legitimacy of a number of claimants to coats of arms. A salacious story about a knight and his retinue seeking accommodation at a nunnery and taking a fancy to one of the nuns, then abducting her and leaving her pregnant, was equally useful: illegitimacy ruled against inheriting a coat of arms. The various stories of how Lollards evaded their pursuers amused him. They had made use of natural features of the landscape: hiding in the boughs of trees in summer, above their pursuers' heads, or under the surface of a river, breathing through a hollow pipe or bundle of reeds while a cap floated downstream, distracting the chasing men.

Between every passage his attention flicked across to the spies' house.

When the hour was up, he placed a smooth horn ruler between the pages of the chronicle and closed it. He stood up and took off the thick robe he usually wore in his study in winter, and hung it on a peg projecting from a beam. Opening the door, he went down the wooden steps to the hall on the first floor, hearing the boards creaking beneath his weight. The staircase was old and needed replacing; the whole front of the building was somewhat warped and decrepit. He did not mind it that way; old things delighted him. The luxury items he had bought for the house after it was damaged by Francis Walsingham's men three years earlier were mostly those that his wife, Awdrey, had demanded. The exception was the glass in the front windows: this was a rarity in any house, let alone one as old as this. It dated back to his first days as Clarenceux, when signs of ostentation had been important to him. These days he saved his money. He did not know when but he was sure that, sooner or later, there would be reason to call upon it. Too many people knew that he was the man who had once had possession of Lord Percy's marriage agreement. The fact that it was no longer in his house meant nothing. He was the way to it. One day, he might have to flee with his family—might find his house set alight. That was what Walsingham's spies were doing now: keeping watch on him and his house lest anyone take action to seize the chronicle. Hence his concern that the number of around-the-clock watchmen had increased.

Standing at the bottom of the stairs to his study, he gently closed the old wooden door. At the back of the house one of his daughters shrieked with laughter and he heard the maidservant, Joan, telling her to give something back. He smelled the oak wood burning slowly on the hearth, at the end of the hall. There were two chests, one on either side of the fireplace, with rich red carpets draped over them. Three new painted cloths that Awdrey had asked him to buy hung on the walls. In the middle of the hall was an oak refectory table that he had bought from a merchant who had taken it from the Dominican Friary at the time of the Dissolution. A small square looking glass and a new painting of Awdrey hung on either side of the door that led to the main staircase, which in turn led down to the front door. The looking glass was not as lavish as the beautiful round mirror he had once owned, and which Walsingham's men had smashed—but then, he thought, there was less pleasure in looking at himself now. In two years' time he would be fifty. Would he last those two extra years? He hoped so—he had his beautiful young wife to keep him going—but he knew he was not his former self. His hair was turning gray and he constantly felt tired. And there was something in his tiredness that told him he could no longer outrun his enemies. His right hip ached regularly. That was one of the reasons why he had started going to Giacomo Girolamo's school of defense at the Belle Savage Inn.

He looked to his right. Here, overlooking the street, was the main window. Beside it stood his elm table, with a single silver candlestick. He ran his fingers along the oval rim of the tabletop. As a boy he had played with carved wooden soldiers on its surface, and had rolled glass beads over the ridges formed by the grain of the wood. He had learned to read sitting at it, and regularly he and his brother Thomas had eaten off it, when their parents had entertained guests at their main table. Along with his father's old sword, it was one of the few family possessions that had survived the destruction of his house by Walsingham's men. At ten years of age he had been beaten by his father for carving his name on it and had had to file away the offending letters. The file marks were still there, patinated now. One day their story would be lost. Most tables were rectangular, and a very few were round. *His* table was oval. It was unusual, well-made, solid, and dependable—all the things he approved of. There was nothing frivolous about it. It was more than a little like him.

He heard the running of his daughters' feet down the staircase at the back of the hall and turned as Annie ran toward him. Her shoulder-length brown hair bounced as she ran, then hung down, framing the handsomeness of her face. She was in her eighth year now, and showing every sign of a sharp, contrary intelligence, like her father. Her younger sister, Mildred, who followed her as fast as her short legs would allow, had just passed her fourth birthday. She was tiny, very pretty, and very outgoing. Both girls were wearing plain woolen cream dresses and soft leather shoes. Mildred had the finest fair hair, like her mother, and was clutching a straw doll wearing a similar dress to her own. Joan followed them, folding her arms as she watched from the doorway at the end of the hall. Clarenceux noticed Awdrey behind her.

Annie rushed out her message in a torrent, looking up at her father with great blue eyes full of excitement. "We were upstairs playing with Mildred's doll Elizabeth and she said that she loved her doll Elizabeth more than anyone else in the world except for Mam, and

Mam heard us talking and said, 'What about your father? Don't you love him just as much?' And Mildred said she did love her dad, and so Mam said we should tell you we love you when you come downstairs because she said you would like to know that we do."

"I love you," said Mildred, looking up at her father.

Clarenceux smiled and knelt down to hold both girls. He stroked Mildred's cheek. "That's good to hear. And I'm glad you love your mother more than your doll."

"I love *you* more than my Elizabeth as well," Mildred said happily. Annie, in high spirits, echoed her little sister. "I love *you* more than...capon."

"More than green cheese!" exclaimed Mildred.

"Enough," Clarenceux said. "I feel much loved…"

"More than warm milk," shouted Annie.

"Enough," he repeated, getting back to his feet.

"More than God!" said Mildred.

Clarenceux shook his head. "Mildred, no. No. You must not say such things. You cannot love me more than God."

"But I do."

Annie looked at him disapprovingly. "But she is telling the truth, and you say we should always tell the truth."

Clarenceux saw the disappointment in Mildred's eyes and the crossness in her sister's. Mildred was uncertain, waiting anxiously for a kind word from him. He knelt down again and put an arm around her, hugging her. He put an arm around Annie too, and spoke to both of them. "You must love God most of all. For we pray that God looks kindly on us, do we not?"

Mildred nodded, her blond locks bobbing as she did so, her eyes moist.

Clarenceux wiped away a tear running down the little girl's cheek and kissed her. He stood again and patted Annie on her head. Then he looked at Awdrey. "I am going out."

"Where?"

He said nothing.

"William, it is very early to be going to swordsmanship. Too early."

Still he said nothing. He walked toward the door through to the main staircase.

"Tell me you are not going to watch Sir John," she said, coming after him. "Promise me you will not go!"

Clarenceux paused in the doorway. "I am not going to let them hang him with no one but jeering crowds there to see him. He was a good priest to both my mother and my brother. He stood by them while they were dying. He gave them the last rites. I want him at least to know there are people who will always appreciate the good he has done in this world before he goes to the next."

Awdrey put one arm around his shoulders and the other hand she placed on his chest. "William, it is too dangerous. Those people across the street, do you not think they will see you? They will know where you are going. Walsingham is probably waiting at this very moment for you to step outside—to arrest you for trying to protect a man he has condemned as a traitor."

He looked at her and saw the fear in her blue eyes. He gently moved a loose strand of golden hair away from her face. "Awdrey, Sir John is my friend in God. I will not let him go to his death without someone beside him. No more than I would you."

He removed her hand from his chest, kissed it, and stepped out onto the staircase. He descended fast, determined not to look back. At the bottom he picked up his long black cloak from the peg nearest to the door and nodded to his old manservant, Thomas, who had heard his master's footsteps but was too late to reach the front door. Thomas was left standing, watching, as Clarenceux strode out of the house, leaving the door open behind him.

Thomas closed it. A child's cry made him look up. In the hall, he found Awdrey crouched on the floor holding Mildred, who was crying. She had dropped her doll and Clarenceux had inadvertently stepped on it as he had left. Annie was standing there too, uncertain what to do.

"He's allowing it to take him over," Awdrey said, looking at Thomas. "I don't know what to say to him. He is living every moment as if he's fighting, scared. He cannot hold a conversation without bringing it back to that accursed document. I wish he would just destroy it and be done with it."

Thomas tactfully waited until an opportune moment came. "He says that he *has* destroyed it, Mistress Harley."

Awdrey cradled Mildred all the more. "You don't believe that, Thomas, do you? That document is like a bad conscience, eating away at him, making him do things that are dangerous."

"Mistress Harley, would it be reassuring if I followed Mr. Clarenceux? We know where he is going."

"Yes, Thomas. Yes, it would. Please. Go with God."

2

Mary Vardine was forty-three years of age and near death. The wounds from the whip on her bare back stung terribly; the gashes were as deep as the thickness of a finger and they would probably never heal. She lay in the dim corner of the jail, starving and frozen on the cold earth floor. Pieces of muddy straw had stuck to the congealed blood on her back She had nothing covering her but the remains of her torn smock. The stench of urine around her was rank, and she had fouled herself. In the last four days she had had nothing to eat but only three slices of stale bread.

She coughed and tried to spit, but there was no phlegm. She closed her eyes and opened them again; all she could see was a gray haze of moving shapes. She heard the clink of a key and the creak of the cage door opening. Two of the shapes approached, and she heard the voices of two younger women prisoners trying to attract the attention of the jailers. One of them was a kindly young tailor's wife who had made sure that Mary had been given a piece of bread one day. If Mary had had the energy, she might have hoped that the warden would choose to lie with her. But in truth she was too tired even to hope anymore. They were all in this hole because they had been accused of felonies; in all likelihood they would be sentenced to be killed on the next visit of the assize judges. For the younger women, there remained the one hope that they could become pregnant before that day, so they could plead their bellies. It was not so much to prostitute themselves that the women called to the guards—it was to find a man who was ready to show pity to them. There was no other transaction except the sexual act, unless the barbarities perpetrated on some of the women by the more vicious jailers counted as a form of payment, by the women.

Mary was too old to plead her belly; the court would not believe her if she did. Besides, she was guilty, and in a cell full of desperate women. Twenty years ago she had found herself in prison for the theft of a silver-rimmed purse from a market stall. The penalty would have been hanging, had she not pleaded her belly. On that occasion she had been in a mixed cell, and among the male prisoners was a young man due to hang the next day; she had let him lie with her all night. After he had been killed, many others had taken his place, whether or not she wanted them to. All she knew about the father of her third daughter was that he had been a criminal. When the girl was born, Mary had been taken out of the cell to give birth in the warden's house; her brother's wife had acted as the midwife and managed to arrange her escape while only women were allowed into the birth chamber, before the clearing up was complete. Such a strategy was now beyond her. Even if her age had not been against her—even if she had not been in such a pitiful state—no one would come to her aid in another nine months. Her brother was dead and so was his wife. Besides, she suspected the jailers here wanted her to face trial and be put to death. She was not facing the noose but the punishment of being burned at the stake—high entertainment in many people's eyes. In her ecstasy after stabbing her husband, she had cried with relief and told many people what she had done. She was not without supporters—a number of women quietly sympathized with her plight and were glad for her—but someone had told someone who in turn had told other men. The High Constable had ordered her to be arrested, on penalty of a heavy fine to be paid by the whole parish. That was how she had been whipped and now faced death by burning: for ridding the world of a vicious drunk, a bully and an abuser of his own stepdaughters.

Mary did not understand why the jailers did not pick either of the women for fornication but came toward her.

"Mary Vardine?" one asked, nudging her arm with his boot.

She did not answer. Somewhere beyond the bars, in another building, was a courtroom, and in that courtroom the evil of her crime would be announced, and her sentence officially spat out. They said that people normally lived to feel the pain even after the fat of their own feet had started to drip into the flames. Death was the only release. It would be better that she just died here, in this cell, of cold and hunger. She did not regret what she had done, and she would stab her husband over and over again if she had to. She might not have saved her daughters from all the indignities and sufferings of life, but she had put a permanent end to one of them.

The second jailer came over to where she lay and, together with the first, they lifted her to her feet. She made no attempt to stand, so they dragged her out of the cage and down the corridor to a chamber where a gentleman, Mr. Philips, was waiting to see her. There they tried to place her on a bench. She blinked in the light, then kept her eyes closed and collapsed onto her side.

"This is the woman?" asked Mr. Philips, looking down with disgust at her bloodied skin and filthy smock.

"It is," replied the first jailer. "She stinks as rotten as her soul. She boasted about her crime. He was found in his own yard, stabbed in a frenzy. The constable had her whipped."

Philips stretched out a gloved hand and lifted one of Mary's eyelids with his thumb. She opened her eyes but said nothing. He withdrew his hand. "Lord Shrewsbury wants her spared," he said.

"If that is Lord Shrewsbury's will," said the first jailer, "then we must obey, but the London justices surely won't like it that he's taken so many women now from an appointment with the Devil."

Philips took off his glove and reached into a pocket. "Be that as it may, I have my orders and now you have yours." He handed each of the men two silver coins. "Take her to Mistress Haig's house; there she can be cleaned up and fed. After that, your custodial duty will be done. Mistress Haig's man will see to the rest, as before."

"Mr. Philips," said the second jailer, whose lank hair fell across his face, "why does Lord Shrewsbury choose this woman? There are many who are hoping to see her burn—and many women far more deserving of compassion. We could easily find Lord Shrewsbury a younger and better-looking woman."

Philips shook his head. "It is his old aunt's decision. Lord Shrewsbury instructed me to follow the orders of Lady Percy's steward, Benedict Richardson, in all things concerning this jail and his rights herein. As you know, Lord Shrewsbury has the power of life and death over convicted felons—an ancient prerogative. What I tell you is simply what Mr. Richardson has decided on behalf of Lady Percy. They are the ones exercising judgment, not Lord Shrewsbury."

3

Clarenceux walked fast, managing the pain in his hip as best he could. He felt conscious of his awkward gait. From Fleet Street he turned left into Shoe Lane, with the smells of smoke from the morning's fires and fresh horse dung in his nostrils. There were only a few white clouds in the blue sky, the mildest of breezes; despite the sharp cold, it was like a spring day. A long barnlike building on the west side of the street was being pulled down for new housing on the site. Several trees from the garden had also been cut and were being sawn up by workers who had half-blocked the road with their wagon. The men outside the cockpit were preparing for the afternoon's entertainment, taking in birds in wooden cages from carts parked there and chalking up prices on a board. Clarenceux passed old houses with low beams and shutters wide open, women carrying baskets, servants cleaning steps, and men setting about their work. At Holborn, on the corner with Fetter Lane, beneath the tower of St. Andrew's Church, he turned to watch the people and carts crossing the Fleet at Holborn Bridge.

A friend of his wife's greeted him jovially with a "Good morrow to you, Mr. Harley," and he acknowledged her with a nod, and a smile; but he turned slightly, indicating that he did not wish to be engaged in conversation. Even after she had gone he could not rid himself of the image of her smile. It was such a contrast: a man was about to be killed for nothing but the crime of being loyal to the Church and kind to his fellow Christians—and she was trying to engage him in idle chatter. *How can anyone say "good morrow" when one of their company is going to be killed for a matter of conscience? The Romans killed Christ for preaching a message of peace and goodwill, and now the priests who carry God's blessing are being killed by the State.* Clarenceux asked himself the question: *After fifteen hundred years of Christ's ministry, has anything changed?* In his heart he had to say: *Yes, the hypocrisy is worse.* But was that just his old age speaking, the timeless grumblings of men past their prime? People seemed to have lost both their sense of right and wrong, and their courage to stand up against injustice. They had learned to smile while the State executed dissenters. They separated their own interests from those of their communities. From now on, more and more people would live their lives as selfish individuals, not as persons belonging to a greater commonwealth.

Thomas knew that Clarenceux would walk along Shoe Lane. He had been twice with him to watch an execution—or, rather, to give succor to a condemned man. At the gate to the city liberties, he stopped, a hundred yards short of the church, where a house on the right-hand side protruded into the street. The mud here stank, having been used as a pissing place by men coming and going from the cockpit. After a minute, and seeing Clarenceux waiting for the procession of those condemned to die, he returned down Shoe Lane and cut across to Fetter Lane to wait for the procession to pass Barnard's Inn.

About ten minutes after the bells of the city had chimed the hour, Thomas saw the Tyburn cart crossing Holborn Bridge. It had high sides, solid wooden wheels, and was pulled by two chestnut horses. Six guards accompanied it, all armed with halberds. Not many people had gathered to watch it go past, not here. Most knew the fate of the six men and three women standing inside it; they would have presumed that the condemned were thieves and murderers, to be pointed out to children as examples. One or two onlookers shouted a curse or an insult as the cart passed them; most, however, were unmoved by the sight of the men and women on their way to execution. It was just another one of the city's routines.

Clarenceux stepped out from his waiting place by St. Andrew's and started to walk behind the cart. "Sir John, remember that God is with you, and the goodness you have done in His name will never be forgotten, and that you are in our hearts," he called in a loud voice.

Men and women stopped what they were doing and stared at him. For a moment there was amazement that anyone—not least a gentleman—would dare speak openly to one of the criminals in the cart. But there was no doubting that that was exactly what Clarenceux was doing; his voice was trained to carry and he was using it to good effect.

Three of the guards stopped and rounded on him; they leveled their halberds at him. "Silence, you! Do not speak to the prisoners," shouted one, as the cart continued on its way.

They resumed their positions and likewise Clarenceux resumed his, following the cart. "God be with you, Sir John," he called. "Tonight you will dine at the right hand of the Lord Jesus. The food of Heaven will be sweet—sweeter by far than the bitterness that people—"

The first clod of earth hit him, shortly followed by the second. "Shame on you, Papist!" yelled a woman. A man with a tall, black hat confronted Clarenceux, trying to stop him from following the cart. "Do you want to hang too?" he demanded. "Show some sense, go home." But Clarenceux simply moved around him, to the other side of the road, close to where Thomas was standing. The guards backed away cautiously, watching him.

Thomas waited as the cart rumbled past the end of Fetter Lane. Never had nine men and women looked more pitiful, he thought. Two prisoners were on their knees—he could see their faces through the side of the cart. Two women were embracing each other. The others just stood with their hands bound, leaning against the wooden side of the cart as it lurched over the uneven road. Sir John alone stood proud in the middle, his head shaved.

"Behold, you, the living! You, the complacent living!" Sir John's voice rang out. "There is still one good man among you. One man of courage, one man of goodness. Do not pray for me; I go to meet my Maker. Pray for him—the good man, the man of conscience! Pray for yourselves, in your viperish and self-consuming sin! Pray for your redemption from the evil that you do in God's name!"

For a moment Thomas lost sight of Clarenceux amid the gathering crowd. Then he heard his master's unmistakable voice singing "*Agnus Dei, qui tolis peccata mundi.*" Clarenceux was on the far side of the street, about fifty feet behind the prisoners. The guards had their halberds leveled at him and were walking backward, trying to keep pace with the cart, but they were no longer trying to push him away. They did not know what to do. They were irritated and confused. "*Miserere nobis,*" Clarenceux sang, before repeating, "*Agnus Dei, qui tolis peccata mundi.*"

Thomas hurried across the street, ready to protect his master. Clarenceux was singing part of the Latin Mass—"O Lamb of God, who takes away the sins of the world"—and the next line would end with the words *dona nobis pacem*: "give us peace." It was threatening in its purity and its irony. He was striding more freely now, committed to his protest. More mud hit him. A gentleman in a fine silk waistcoat and doublet tried to have words with him. Clarenceux pushed him away, still singing.

At the top of Chancery Lane, more people started to gather. Still Clarenceux went on singing—and in chanting the *Agnus Dei* he was joined by several of those in the cart, who, even if they did not know who he was, realized that he was singing it for them, and making a spectacle of himself for them, in defiance of the guards and the crowd. On they went, still singing the *Agnus Dei*, and when they passed the grounds of Lincoln's Inn, where the road left the houses and there were fields on both sides, the sound of the singing seemed to be stronger. People paid no attention to the prisoners but cajoled and cursed Clarenceux, accusing him of wanting to let murderers kill innocent people and Catholics assassinate the queen; but few followed the cart very far. When it approached the village of St. Giles in the Fields, only six people were still following. Clarenceux was one, Thomas another, and the other four were also singing the *Agnus Dei*.

No one in the parish of St. Giles challenged the protesters, although the people in the high road looked askance at them. The guards did not bother them either, their halberds back on their shoulders. The prisoners took heart from this and continued singing through St. Giles and beyond, out along the road that led to Tyburn. But here the four men with Clarenceux fell away and returned to their own business. Thomas stayed with him, walking alongside, watching out. People going to Tyburn to see the execution caught up with them and then hurried on, often shouting an insult as they went. Washerwomen in the fields briefly stopped laying out their laundry and stared. But as the men and women in the cart saw how near they were to Tyburn, their singing turned to fearful wailing. One of the women began to scream hysterically. Sir John turned and tried to comfort her, and when she paid him no heed, he tried to rouse the others to sing again, but their hearts were not in it. They were people who preferred the tavern to the pulpit and had no wish to go to their deaths singing part of the old Mass. Those walking to the place of execution continued to shout abuse at the condemned as they passed the cart. Then even Clarenceux fell silent, simply repeating, "Hail, Mary, mother of God," as he walked.

There were more than a thousand people gathered at Tyburn. It was the first of several law days in the city, and it had been some weeks since the last jail delivery, so those looking for some gruesome entertainment had all turned up early, hoping to secure the best view. As the cart drew nearer to the gallows, the distress of the prisoners became more extreme. Thomas saw there were children in the crowd: a boy of about nine was playing with a dog, and a young girl was chasing another child between the standing onlookers. He heard joyful shouts and saw a young woman being lifted into the air by a group of young men. Around him came careless shrieking, insults, and the singing of rude songs. He saw the face of a man in a leather jerkin who, realizing he had been swindled, lashed out at the coney-catcher who had tricked him. There was a woman being lasciviously kissed by a man at the back of the crowd, his hands groping her breasts. "Surely the Hell to which the most miserable sinner is condemned is no worse than this," Clarenceux shouted to Thomas. But then the crowd surged forward. The people were not angry; they were singing and dancing and gesticulating and laughing, shouting jokes and throwing mud at the prisoners simply for the sport of seeing if they could hit them. The cries of the prisoners and the screams of a woman only made them laugh more, and the guards had to fend them off with their halberds.

Within a few seconds, Clarenceux, Thomas, and the cart were engulfed. The cart was almost stationary now with the press of the onlookers. Thomas tried to keep as close to Clarenceux as he could but it was difficult in the festive, jeering crowd. The six halberd bearers were assisted by a dozen soldiers who had been waiting at the gallows since early that morning, but it was all the guards could do to keep the crowd from climbing onto the cart. Thomas hoped that Clarenceux would back off, but he did not. Instead he pushed forward to seize hold of the back of the cart, and held on to it all the way to the gallows.

The gallows itself was a large timber frame of three interlocking beams—an oak triangle—on three huge upright oak supports. From each side of the triangle hung three nooses, ominously empty. The entire structure, massive though it was, could be seen to move slightly as the crowd pressed in around it, causing the empty nooses to sway. The cart came to a halt beneath the first of the great beams and two executioners placed sackcloth bags over the heads of the first three victims followed by the nooses. Then the back of the cart was let down. No one paid any attention to the priest at the foot of it, who tried to read words of consolation to the prisoners. One of the women and two of the men stood shivering and crying, muttering prayers until suddenly the cart gave a lurch and moved off. A huge roar went up as the crowd saw the three bodies twisting and spinning on the end of the ropes. The men with the halberds pushed them back, to make way for the cart to turn, as the three hanging prisoners began to twitch, their bodies struggling for breath.

After the next three prisoners had been left choking on the end of a rope, it was the turn of the last three, including Sir John. The cart turned and came to rest directly beneath the third beam. As the executioner climbed up onto the cart and started to put the hoods over their heads, Sir John stood grim-faced, looking down at the crowd, waiting his turn. He was second-to-last. Next to him stood a terrified young woman. "I am innocent," she wailed. "Tell my girls I died an innocent woman. It was John Lucas who took Mr. Robert's linen." But the crowd simply laughed at her and mimicked her plea. To their great delight, the executioner forced a kiss upon her lips and squeezed her breast before covering her head too and placing the noose over her neck and tightening it.

Thomas closed his eyes. He wished the whole lamentable business was over. But when he opened them again, to his horror, he saw Clarenceux climbing up onto the back of the cart. He tried to get to him, but Clarenceux had already started to declaim to the crowd. The people closest to him were so startled to hear such a voice booming out that they fell silent, and soon the whole crowd was wondering who this was and what he had to say.

"You laugh—you laugh today at these unfortunate creatures before you and those"—he gestured toward the six now motionless corpses—"and you laugh away your humanity. These are not all villainous murderers dying here. These are not all thieves. There is a good man here, a priest, who would stand up for his fellow men. He would stand up for you, even though you are strangers. When you laugh at him, you laugh at the ties that bind us to our fellow men. You laugh at what is good in you. You laugh at kindness; you laugh at the courage to stand up against the constables who would rule your lives with an order and a knife…"

A clod of earth was thrown. It missed Clarenceux, who carried on regardless. "Sir John is destined to be killed because what he believes is unwelcome to the State. And the State insists that it must come first—before your friends, before your family—yea, even before your faith. Who here, doing the business of the State, loves the State more than his own kin? Who here would put the queen above God? Do you not see what the destruction of the Church has brought upon us?"

Already there were mutterings. Then the jeers started. The crowd had not come to be preached at. They had come to watch a spectacle, to meet people, perhaps have an illicit assignation or cut a purse from a stranger's belt. They wanted to be entertained—and to that end they did not mind hearing a gallows speech from someone less fortunate than themselves. But they did not want to be spoken to about the queen; nor did they wish to hear anything concerning the Church. They resented Clarenceux's intrusion. But they laughed again—heartily—when the executioner picked up a sackcloth bag and placed it jokingly over Clarenceux's head. As the hooded figure of Sir John called out, "God be with you, William," and the crowd erupted with noise and cheering, Clarenceux tore off the bag and threw a punch at the executioner, hitting him sooner than he expected, so that he struck the man hard on the nose, and he himself toppled backward. Both men fell off the cart into the crowd. Before he could regain his feet, the crowd had taken over the executioner's role and smacked the horses into life, pulling away the cart and leaving Sir John and the other two prisoners hanging.

Clarenceux struggled to his feet and waded through the jostling mass to the figure of Sir John. Thomas joined him as he made the sign of the cross. Together they reached up, took hold of Sir John's legs, and jumped with all their weight, pulling him down suddenly and breaking his neck. Several men did likewise with the young woman whose body was jerking beside the still form of Sir John.

Clarenceux stood panting, with mud on his face. He looked at Thomas and placed a hand on his shoulder. No sooner had he done so than one of the guards knocked his arm away with the shaft of his halberd. Two others seized his arms and proceeded to tie his hands behind his back. "You will face the justices tomorrow," said the first guard. "Take him to Newgate. Since you want to be on that cart so much, we'll see you get your chance."

4

In the small dining room at Cecil House, Sir William sat alone at table. The door was shut. Before him was a silver salt cellar, a silver dish containing a roast capon and some slices of roast beef, two silver saucers—one with a mustard sauce, the other with a white wine and onion sauce—some bread, a drinking glass, and a flagon of wine. He did not feel hungry. Or, to be exact, his yearning to have some time to himself outweighed his hunger. He broke the bread and set it down on the white linen tablecloth, looking at the crumbs, playing at them with one finger. He then glanced up at the portrait of his wife, Mildred, that hung above the fireplace.

Life is a labyrinth, he thought, as he pushed the crumbs into a line. *The way in is simple enough, at birth, and the way out easy enough, at death; and no one can fail to find a path between the two. Yet how few people find their way to the mysteries at its heart? Most of us are lost. Most of us depend on maps which are in themselves labyrinthine. The Bible is one such map, poetry another.* The breadcrumbs were arranged in a neat row; now he moved them into a circle. *For the most part we rely on direction through simplification. The art of government, like the arts of writing, astrology, and navigation, is to make such simplifications meaningful. Politics is the art of meaningful simplification—purposeful lies.*

He reached forward, cut a slice of beef in half, picked up one piece with his fingers, and dipped it in the mustard sauce. The rich taste of the meat made his mouth water. Its robust flavor, coupled with the smooth piquancy of the mustard, which affected his nose, gave him an instant of pleasure, and he rediscovered his hunger. He took a piece of bread and dipped it in the white wine sauce. That too was good. *French sauciers are the best*, he reflected, reaching forward with his knife to cut a slice of capon. He dipped this in the same sauce, as one of his ushers knocked at the door.

"Do not disturb me," he said.

There came another knock.

Cecil hurriedly picked up another piece of beef with his fingers, dipped it in the mustard sauce, and pushed it into his mouth. Still chewing, he sliced a second piece of capon and dipped that in the white wine sauce. *Every moment a new opening appears in the labyrinth.*

The usher knocked a third time. "Sir William, Mr. Walsingham has come to see you. He craves your attention most insistently."

Cecil finished chewing and started to cut himself another piece of capon. "Send him in." He took his time now, pretending he was dining in slow luxury.

Walsingham entered, wearing his usual thin ruff, black doublet, black skull cap, and deep frown. He was thirty-three years of age, the same age as the queen, yet anyone who did not know them would think them a generation apart. He had the demeanor of a man ten years older, while Elizabeth could be as playful as a girl when she felt so inclined. Cecil wondered whether Walsingham had ever been playful—even as a child.

"Sir William, I have received a report from Scotland—about the christening of the royal babe—the nature of which I presume is not unknown to you."

Cecil gestured to a chair. "As you can see, Francis, I am dining. Could this not wait?"

"If I waited every time I needed to discuss matters of State with you, you would be much the more ignorant and I would never have the answers I need. If you will, I shall return another day. For my part, the business of the State takes priority over my mealtimes."

Cecil wiped his mouth on a napkin and put it back down on the table. "Quite. Yes, absolutely, Francis. I will have you join me. You must try the capon in the white wine sauce—it is excellently pleasing." Cecil got to his feet, went to the door, spoke to the usher waiting outside, and closed it. "So, what is the news?"

"You know about the baptismal font?" replied Walsingham, clearly agitated.

"Of course. It is no secret: twenty-one pounds of pure gold—and the finest workmanship. They'll melt it down, of course, but in the meantime it should make quite an impression."

"And the queen used it to buy the right to name the child James—is that true? And if it is true, does not that signify that she sees him as her successor?"

"Her majesty was determined that the child not be called Charles, despite his mother's wishes. I supported her majesty in that and so I suggested that she make the gift of the baptismal font. Her majesty confirmed on the ninth of December that the child was to be christened James. The christening should have taken place two days ago, on the seventeenth. Presuming that happened as planned, the babe is now James Charles Stewart, or Charles James Stewart, prince of Scotland. Either way, he will be called James."

Walsingham thumped the table. "For years we have been asking her majesty to confirm her intentions regarding the succession. In this present parliament that now is sitting she has declared that no one may discuss the succession—on pain of death. And yet she goes so far as to give a name to her legal heir, and a name contrary to that chosen by his own mother. In so doing she has practically named the boy as the next king of England."

There was a knock at the door. A servant brought in a silver plate.

"The queen may yet have children of her own," objected Cecil.

"She has done precious little about it yet," replied Walsingham, cutting some capon and putting it on the plate now set in front of him. "If she names her successor, then we know whom to guard against and whom to protect. If her successor is a Catholic, he will throw this entire nation into chaos and confusion. She will give succor to the Catholic cause. The alliances and schemes I discover—are they signs of future loyalty or indications of an incipient attack on her majesty? How can she name a prince, the child of both her cousins, and the child not be seen as her heir? The child has been baptized a Catholic. Both his parents are Catholic. She has taken a role in naming that boy in a Catholic ceremony. How can she do this and expect no reaction from the Catholic community? She has named her killer—or at least the boy in whose name she will be killed."

Cecil leaned forward and took a whole slice of beef. He rubbed it in the mustard sauce, then put it in his mouth and chewed slowly. He swallowed. "Whether she is killed or not is very much your responsibility, Francis. But as you know, many things may—and will—happen between now and the next reign, and let us hope to God that many years pass. The prince may not live. Catherine Grey's sons might be restored to favor; and as you know I am trying to persuade her majesty that some leniency toward their father, Lord Hertford, is highly advisable, especially if he permits their education in the Protestant faith. No less significant is the possibility that Mary herself might not live."

"She has only just turned twenty-five."

Cecil shrugged. "How are you getting along with that new wife of yours?"

Walsingham paused with a piece of beef on the way to his mouth. "What has that to do with the matter in question?"

"Mary of Scotland does not get along with Lord Henry Stewart. As husbands go, he leaves a lot to be desired."

"I'm not surprised—after he murdered her lover, David Rizzio."

"Rizzio may or may not have been her lover. Personally, I doubt it. However, he *was* her informer. Lord Henry Stewart had him killed because of what he knew, not what he did. As it happened, he was too late. Rizzio had already passed on his information, just moments before he was killed."

Walsingham set down his knife. "And that was?"

"That if the child that Queen Mary was then carrying turned out to be a son, then Lord Henry Stewart would have her murdered. He would then rule Scotland in the minority of the child. Of course he would also be the sole potential Stewart heir to the throne of England. If Elizabeth died before the child grew to be of age, Lord Henry would rule both countries during his son's minority."

Cecil watched Walsingham get up and walk to the window. "That is…sickening."

Cecil stopped eating. "I have never seen you so taken aback, Francis. I am surprised. You know as well as I do that Lord Henry Stewart is a drunkard and a killer."

"And your counsel to her majesty is—what? To take advantage of Lord Henry killing his wife? The queen of Scotland is Elizabeth's cousin once removed."

"So is Lord Henry. But Mary is forewarned now—Rizzio did not die in vain—and her loyal subjects are alerted. She is by no means without friends. In fact, she has many more friends than Lord Henry north of the border. His strongest supporters are mostly in England: the Catholics who see him as the savior of the old religion, or family connections like his mother, Lady Margaret Douglas, although what good she can do him in the Tower, I am not sure. I trust you have ears and eyes around her too."

"Of course. There is a rather sour gentleman with spectacles who pretends to go by the name of John Black and who brings messages to her—where from, I do not know. I am reliably informed that John Black is actually a Catholic priest called Maurice Buckman. No doubt he is her confessor too. But I am intrigued by your idea that Queen Mary and Lord Henry Stewart will destroy each other. You think that the new prince will be the heir, sooner rather than later?"

"If he lives, yes."

"And if he does not?"

"By then, with God's grace, our queen will have her own heir."

Walsingham scoffed at that. He sat back down, helping himself to the last piece of beef. "Have you ever really studied her, and looked at her as a woman, not as a queen?" he asked Cecil.

"It is impossible to forget she is the queen."

"Exactly. She never lets anyone forget. And you cannot see her as a woman. You cannot desire her; you cannot imagine treating her as a woman. You can tell a woman what to do—you can give her orders, you can expect her to obey you, and you can beat her if she refuses.

You cannot do that with a queen. But truly, deep inside Queen Elizabeth of England is a small, frightened girl whose father killed her mother and who lived in terror of being killed by her sister. Fear conditions her every move. But she is supremely intelligent, as we all know. She has seen what she needs to be in order to survive. She has created herself, designed herself, and changed herself into something magnificent—much more than a woman. She can command, she can control, she understands. She has made herself master of many manly skills and yet she has preserved the spiritual or mystical virtues of her womanhood. She is merciful—she listens to her subjects, she does not crush them beneath a rod of iron but commands them with a white wand to do their duty for the nation. And she can be a destroying black angel too. She is not a woman. She does not want to be a woman; she wants to be an angel. She wants to be worshipped, to be adored, to be loved and yet still remain pure, divine, both great and, above all, safe."

"But she cannot escape the fact that she is a woman," Cecil put in.

"I agree." Walsingham nodded. "Inside the angel, she *is* a woman—and that is her vulnerability. If she marries, the woman will be revealed—stripped of her divine purity and seen to be all too mortal. If she falls pregnant, she may die in childbirth, like a mere mortal, handing power directly to her next successor, the Catholic queen, or the prince. She must therefore do all she can to stay alive—and that means not marrying, not becoming pregnant, not being seen to be womanly or weak, but playing the part of God's angel in England."

Cecil poured wine into his glass, drank from it, wiped the edge with his napkin, and offered it to Walsingham, who accepted it. "If the privy council deem it expedient, she will marry," he said. "Her fears are not above the interests of the nation."

"She is more than a match for the privy council. Do you think it merely an unfortunate coincidence that she favors both you and Lord Dudley? If it weren't him it would be someone else that she would use to balance you and to check your influence."

Cecil was not amused. "I flatter myself that I know her better than you."

"That is what blinds you. That is why you cannot see the facts. You are too involved in the elaborate intricacies of things. If she does what you suggest, and marries to please the privy council, she will have second thoughts very soon afterward."

Cecil frowned. "Well, Francis, I have answered your question about the queen naming the Scots prince. I have told you what I think will happen between the Scots queen and her husband. I will reflect on what you say about the queen marrying. In return, I will give you a further piece of information on which to reflect. I mentioned earlier that Queen Mary is not without friends in Scotland. In November she met her loyal magnates, ostensibly to discuss the baptism. However, it was decided then to end the royal marriage—either by divorce or by some other means, for the lords would not accept being ruled over by Lord Henry Stewart, who they believe will prove a tyrant if he succeeds in killing Mary. It is either him or her. One of them is going to dispose of the other. And it is going to happen soon. The royal couple have planned a reconciliation in January—and that can only be because one wants to get close enough to the other to perform the final cut."

Walsingham rubbed his chin. "It was always the way with the Scots. How many murders and black deeds have they performed over the centuries? Has an Irish or Scottish king ever died in his bed? By comparison, we English are mild and meek."

Cecil laughed. "Listen to yourself—think about Edward II and Richard II, Henry VI and Edward V. We have had our share of royal butchery. But anyway, that's not the issue. Be aware that one heir of Scotland is set to kill the other, and that if Lord Henry Stewart is the victor, you can expect his attentions to turn to England very soon thereafter."

Walsingham nodded and got up to leave.

"There's one other thing," said Cecil, lifting the glass of wine. "Please would you be so good as to release the herald, Clarenceux?"

Walsingham stopped. "Clarenceux was arrested for breaking the peace at the hanging of John Blackwell, the traitorous Catholic priest. He was heard by the whole crowd to speak openly in favor of the man, and to encourage them to throw off the control of the civil authorities. He cannot be allowed—"

"Yes, yes, I know. I had spies there too. It's nothing he has not done before. Let him go."

"Given his custody of the Percy-Boleyn marriage agreement—which you never seem to speak about anymore—I have reason to believe he is safer in my keeping than he would be in his own home."

"If you are worried about him, you can put him under watch. I am sure you have considered that already."

"Morning, afternoon, evening, and night. Nevertheless, I can assure you that you are making a mistake."

Cecil looked Walsingham in the eye. "I would rather make a mistake than follow the advice of those who claim never to make them." Cecil leaned back in his chair and surveyed the table. "Now, I think I am ready for my custard tart. Good evening to you."

5

Sunday, December 22

Rebecca Machyn awoke early in the little cottage in the village of Portchester that she shared with Widow Baker. It was still dark, and her mind was echoing with a dream. In her heart she felt a tremendous sense of loss, for she realized the dream was just that: a dream. A moment ago, asleep, she had been happy. She had been lying in a bed in an inn with William Harley, Clarenceux King of Arms. They had been traveling somewhere and pretending that they were man and wife; she had been wearing just her smock and he his drawers, and in the darkness he had kissed her and held her, and moved his hands over her body. She had felt so loved, warm, and when his hands had brushed her nipples, her body had sung like the strings of a lute. Now the lute was silent, the strings slack, and she was alone in the darkness. Even Widow Baker was abroad, having gone to nurse a woman in the next village.

For a moment Rebecca lay still, divided between the luxury of the dream and cursing herself for her self-pity. She pictured Clarenceux—his curly dark hair, his grim but handsome face, his height, his brown eyes—and wiped away a tear. *Even now, even after all this time, he can move me.* She cast her mind back to their meeting, when her husband, Henry Machyn, had still been alive. Henry had been a merchant taylor, no one important, but he had idolized Clarenceux and referred to him as "the most noble gentleman of my acquaintance." This was why Henry had chosen Clarenceux to be the recipient of his precious chronicle. Clarenceux had taken to her, and his looks had increasingly lingered on her. After Henry was murdered, she and Clarenceux had been chased by Walsingham's agents and together they had discovered the secret contained within the chronicle. He had looked after her, cherished her, desired her, loved her. Gladly she would have sworn to be with him always—but it could not be. He was married, and he loved his wife no less than he loved her.

She had not seen him for two years now, since the autumn of 1564, when she had gone back to London to collect the last of her things from the old house. On that occasion, a bright October day, she had traveled with the cart along Fleet Street. Approaching Clarenceux's house she could not help but look at it, and remember him, and feel close to him. She had not meant to say good-bye in person, but at that moment he had come to the window and seen her, and rushed out of the house. That final meeting in the street had overwhelmed her. She had dismounted and he had embraced her, and they had talked. He had politely asked her about the old house and she had explained that it was all John Machyn's now, Henry's son. She was going to live in Portchester, where she had found acceptance and happiness in her work at the military hospital in the castle. Clarenceux told her how he wished her well. There had been a long pause, when neither of them had said anything. He had embraced her then, and she had known in the way he held her and the way he kissed her that his feelings for her were still strong. Hers for him were equally so. But there was nothing they could do. He had simply whispered good-bye to her and had waved her on her way.

Why was she even thinking of him now? The previous day, Mr. Wheatsheafen had told her that two young men had come looking for her. That fact had unnerved her, and she had searched her mind wondering who they could be. Although she did not want to admit it, there was a chance they had come from London. No one there knew where she was—except Clarenceux and her stepson, John Machyn.

Rebecca got out of bed, felt for her shoes, and pulled them onto her feet. She put her dress on over her smock. Hunched forward to avoid the low beams, and with her hands stretched out in the darkness, she made her way to the opening and down the ladder to the room below. The faintest glow of the embers on the hearth could be seen, and finding a loose stick, she raked off the surface and crouched down to blow on them. Soon there was a small flame. She broke a few more sticks, built the fire a little more, and then fetched a candle.

If the two young men had come from Clarenceux, she thought, perhaps this was good news? But he would be unlikely to send two men, and certainly not two *young* men to her. He knew how harshly young men with strength and authority treated an attractive woman with neither husband nor father to protect her. Clarenceux was more considerate than that.

She put the candle into a lantern, set it beside the basin, and rinsed her face and hands. Taking the lantern, she went back upstairs to rub herself clean with linen and to dress in her best clothes, ready for church.

6

Clarenceux led his daughters by the hand through the churchyard to join the queue of people entering St. Bride's. The great bell was ringing in the chill air above them. Occasionally he caught someone's eye and nodded a brief greeting. Annie was feeling the cold and about to complain, so he held her hand a little tighter to remind her to be quiet. She would warm up soon enough in the church, with the heat of all the people.

He looked up at the vicar's room above the porch. So many vicars had come and gone, so many changes had taken place. One had even gone to the stake. Now there was no vicar: William Living had resigned the previous year to go to St. Mary Abchurch, and a series of chaplains held the services. The present one was a nervous man with short black hair called Mr. Bowring. His sermons were too enthusiastic for Clarenceux, too idealistic, copied from Mr. Bowring's more able heroes.

Clarenceux had first come here at the age of seventeen, before old King Henry's dissolution, when the rector and right of patronage had been with the abbot of Westminster. It had then been one of the most beautiful religious buildings in the environs of the city, and he had marveled at it. The columns in the nave had carved stone vines twisting around them—a monument to a rich man called Vyner—and they had been painted, as if growing up to the roof. The walls too had been painted and the windows filled with rich glass. There had been six altars in the church, including a fine tall altar to St. Katherine in front of the rood screen. The printer Wynkyn de Worde was buried just in front of it. And each of those altars had had a painted screen behind it with sculptures of the highest quality, and an altar cloth around its front, and beautiful silver-gilt furniture. Above the high altar had been a great wood-and-silver cross. The whole nave had been a wonderful cave of color, light, and music. Chantry priests had sung through the day, until compline in the early evening; the organ had played during services. Now almost all of that had gone. The altars had been torn out, their sculptures smashed. The paintings had been covered in whitewash, the rood cross had been burned, the chantry priests all thrown out and the chantry hall sold off. The organ had been abandoned and was no longer used. No one dared sing anything but psalms these days. Tombs had been defaced, altar cloths turned into kitchen rags, and treasure melted down. Even the beautiful vine carvings on the columns had been purposefully damaged, the paint scraped away.

He entered the church and sat on the plain bench pews in the nave. Around him, people found their places, and sat or knelt. He looked up: traces of sculpted beauty remained but most had gone. His daughters would never know the lyrical majesty of their parish church, which, like the vine, had once drawn the eye in many directions. They would only know the one altar, the stern dictatorial commandment to look east. To them, church attendance would not be a matter of community but duty—to take their place obediently behind the profusion of private pews of various types that now filled the nave, and to listen to the didactic and sanctimonious speechifying of an impostor priest. It was a sign of the times: people were no longer members of a community but individuals, cut off from each other, as if they were all choosing to stand alone in the eyes of God. It made him bitterly sad to reflect on so much destruction. It was not holy. Destroying beautiful things and fragmenting society could not be justified, and the smashing of the sculptures had been particularly vindictive.

He knelt down, shut his eyes, and prayed for the mystical true faith to find another way to enter their lives, to allow a better understanding of God's guidance. He prayed for the safety and security of his wife Awdrey and their daughters. He prayed for his closest friends, especially Julius Fawcett of Summerhill, Sir Richard Wenman of Caswell, John Hooker of Exeter, and especially for Rebecca Machyn. He prayed also for his servants, Thomas, Joan, and Nick, and the community of which he felt a part. Then he opened his eyes, and resumed his seat.

A strange gentleman, seated not far away, was looking at him. He had a distinct air of being out of place. He showed no sign of connection to those sitting beside him. His hair color was extraordinary—it was white, even though he was clearly not old. His clothes were just as distracting as his hair: despite the cold, he was not wearing a doublet but only an extremely fine linen shirt embroidered with gold and silk. He seemed not to know how to wear that properly either; the ties at the collar were hanging down and he wore no ruff. His cuffs too were loose. On his lower body he was wearing soft leather breeches and silk netherhosen.

Clarenceux met the strange gentleman's gaze twice. The first time he held his eye. The second, he felt uneasy. He glanced at Awdrey, who turned to him. When she understood his expression of concern, and had herself seen the white-haired young man, she shrugged, to say she knew nothing about him. But from the corner of her eye she studied him, watching his movements.

At the end of the service, Clarenceux and Awdrey led their daughters straight out of the church. The white-haired man was caught in conversation with another gentleman who had been sitting on the benches in the nave, and who wanted to know more about him. He did not catch Clarenceux's eye again.

7

Rebecca caught up with Mr. Wheatsheafen after the service in the church in the precincts of Portchester Castle. He was walking back to his lodging slowly, appreciating the sunny morning.

"Good morrow, Mr. Wheatsheafen. A fine day for December, is it not?"

He turned around and caught sight of her long brown hair and smiling eyes. "Ah, good morrow, Rebecca. It most certainly is a good day. I was just reflecting that, at my age, one appreciates every day that bit more, regardless of whether the weather be good or bad. One knows one has relatively few days left to enjoy. But if all days are good, then it follows that the fine ones are doubly pleasant."

She walked alongside the physician, comfortable with him. He was a good Christian man who genuinely cared for people regardless of their status in the world.

"Did you see Philip Camp in the congregation?" she asked him. "To think—two weeks ago we did not expect him to live another day."

"Indeed, it is something to give thanks for. The Lord is merciful as well as bountiful."

Rebecca went on for a few more paces before turning the

conversation to her prime concern. "You remember, yesterday, you told me that two young men had been looking for me?"

"I do."

"Can you tell me more about them? Did you notice anything in particular?"

Wheatsheafen turned to her. "Such as?"

"Well, I do not know exactly. But…were they kindly disposed toward me?"

They had reached the gate leading out of the castle. The great gate was closed but a smaller side door was open, allowing people to come and go freely on foot.

"Well, I would not go so far as to suggest they were unkind," Wheatsheafen said after thinking hard on the matter, "but nor would I say they were friends of yours. They both had strange accents, from the north, I believe. One of them was—well, ugly. He had swarthy dark skin, like an Egyptian, and his eyes were too close together. I cannot imagine your beautiful brown eyes settling happily on his and not being a little disconcerted. You know what they say about the Egyptians. It is just as well consorting with them has been made a felony."

"And the other one?"

"I can recall only one thing about him—I do not think he was a man."

"You mean he was a boy?"

"No, no. The Egyptian seemed to be taking direction from this smaller, smooth-skinned person, who did not speak at all. I had thought his demeanor odd at the time; being a physician I had looked at his hands—but he was wearing gloves. I also looked at his throat but he had covered it up. Later it struck me that this is exactly what a woman who dressed as a man might do to conceal her identity. So my best guess is that this second man was a woman in disguise."

Rebecca stopped. "Did you not see fit to tell me this?"

"I only thought about him being a woman after I sent to you. Would it have made things different? Would you have known them? My dear, you have to admit, you are something of an enigma. It is nearly two and a half years since we first met and yet I know so little of your life before then. You keep many things hidden. I would ask, but I am afraid of appearing to pry into matters that you very clearly wish to keep to yourself. I recall a man coming here not long after you had arrived. Immediately you had to go to him. I knew then that you had a past that you could not wholly leave behind."

"That was Mr. Clarenceux."

"Is he a past lover? Or, let me put it more discreetly: do you love this man from your past?"

"With all my heart."

"Then you should go to him. We may need you here, but you must follow the path of your emotion. Feelings are the Lord's way of guiding people in life, I believe."

Rebecca shook her head. "He is married. He loves his wife, and she is much younger than me."

"Ah." Mr. Wheatsheafen looked down the lane toward his house. "In such unfortunate circumstances, the Lord Almighty can sorely tempt us. Perhaps that is what He is trying to do—test you, by making you love a man who does not love you. Virtue is your guide and your target."

"It is not that he does not love me. I know that he does. He and I shared an intense experience three years ago. It was very dangerous; we became very close. He would look at me and his eyes would linger, always that moment too long, and I would hold his gaze. But the fact is that he is married and loves his wife dearly; the affection he feels for me is secondary to that fact. But such things are settled—this is not about affection. If someone is searching for me, and knows I am here, then they have good information yet they are not friends. That in itself is worrying. Why are they looking for me? If it has anything to do with my experiences with Mr. Clarenceux, then I might be in serious danger, and so might he."

"Is that likely?"

Rebecca looked over her shoulder. There was no one in sight; the lane was empty. She spoke in a low voice nonetheless. "You must not repeat this to anyone, Mr. Wheatsheafen. Not even your wife. Mr. Clarenceux has possession of a document that could destroy the queen—it proves that her mother was previously married to Lord Percy and so the queen is illegitimate. It was given to him by my late husband, Henry. Needless to say, there are a number of Catholic plotters who are prepared to do anything to seize it. My husband was killed by Francis Walsingham simply because of a suspicion that he would use it for revolutionary Catholic purposes. Two years ago last May, when Mr. Clarenceux came here to Portchester, it was because the document had been stolen. I believe he recovered it, although I never asked him and I have not been in communication with him at all since October of that year."

Mr. Wheatsheafen listened with the same careful attention with which he listened to patients telling him of their illnesses. At the end, he considered his prognosis and spoke solemnly. "On the one hand, Rebecca, I have always said you had some dark secret and that your past was not yet over. In that I am satisfied; the enormity of your situation does not disappoint. But I am not glad to be right, for I can see that it saddens you and makes you think about the past perhaps a little too much. There is a man there you must forget; you must leave both him and that awkward situation behind and live your own life, guided by God." He put his hand on her shoulder. "As for your affection, I do know also that it is possible for a man to love two women. I still love my first wife dearly, God rest her soul. I also love my present wife. I therefore love two women. Although one might now be permanently in the past, if she were alive today, I would love her all the more. Likewise, I cannot say that I would not love my present wife if my first were miraculously to return: love is not just a matter of timeliness. So, if it be that I go to Heaven, and trusting that both my wives will be there too, I will find myself living in a state that contradicts the scriptures."

They fell silent, looking at each other. Eventually Wheatsheafen said, "Rebecca, I think you are wise to be cautious. I do not believe those men—or that man and that woman—meant you well."

8

Monday, December 23

Maurice Buckman waited in a panelled chamber in the inn in Grantham, in Lincolnshire. He was a fifty-two-year-old man with a round head and very little hair. What little there was amounted to the merest halo of white. His vision was poor, so he wore wooden spectacles with very thick lenses, and he blinked much more than most people—but nothing about him otherwise was blurred, and when wearing his spectacles, which had been made for him by a Milanese craftsman, that visual vagueness became a hawklike precision. For a man in his fifties, he was quick-thinking and agile, capable of intense concentration. He regularly wore an old black cassock, which left people wondering whether he was a priest (which he was) or merely a poor man (which he was also, although by choice). Beneath that cassock was a rough canvas shirt, and beneath that uncomfortable shirt, a heart that beat with a passion for the Catholic faith.

Placing another log on the fire, he sat back at the nearby table and sipped the glass of sack. It would not be long now. It had been a long journey, he reflected: four and a half days. But Lady Percy's instructions had been clear. Everyone coming or going to see her was followed—Walsingham kept her houses under constant surveillance—and if Buckman was noticed coming to her from the Tower, he would be arrested, interrogated, tortured, and hanged. The route was therefore extremely elaborate. Also, speed was imperative: he had had to arrive at this inn many hours or even a day before her ladyship, so those spying on her would not see him enter the building.

From his lodging in London he had crossed by wherry to the south bank of the river at Greenwich and joined the southbound travelers taking the ferry along the Kent coast to Gravesend. Most of them had then transferred to the Canterbury road, hiring carts and coaches for the rest of their journey, but Buckman had noticed that one young man did not. When he had boarded one of the crayers that went up and down the coast, the young man had boarded another boat and followed at a distance. Buckman had accordingly deviated slightly from his intended route and landed on the Isle of Sheppey, near Shurland Hall. No one went there anymore; it was a desolate place. But he knew it well—he had grown up nearby. Any paint still left in that vast mansion was peeling. The elaborate plaster ceilings were damp and stained; in some cases they had crashed down onto the floorboards. Windows with armorial glass had lost quarrels or housed cracked panes, and were strewn with cobwebs and dead flies. The shutters of unglazed windows hung at angles where their hinges had given way. Several fireplaces were strewn with twigs where birds' nests had fallen down, sometimes with the dead birds. And in the great hall, the tapestries' wooden frames lay bare.

Buckman had allowed himself to be seen heading along the lane toward the hall. At a suitable point, he had turned and watched his pursuer through the long grass near the gatehouse. The young man was rash, too keen in the face of danger. Buckman had withdrawn into the shadows of the empty house and ascended a staircase that had lost its balustrade; from there he had observed the young man, who hesitated at the door. Had the young man's nerve failed him, he would have lived. But he had entered—and he too had ascended the staircase.

It had been an easy kill. Buckman had drawn him toward the privy chamber with the creaking of a floorboard and the closing of doors. He had seen that the young man was carrying a pistol but he too had a gun. Gradually, room by room he had lured his victim to the long corridor that ran between the great chamber and the privy chamber. This corridor had a west-facing window at the end—and the glazing there was all broken; at that time of day, it was glaring with late afternoon light. Near that window was a doorway into the privy chamber. That large room was completely dark. The windows had been boarded up long ago, before the house had been abandoned.

Buckman had waited there in the darkness. Eventually the figure of the young man had appeared clearly silhouetted in the doorway, twelve feet away. There he had stopped, looking into the room and seeing only darkness within. That was when Buckman had shot him in the chest. The gun's report had echoed around the mansion, through its courtyards and across the parish but he had not been worried. Rather he had walked forward slowly and stood over the young man, whose chest was burst open with the bullet. The dying man's mouth was making soundless words and he was staring up. Buckman had used the young man's own pistol to finish him off, firing it into the back of his head to obliterate his features. He had then dragged the body over to the window and thrown it out. Back downstairs, he had lugged the corpse across the unkempt grass to the great fish pond, weighing it down by placing stones in the young man's clothes.

Afterward he had walked to Eastchurch to take a boat across to the small port of Brightlingsea, then continued on his journey—by land to King's Lynn, by sea to Boston, and by hired horse to Grantham.

There was a knock at the door. Buckman's hand reached inside his cassock to feel the stock of his pistol.

"Come in," he said. His voice was relatively high in tone and had a nasal sound.

The man who entered was in his late twenties, dark-haired, handsome, and thin, with a small beard. His ruff was neat and not too wide, his clothing correct. Buckman relaxed. This was Benedict Richardson, who had begun his career in Lady Percy's household at the age of fourteen and had gained her trust soon afterward. At twenty-five he had become her chamberlain; now he was her steward, overseeing the administration of her manors and the order of her household.

Buckman knew better than to greet him by name. "It is good to see you, my friend. Is her ladyship here?"

Richardson bowed a polite greeting. "I thank you for your cordial welcome. Her ladyship has arrived." He looked around the room. "I trust you had an untroubled journey?"

"Like any other traveler, I am used to picking up and throwing aside the small obstacles I find in my way."

Richardson smiled. "I will tell her you are ready."

Ten minutes later, there was another knock and Benedict Richardson showed Lady Percy, dowager countess of Northumberland, into the room.

Lady Percy was in her midsixties. These days she habitually dressed in black satin and walked with two sticks. Her gray hair was neatly coiffured, she wore a farthingale that spread the hem of her skirt out wide around her ankles, and her ruff was fashionably starched. Buckman noted the signs of age: the loose skin beneath her chin, the lines around her eyes, and the wrinkled skin of her hands. Her eyes themselves were gray and full of intelligence beneath a frowning brow. He bowed. Lady Percy brusquely gestured for him to be seated and took a seat herself at the table. Mr. Richardson stood beside the door.

"I thank you for coming to me. I know it is not easy."

"My thanks go to you, my lady," replied Buckman, bowing again. "Someone tried to follow me from Gravesend but that was all. He will be missed but he will not be found."

"Good." Lady Percy was silent a long time. She looked into the fire, composing her thoughts. "One thing has been much on my mind. Was my sister killed? Did Walsingham torture her to death?"

Buckman put his hands together, the tips of each finger touching as he considered his reply. "I saw her in the Tower but once. Lady Margaret asked me to administer to her, to hear her confession. It was about a week before she died. She was not well; she looked very pale and drawn, and her eyes were bloodshot. She did not speak of torture—but that does not mean that she was not hurt. Her confession was very formal. I believe she knew the end was coming. Lady Margaret later told me that she had seen a small, shrouded body being carted away from the White Tower—not your sister's usual dwelling—and the same day she had asked a warden if she could see your sister and was told that she was dead. Therefore I strongly suspect the answer to your question is yes, she was tortured to death."

Slowly, like a feather settling through the air, Lady Percy's eyes lowered, her mouth moved silently. She had loved and admired her sister—a love and admiration made all the stronger by their being involved in the same risk-filled ventures, without actually having the inconvenience of living alongside one another, for "Mistress Barker," as her younger sibling had been known, had kept watch for her in London.

"Permit me, please, Father, a moment of reflection."

Buckman bent his head in prayer as she prayed, and waited.

"I knew that she would die in the Tower," she continued, "but hearing the news…it wounded me deeply. I say 'wounded,' but the truth is that it was not pain I felt but emptiness, which in some ways is worse than pain. I felt sad also, because all we fought against still plagues this land—all the sinfulness and indulgence, the pettiness and the self-righteousness. If I could have had just one wish, it would have been to whisper in her ear as she lay dying 'Elizabeth is dead, Lord Henry Stewart is riding south, and the holy Catholic child rides with him.'"

"If it is any consolation, my lady, I do believe that Lady Margaret spoke to your sister about the plans ahead, telling her how Lord Henry would rescind all the heretical laws and restore the faith. She must have taken some comfort from that."

Lady Percy silenced him with a look. "True consolation would have been to cut Clarenceaux's throat. True consolation would have been to strip the shirt off the back of that whore Rebecca Machyn and have her flogged until the whip ends cut so deeply into her flesh they stuck there when the whip was pulled back. It was their fault. If they had used the document appropriately, as they said they would, none of this would have happened. If Clarenceux had declared Elizabeth illegitimate and then proved it, as was his duty, our Spanish and French friends would have arrived by now—in force. The righteous in England would be up in arms. But he was just too scared. Instead he led Walsingham straight to my sister." She paused, looking at Buckman, challenging him to doubt her words. "It was not an accident. I will be revenged—on them both."

Buckman had expected this. "I spoke to the first of the women you sent. She was impressive. Immoral but impressive."

"They all are, Father. Each and every one. I might be practically imprisoned, unable to escape the attentions of Walsingham's men. They are outside even now. They follow each and every one of my servants. But some places they cannot go. And while they are watching me, they do not know whom I command." She gestured to Benedict Richardson. "My steward here makes the inquiries through the courts controlled by my family. In several places we still enjoy the legal privileges of life and death. Women who are sentenced to hang or to be burned alive are offered a reprieve from the gallows or the stake. If they undertake my command successfully, then they will be allowed to escape their sentence. They have nothing to lose. That is their first great virtue."

"Their first?" He blinked several times.

"The second great virtue is that they are not men. That was my mistake in the past: to trust men. Men are weak. Men let us down because they are too easily frightened. Men are unreliable—they can be seduced." She noted the look in Buckman's eye. "Yes, I hate to say so, Father, but even some clergymen can be swayed. The third great virtue of these women is that no one, not even Walsingham, imagines that I would choose *women* to cut the throats of my enemies. Walsingham's men are too busy looking for soldierly-types. My women slip between them like smoke."

"But how do you ensure their loyalty? If these women are all thieves, murderers, traitors, and witches—why do they not escape as soon as you send them on a mission?"

"They all have children," answered Lady Percy immediately. "More particularly, they all have daughters, vulnerable daughters. If they defy me, their daughters will suffer the same fate that they would have suffered."

Buckman nodded. "Have you yet hanged any of them?"

"It has not been necessary. One woman proved uncaring of her offspring from the outset—I used her as a test for the others, to see if they had the resolve to kill her. One did, the woman you have already met, and she did so admirably. But, rest assured, I will carry out my threat. The negligence of the mother and her defiance of my orders will be additional crimes to that for which she faced death in the first place." She held his gaze. "Were you able to assist the first of my revenging angels?"

"It was not difficult. Widow Machyn's house was directly opposite that of your sister. She left London two years ago and now nurses the injured soldiers in Portchester Castle. Her stepson told us where she was—for the price of a quart of wine." He leaned forward and picked up his glass of sack. "You are right: some men are easily seduced—and not just by the pleasures of the flesh."

A flicker of a smile crossed Lady Percy's lips. "Do you hunt, Father?"

"No. It is not possible in the city."

"As you spoke those words just now, I had an image of one of my hawks in flight, swooping in for the kill. And you are like my falconer, calling in and sending out my beautiful birds. They have the talons, and they can spiral high, looking for their prey."

Buckman sipped from his glass. "One of them will drop silently from a great height soon and seize a small, frightened rabbit near Portchester."

9

∾

Joan Hellier lay on the hay in the darkness of a barn. An owl hooted outside. Everything seemed so precarious: her life, her daughter's life—the next meal, even. She was cold but not as cold as she would be if John had not found this barn at dusk. He was her godsend—and yet being with him brought more problems. He had been known back in the north as "Egyptian John" or "John the Egyptian"—he being the illegitimate son of an English prostitute by an Egyptian vagabond. Those features were clearly to be seen in his face, which meant he was distrusted at best, and hated at worst, wherever he went. She could be arrested just for being with him.

She felt John behind her. He reached around and cupped her breast in his hand. She let it lie there for a moment, but when she felt him fondling her, she pushed his hand away.

"Not now."

He moved his hand. "What then? You want to sleep?"

"I want to think."

"About the woman?"

"About Jenifer. About the assizes. About Lady Percy. God's breath, I wish I could wipe the smile off that judge's face. And Lady Percy's too. They sicken me. I wish it could be them that we had to kill and not this poor woman. What does she do except help sick soldiers?"

John moved, trying to dig himself deeper into the hay for warmth. "She is alone in the cottage. We could go back and do it now."

"Too dangerous. If she cried out, the whole community would come running—and they know the lanes and alleys; we don't. They will have lights; we'll be hunted down. And remember, it's not just a matter of killing her. Father Buckman gave us precise instructions."

"Then we don't let her cry out."

Joan remembered how scared she had been when Lady Percy's officers came for her in the prison. And how nervous she had been later, at Sheffield Manor. She and two other women, Jane Carr and Sarah Cowie, had been told to kill another condemned woman in front of Lady Percy. Sarah had proved weak-willed; Jane simply weak. Joan had done the killing almost alone, using the hem of the victim's own skirt to throttle her. Then, slumped in the torment of what she had done, she had seen her seven-year-old daughter Jenifer carried into that same great chamber, and the other women's daughters too, including the daughters of the woman she had just killed. The memories were horrible: the dead woman's petticoat, the crying of the children. She had been told to go to London and call at a certain tavern, the Black Swan, where a priest in a dark attic room would give her instructions. Given what she had already done, the prospect of killing this middle-aged, lonely nurse had not worried her at the time. Only now, faced with the necessity of killing again, with these houses and these people around her—all of them southern, strange, and untrustworthy—did it unnerve her. Also, the sense of being someone else's instrument made her feel as if she was owned. Like a slave.

She settled herself into the hay. The owl outside continued

hooting. Soon afterward she heard John snore. When the memories of Lady Percy came into her mind she beat them back, each time saying a prayer for Jenifer, wishing her more and more good things—wishing her a smile.

10

∽

Tuesday, December 24

The weather was a mixture of weak sunlight and gray cloud. Clarenceux looked at the sky and across the road, and pulled out his piece of paper. He marked "Greybeard" and "Tom Green" as the two men watching the house. However, today there was a third man too. He did not see his face clearly through the distorting glass, but he was tall and clean shaven, and wore a black felt cap, bright white shirt, and velvet jerkin. The last item was more the sort of garment that would be seen at court than at a house in Fleet Street. The way he carried himself reminded Clarenceux of a naval captain he had once sailed with on a diplomatic mission. This man had authority. There could be little doubt that the house of spies had a new master.

Clarenceux created a new column on his piece of paper and headed it "captain." There were now eight men coming and going from the house. At some points there had been as many as five in the building at one time.

Turning from the window, he put the paper away and tried to concentrate on the preparation for his visitation of Oxfordshire. There were piles of bound books and unbound manuscripts all over the table and floor. His heart was not in reading them, however; he could think of nothing but the growing threat across the street. He chose instead to stack them away in the book press by the door. But in so doing he picked up the chronicle of Henry of Abingdon.

It was a most unusual volume. The best parts were all the things the author deplored. One concealment of two Lollard knights at Thame Abbey was particularly obnoxious to Henry and thoroughly entertaining for Clarenceux. Henry had not written to praise these men, who were Lollards and therefore heretics in his eyes, but to show what evils lurked in the Church. He had been appalled that the abbot of Thame—a Cistercian, no less—should have sheltered two such men and even facilitated their escape. He was no less outraged that the abbot was never prosecuted. Clarenceux made a note to point out the passage to Sir Richard when he returned the volume, for Sir Richard was now the owner of Thame Abbey.

The bell of St. Bride's chimed eleven. Entering the hall, he saw Thomas lighting the fire and the table laid out, with his elder daughter, Annie, positioning the salt and the butter dish in front of his place at the head. Awdrey rushed in, carrying a tablecloth. She looked anxious.

"Do you have the time to help?" she asked pointedly, moving the salt and the butter dish out of the way. "Perhaps you have not noted how much work goes into the preparation of a Christmas meal? Joan and I are both hard-pressed. Even Thomas lent a hand with chopping herbs. You and the children seem to be the only ones in this household with time on your hands." She did not stop for a reply but went out to the back landing.

Clarenceux stood still as he heard her rapid footsteps on the back stairs, heading down to the kitchen. "Thomas," he said, walking over to the table and straightening one corner of the newly laid cloth. The old man looked up from the hearth. "Do you have any idea why Walsingham has increased the guard?"

"I do not know, sir. But I do fear it, as I know you do. I do not know how to counsel you." He rose to his feet. "I will say this, though. You carry a heavy load. You do not seem yourself, and that affects us all—Mistress Harley most particularly, but also Nick, Joan, and me. I do not think it was wise to banish Nick to the stables, sir. I do not believe he was consorting with them."

"What else should I do? Run the risk of having a spy in my house on the chance that Nick is innocent? What if I should be wrong? It is better to be cautious and wrong than to be wrong about his innocence."

"Sir, it is very cold these days. Normally out of mercy you would have let him inside the house. Now you have made him like you less."

Clarenceux sighed and rubbed his face in his hands.

"Sir, I wish I could alleviate you of it, this anxiety. So too does Mistress Harley. She feels that you are worrying over what might never happen."

"Might never happen?" Clarenceux took his hands away. "It is happening. What does she want? For me to pretend all is well until someone holds a gun to my head, or to hers, and demands the document?" He turned and looked at the brightness of the glazed window. "Jesus is our Savior, Thomas, but I have been pushed past the point of prayer. I have been pushed past the point of trusting her majesty to protect me too. That document is the point of a dagger and the weight of England is resting on it. It pushes into me; it pierces me. And I do not know what to do. All I know is that Walsingham fears that something will happen soon—and that is why he has increased the guard."

"Sir, you could go and ask Mr. Walsingham why he has made this change."

"I was thinking much the same thing. My wife's priority might be setting the table, but my obligations…" He decided and moved to the door. "I will do so now. I will be back before dinner."

He went down the front stairs, took his cloak and hat, and stepped out into the street. He could not help but look up at the house opposite: there was a flash of light, as if a man's shoulder buckle had caught the light. A man's face moved in the first-floor window— and quickly withdrew.

"May your heart pour with shame and your eyes weep torrents of regret," shouted Clarenceux.

A fine rain had begun to fall. The ground, still frozen after last night's cold, would soon soften into mud. He looked down the hill to Fleet Bridge and up to Ludgate, with the cathedral tower, lacking its spire, frowning down on the scene. A wherry journey to the Tower would be frustratingly slow, since you could never get the watermen to put their backs into rowing against the tide, especially when it was raining. Back at his house, he opened the gate and went into the yard. "Nick!" he called.

Nick had been in the hayloft. Hearing the call, he took two steps on the ladder and jumped the rest of the way to the straw-covered ground. Clarenceux went to the stable door and looked in. Nick unlatched it. The tall black stallion, Brutus, welcomed his master by throwing his nose in his direction. Maud, the chestnut mare he kept for his wife, bucked her head in her stall and snorted. He patted her too. Both horses had been cleaned out; hay was in their manger and fresh straw on the floor.

"Was it very cold in here last night, Nick?"

"I kept myself as warm as I could, sir, in the hay upstairs. But, truth be told, it was indeed cold."

The boy needed a wash and a clean shirt. Even by the standards of stable boys he was dirty. "I am sorry I spoke sternly to you the other day," said Clarenceux. "Tonight you can sleep by the kitchen fire."

"Thank you, sir."

"Do you have family with whom you want to share Christmas dinner? You are welcome to stay with us should you wish, but if you would rather go to your kin, you may."

Nick seemed brightened by this news. "Thank you, sir. I did ask Mistress Harley if I might spend Christmas with my cousins in St. Dunstan's parish; she said she would speak to you about it."

"Well, you have my permission. Now, if you will help me saddle Brutus, I have a journey to make across the city."

11

Joan Hellier kept watch on the back of Widow Baker's cottage as John tried the door. It was locked and there was no keyhole: it was bolted on the inside. He stepped back and looked up. A shuttered window ten feet above the ground looked as if it might not be locked, or only fastened with a loose catch. Although it was only small, about a foot wide and about the same high, Joan was slim enough to get through such a gap. There were two buildings in the small yard: a henhouse and an ivy-clad ruined carthouse. By the henhouse John found a crate packed with hay in which Widow Baker stored apples. Emptying the apples out, he carried it in one hand as Joan walked around the yard seeing what else could be used. A wooden pail, a block of wood used for chopping firewood, an old wooden churn. They tried various combinations. Five minutes later, with John balancing on the churn on top of the upturned crate, and Joan standing on his shoulders, she was able to slip a knife between the shutter and the jamb, lift the catch, and haul herself up and into the dark chamber of the cottage.

She crouched on the floor of the bedchamber of her intended victim. Even though they had knocked on the door repeatedly and believed no one was home, she was still apprehensive. Reassured by the silence, she straightened herself as far as she could, as the roof was low, her eyes adjusting to the light. The room was very neat, with nothing scattered about or left to one side. There were two beds, a chest beside the window, and another chest by the opening to the ladder that led down into the main living space of the cottage.

Joan went down the ladder. Halfway there she paused and looked around in the gloom of the shuttered space. There was a cauldron of pottage near the fire, some embroidery on a bench by the closed window. These were signs that someone would return soon. She descended the rest of the way, smelling the lingering smoke of the fire and boiled vegetables. The ashes were still warm. Her cautious eyes tried to take in as much as possible: a pair of old bellows, the leather-work needing repair; two flitches of bacon above the fireplace; a table board and trestles in a corner.

She went to the back door and unbolted it. "John," she whispered, "put the pail and block back where we found them. Nothing must appear disturbed. Then come in here and bolt the door after you."

12

Clarenceux rode through the street toward the Tower, impatiently pulling Brutus to the left, then to the right, trying to avoid pedestrians, and spurring the horse when there was an opportunity for speed. The timber jetties of houses hung darkly over the narrow alleys, with little more than a strip of gray sky to be seen above. At London Stone, several coaches blocked their road where merchants' wives had bade their coachmen stop so they could chat without descending. This infuriated Clarenceux, who turned Brutus north along St. Swithin's Lane and then right into Lombard Street. In galloping, however, he almost knocked himself off the horse when, standing in the stirrups, he struck the overhanging beams of an old house with his shoulder.

At Walsingham's house, the servant who answered the door brusquely informed him that Walsingham was away on the queen's business. No matter how much Clarenceux harangued the man, he would not say where. Leaving with a few choice curses, he galloped away, riding in a blind fury. People turned their heads and shouted at him to slow down. He almost careered into a wagon crossing Cornhill; another time a young woman had to throw herself out of his path. Only that last close scrape brought him to his senses. A moment later he reached Aldgate and the road heading east. There was no point going further.

Thomas is right, he thought, wiping his face. *It is burning through my mind like spirit of vitriol.*

He looked at the people coming and going through the city gate—women with baskets, men driving small carts, servants carrying firewood or provisions, and one or two people on horseback—and felt suddenly purposeless. *My family would be better off if I were dead*, he thought. *If I were to destroy the document and myself in some way, publicly, no one would bother them again.* Brutus snorted and waited, the fine rain still coming down. Clarenceux kicked him into a slow walk back along Leadenhall beneath the expensively glazed windows of fine houses.

If it came to the worst, he could defeat them all—all his enemies, those within the queen's government and those who wished to overthrow her—by an act of personal sacrifice.

The horse broke into a trot, the rain coming down harder on them both. A wide street lay ahead, almost empty because of the rain. He began to canter, then gallop. Onlookers were shocked to see someone galloping straight through the street. Some shouted, some tried to wave at him to slow him down, but Clarenceux's mind had gone beyond the day-to-day reasoning of polite conduct. He rode hard, swerving this way and that. Coming to Gracechurch Street he turned right and rode to Bishopsgate, under the arch and out along the road to Hackney, past Bedlam Hospital to Hog Lane, where he turned left along the track. A woman in the field to his right had been caught out by the weather and was hurrying to gather up the laundry she had laid on the hedges to dry. Next he had the windmills on his right: four tall wooden buildings, sails unmoving in the wet air. Chiswell

Street brought him back into the suburbs of the city, where handsome houses stood with large gardens. He had once wanted to own just such a house. It would have been the way to bring up his children—his son, if he ever had one.

He would never have a son.

Clarenceux slowed. The madness of his ride, and the foolish euphoria he had just felt, settled on him like a cloud. How selfish he had been, risking crashing into someone in the street, endangering so many pedestrians, including children. What had so excited him? The thought of his own destruction. The thought of leaving his wife a widow and his two daughters fatherless. He stopped, dismounted, and felt the rain running down his back, under his collar. His sleeves too were beginning to let in water. Destroying himself might crush all the aspirations of his enemies. It would save his family. But they would all pay a price, and his wife and daughters would pay almost as heavily as he. Clarenceux was suddenly jealous: his self-sacrifice would end with another man lying with Awdrey, having children by her. His daughters would lose the love of a father.

At the turning of Aldersgate Street into London he stopped and rested his forehead against Brutus's neck. *Get a hold of yourself, William. There is a way through this. True, I could end it all, but such decisions can wait. First things first: I must find out why Walsingham has increased the guard on my house.*

13

It was late afternoon. Rebecca knelt down by the bed of the feverish young man in the long hall of the hospital in Portchester Castle and started to unwrap the bandages on his leg. Sweating, and uttering involuntary cries of pain, he looked down at her. Like so many sailors and soldiers before him, he saw the kind face, her dark hair and brown eyes with their haunting sadness, and was warmed by her looks, which were even more appealing in the candlelight.

She reached the innermost section of the bandage, still stuck to the skin, and smelled the familiar odor of pus and bloody flesh. Over the last two and a half years she had grown used to the sights and smells of calamitous injuries. She had assisted in more amputations than she could remember. The French war might be over and the number of patients was not as high as it had been when she arrived, but even so, a steady trickle of naval injuries kept arriving. Some had fallen from the rigging of ships onto the deck; some had been blasted by gunpowder or hit by the recoil of a cannon. This young man had slipped when passing between two boats at sea. His lower left leg had been trapped between the gunwales of the two vessels as a wave brought one hard against the other, breaking both of the major bones. He was lucky. Rebecca had seen a man whose whole pelvis had been crushed in a similar accident; he had been brought in quickly, but even so he had not lived long.

"What is your name?" she asked.

"Martin," he replied, his face contorted as he tried to control the pain. "Martin Milton."

Rebecca lifted off the last part of the bandage, pulling it away from the sticky flesh and caked blood, and Martin cried out. Very carefully, she turned the now-exposed limb. One of the bones had punctured the skin. It had not rotted: all the flesh was still bloody and pink, and there was healthy skin around his lower leg and foot. However, the jutting broken bone made her uncertain whether to deliver the good news herself or to leave it to Mr. Wheatsheafen, just in case he decided that it had to come off.

Three beds away, Mr. Wheatsheafen saw Rebecca studying Milton's leg. He dried his hands on a towel and walked across to look over her shoulder. He peered curiously, then came around Rebecca and examined the wound more closely, standing right beside the bed. "Well," he said carefully, taking plenty of time to consider the situation, "this is definitely a job for the bonesetter. He *may* be able to put you on your feet again. If not, that bone is good enough for the pot—it won't go to waste."

With that he patted the injured man on the shoulder and moved on to the next patient, who had a large bandage covering his skull.

Rebecca grinned at Martin Milton as she set the old bandage to one side and began to wash the wound, cleaning away the dirt and pus. "You can trust Mr. Wheatsheafen," she said as she worked. "If he makes a joke about your injury, you're as good as cured."

Martin Milton said nothing. He merely grimaced an attempted smile at her through the pain.

"I only wish he would make more jokes," she said, thinking back to some of the men she had had to deal with. Every morning she dreaded the moment when, entering the hall, she discovered that a man who had been a patient the night before was now a corpse. "I am sorry, Martin, this is going to hurt—but if it becomes unbearable, remember this: you are one of the lucky ones."

When Rebecca had dealt with Martin and re-bandaged him for when the bonesetter arrived, she changed the linen on the beds that had been vacated over the day. This hall had forty-two beds; a third were empty. She left just two made up in case of urgent need. Bundling the canvas sheets and bandages together, she carried them down to a buck basket by the door and dumped them there.

"It's getting dark. You can go home if all is to your satisfaction," said Mr. Wheatsheafen as he ticked names off a list at a table.

Rebecca made one more trip up the central aisle, closing the shutters above the beds and wishing the patients a pleasant night's sleep. To Martin Milton she made a special visit, to make sure the bandages she had applied to his broken leg were not too tight and causing him unnecessary pain. A lantern burning halfway down the hall was sputtering, so she righted the candle inside, corrected the angle of the aperture, and watched it burn again with an even flame. After one last check, seeing the glow of the four lanterns lighting the hall and the beds, she wrapped her cloak around her shoulders and made her way out into the dusk.

Inside, it had been nearly dark. Outside, however, there was light from the last traces of the sunset in the west. She walked across the muddy path to the main cobbled lane running through the outer ward and over to the gatehouse on the landward side. The huge tower and defensive walls of the medieval castle were still menacing despite the passage of centuries. A seagull perched on the battlements, surveying the scene before taking wing and flying out over the bay.

Passing under the gatehouse, Rebecca decided to walk the longer way home. Widow Baker was away and unlikely to return until after Christmas; there was no need to rush. Turning left, she wandered along the shore, just feet away from the castle wall, listening to the gentle lapping of the water. There were several ships in the bay and she thought of the men aboard those vessels. How many of her old patients had gone on to see the world? How many had fallen prey to diseases in a hot climate, or been washed off deck in a storm? How many would grow old? Precious few, she knew that. As long as men went to sea, they faced the likelihood of a violent end and a watery grave.

A cold breeze blew off the water. She heard footsteps on the shingle behind her and turned to see it was Mr. Wheatsheafen. He was heaving his portly frame along at quite a rapid pace to catch up with her. "Rebecca," he panted, "it occurred to me that I should not let you go home alone to a cold cottage, not on Christmas Eve. Come and sup with me and my wife. We would be glad to entertain you."

"That is indeed kind of you, Mr. Wheatsheafen, but I do not want to put your good wife to any trouble. Besides, I have my own supper prepared at the cottage."

"Perhaps tomorrow then, after we've seen to the patients?"

She pulled the cloak tighter and smiled. "Yes, tomorrow." She walked with him slowly, as he caught his breath. "Do you think that the bonesetter will really be able to fix that leg? It is broken so badly. And the way he was injured—it reminded me of that man who died here after he was similarly crushed."

"He's young and looks strong. He'll cope with the pain. You've taken a shine to him, then?"

"As I do with almost all the young men who come here and are subject to our ministrations."

"You should train to be a surgeon. The Church grants licenses to women as well as men. I hear there's a woman of Bodmin about to be examined—and my source in Exeter tells me that she is the equal of any man. You could do the same. You have the skill and you care."

"You are too kind, Mr. Wheatsheafen. You exaggerate my skills and my aptitude. And I know full well that I could not make a surgeon. I am not like you. It is the people that move me, not their sicknesses."

Wheatsheafen smiled. "You do me a disservice, Rebecca. I care very much for my patients. But you are right in a sense. You have to love the understanding of how God orders the body, and a good physician will always put that first before any single patient. You know how a gambler loves to gamble, regardless of whether he wins or loses; it is the same with a good physician. He loves to be the instrument of God's mercy, regardless of how God eventually determines the fate of the patient."

Rebecca looked across the wide bay, with the sky darkening. "I do not much care what is wrong with these men. I just want to make them better, to give them some hope." She walked on a little way.

"There's a special dish I am planning to bring in tomorrow, for the Christmas dinner. I bought some cured fish not long ago, and with eggs beaten and fried, it is particularly good."

"You know the way to the men's hearts," commented Wheatsheafen, then he looked up. "It's getting dark. I'll walk with you to the crossroads."

Five minutes later, Rebecca said good-bye to Mr. Wheatsheafen.

He ambled off to his house; Rebecca wandered to hers. She felt for the key to the cottage in the pocket of her kirtle and had it to hand as she approached. It was almost dark now; as soon as she was indoors she would have to light the fire. There was tinder by the back door, some dried lichen on the shelf by the hearth.

She reached out, placed the key in the lock, and turned it, feeling the familiar resistance of the levers. It caught, as it so often did, and she wriggled it slightly, finding the angle that would allow the lock to open. The door swung into the dark interior and she entered, leaving it open so she could see the outline of her way across the hall to the back door and the tinder box.

In the dimness, she did not see John the Egyptian before she felt him grab her from the left. He threw her onto the floor, falling on top of her. Rebecca shrieked as she fell, and hit the ground hard, landing on her back. The breath knocked out of her, she scrabbled in panic in the darkness to get to her feet. Gasping, she tried to scream but he held his hand over her mouth. She felt his weight on her and raised her knee to push him off—but then the knife was driven into her abdomen. At first it felt like a thin spike but it kept entering her, opening her up, and with every fraction of an inch that it moved into her, the pain increased tenfold. Swirling in her own fear, she felt the man tear the knife out of her and plunge it into her with a second agony. He stabbed down a third time, toward her heart but hit the bone. The knife entered her a fourth time, again striking her bone. She thought of the pain of the man she had tended that afternoon, who had grimaced and cried as she had turned his leg. A greater pain was overwhelming her—a whale about to swallow her, Jonah-like. All the pains she had ever caused were overwhelming her now. She yearned for someone to take them away. She saw Mr. Wheatsheafen hurrying along the shoreline, Widow Baker lighting the fire, and a huge hall of patients—thousands of them in a hospital ward that seemed to go on forever. Then she looked at one of the beds and saw her first child lying dead there, and in the next two beds were her next two children, both dead. Nearby she saw her late husband, Henry, crouched over his manuscript in the light of a candle. And behind her she sensed Clarenceux, standing with his hand on her shoulder. She turned and tried to embrace him, but then there was only the cold ground there.

When the knife entered her a fifth time—how much later she could not tell—she was expecting it. She recalled lying in bed, in childhood, feeling sick and being looked after by her mother. There was bright morning light coming in the window, and all she had to do that day was keep warm. She could hear her mother in the hall singing to herself. The breeze moved a cobweb in the window of the chamber, just inside the open shutter: it entranced her, sending images of dancing angels of light shimmering into the room. It was a perfect moment in a beautiful world, even though she was unwell. She felt no hatred for the man who was now bringing her life to a close. She had no wish even to think about him in these last few instants. There were more wonderful things—light, beauty, kindness. Such a man did not belong in her world anymore. She refused to allow him to follow her.

Then, sadly, she said good-bye to the light, to the world, to her heart, and to everything she had ever known.

14

Christmas Day, Wednesday, December 25

Awdrey had been up late the previous evening decorating the hall. The tops of the walls were all woven with strands of ivy and mistletoe, which she had bought from a street vendor the day before. Each door was arched with sprigs of holly and juniper. In the morning the girls had been delighted with the scene; they quickly learned that the holly was sharp, so had taken to walking through the doors very slowly and carefully so as to avoid the prickles. They had seen the table laid with a pristine white cloth and laden with a ham, marchpanes, and pewter plates, ready for the feast, and they had complained bitterly when they realized their father was not going to allow them to breakfast at all, let alone on this feast, before taking them to church. But they had both submitted. Mildred had stomped her feet and sulked for a minute before her sister told her that there were mince pies and capon in the kitchen, as well as beef and mustard. Annie had laughed at the way the younger girl's eyes had opened wide.

Thomas accompanied them to church and then bade them a merry feast at the church gate, as he had promised to dine with his nephew's family. Only Joan was left in the house, and this made Clarenceux anxious. He had visions of the place being overrun while he was out, and everything being destroyed in a frantic attempt to find the document. He was even more concerned when he noticed the white-haired gentleman there too, in the same pew as before. This time the man was more suitably attired, in a black doublet and matching hosen. Only once did Clarenceux catch his eye. He did not attempt to speak to him, but he did ask several parishioners if they knew the man. None did.

As the children ran around, excited by the huge spread of food that was being prepared for them by their mother and Joan, Clarenceux looked out the hall window. In his hurry to get to church with the family, and to guard against attack, he had failed to note who was watching the house. He cursed himself, clenching his fist against his mistake.

While Awdrey and Joan fetched the food up from the kitchen, he stole up the stairs to his study and picked up his best sword from where it rested on the top of a book press. He returned to the hall and then went down to the front door, where he placed the sword on a hook behind his cloak, covering it there. He walked along the ground-floor passage, past the buttery, to the kitchen at the back of the house. Awdrey had her hands full with a platter of roast beef, and Joan was behind her carrying a tray of sauces.

"I feel I should be playing my part today, in the old style," he said as they passed him.

"In the old style?" asked Awdrey.

"The Lord of Misrule. The custom is for the servants to sit in the best place and the lord to serve them, and for the men to play the women's roles."

"You are behaving very strangely, William. Is there anything you need to tell me?"

"No, I just thought it would be an entertaining gesture. Yesterday you told me that I ought to help more."

Joan smiled. "I think Mr. Harley is a most considerate employer. If he wishes to wait on me at table, I will not protest."

Clarenceux performed a mock bow and took the tray from her, following the women up the stairs to the hall. There Awdrey and Joan settled themselves while he fetched the rest of the dishes and plates, taking advantage of his time alone downstairs to ensure that both front and back doors were bolted. He took up flasks of wine from the buttery and gave some to Joan as well as Awdrey—which made Joan laugh nervously, as she was not used to wine. He himself did not drink. Even when carving the roast beef he did not relax but kept his attention on the sounds of the house beyond the hall, listening in case, and every so often walking around the window end of the table so he could glance out at the house opposite.

Nothing happened. No one broke into the house. No one called.

"What is the matter with you?" asked Awdrey when they had a quiet moment together in the kitchen after the meal.

"I am truly worried."

"I can tell. Everyone can tell. I too am worried—about you. Whatever is in your mind is taking you over. But why now? What is it?"

Clarenceux shook his head.

"Come, William, you are worrying me now. I need to know what it is. Share your troubles." She stepped closer to him and put a hand on his arm. "You have got to tell me, please, for my peace of mind. I can feel that you're like iron. If I hit you across the shoulders with a crowbar now, it would bend. Please, William, confide in me."

He took a deep breath. "Across the street is a house full of men who have us under surveillance. They have been watching us for months. Three weeks and six days ago, the regular watch was increased to two guards per shift. Now it has increased to three, with a well-dressed captain attending in person. In addition we are being watched in church—you might have noticed the white-haired gentleman…"

Awdrey looked at him. "But what makes you think such people are our enemies? Might they not be Sir William's men watching out for us? Have you spoken to any of these men?"

"One, who called himself Tom Green. He was not friendly."

"This Tom Green might just be curt in his manners. His captain might be more affable. But…what am I trying to say?" She looked at him with pleading eyes. "I know how seriously you would take any threat against us, and I understand how diligently you work to safe-guard us, but can you not relax for today? It is Christmas."

"I know, I know. I wish I could be other than this. But I cannot be, for I must be alert to the dangers. Perhaps it seems to you that I am being overcautious, but it is the friendly stranger who will threaten us. We will not be given any warning."

A clear, deliberate knocking rang out on the front door. Four loud blows, in rapid succession.

"Look to the children," said Clarenceux. "I will answer."

He watched Awdrey turn and run up the stairs. Then, slowly, he walked along the passage to the front door. Taking his sword, he held it behind his back. *Thy will be done.* He seized the top bolt and shot it open, turned the key in the main lock, and finally undid the lower bolt.

A man stood in the daylight. Clarenceux recognized his livery as that of Sir William Cecil's household.

"Sir William bids you heartily a good Christmas and hopes that the feast finds you well. He asks you, Mr. Clarenceux, if it pleases you, to wait on him on the morrow at his house, at three of the bell. He asks me to add, for the avoidance of doubt, that this invitation is for you alone. May I assure him that you accept his invitation?"

Clarenceux mumbled his acceptance with some relief and closed the door, noting that the man on duty in the house opposite was watching them from the first-floor window. Only after he closed his front door did he start to think. *I did not recognize that man. Is this a ruse to separate me from my wife and family? Is it to kidnap me or to make sure the house is undefended?* He walked up the front stairs slowly to the hall, reflecting on the dangers that lay all about them, and the equally real responsibilities.

"Who was it?" asked Awdrey from the table.

Clarenceux looked at her and the children and Joan, sitting together. All of them were staring at him. This was no Christmas jollity. The weight on his shoulders was dragging down Awdrey too, and the children and Joan could not help but sense something was wrong.

"It was a message from Sir William—he wants me to see him alone, tomorrow."

"On St. Stephen's Day?" asked Awdrey. "He should have asked us all. Will you go?"

Clarenceux nodded. "I can hardly refuse."

Normally there would be nothing strange in Sir William wanting to talk to him alone about some matter of business on a weekday. Sir William was interested in heraldry and history, and he knew that Clarenceux had considerable experience not just in these subjects but in the practical matters of diplomatic missions overseas. But such business was not normally conducted on the day after Christmas. And St. Stephen's Day was not a time to invite him to pore over a heraldic treatise or a historical manuscript. All this lingered in the air between them, going over the children's heads and ignored by Joan who knew better than to involve herself in her master's affairs.

When Awdrey did speak, she did so in a cheerful voice. "Let us lock all the doors and bring out the wine," she said. "Let us answer the door to no visiting neighbors, not even for wassail and hippocras. Let's pretend we have gone away together to some strange land and know no one and are spending the feast alone surrounded by..."

"By blackamoors!" shouted little Mildred excitedly. She had only recently seen some slaves from Guinea exhibited in a street near the cathedral.

"And Indians," said Annie. "Or the Caribs, who are going to eat Mildred up for their Christmas feast!"

"And Joan," said Mildred, smiling at the servant. Joan pretended to be horrified at the thought of being eaten by Caribs.

Clarenceux looked at Awdrey. Nervously she smiled at him. And at that moment he felt he had everything that was precious to him close at hand. Everything he feared losing was not yet lost.

"Well, the front and back doors are barred against Caribs, Indians, Moors, pirates, thieves, robbers, housebreakers, Lutherans, and Anabaptists. And Francis Walsingham's men. We are safe. So let us drink to the protecting grace of Our Lord and Savior, and eat and be merry while we can."

15

Mary Vardine sat on the bed in the chamber where she had been locked for the last two days. She did not know the name of the house where she was being held, but it clearly belonged to a wealthy and influential man. She had seen a wide stone front with huge glass windows when she had been brought here, in a cart. There was glass even in the window of her chamber and rush matting on the floor. A latrine adjoined the room, with a green baize seat and a blue cloth-covered cushion over the hole. Her bed was soft, and the sheets were clean and made of something much finer than the canvas she was used to at home. The clothes she had been given too were of good quality—better than she would have bought for herself. A surgeon had come to see her for the first two days and then again yesterday; he had applied ointments to her skin, which had healed quickly. Every mealtime she had been given good broths containing lamb, chicken, or rabbit. A woman had come to wash her hair in a brass basin on the third day. A week ago she had been hoping to die before they could burn her alive. Now she did not know where she was—only that she was imprisoned. The physician and servants who came to her room clearly had instructions not to speak to her about anything other than her physical condition.

She had lost track of time in the jail. But she was aware that something out of the ordinary was happening in the house. She had heard a lot of clattering earlier, and someone had been shouting in the stable yard, which was visible through the glass of her window. Beyond the stables she could see the rise of a hill; a hunting party had ridden that way in the early morning sun. Now she felt hungry.

Soon she would hear footsteps along the corridor and the sound of the lock turning. The door would open and one man would place a bowl of pottage and a hunk of good bread on the table while another man stood outside the door. Then they would close the door and lock it until dusk.

Today, however, when the door opened, there was no food. Instead, one of the men spoke to her. "Your dinner is served in another chamber."

She followed the guards along a corridor with bare floorboards and plain plastered walls, wondering if now they were going to take her somewhere to burn her. She doubted it. There was no need to send a surgeon to heal a condemned person. After descending a narrow servants' staircase to the first floor, she found herself walking along a corridor with a much higher ceiling. Here the leading guard stopped and unlocked a door.

Mary entered a high, long chamber with a fire burning in a hearth to one side. The ceiling was decoratively plastered and painted with heraldic symbols and semi-naked figures, some with weapons. Huge glass windows allowed light to flood into the room. Two servants stood by a door on the far side, and in the middle was a long table, laden with food. Two women were seated there, looking at her. They were not wealthy-looking—quite the opposite. They were women like her, who had looked old from the day they turned twenty-one, having seen enough hardship in those first formative years to mark them out forever. One had a fine face but a cold eye and a sneer; her blond hair was unkempt and uncombed, her fingers callused. She was about thirty, and hostile-looking. The other woman looked to be a similar age. She had freckles and reddish light-brown hair. She did herself no favors by breathing through her mouth, so it was always open and her bottom lip protruding.

The woman with blond hair leaned on the table with one arm. "It seems we three are required to share this Christmas dinner together. Only Mr. Richardson said to wait until our host has arrived with the chaplain." She gestured at the cuts of meat and the cheeses, the salad dish and the saucers. There were near three-dozen dishes on the table.

Mary too looked at the table. "I have not seen such food since…" She could not remember when she had seen so much meat set out before her.

The freckled woman openly snatched a piece of chicken. "I'm not waiting," she mumbled, putting the meat in her mouth. "And what is anyone going to do? Kill us? We're already sentenced to die."

"You are?" asked Mary.

The freckled woman shrugged as she ate, chomping on her food.

The door at the far end of the room opened and the guards stood to one side. A man in a rich suit entered, with a white satin jerkin trimmed with brocade. He turned and bowed, and in came an old woman in a black satin dress, wearing an expression that would not have looked out of place on a judge. Her skin was very pale and wrinkled, her forehead knit in a deep frown. She walked with a pair of sticks. A priest followed her, and behind the priest came four more men.

"You are seated," she said, looking at the first two women. "You have not got to your feet. And *you* have started eating despite my orders to wait."

Mary watched her, scared, even though she was not talking to her. The woman's unblinking eye was hawklike; she looked at Mr. Richardson, who had led her in.

"Punish her."

Richardson gestured to two of the guards, who stepped forward quickly. The woman started to get up from her seat and shouted, "Don't you come near me!"

The noblewoman shouted in a shrill voice over her. "You are a condemned woman. You are beneath the law. You would be dead if it were not for me. You owe me your life—yet you cannot obey a simple order even to delay eating."

The guards tore the woman's dress as she tried to beat them off. Her breasts and back exposed, she struck out at them, knocking one to the floor. She sprawled on the ground after him. Several pewter platters went flying as the men lifted her and forced her across the table, facedown. Another man came forward with a wide length of leather, like a sword belt, with a buckle in it. The noblewoman nodded, and he brought it down across her back with as much force as he could manage, leaving a great red weal and a deep cut. A second time he struck her, with the same results, and a third. Then the noblewoman held up her hand, and he stepped back. The half-naked woman remained where she was.

"Two of you are sentenced to hang, one of you to be burned to death. I know all about you. I know where you are from, I know where you lived, and I know the people who condemned you. I know your families, your children, and your enemies. And like three of the first four women I snatched from the hangman's grasp, I am going to give you a chance to live again, to regain your liberty. But I require total obedience. One woman was not obedient. I ordered her fellow prisoners to kill her there and then, with their bare hands, in this very room. One brave woman did so, and I was most pleased. I would ask the same of you—except for the fact that today is Christmas Day. There will be no killing today."

There was silence for a long time. "What do you want us to do?" asked Mary eventually.

The noblewoman looked at her. "To reclaim a piece of property belonging to my late husband. A document, to be exact. A vitally important document—one for which I would gladly kill a thousand men."

"Who was your husband?" asked the blond-haired woman.

For this question she was given a stare of contempt. "I was married to Lord Henry Percy, earl of Northumberland." Lady Percy turned her attention to the freckled woman, who was still lying across the table. "You, Helen Oudry, sit down. The surgeon will see to your wounds later. First, grace." She raised a hand and, without turning around, beckoned the priest forward. "Father, if you would be so kind."

The priest bowed and uttered a short blessing in English, appending a short Latin grace. He bowed again and stepped back.

"Thank you, Father. You may leave us." She looked at Mary. "Are you going to stand there all day? Let us eat."

Mary took her place on the bench opposite the other two women. She began by helping herself to some chicken breasts that were on a nearby dish. But she hesitated. Like the freckled woman who breathed through her mouth, Lady Percy ate very noisily, as if she was putting as much effort into opening her mouth as closing it. The noises distracted her for a moment until the juices of the roast meat proved too pleasing.

"I want to forgive you," Lady Percy said. "You don't have to answer. But I do expect a modicum of gratitude for saving your lives."

"A modicum?" asked the blond-haired woman.

"I do not expect more. I do not expect your love, Ann Thwaite. Besides, what I have done for you in sparing your miserable lives is nothing by comparison with what I hope you will do for me. Succeed, and I will give you gold as well as your liberty."

"And if we fail?"

Lady Percy stretched over to a plate on which a roast partridge lay. She picked it up and broke it in half with her fingers, put half back, and sliced some meat off the half she had taken, picking up the pieces and dipping them in the nearest sauce. "That depends on how you fail. You all have children. Ann, six; Helen, three; Mary, two. They are the reason you are still alive. If you give your life trying to fulfill my request, then I will release your children and entrust them to those who will look after them. If you deliberately fail—that is to say, if you desert the cause—I will hang all of your children in those woods you can see over there." She pointed through the window.

"But they are children!" exclaimed Ann Thwaite.

"And you are felons. The cause of the Holy Catholic Church is greater than that of the children of felons. Your lives are forfeit, and the lives of motherless children are short. I want that document, and I want the traitor who hides it dead. England has a new heir in Charles James Stuart of Scotland. I will have his grandmother Lady Margaret Douglas released from her wrongful confinement in the Tower. And I will have the Catholic religion restored to every altar of every church in the realm."

Mary had stopped eating. The countess's words had suddenly made the food in her mouth taste dry and unappealing. Lady Percy noticed. "Mary Vardine. I know you have already killed a man, and that you are sentenced to burn. I have a special plan in mind for you."

16

Clarenceux stared at the piece of paper by the light of the candle on the table in his study. Even though he was wearing a thick robe he was cold, shivering. The fire in the hearth was almost out, and apart from a few loose sheets of paper, he had put nothing on it for an hour. He should have fetched a Yule log, he thought, and lit it with the remains of last year's log for luck. Instead, he had burned the carefully saved remains of last year's log downstairs at suppertime, with nothing for next Christmas.

He heard footsteps ascending the stairs. The door creaked open and he saw Awdrey's face, golden in the light of her candle.

"You are not working now, are you?" she asked.

He shrugged. "Dethick wants me to complete this visitation of Oxfordshire by the end of February. He expects me to start as soon as the Christmas feast is over. Part of me says I should go, and you will be rid of me and the risk, and part of me says exactly the opposite: that I should stay because you will be vulnerable."

"Have you considered coming to bed?"

"I cannot sleep."

"I wasn't suggesting that you should sleep."

He smiled, then closed his eyes. He did not know what to say. In truth, he did not desire her at that moment—he desired her safety more. But she came toward him and set her candle down on the table. She leaned over him and kissed the side of his face, his ear, then his cheek. "We have to live," she whispered, "and there is much more to living than constantly avoiding death. Besides, you're worrying so much you're almost killing yourself. Soon there will be nothing left of you but an epitaph. 'Here lieth William Harley, a worried man.'" She kissed the side of his face again. And again. After several more kisses she started to kiss the other side of his face and saw the tear in the candlelight. She kissed that too.

"If we are to be parted," he said, "whether that be through your death or mine, I want you to know that I love you. I know I have not always been the most faithful husband, and that I have at times been distracted. But they were, and are, just other stars in the firmament. You are my Pole Star, and you always have been. You are the guiding light of my life."

She kissed his hair. "We Pole Stars have difficulty making you sailors follow our light. You wander about until you are threatened by darkness, then you look for us. I know you. You are a man, and men lie in their words—but not in their deeds. I want you to show me that you love me more than everything you fear out there. Show me, do not tell me."

He put a hand to her face. "Bless you, Awdrey, my Etheldreda, my love."

17

John the Egyptian reached out in the darkness and felt Joan lying beside him. He ran his hand over her clothed body, over her breasts. She lay awake, not moving, not wanting him. She wanted only to sink in the straw and find herself anew, somewhere else. She turned away from him.

"What is the matter?"

"What do you think?" she replied.

"I was the one who killed her. I did it for you. You owe me something."

She turned back over, angrily. "I owe *you?* Do you mean…Oh, let me not waste my breath."

John reached out and held her wrist tight. "I used to break into houses, lift clothes through windows with hooks, and trade stolen goods in markets. I used to take horses, play with false dice, and trick travelers out of their money. I did not kill women just because some haggard old countess wanted them dead."

"Don't pretend that you were an innocent. It makes no difference— theft or murder, you'll still swing for it one day."

"I had no reason to kill that woman. Jenifer is not my daughter. You owe me."

Joan lay motionless on the hay. Suddenly she reached down, lifted the skirts of her kirtle and smock up high, above her waist, reached for his hand, and pulled it violently toward her, placing it between her legs, which she spread wide. "Go on, just do it, since you feel that I owe you. Get it over with. Me, I am thinking of my daughter. I am also mindful of that woman we killed. I can't forget that her head is in a sack over there. You might have killed her, but it was me who cut her head off. Now do you still wish to use me for pleasure?"

John grabbed her thigh. He pinched it tightly as he moved over her. He put his other hand around her throat. "Yes, I do. Because I want you to know I am not just your tool in this matter. You are my doxy and you'll stay that way, even after all this is done. Your daughter is your business, but you are mine. I am helping you, am I not? That is because I want you. I'll help you all I can—but I will have you when I want you…" He let go of her neck and thigh to unfasten his breeches and push them down. Forcing his left arm under her back, he grabbed her left arm and pressed himself against her, pinning her right arm as well. Then he entered her. He was not violent in his movements, but she felt him bruising her left arm with his grip.

"This is good," he said. "Oh, this is good…" But then he said nothing more until he had finished.

"You bastard," she whispered. "It's all the same to you, isn't it? Killing and fucking and stealing. Always having things your own way."

"I *am* a bastard," said John between gasps as he recovered his breath. "I will always be a bastard. It is what I am. But when I have you, I don't want to be anything other than the half-Egyptian bastard I am. I don't want to be all-English, and I don't want to be anywhere else, or richer, or dressed in fine clothes, or with anyone else. I just want to be naked, holding you, having you."

"There are better sorts of loving," she said, turning away from him.

"None more honest."

18

Thursday, December 26

Clarenceux looked up at the portrait above the fireplace in Sir William's writing room. It showed a proud man in his prime. *Sir Wyllyam Sessylle, aetatis suae xxxii* was painted in gold in a corner. He reflected that there was something slightly naive about the face. This was the most intelligent man in the realm, or so many said, and yet this face lacked something that the older Sir William possessed. It took Clarenceux several minutes to work out what it was. Humility.

He had arrived promptly at the appointed hour, three o'clock, full of apprehension, and had been told to wait in an antechamber not far from the great hall. After about a quarter of an hour, he had been shown into this room. There was a fire on the hearth, which must have been burning awhile, as it was beautifully warm. A pewter flask of wine was on the table to one side, and two glass goblets of Venetian design. But the room was dominated by several large book presses, each taller than he was and containing two to three hundred volumes, with carved scrollwork at the top. They seemed to be mostly English and Italian humanist works, and several Italian volumes on architecture and design. He lifted down one leather-bound volume and read *An Abridgement of the Chronicles of England, gathered by Richard Grafton, citizen of London. Anno Do. 1563.* He knew Richard Grafton well enough to know that abridging chronicles was his forte. Grafton believed that copying other people's historical work was not immoral—for how could anyone have a monopoly on the truth? Clarenceux also knew John Stow, who was enraged by the copying that Grafton had already done of his work and bitterly resentful that Grafton planned to produce another volume of "his" chronicles, stolen entirely from him, Stow. Clarenceux's sympathies lay with John Stow; the normal state of the past was for it to be lost. If, then, a man preserved something of it, and made something new out of it, it was not free to be stolen.

He put Grafton's book back on the shelf and pulled down the adjacent volume, a slightly older *Bible in Englysh.* There was no name on the cover but he knew that this too was Richard Grafton's work, as a printer, rather than a historian. He shook his head; Grafton claiming other chroniclers' work as his own was akin to him claiming the work of ancient writers as his own too—even the writers of the Bible. He was not at liberty to claim the work of the Church Fathers as his own, so why should he be allowed to claim that of his contemporaries? He put the Bible back also. Still Sir William had not come, so he pulled down the next volume. This was *The Castel of Memorie: wherein is conteyned the restoring, augmenting, and conseruing of the Memorye and Remembraunce, with the safest remedies and best preceptes therevnto in any wise apperteyning: Made by Gulielmus Gratarolus Bergomaris Doctor of Artes and Physicke. Englished by Willyam Fulwod.* Clarenceux was impressed: Grafton, Grafton, Gratarolus—Sir William had arranged his books in alphabetical order of printer or author. Curious, he started reading the first section of Gratarolus:

Memorie is by the whiche the mynde repeateth things that are past. Or it is a stedfast perceivyng in the mynde of the disposition of things and words. Or (as Aristotle supposeth) it is an imagination, that remaineth of such things as the sense had conceyved. Also by the sentence of Plato, Memorie is a sense & a safetie (or a safe reteining of things): for the soule obtaineth by the office of the senses whatsoever things chaunce under the sense, and therefore it is the beginnings of an opinion. But by the mynde itselfe it considereth intellectuall thynges, & so is it become intelligence.

He put his finger on the words "Aristotle supposeth" and read that sentence again. "Memory is an imagination." *If that is so,* he reasoned, *then all recorded memory is merely fable. And the document I guard, which speaks of the marriage of Lord Percy to Anne Boleyn, is also nothing more than fable. The illegitimacy of the queen herself thus becomes untrue.*

But the truth is the truth, and always will be; so the truth of the past is unchangeable even if God alone knows it.

The door to the library opened and Sir William entered hastily in his robe. He was much older now than his picture, only two years younger than Clarenceux. His beard was heavily gray, with just a little reddish-brown in the mustache. His graying hair was concealed beneath a black cap and his doublet was made of black velvet with gold trimmings and pearl buttons. The effect of the black robe over the whole black and jeweled ensemble was strikingly rich and dramatic.

"I am sorry to keep you waiting, William," said Cecil. "I was with her majesty this morning—and she thrust a bundle of petitions at me and asked me to look through them. I tried to give my apologies but, well, you know what she is like in a bad mood. Looking through them took me an hour—thus detaining me longer than I expected at the palace."

Clarenceux put the book back in the press. "Does your wife ever see you these days?"

Cecil smiled at Clarenceux. "It is the secret of our beautiful marriage," he said as he took off the robe and placed it on a bench by the wall. "I am never a burden on my wife. Wine?"

Clarenceux shook his head. "No. It has lost its savor somewhat these days. Inebriation makes me feel vulnerable."

"Then only drink a little," said Cecil as he poured himself a glass. "That at least should embolden you against your enemies."

"I have too many enemies."

Cecil nodded. "I hear you attend sword practice these days at the Belle Savage?"

"Who told you?"

"Walsingham, of course." Cecil sipped his wine. "I always thought you were too proud to admit that you might need lessons in anything, swordsmanship especially. Scholars who can defend themselves with real weapons as well as wit are few on the ground. Most think wit is enough and only find out too late that it has its limitations."

"Why did you summon me?"

"I did not summon you. I invited you. And you know why. I must have the Percy-Boleyn marriage agreement. The time has come for you to hand it over to me."

"Last year you were happy for me to keep hold of it. The year before that too. What has changed?"

"The Scottish marriage. Charles James Stuart. The queen herself admits that she cannot pretend anyone has a better claim—at least, not until she herself has children. It is ironic: her majesty has forbidden anyone from discussing the succession and yet precisely for that reason we do little else but discuss it. Walsingham thinks she will never marry because she sees the monarchy as indivisible from herself, alone and ethereal, like an angel of England. I disagree. I think she will marry—not for the sake of company nor even for the sake of her father's dynasty but for the sake of religion. If she does not, the Catholic boy in Scotland will inherit the throne of England."

Clarenceux disagreed. "If you have not persuaded her to share power with a husband yet, you never will."

"But the Catholics have a champion in that boy, and he has a powerful protector in his father. Remove Elizabeth now and a Catholic will inherit—there is no doubt about that. The document you hold used to be just a curiosity—something that your London revolutionary friends toyed with. Certainly it was dangerous; it inspired their imaginations and made them feel important. They could have done much damage with it. But they were never sufficiently well connected to wield its true power. In Lord Henry Stewart's hands, however, it becomes the means to persuade foreign powers to assist the Catholic cause. That is why I must ask you to surrender it."

Clarenceux looked at the fire. It was burning low. He walked to it, crouched down, and picked up a log from the pile. He tossed it onto the flames. He did the same with a second log. Still looking at the flames, he replied, "I cannot do that."

Cecil lifted his wine glass to his mouth. "I trust you will explain."

Clarenceux remained looking into the flames. "I have had a long time to think about that document and I have come to realize certain things. If we were to have an open meeting—in the Guildhall, for instance—and if at that meeting I was formally invited to hand the marriage agreement over to her majesty, or you, or anyone, and did so in the presence of the leading Catholics of the realm, then I would gladly do so. But you cannot allow that to happen. If you, the queen's secretary, were even to acknowledge that that document exists—that it *ever existed*—you would start a civil war. Its very creation renders the legitimate line of old King Henry extinct and Mary of Scotland the rightful queen of England."

"Something could be arranged. A private gathering, perhaps."

Clarenceux put another log on the fire, and then a fourth. "No. Not even Elizabeth herself would be able to assure me that I will be allowed publicly to hand over that document. It is no good the handover taking place in secret, for the followers of the old religion will be left in the dark as to where it is, and never have anything official to show it existed. For it is knowledge *of the truth* that you must deny. In some respects Aristotle was wrong to say that memory is imagination; our consciences are not the same as our imaginations. But in the matter of politics he was quite right. You can claim that we do not remember the circumstances of our queen's parentage; we merely imagine it. Political leaders have a tendency to turn memory into imagination."

Cecil approached the fireplace and crouched down beside Clarenceux. "I do not disagree," he said. "Only I word it differently. 'Politics is the art of purposeful lies' is how I put it. But that is the point. They are *purposeful*. Anyone can tell the truth. If governing the country was just a matter of telling the truth, then we would have no secrets. We could leave it to a machine—like a water wheel or a mill. Telling the right lie at the right time, or concealing a particular truth at the most necessary moment—these are things that a machine cannot do."

"You can tell the truth if you believe the truth is God's will."

Cecil picked up a stick and adjusted the position of one of the burning logs, then threw the stick onto the fire. "William, you have to choose sides, you know. You cannot remain alone, defiant of the State and in defiance of the Catholic cause. If you choose to follow your faith, you will become a traitor."

Clarenceux looked into the flames, which were now rising higher. "I am not alone. I have God on my side. I do not believe that God is on your side simply because Elizabeth is queen now. Nor do I believe that God is on the side of those who would overthrow her. But I do believe He is on my side, for I follow His direction. So, Sir William, while you think I am outnumbered, the truth is that you are."

He got up and walked away from the fire. Cecil slowly also got to his feet.

"You understand how dangerous your way is. You know there can be no return, no path of redemption. You and your family will always be watched. Pursued. Threatened."

"Why has Walsingham increased the guard on my house?"

"You'll have to ask him. I know he has you watched. In doing so he is only following my orders. It is for your safety."

"And the safety of the document?"

Cecil said nothing.

Clarenceux poured himself a glass of wine. "I'll drink this because I am in good company," he said, raising the glass. "I know you are a remarkable man, Sir William. One day the chronicles will be filled with descriptions of your deeds. But I cannot give you the marriage agreement. It is not that I do not trust you—it is that I know you will prove wholly loyal to her majesty, not me. One day the time will come for me either to use it or destroy it." He drank again. "And maybe I will destroy myself too. In this I will perform the will of God, not the will of her majesty."

"Elizabeth does not even know the document exists," muttered Cecil. He walked over to the bottle of wine and poured another glass. "William, do not sacrifice your life."

"The thought is not entirely unwelcome, if thereby I can end my worries, frustrate the rebels, and guarantee my family's safety."

"You love them that much?"

"Just as you do your family."

"True." Cecil drank. "However, I would feel an obligation to put her majesty and the State before my family. God knows I love my wife and children, but I know my capacity for loyalty is greater than my capacity for love. I pray that I am never again forced to choose."

"Never again?" asked Clarenceux.

Cecil walked over to the door. He opened it and called out, "Mr. Tasker, more wine up here, please—a quart of the Rumney, if there is any left." He shut the door again. "We will wait a moment; I do not wish to be overheard." Then he added, as if a little inebriated, "Do you like the wine?"

Clarenceux nodded. "It is strong. Strong is good." He lifted his glass—but he did not drink, not this time.

When Mr. Tasker had supplied the flask and left, and glasses had been refilled, Sir William Cecil dragged a bench close to the fire, which was now burning heartily. He drank half of his glass in one go and began his story.

"Where were you when the king died? King Edward, not the old king."

"I was Norroy herald in those days. Where was I? All over London—it took a long time, his death. I remember leaving Skinners Hall and walking down to the river to pick up a wherry. A stranger told me that the king was dead. I was not sure whether to believe him, so I went back to the river and asked the boatmen there. The news had already circulated among them. It was then I began to believe it, at the riverside, watching the swans."

Cecil shook his head. "When he lay dying, Edward decided that the most important thing for England was that it remain a Protestant kingdom. To that end he decreed that he could alter his father's Succession Act. Normally he would have been quite right: a king can alter his predecessor's orders, even with regard to the order of succession. The problem was that his father was very shrewd and had had his orders for the succession enshrined in law, by Parliament. Edward left it too late; there was not enough time to summon Parliament to reverse the Succession Act. But the young king would not be deterred: he drew up his 'device' declaring Mary and Elizabeth illegitimate and making Lady Jane Grey his heir. That was the point at which we were forced to step onto the whale's back of the law."

Clarenceux had often wondered how Cecil, who had signed the declaration that Mary and Elizabeth were illegitimate, had not only managed to survive but had risen under both queens.

Cecil drank from his glass. "Who really governs this realm? Is it the monarch alone? Or the monarch in alliance with her people, the major householders of the kingdom? In truth, it is a two-way thing: the making of laws and the implementation of them. But the making of them is a matter for the monarch alone. So when the poor boy was dying and so insistent that his Protestant cousin should inherit, there was nothing we could do. You know what happened. You know what I did. The only reason I am alive today is that I insisted I was merely signing as a *witness* of the king's will and on the advice of his chief ministers."

Clarenceux lifted his glass to his lips. This time he too drank.

Cecil looked directly at him. "There will come a time when you know that your life is in the balance, and you will write to your wife for the last time, as I did in June 1553. Not to sign the device, the king told us, would be considered treason and we would be made examples of; we would be executed. Realizing what lay ahead of me, I went to my study, picked up my pen, and began a letter: 'Dear Mildred.' In that letter I bade her look after my children by her and also my first-born son, Thomas, by my first wife."

Cecil curled his knuckles and bit them, looking away from Clarenceux. "I gave that letter to Sir Nicholas Bacon, my brother-in-law. I would like to be able to say that I prepared for death then, but all I remember from those hours is that one cannot prepare for death. Death is nothing to prepare for. How does a lamb prepare for the slaughter? It can only carry on being a lamb."

Clarenceux said nothing for a long while. Then he said: "Sir William, you committed yourself to the Protestant cause—even facing death. You gambled and won, for now. But I am not a gambling man. I have no need to be."

Cecil smiled and sighed a little. "I would like to get drunk with you—properly drunk—but I know that if I suggested that, you would simply think I was trying one of my Protestant tricks on you. I don't want that." Cecil's smile passed, and he became solemn. "You and I are like brothers at war—we have no hatred for each other, but we are not on the same sides. The most likely reason why Mr. Walsingham has increased the watch on your house is because Lady Percy's sister is dead. She died in the Tower on the twenty-eighth of November."

Clarenceux set his glass down on the table. "I must go. Tomorrow I have a long journey. I am preparing for a visitation of Oxfordshire.

And you know I have to make certain other provisions beforehand, for the safety of my family."

Cecil nodded. "As I said, the time will come, William, when you too write a letter to your wife, asking her to look after your children. And you will hand that letter over to your last true friend in this world, the person you trust most to stand in your stead and face your enemies after you are gone."

Clarenceux ran his fingers through his hair, holding his head. "I know." He looked back up at the portrait of Cecil as a thirty-two year old. "If you were thirty-two…That was the year, was it not? The year the king died?"

"The painting was done a few months before, when I was riding high in the king's favor and he was expected to live for many years."

Clarenceux bowed to Cecil. "When I write that letter, I will entrust it to you."

19

Friday, December 27

Clarenceux lay awake in the darkness. Through the gaps between the shutters he could see the full moon. It was cold enough for a frost. That was good; for if ever the guards opposite were likely to close their shutters, it was when it was very cold. He knew now where he needed to place the marriage agreement, and that meant going to fetch it from where it was hidden: in a barn near Wargrave in Berkshire.

He had placed it there two years earlier. Under the pretext of visiting Awdrey's sister in Devon he had made a long journey westward, taking every opportunity to stray off the road and visit a nobleman or an armigerous gentleman. In Berkshire he had heard of what he wanted: a modest cottage in a remote yet easily accessible place. He had purchased the property together with some land and had let the smallholding to a local man, John Beard, and his wife, Agnes. There he had hidden the document. John was an unquestioning soul who could be trusted not to take a flame into the barn under any conditions, as Clarenceux had stipulated. He also could be trusted to keep the hayloft loaded with hay and to keep watch for anyone suspicious paying attention to the barn.

He carefully clambered out of bed in his shirt, making sure not to shift his weight too suddenly off the ropes beneath the mattress. Awdrey did not stir. He crept around the bottom of the bed to find the jug and basin, pouring a little water onto his left hand to rinse his face and wake himself completely. He felt in the darkness for his clothes, pulled on his hosen, and held his shoes, doublet, and breeches close to his chest as he crept out of the room. The back stairs creaked terribly as he made his way down. He paused outside the door through to the hall but he heard nothing. Thomas, it seemed, was still asleep. There on the back landing, he hurriedly put on his doublet and breeches. He descended the next set of stairs just as carefully, carrying his shoes in one hand and feeling his way with the other. He paused; still there was no sound. At the bottom he walked across the flagstones past the buttery and into the kitchen. Here a little light from the fire was still playing across the floor, illuminating the ragged edges of the canvas-covered mattress on which Nick was sleeping. He shook him awake.

"Nick," he said quietly, feeling the boy wakening beneath his hand. "Can you saddle Brutus for me in silence and without a light showing from the stable? I need to make a journey."

The boy threw off the blanket. "Sir, yes."

Clarenceux took two candles and lit one from the fire. He put it inside a lantern, closing the aperture so no light escaped, and handed it to Nick. "Be as quick as you can," he said in a low voice. Then he lit the second candle and set it in a holder on a table; by its light he searched the kitchen for food for the next two days. He settled for a hunk of bread, some cheese, and a lump of ham that he sliced rather badly. Then he thought of what he had to do and wrapped the whole of the ham in a linen cloth, and placed it and the bread in a leather budget. He went into the buttery with the candle and felt around for a leather bottle. Having found one and filled it with wine, he crept back up the stairs to Awdrey and very gently shook her shoulder.

"What time is it? Is everything all right?" she asked sleepily.

"Everything is fine," he whispered. "It is early in the morning—no need for you to be up yet. I am going away for a few days. I cannot say where. Tell anyone who asks that I have gone ahead to Oxfordshire, to make a start on the visitation."

Awdrey was awake straight away. She pulled herself up in the bed and reached for him. "Why do you have to go? When will you be back?"

He held her hand and kissed it. "Five days at the most. Maybe just four." From his clothes chest he took two clean linen shirts, a clean pair of braies, and two pairs of linen socks.

"Look after our daughters. Go and visit Lady Cecil—it can never hurt to remind her of her connection with us and her godmother's obligations to Mildred." He kissed her. "I will be back in a few days, I promise."

"I will pray for you."

He kissed her again, then crept out of the chamber past the door to their daughters' room, and down the stairs, picking up his travelling cloak from the front of the house. He left through the back door. Moonlight was reflected in the ice formed on a puddle in the yard. He let himself into the stable and waited while Nick got the horse ready.

"Nick, I want you to lead him down the road. Walk, don't ride him. Keep him to the soft mud of the street. Tie him up at Queen Eleanor's cross and then come back, slowly and quietly. I will not be far behind you."

Clarenceux watched the boy, wondering whether he would ask questions. Nick, however, merely nodded and did as he was told, thinking even to extinguish the candle before he left the stable.

Clarenceux accompanied him to the gate to the yard and watched him leading the great horse softly away, its breath silver in the moonlight. After they had gone he too walked silently along the passage from the yard to the street and looked up at the house opposite. The shutters were still open, as they always were. There was a faint glow of a candle in the lower room but he heard no voices. No one left the building. He waited for about five minutes; then, satisfied, he walked along the street as quickly as he could.

Seven hours later, four hours after sunrise, Clarenceux found himself riding along the road toward Bath. Birdsong seemed to be coming from everywhere around him; the sun was shining, and the warmth of the light was making the cold frost rise from the ground in small clouds. For these minutes he was able to lose the grim determination that had tyrannized him in the city—he was sure that no one was following him. He was tempted simply to continue riding, to rid himself of the worry, and carry the curse of the document far away from London. He could take it and give it directly to a leading Catholic member of the gentry; everyone would then know he no longer had it, and his wife and daughters would be safe. But in so doing he would start a war. There would be a proclamation of its contents; it would be used as a rallying call to all loyal men of the old religion. He would be indicted as a traitor. In the Low Countries, the Spanish duke of Alva was massacring men and women in the name of religion. In the last reign, Protestants had been burned in the name of Jesus. There were many who sought revenge—so much for "turning the other cheek." He wanted the old religion restored, but not at the cost of thousands of lives or burning pyres. Nothing would guarantee the destruction of the old religion more certainly than the blood and ashes of conscientious Englishmen and women.

He did not stop to eat but took some bread and cheese from his saddlebag and consumed it as he rode. On he pressed, not riding fast but making sure no time was lost. Travelers he was polite to, carters he saluted, women bearing loads he greeted with a smile, men driving animals he made way for. Whenever woods were too close to the road, he swept his cloak back, revealing the sword at his side. At fords he rode straight through on his great horse; at bridges he clattered over, or made way for the carts that queued up to cross.

Coming to a large elm at a crossroads at about three in the afternoon, he pulled on the reins and led Brutus along a narrow lane past a farmhouse. He wanted to ride on, and faster, to find out whether the document was still safe, but the track here was muddy and uneven. It was still frozen in places, where overhanging trees had shielded it all day from the sun. He dismounted and led Brutus the last few hundred yards along the rough track leading down the hill to his cottage, where John Beard lived.

The cottage was a single-story cob building on the edge of a copse, with low, thatched eaves covering the firewood stacked outside and darkening the open windows. The shutters were small and propped open. The thatch itself needed attention, especially high up, where moss and fern were growing in it. In the yard to the left of the house, where Clarenceux tied Brutus, there was an old cart with a broken wheel, its wooden planks rotted in places where too many seasons in the rain had taken their toll. Two brown pigs were roaming loose. There were two barns, one on the far side of the yard and a second, longer barn—*the* barn—on the left. Both had their doors open, and five or six chickens were coming and going, pecking here and there at grain in the cold mud.

He walked to the door of the cottage and pushed it open. Inside was so gloomy and smoky that it took him a while to realize that a woman was crouched by the hearth, tending to a dish over the embers. She was about thirty, thin, and wearing what looked like a black cassock; but as Clarenceux's eyes adjusted he saw it was not black but brown. Her dark hair was tied back; her eyes were worried and tired. She was looking straight at him.

"Are you Goodwife Beard?"

"I am. And you, sir?"

"My name is William Harley."

The woman paused, trying to place him. "Oh, good God, Mr. Harley!" she exclaimed suddenly. "The rent—oh, sweet Jesus—you'll be wanting to speak to my husband, John…Sir, we were not expecting you. We did never expect you this quarter."

Clarenceux ignored her worry and looked around the space of the cottage. The floor was nothing but earth and old straw; the gray walls were whitewashed cob, not even plastered. There was no ceiling, the house being open to the roof, with just one inner chamber for sleeping. The beams and under-thatch were black with soot from the fire. The windows were small and dark, the light kept out by the overhanging eaves. There was no sign of any children. It was obvious that little or no rent would be forthcoming.

"Where is John?" he asked.

"He's gone to sell some chickens to his brother. He'll be back before long. Do you want to wait for him? Or shall I say you called?"

Clarenceux detected a desperate hope that he would go away. She clearly feared him demanding money, which obviously they did not have, even though last quarter's rent had been due at Christmas. "I would like to look in the long barn, if I may."

"Sir, you are most welcome. I will look out for John and tell him you are here." She set down a ladle on a wooden plate beside the fire and rose to her feet. Smiling nervously at him, she led the way out into the yard, stepping over the puddles in wooden-soled shoes.

Clarenceux walked straight to the barn and entered. After his eyes adjusted quickly to the dim light he found a ladder lying down alongside a wall. Lifting it, he set it up against the platform of the hayloft. He ascended, went over to the rear right-hand corner, and started moving the sweet-smelling hay with his hands until he felt the wooden timbers where the document was lodged. When he had first bought the barn he had placed the document on the floor and nailed three boards down over the top of it, as if they were a patch in the floor. He felt the boards, still fastened tight.

"Goodwife Beard," he called down. "Does your husband have a crowbar?"

She did not answer. He stepped back to the edge of the platform. All he could see was the open door and a chicken strutting about on the ground. "Goodwife Beard?" he called.

Still no answer.

He climbed down the ladder and walked out, squinting into the sunlight. She was away up the lane, hurrying up the hill, holding her skirts. A moment later she disappeared from sight.

Birds chirruped and cheeped around him, and a slight breeze blew a few wisps of straw across the scene. Searching for something to lift the boards in the hayloft, he found a pail that contained some tools, but nothing substantial enough. In the other barn there was a cider press, crates of apples, some grain for the chickens, a pile of empty sacks, and a few sheaves of corn. Apart from their few animals, John Beard and his wife had almost no food laid in store.

He strode out of the barn and looked up the lane. Two figures were coming back down the hill, one striding much faster than the other. The second one was the woman, struggling to keep up, recognizable because of her brown dress. Ahead of her John Beard was moving purposefully down the hill. He jumped the small stream that ran across the path at the bottom of the descent, just before the yard. Clarenceux noticed the unkempt hair, the plain leather boots. The man's shirt had once been white linen but was dirty, his hosen gray and old, his doublet leather and hard-wearing.

"Mr. Harley, sir," John gasped, "I am so sorry I was not at home. My wife should have entertained you, offered you something. It has been a long time, I know."

Clarenceux nodded, smelling the earth of the yard and hearing the birdsong still. He felt strangely at peace. "Regain your breath, Goodman Beard. I can wait for a few moments." He looked to Agnes, who was walking toward them. "You and your wife are well?"

John looked around at the near-squalid cottage and its buildings. "We have had our struggles, sir, to be honest. I have a confession to make. About the rent: I know it is due but there was a big storm here at the end of the summer, and then the cows died. We lost almost everything."

He had aged quickly. Both he and his wife had bags beneath their eyes, and a weariness there. It was as if their very lives were roofless buildings and they were forever battling to keep out the elements.

"You are doing well for chickens," remarked Clarenceux, pointing. "And not so badly for pigs either."

John glanced at his wife. "We lost our crop, a disease killed our cows. Almost everything valuable we had disappeared in three days. Then our daughter, Dorothy, fell sick too. We had no money. So I borrowed from what we had set aside for your rent, sir. I bought four dozen chickens. Widow Grey told us chicken broth would make Dorothy strong again, and eggs would be good for her too. But it was not to be. She died in October. We have eight chickens left—foxes took some, and we've sold or eaten the rest. We kept the pigs and the hay, for without them we'd have nothing to sell to pay you back what we took from you."

Agnes reached forward and took her husband's arm.

"Speak truthfully to me, Goodman Beard. How much money do you have of the seven shillings four pence you owe for the last quarter?"

John looked down. "To speak truthfully, sir, I have one shilling and threepence in my hand." He showed the silver coins. "And I have another eighteen pence in the house."

"That is all?"

"That is all, sir. As God is my guide and my redeemer."

"It does not matter. I did not come here for the rent but for something I hid here when I bought this cottage. We can talk about the rent afterward. Do you have a crowbar or some heavy metal implement with an edge?"

"I have an ax." John walked toward the house and reached behind a pile of chopped wood. He handed the ax to Clarenceux; it was old and blunt but it would do.

"Good." Clarenceux immediately went back into the longer barn and up the ladder. John followed and watched him as he felt for the boards. Waiting a few moments more for his eyes to adjust to the dimly lit target, Clarenceux drove it into the crack between the two pieces of wood. Twice more he struck. The first board lifted a little, forced up by the thickness of the ax blade. Using the edge of the ax he levered it up.

He could see nothing but the board beneath.

He swung the ax again, driving it into the crack. Again, he struck, harder. Soon this second board too was lifting, half-splintered by the blows. Kneeling down, he yanked it up and felt for the document. A moment later he touched vellum. He was relieved beyond measure. The profound blessing that poured into his heart was like the rejoining waters of the Red Sea in the Bible, drowning the Egyptians.

He pulled the document out, handed the ax back to John, and climbed down the ladder. He unfolded the vellum in the sunlight of the yard. The document had acquired a couple of holes where an insect had eaten through, but otherwise it was as he had left it, with its seal still attached.

"What is that, Mr. Harley?" asked John, looking over his shoulder.

"Believe me," said Clarenceux, folding it up again and tucking it inside his doublet, "you do not want to know. And I will not add to your troubles by revealing its contents to you." He smiled at John and then at Agnes, and slapped John on the back. He looked at Brutus. "Do you have any oats?"

"Not much in the way of oats, not since we sold our own animal."

Clarenceux went into the cider barn and came out with an apple, which he gave to the horse. "I'd appreciate it if you could feed him whatever you can. I'll repay the expense."

"No, sir, we are in your debt," protested Agnes. "Go on, John, there are some oats still."

As John went to fetch the oats, Clarenceux looked at Agnes. She was young enough for them to rebuild their lives and family. "What were you cooking when I arrived?" he asked.

"A broth, with some chicken bones and cabbages. You are more than welcome to partake, sir, but I doubt it will be pleasing to you."

Clarenceux heard the word "chicken" and was shocked. It was Friday; one had to have a license to eat meat on a Friday. It was rightly a fish day, in line with the old religion. That was why he had not touched his ham yet. But then, out here, the fish days of the old religion did not make that much difference, he realized. "It will be pleasing indeed," he replied. "I can offer you some ham in return—although I would ask that you not eat it until Sunday." Agnes looked abashed. John returned with a small bag of oats and started to feed Brutus.

Clarenceux looked around at the barns and the house, and the hills in the late afternoon sun. He reflected that, if only one could live in the country and be sure of enough food, it would be an idyllic existence—with so few threats and so many friends living close by, and all the garden produce and unpolluted water around. No stenches from overflowing city latrines. No one to tell you what to eat or to inform on you. No cascade of bells raining down on the city every hour. All he could hear was birdsong. There was more peace and freedom here than one could find in a city. These people were better off than they realized—if only they could earn enough to keep themselves.

20

Saturday, December 28

Joan Hellier realized that John was not following her. He was seated on the black horse that he had stolen from a stable in Hampshire on Christmas Day, but he was motionless, fifty yards behind her. She reined in her own stolen horse and let some travelers on the London road move out of earshot before she rode back to him.

"You will not come?" she asked.

"You know it would be madness. Anyone with dark skin is abhorred, and towns are worst of all. London would be the death of me. Just imagine if a market trader saw me and accused me of stealing something—the crowd would kill me in a minute. I will wait for you wherever you say, and I will count the days until we are together again, but I will not move closer to the city than this."

"Then you are a coward. Any man who loved me would not fear entering the city, no matter the color of his skin."

"Please—"

"I think it is time I found myself somebody else."

"Do you have no pity for me?"

"I have lost my daughter; you have not. Why should I pity you?

You have helped me and I have pleased you well with my body. But I do not care for you as I do for my daughter. I cannot pity you—for all my pity is reserved for her." She listened as a breeze rustled the leaves of some nearby beech trees. "I wish you no ill, John. Truly. I know I am unkind to you, and that you love me more than I love you. But the truth is that I cannot allow myself to love you. I have to go into the city now, and I have to take this stinking bag with me. If I were to let myself love you as well, I would be weaker than I am. I am prepared to seduce this man, kill him, and kill his wife and daughters to satisfy the countess. And if I do not do those things, I will let down an innocent girl who is facing death for my crimes—mine, not hers—and who has no one else left in the world to look after her."

She moved to one side, so he could see her face. Blue eyes, slightly milky; very light brown hair; white skin; ample breasts; and strong shoulders—the shoulders he so loved to kiss. It was not that she was pretty; it was that there was a great fear within him, and a growing terror of the loneliness he knew he would feel without her. She had given him more love than any other woman he had known. She had shared his suffering.

"I am going to ride on now, into the city. The priest I have to see is staying in a tavern called the Black Swan in the parish of St. Dionis Backchurch. If you change your mind, that will be the way to find me."

John swallowed, fighting his emotion. "I will never see you again."

A cart rumbled by. Joan waited for it to pass. Then she held up a hand and rode on. "Good-bye, John. Good luck."

He never saw her weep a single tear.

21

It was dark when Clarenceux arrived at Caswell, Sir Richard Wenman's house in Oxfordshire. He was exhausted. He rode around the old gatehouse, its arch now blocked by timber, and crossed the bridge over the old moat that had once surrounded the fortifications of the place. There he found he could barely dismount, so great were the aches in his limbs. Yesterday he had traveled thirty-six miles; today he had covered forty. He had slept in the barn of the cottage in Wargrave and left in the early hours of the morning. The fine weather meant he had made good progress and had resisted the temptation to stay at an inn. All the time he thought of his wife and how he had promised her that he would be back soon, within five days at the most. With so little light, that was difficult. Nor was it just the light. He was not as fit as he had once been; twelve hours in the saddle was more than his body could easily bear.

Sir Richard had greeted him with a great show of affection, however, which raised his spirits. Sir Richard was in his early forties, four or five years younger than Clarenceux. He was one of those country gentlemen who took their independence and liberty for granted—and despised anyone who thought otherwise. He expected men to be honest and passionate, and to maintain their integrity—not to comb their nature neatly into place. He made no bones about disliking the new religion and said so, regularly. Nor did he like the queen's favorite, Robert Dudley, and roared his disapproval of the man at every opportunity. When his father had learned that the Dudleys had been given the lordship of the manor of Witney, where much of their property lay, he had been furious. His son had inherited that fury and maintained it now as a matter of honor.

There were many candles burning in the hall at Caswell when Clarenceux came down for supper, having washed his face and hands and changed his shirt. Some lights were set on a candelabrum in front of the table; others were raised on a circular chandelier above them. There were tapestries attached to the walls and a painting of the Blessed Virgin Mary above the door. Most of the household had dined earlier; it was just Clarenceux and Sir Richard sitting down at the table. Isabel, Lady Wenman, had greeted him on his arrival and then withdrawn.

"I thought you said you had already eaten," remarked Clarenceux as he watched Sir Richard inspect the boiled and roast fish in various sauces.

"I have. But I cannot let you eat alone, especially on a fish day. You might suspect I was not providing you with the best."

Clarenceux, who already had a mouth full of roast halibut, lifted his wine goblet in salutation.

"How is the work for the visitation coming along? Has that chronicle I lent to you been of any interest?"

Clarenceux swallowed. "It has been a revelation to me, Sir Richard. I cannot thank you enough."

"Good, good. I know there's no chance of finding the Dudleys guilty of illegally usurping their coat of arms—more's the pity—but there are some people in Witney to whom I would like to see you pay special attention. The number of wool merchants who have rebuilt their houses with a courtyard, and had chimneys and planchings put in, and then had heraldic glass inserted—it is truly shocking."

Clarenceux knew that the Wenman family of Witney were originally "wainmen"—carters who had brought wool into town. They had made their money in Calais, running the wool staple there, and had bought their coat of arms from Henry VII. About this, however, he said nothing. He drained his goblet of wine. "We can discuss coats of arms in due course. But that is not why I have come to see you. What interests me more at the moment is Thame Abbey. It is mentioned many times in the chronicle of Henry of Abingdon. I think Henry must have stayed at the abbey for a while. Whether he did or not, I want to check a number of stories that he tells, and that can only be done through visiting it in person."

"Stories?"

"One concerns two Lollards, in the reign of Henry V. They were both knights, both fervent and religious…"

"And both perceived as traitors to their sovereign and heretics in the eyes of the Church," added Sir Richard, breaking some bread.

"Like you and me," agreed Clarenceux.

Sir Richard nodded. "Indeed. Good men. Go on."

"They were fleeing the king's officers when they came to Thame Abbey. They asked the almoner if they might take sanctuary in the abbey. The almoner refused, saying that he could not shelter them in a closed order for it would be held against him. But one of the Lollards asked to speak to the abbot and through a cunning ruse persuaded him to let them take shelter in a certain hiding place." Clarenceux broke off to eat some more halibut. "Henry of Abingdon is a boring writer when he talks about theology but full of life when he talks about the goings-on at Thame. He also mentions a number of pieces of heraldic glass in the church and certain effigies there too, which will help me."

Sir Richard saw the halibut disappearing fast and helped himself to a significant portion. "So you want to inspect the abbey. That is all well and good—of course you have my blessing. Only, why now? Normally you'd do all that heraldry on your visitation, with your clerks and pursuivants and strangely attired officers assisting you. I've seen you on a visitation, old friend—you travel with more men than most lords."

This was an exaggeration, but it was true that Clarenceux did like company when he worked in the field, going from house to house and church to church. "I need to know what is at Thame and to be sure I can gain access if there is much there," he said. "Taking a large number of men to an abbey only to find nothing worth recording would be a waste. It would be even worse to go and find the church and other buildings full of detail but forbidden to me."

Sir Richard picked up his goblet and turned it in his fingers. "You really are a very poor liar, William. You want to look around my abbey for yourself. I am trying to imagine why; I confess I cannot. Will you not be honest with me? You have nothing to fear on the religious score."

Clarenceux finished the food on his plate. "You know me too well, Sir Richard. But you also know that honesty is not the same as transparency. I should not have to remind you—there is such a thing as an honestly kept secret."

22

Sunday, December 29

Awdrey took charge of the family journey to the church. She did not hold with her husband's policy of leaving one of the servants behind to guard against thieves. Thus Thomas, Joan, and Nick all accompanied her and her daughters to St. Bride's that morning. The dinner was prepared; the fires had been lit in the kitchen and in the hall. There was a lamb roasting and green vegetables, eggs and herbs for a salad. Her husband had told her that it was good to eat natural things, as God had provided them for the benefit of all creatures, and this nonsense about their being bad for the humors was not to be trusted. He had been in Italy and France and eaten salads without any harmful effects on many occasions.

Mildred had had a tantrum at the prospect of going to church and had stamped her foot and declared, "I don't *want* to!" Awdrey had roundly scolded her and picked her up, forced her into her Sunday clothes, and carried her down the stairs kicking and screaming. Then in the street, with their breath billowing in the cold air, she had given her such a telling-off in front of everyone that the child had cried more. This had not gone unnoticed by Annie, who saw that she had an opportunity to prove herself well-behaved in comparison with her little sister.

As mother and daughter were having this confrontation in the street, the door to the house opposite had opened and the tall, white-haired gentleman came out. Awdrey remembered him from church. "Good morrow, Mistress Harley," he said in a Northern accent. "You are on your way to St. Bride's, I presume?"

Awdrey considered him. He had the wealth of a gentleman, judging by his clothes: a black velvet jerkin and white shirt, black velvet breeches and white stockings. His movements were graceful and fluid; she noticed he was light on his feet. At first she thought he was a couple of years older than her, maybe twenty-nine, on account of his agility and the energy in his movements. He was clean shaven and his clothes were clean too, albeit tucked together with a certain careless-ness. Looking at his face more closely revealed he was at least thirty, probably a little more. His shock of white hair was obviously not due to age, but she could see other signs of maturity in his face—the slight lines, the weather-beaten texture of the skin, the experienced way he looked her over with his gray eyes.

"Your name, sir? We have not been introduced."

"John Greystoke. I am newly in this parish. I was in Italy for some years and since then in Paris. I returned to London this time last year."

"And since then you have been staying?"

"In the households of various gentlemen. Most recently that of Francis Walsingham, whom I believe you know."

Awdrey began walking toward the church, with Mildred's hand in hers. Thomas walked on her left. Joan followed behind her with Annie. Nick took up the rear.

"You will know then that my husband and Mr. Walsingham are

not on friendly terms," Awdrey said to Greystoke, finding him amiable and good-looking company but nevertheless wishing he would go away.

"Yes, yes, I do," replied Greystoke with an earnestness that Awdrey did not find convincing. "But it is all a misunderstanding. Your husband and Mr. Walsingham have much in common. Truly, they are both men of great integrity and sophistication."

"You do not know my husband, Mr. Greystoke. You may spy on us from that house, and you may measure our comings and goings, but you do not know us. Should you wish to make our acquaintance more formally, I suggest you speak to my husband."

"Of course, Mistress Harley. Forgive me for being so rude. Where is your husband?"

Awdrey stopped. Thomas, who had been listening, stepped in front of her protectively and looked Greystoke in the eye. "Do you not understand? My mistress has no wish to talk to you. Take yourself to church, sir, and bother yourself not with our business."

Greystoke bowed. "My sincere apologies, Mistress Harley, Goodman Terry." And he walked off smartly into the crowd of people heading toward the church.

"He knows who we are," said Awdrey, watching him go.

Thomas also watched him. "That does not surprise me. Mr. Clarenceux has been observing that house for weeks and telling us that they are spies from Walsingham. Now we have it from the horse's mouth." They started to walk again. "But I am sure that was not the sole purpose of that little interlude."

The service was long. Mr. Lynton, the chaplain administering today in place of Mr. Bowring, was no more inspired than the others Awdrey had heard. There was no fire in what he said; there was merely duty. When he spoke of returning the Church to the values it had known in Biblical times, he was being unrealistic. She grew increasingly irritated. He was refusing to face the fact that the simplicity of the early Church was built in a society in which the Church was a new thing. There was no use trying to turn the clock back and pretend that Christendom was not covered in monasteries and churches. Saying that all clergymen should give up their wealth and do nothing but preach to their loving flocks was nonsense. Those flocks in the old days had all been willing converts who had been unable to read the word of God for themselves. Today people did not need priests—they could read the Bible and think independently. In fact, the task of reforming the Church was much harder; it involved caring for the uncaring and converting the unconvertible.

After the service, Awdrey kept her distance from Greystoke. However, she watched him from the corner of her eye. He spoke to no one else, which confirmed her suspicion that he had spoken to her more out of interest in her husband than in neighborly relations. What worried her more, she reflected as they walked back toward the house, was that he had been so unsubtle. Did Walsingham really think he could send a man to spy on them, and then for that man to ask her directly where her husband had gone?

They entered the house through the front door, Thomas taking the key from Awdrey and unlocking it. Memories of it being overturned by Walsingham's men in the past haunted her, and it was not without a feeling of apprehension that she walked up the steps and entered. Nothing seemed to be amiss, but all one could see from the door was the corridor through to the buttery and the front stairs leading up to the hall. The girls ran ahead up the stairs. Nick, Thomas, and Joan respectfully waited to follow Awdrey.

"Joan, will you see to the kitchen fire, please," she asked as she started up the stairs. Nick went with Joan through to the kitchen. Looking into the hall, everything was as it was. "Thomas," Awdrey said, turning to rest her hand on the old man's shoulder, "I am becoming like my husband. I worry about everything. Unnecessarily." She looked around the hall again; the pictures were in their frames, the chests covered with their carpets. She walked across to the main table, pulled out a form, and sat down.

"Shall I prepare for the dinner?" Thomas asked, seeing her distracted.

"Yes, please." Then she added, "I wonder where he is."

"No doubt he will be home as soon as he can. He is a careful and clever man, my master. Whatever he is doing, and wherever he is doing it, I am sure it is for the best, and necessary. He would be here, looking after you, if he could."

The girls, who had run up to their bedchamber, ran down the back stairs again and into the hall, shrieking and laughing. Awdrey reached out and caught Mildred as she ran past. "That's enough," she said, "you'll cause an—" Before she could finish her sentence there was a terrible scream from somewhere: not a woman's high-pitched scream of terror but a man's yell of physical shock.

She looked at Thomas, who was already moving to the back stairs. "Wait here, look after the girls," he said.

"What is it, Mam?" asked Mildred. "What was that man shouting for?"

"It is nothing to worry about," she replied, lifting Mildred onto her knee and beckoning Annie to come close too.

"Why are you shaking?" asked Mildred.

Awdrey stood up, lifted Mildred, and walked across the room and then back to her seat by the dining table. Inside, she was praying that it was nothing. She wished that her husband was with her.

"Are we going to eat lunch soon?" asked Annie, sitting at the table on the bench that Awdrey had vacated. "I hope it's capon. Mildred will want it to be cheese."

"Be quiet," snapped Awdrey, hearing voices below. Then she could stand it no longer. "Annie, stay here with Mildred." She put the girl down on the same bench as Annie. "Stay here with your sister. Do not move, do you understand? Stay here." Then she walked quickly to the back stairs and went down.

Thomas was beside the kitchen door with Nick and Joan. Nick was in tears.

"What has happened? What is it?" Awdrey demanded.

Thomas cleared his throat. "There is a woman's head on a stake in the yard, mistress. It is partly decayed and horrible to see. But I believe it is the head of Rebecca Machyn."

"Oh my God," whispered Awdrey. "Oh my God!" she cried aloud, running to look at the monstrous sight that she knew meant the end of all denial, all safety, and all peace.

23

Clarenceux rode the twenty-five miles to Thame with Sir Richard and several of Sir Richard's servants that morning. They set out with gray clouds above them and expectations of rain. The wind blew chill from the east, which did not bode well, but the rain held off until just after they left Oxford. Water caught in the saddle of Clarenceux's horse, and his loins were soon chilled as the breeches let in the cold water. Before the rain they had talked amiably; after it started they fell silent.

His first view of Thame Abbey was through a gray mist of drizzle. Although only twenty-seven years had passed since the last abbot and twelve of his monks had surrendered the place, trees had grown up all around the site. Much glass was broken in the tall, arched windows of the church and the west front was like a rocky beach of piled rubble. This, however, was a Cistercian monastery, and the Cistercians had never spent out on elaborate statuary—at least not images of people. The carvings were of flowers and birds and fantastic animals. The roof still had its lead, and so did the abbot's house and much of the monks' living area.

Clarenceux dismounted, and after wiping the rain from his face, he took his horse's reins and followed Sir Richard and the other men through an arch and into the undercroft of the lay brothers' dormitory, which had been partly converted into a stable. Sir Richard led his horse across the cobbled floor to an empty trough. "Is there nothing for the horses?" he called, his voice echoing around the stone-vaulted space. "John, go and find something from one of the locals." To Clarenceux he said, "My father-in-law, Sir John Williams, used to stay in the abbot's house from time to time. He told me he wished to pull down the monastery and rebuild it as a proper house. One day soon I will do just that. Trying to live here would be like trying to make oneself comfortable in a coffin."

Clarenceux left the undercroft and entered the old cloister of the monastery. Many pieces of carved stone lay here, weeds and nettles growing around and up through them, their leaves shuddering under the blows of raindrops. The buildings around the perimeter, however, still had their roofs, although the decoration was in need of considerable repair. The church was on his left, on the north side of the cloister. Opposite it, on the south side, was a warming room and a kitchen. On the east side was the chapter house, with a fine, carved doorway, and to its right, the steps up to the refectory, which was raised above the level of the cloister. Entering the chapter house, Clarenceux saw stone benches all around the room—silent witnesses to the destruction. The east window in here was broken and the floor littered with twigs and bird lime. The wind pulled at a piece of vellum in the mud: a faded fragment of a page of an antiphonal. The glass was broken and the paint on the walls and vaulted roof was peeling. It was a sad sight.

He went back out to the cloister and walked through a side door into the church. Timber was stacked in here, waiting to be reused or burned. The choir stalls had been dismantled—chopped up and piled against the wall of the north transept, and so had almost all of the rood screen. Only one part at the northern end still separated the nave and the chancel. The whole building was huge, more than two hundred feet in length from the west end to the smashed stonework of the east window. Clarenceux stopped and listened; there was a whistling of wind through the carved tracery of the windows, nothing more. The graves of benefactors lay still, their colored stone effigies covered with paint that was rubbing away or washed off. Here a one-legged alabaster effigy of a knight lay on a table tomb, with his hands together in prayer; his fingers were broken, and the leg that had been removed lay in pieces on the tiles of the floor. Looking at his shield, Clarenceux could make out some red and a martlet in the dexter upper corner but that was all.

Once, this place had symbolized fidelity to God—eternity. It had been a place where people could make their prayers and leave their bodies, secure in the knowledge that forever, here, their deeds would be remembered and priests would pray for their souls. No more. It felt as if this were a cadaver of his religion and he was picking through its skeletal remains. Strands of flesh were hanging on to these ribs, to be examined by carrion eaters; and yet at the same time it was strangely beautiful, hauntingly so. The arches were no less graceful than when they had contained glass. The sculptures of birds and leaves no less lovely for their weathering. And everywhere was an overwhelming silence, an enormous emptiness.

He went back out to the cloister. On his left, the half-rotten door of a wooden book press hung from a single rusted hinge, its red and green paint faded. An image of the Risen Christ painted on the wall had almost been obliterated. Yet there were still things here from which the experienced antiquary could learn. He could maintain his half lie to Sir Richard about why he had come. There were inscriptions in the stone that confirmed entries in Henry of Abingdon's chronicle and enough fragments of painted heraldry for him to say something of the people buried here, and their dates and epitaphs. There was the unusual layout of the buildings too. Normally Cistercian houses were built according to a strict plan. This one was unusual. The refectory was adjacent to the chapter house and the kitchen was on the south side of the cloister, so all the food had to be transported through the cloister to the refectory. Another unusual feature was the abbot's lodging to the south of the kitchen, angled off the lower end of the lay brothers' dormitory, creating a separate southern courtyard. Oratories, empty buildings, and stone rooms stood at junctures of the cloister and other corridors: echoing, cobwebs wafting from their corbels in the dusty silence.

Passing the door to the chapter house, Clarenceux walked up the stone stairs to the refectory. The door was ajar, the old key in the lock. It did not move. Decades of abandonment meant that it had seized, unlocked, open forever.

In its day, the refectory had been a great room. The wooden floor was strewn with old stale rushes and there was still one long trestle table in here. At the far end was the stone lectern where one of the monks would read to the others while they ate in silence. Not far from it was a narrow opening in the wall, leading to what had once been the latrine. But the windows were the chief glory of the room; they were the same shape as the windows in the main church and almost as wide. Four of them faced south; the last faced east. Hardly any of the glass had been broken. Sir John Williams must have preserved them against their reforming attackers. Even in this gray weather they let light flood into the room, illuminating the wall on the opposite side, the north, where lines from the New Testament had once been written. As Clarenceux walked up and down the room he could see black letters and words under the whitewash that had been daubed over the paintings. The whole room was so elegant, so wonderfully bright, it felt very modern, like a nobleman's house, covered in glass. There was even a fireplace in here, albeit one littered with sticks and fallen fledglings that never saw their first summer. Peering up inside, he saw daylight at the top of the flue.

For several minutes he stood in silence in that room, hearing the wind batter flurries of rain against the glass, imagining the words of the lessons, the slurping of soup and hand gestures as the monks asked soundlessly for this or that to be passed to them. He crossed himself and prayed until he heard Sir Richard enter the room.

"This building, the kitchen, the cloister between them and the abbot's house will be retained—I don't intend to keep any of the rest. So if you want to record any of it for posterity or your visitation, I should study those parts now, while you can."

Clarenceux nodded. "If it is not displeasing to you, I would like to remain here awhile, a few minutes more, and compose my thoughts on the place."

Sir Richard looked around the room. He pointed out a boss in the ceiling which still preserved its paint. "I love the detail in here. Look at those hares, with their ears all joining. Sir John used to say that that was a symbol of the Trinity."

"You find it in many old churches."

Sir Richard paused, staring up. Then he clapped Clarenceux on the shoulder. "Take as long as you want. I don't intend leaving here until the storm is over."

Clarenceux looked out the window at the abbot's house and the courtyard, and the clouds swiftly chasing each other across the sky. He heard Sir Richard shouting outside. It was time. He would hide the document in here.

24

The weather did not improve. At dusk, Clarenceux and Sir Richard were still sitting beside a fire in the abbot's lodging, the only comfortable part of Thame Abbey. When it started to grow dark, they abandoned shelter and rode the mile into the town of Thame, to call at the Saracen's Head. The landlord was an amiable balding fellow called Simeon, who started telling Sir Richard stories about the abbey before the Dissolution. As a lad, he said, he had often been paid a penny to guide travelers there after dark. With many tales to tell and with no other guests staying that night, Simeon had accepted their invitation to join them drinking wine by the fire. Late into the night they drank, Simeon growing more effusive with the wine and the hour. Eventually Sir Richard drank himself into a stupor and was helped up the stairs to his bedchamber.

Clarenceux suggested that Simeon share another pint or quart with him. He wanted the evening never to end. Tomorrow he would start riding back to the city and the torment of waiting for the attack on his family. By the light of the fire, the talk moved on to epitaphs and what a man should choose to put on his tombstone. Clarenceux was drunkenly mulling over some words he had read in Sir William's copy of Gratarolus: *Judge me as I am worthy*. Simeon had ruled that out, on the grounds that an educated man like Clarenceux should not use words written by another writer. Simeon went on to philosophize that literary men should not be allowed to select an epitaph. Someone else could select a line for them from their work, on the understanding that the author had encapsulated something of his essence. That led on to the matter of literature. When Simeon revealed that he was the proud possessor of a dozen books: poetry, history, medicine, and theology, Clarenceux was impressed and ashamed that he had presumed his host was illiterate. But his amazement was even greater when he learned that Simeon had never even been to school. How had he learned? Simeon held up his copy of the Bible. "This," he said proudly. "God taught me to read."

The next morning, Clarenceux was awake at first light. He roused himself and splashed water over his face, washed his hands and mouth, and went downstairs. Simeon was about, as bright and breezy as if he had had a full night's sleep. Sir Richard was still snoring. Clarenceux settled their bill and called for his horse. After saying his farewell to Simeon, he started out for London.

The following evening he ate alone at an inn in Denham. The innkeeper here was quite unlike Simeon: an illiterate bore. The herald slept little, despite it being a comfortable bed, and awoke feeling anxious.

25

Tuesday, December 31

The weather remained cold and wet all the way to London. Beside the road, ivy crowded the bare trees, reaching out along the skeletal branches. He looked for greenness, a sense of spring, but there was nothing to give him that uplifting feeling of renewal. It was just the hard knife-edge of winter, cutting deeper and deeper. A raven sounded out *ka-ark* as it flew over him, and the sound was as desolate as he felt. He had achieved nothing, he told himself. He had simply moved the document—and left his wife and daughters unguarded in all the time he had been away.

He did not feel he was coming home but riding into a strange town. People seemed to be looking at him oddly. He told himself he was being overcautious; these people did not know him, or only knew him by sight. At Charing Cross he looked toward the gray river, the cold muscle of the city. It did not look welcoming. Passing Cecil House, the windows with all their glass quarrels seemed to frown at him—so many eyes watching, so many ears listening. And then, clopping through the mud of Fleet Street, the desire to see his family was like a flame burning quietly in the dark cave of the night.

Immediately, he saw that the windows of the house opposite had changed. All but one were closed.

Clarenceux dismounted and led his horse down the side passage to his stable yard. He tried the latch on the gate; it was locked. "Nick! Thomas! Is anyone here?" he shouted.

After a moment he tied the reins to a post by the gate and walked back to the front of the house. He did not have the key with him so he hammered on the door. He took his knife out and knocked with the hilt of that too. No one came.

The cold wind bit into his face and hands.

He hit the door again, harder, more out of frustration than hope that anyone would answer. The noise of his striking echoed away inside. He went back down the alley and climbed over the gate into the yard. The back door was bolted and the shutters barred. Even the stable door was locked. He could hear Maud inside stamping in her stall. But at least this lock was breakable. He unbolted the gate, led Brutus into the yard, and went back outside into the street to search for a suitable stone. As he went along the passage, however, he glanced at the house opposite, and its closed shutters.

They know there is no one to watch.

He went across to the house and drew his knife again, and was about to hammer on the door when he thought to try the door without knocking, to take them off their guard. After all, why would a house of spies have anything to fear? He tried the handle and went inside. It was almost wholly dark in there—lit as far as he could see only by the light behind him. He paused and listened: nothing. As his eyes adjusted he could see two ground-floor doors and a narrow staircase. The open window he had seen from outside had been on the first floor. He walked carefully to the staircase and ascended. On the landing there was one door open, one source of light. He walked toward it.

John Greystoke was lying on his bed in a loose white shirt, reading a book, when Clarenceux walked in. The rest of the room was empty except for a table where there were three swords, a pile of clean linen shirts and a couple of doublets, and four more books. Greystoke's shoes were neatly arranged beside the bed. He did not look up until Clarenceux was in the room.

"I'm glad you're safe," he said.

Clarenceux recognized the white-haired man from church. He now realized that this man and the captain he had seen were one and the same.

"Where are my wife and daughters? My servants? What have you done with them?"

"Me?" laughed Greystoke, getting off the bed and walking over to place the book on the table. "I have done nothing with them. I am simply here watching your house on behalf of Mr. Walsingham. Your wife left on Sunday, not long after returning from church. As to where she is now, I have not heard that she has removed herself from Cecil House, which is where she has been ever since."

"Why are you watching us?"

"Mr. Walsingham is very keen to know where you are at all times. He asked me to help look after you, to watch over you as it were. He knows how great the danger is."

"I do not need protection."

"Mr. Clarenceux, you do not know what you face. Do you not realize Lady Percy has been planning your downfall now for the last two years? When you did not use the document in your possession, she swore to make you pay for it. When you betrayed her sister, Mistress

Barker, she swore that she would make you pay with your life. Now her sister is dead, she wants nothing more than to make you suffer— and to use the document to start a war to rally all the Catholics in England to the cause of Lord Henry Stewart. To that end she has sent a small army after you."

"I did not betray her sister. And Lady Percy is an adherent of the queen of Scotland, not her husband."

Greystoke shook his head. "That may have been the case, sometime before the marriage. But Lady Percy is a great friend of Lady Margaret Douglas, Lord Henry's mother, who is, as you know, a prisoner in the Tower. Lord Henry now has a son who is the unquestionable heir of both kingdoms. Together Lady Percy and Lady Douglas seek to rid England of Elizabeth and have Charles James Stuart proclaimed king of England, uniting the whole of Great Britain under one Catholic monarchy."

"This should have nothing to do with me or my wife, let alone my daughters."

Greystoke picked up his swords. "Don't play the fool with me, Mr. Clarenceux. You know well why it affects them too."

"No. Tell me."

"They are your greatest weakness."

Clarenceux was silent. He thought of Awdrey: her face, her voice, her touch. He thought of Mildred and her round cheeks and bright eyes, and her funny expressions. He recalled her childish prattle, saying that she loved him more than God. He remembered Annie running around the house and arguing with him whenever she was told anything with which she could disagree.

"I must go to them," he said, turning back to the stairs.

"One more thing," called Greystoke after him. "The army she has sent is made up of women. You might find that information useful—when they come after you."

⁓❀☙

"Father!" exclaimed Annie when she saw the door open to the second-floor chamber. "Dad!" shouted her sister, who was standing beside the fire. "Look, Mam, it's Dad."

Awdrey had not slept. Her eyes were rimmed with tears, and her hair was hanging down, awry. Clarenceux knelt, hugged his daughters, and waited for the servant to leave the chamber before going across the room to embrace his wife. He held her for some long moments before breaking away.

"What happened?"

"Rebecca Machyn is dead. We came back from church and…It was awful. Her head was on a pole in the middle of our yard."

Clarenceux stared at her, open-mouthed. He could not believe what he had just heard. He looked down at his daughters, both of whom wore worried faces. "What was she doing in London?" he asked, a lump in his throat.

Awdrey shook her head. "I do not know. You told me she was happy in Portchester. I hoped she would stay there."

"Have some pity," said Clarenceux. The memory of her brought tears to his eyes. He felt hollowed, winds of emptiness howling through the broken-windowed hall of his soul. He longed to hear her voice again.

Awdrey looked sharply at him. "Pity? I don't have the time for pity. What is going on? Who is going to be killed next? That white-haired gentleman stopped me in the street as I was on my way to church. His name is John Greystone—he has been spying on us for Walsingham."

"I met him just now. He told me where to find you." The pain of Rebecca's death tore at him. He tried to put it out of his mind.

Awdrey plunged her face into her hands. "Oh Christ, I feel sick. It will never end."

Mildred started to cry. Awdrey ignored her and walked away, toward the window. Clarenceux lifted Mildred, saying, "Shhh," to soothe her.

"You have got to bring this to an end, William, once and for all. You have got to get rid of that document. Give it to Sir William. Get it out of our lives!"

Clarenceux held Mildred tight, pressing her against his breast. "Do you think that that would make any difference? It does not matter whether we have the document or not. We are the ones who are known to have it. It will not save us, to give it away."

She looked at him as though he were speaking lies to her face. "What do you mean? You will endanger our lives! Sir William will help us."

Clarenceux put Mildred down and smoothed her hair. He stepped close to Awdrey, so the children would not hear him. "Awdrey, our lives are at risk but so is the safety of the State—and if Sir William has to choose between the two, then he will prefer the State over our safety. Sir William and I have already spoken about that document, and he has already asked me to hand it over. I refused—"

"Then you are cruel and selfish and you do not love us!" she cried. "You will get us all killed!"

Clarenceux grabbed her wrists. "Listen to me. If I give up that document, we are as good as dead. Not having that document did not save Rebecca, God rest her soul. Without it we will be victims too—we will be the innocents that the plotters use to frighten Sir William or whoever next has the document."

"Damn you! Sir William will not give in to such blackmail. Give it to him."

"Giving it away is not enough," Clarenceux insisted. "We have to get rid of it in a way that the Catholics in England know we have given it away. But Sir William cannot allow that to happen. He cannot let it be known that that document ever existed. The only solution is to destroy it publicly."

"Then do so, William," said Awdrey. Mildred was crying again; this time her mother bent down and lifted the girl.

"Where is Rebecca's head now?" Clarenceux asked.

"Thomas took it in a bag to the church but both Mr. Bowring and Mr. Lynton refused to bury it without a coroner's inquest being held, so he brought it back again. I was distressed and angry, so I took it back to the church and left it there, in front of the altar."

"You left it there? Did they see you?"

"I don't know. I don't care. I was upset. They know where it comes from. The coroner should have done his business by now anyway. I don't want to think about it. I just want life to be normal again."

"Why are you crying, Mam?" asked Mildred.

"It is nothing, my sweet. Nothing." Then she closed her eyes and let the tears flow. When Clarenceux stepped forward to embrace her, she put Mildred down and held on to him, weeping openly.

A minute later Annie asked, "When are we going home?"

"I don't know, sweetheart," said Awdrey.

"We cannot stay here," muttered Clarenceux.

"What do we do, then?"

"I don't know. Wherever we go, men will track us down."

"Perhaps we should accept the help that Walsingham has sent us in the form of Mr. Greystoke?" she asked. "I was abrupt with him, perhaps too much so."

Clarenceux shrugged. "If we were to go to Chislehurst to stay with Julius Fawcett, how long would it be before they tracked us down there? We would bring danger to him. If we were to go to your sister's house in Devon, we would place them in danger."

"Not if they could not find us."

"They will find us. All they need to do is to follow the messengers from the properties that supply us with our income. If they found Rebecca Machyn in Portchester, they'll find us wherever we go."

"Do we just go home, then?"

Clarenceux nodded. "We carry on. As long as the document cannot be found, we are relatively safe. Our attackers will at least want to keep us alive."

26

Wednesday, January 1, 1567

The skies above the bullring were dark with rolling clouds in Sheffield. But no one was looking up. Everyone was concentrating on the bull, a muscular brown animal with a rugged, thick neck, four hundred pounds in weight, tethered by a chain and a wide leather collar. People were shouting and clapping: men and women, young and old. As the fight moved in one direction, so did the circle around them, shifting about the central point where the bull was tethered. There was a smell of blood and sweat in the air. Two dogs were dead, two still fighting.

The bull, which had been so aggressive when first led into the ring, was exhausted. It stood panting, blood running down its neck on one side. Two men stood guard with spears as the bull stared at the remaining dogs, one of which was yapping. The lull in the fight only increased the enthusiasm of the crowd. They knew the kill was near. Two children watching from the chamber above a clothier's shop were cheering, enjoying the spectacle. A couple of young women in the room above the shop next door had screamed in excitement when the bull had gored one of the now-dead dogs on its horn—and screamed even louder when a dog dashed in close enough to bite the skin on the bull's neck.

Benedict Richardson stood beside Lady Percy's seat. He had been watching the windows overlooking the bullring more than the fight, nervous of an attack. She had waved away his concerns for her safety, declaring that if she was too old to ride with the hounds and too cold to fly her falcons, then watching the bull baiting was the only sport open to her. When he had further protested, she had pointed out she was expecting to receive a message and could hardly do that at the manor without attracting attention. This was, in that respect, safer.

The bull lowered its horns, seeing one of the dogs about to run at it. The other dog ran across from the other side, distracting the creature. It turned its head, tracking the dog's movement, and the first dog ran forward, fastening its teeth into the loose folds of skin below the bull's jaw. The bull rounded instantly, its muscular legs stomping the ground hard as it bucked and lifted the dog and shook its great head to throw it off. But the dog held on, tenacious in the extreme, trying to break the skin. Down went the bull's head, and its shoulder followed, but not with any sense of surrender. Instead the bull was trying to use its weight to crush the dog, to drive it into the ground.

The crowd shouted and cheered, wanting to see the struggle rise into a greater fury. The bull whipped its head around, and the dog spun with it, still holding on, even as the bull swung its head back again. Down went the bull's head once more, but this time the second dog ran at it from the other side and also took hold of the bull's neck-folds, pressing back with its paws, trying to tear the neck. Swinging its head madly now, the bull caught the second dog's underbelly with its left horn and gored it. The creature opened its mouth to howl in agony and let go, flying off, as the bull pulled its huge weight around and stamped on the ground, then swept its head back again, trying also to gore the first dog. A man with a stick beat the wounded dog back into the fight, not allowing it to back off, and it limped around the powerful animal, frightened and bleeding. The bull snorted and again tried to shake off the first dog but this time it charged, running straight toward the crowd of shouting onlookers, snorting loudly and thrashing around in its fury. Two boys waving sticks at the bull were pulled back by their parents as it reached the end of its tether and was jolted back. Its head flew back and twisted; the dog, surprised, loosened its grip and landed on its back. Before it had regained its feet the bull was on it, driving its horn under the dog's jaw into its throat.

Lady Percy beckoned Benedict Richardson. "See if you can acquire this carcass when it's dead."

"I have already asked for the first option."

"Good." She looked across the crowd. "Is that man in the green jerkin one of Walsingham's spies?"

"He is, my lady. We have lured him by means of an assignation with the daughter of the landlord of the Golden Fleece, behind the inn's stable, after the fight. John Parker and Richard Braithwaite will be there to take him when he arrives."

Lady Percy looked at the doomed man. She turned away from him when two new dogs were shown the steaming bull, men straining to hold their collars, rubbing their noses with blood. "Men are so weak," she muttered. "Weak to resist what they desire and weak in pursuing what they want." She looked at Richardson. "You are an exception."

She turned back to the bull baiting as a yelping dog flung itself at the bloody neck of the bull. The second dog bit the bull's upper leg—a mistake, for it was unable to avoid the bull's sweep of its horn.

Dismayed by the dog's blood being spattered across the earth so soon, the crowd sighed but then cheered when two more dogs were sent into the fight.

"The messenger has arrived," Richardson told her discreetly as a man in the crowd nodded. "The signal has been given."

The bull swayed and crashed to its knees, and then fell onto its right side. The surviving dogs rushed at it, barking and ripping the skin before men with sticks beat them off and put them on leads again. The audience, cheered by the spectacle, began to depart. A pair of Flanders horses with a chain linked to a yoke was brought into the ring to drag the dead bull away. Before the chain was attached, a man stood over the bull and drove a chisel into its brain and pulled it out. Brilliant red flowed onto the dusty ground.

A man in a traveling cape and leather breeches came close to Lady Percy. "Your friend in London sends his greetings in Christ. He wishes me to tell you that Rebecca Machyn is dead. She was killed as you instructed. Her head will by now have been presented to Clarenceux."

"That is very satisfying," said Lady Percy.

"I came as soon as the Hellier woman arrived in London. It will not be long until you have brought Clarenceux to his knees, my lady."

Lady Percy looked at the messenger. "I intend to drive him into the ground, not just to his knees." She picked up her sticks and rose to her feet. "Ride to Scotland now. Walsingham's men will find it difficult to follow you over the border. Go to Lord Henry Stewart; inform him of what we are doing to procure the document for him."

27

Thursday, January 2

Clarenceux reached across the table for an apple as Joan cleared away his platter. "Did you enjoy that, Mildred?" he asked.

Mildred beamed. "My favorite!" she exclaimed, putting her spoon in her bowl and pushing it to Joan, who smiled.

"And you, Annie? How does baked chicken agree with you?"

"I don't like the little bones," replied Annie, looking at the leftovers on her plate.

"But it tasted good," said Clarenceux, trying to sound positive. "We cannot have things exactly as we want them all of the time." He glanced at Awdrey and thought of the previous night. He had kissed her as they lay in bed, and soon afterward she had pulled him toward her, tearing off her smock despite the cold and climbing over him, making love with him frantically, as if this was their last chance.

"It is Thursday," she said. "Are you going to the Belle Savage?"

Clarenceux got up from the table and went to the window overlooking the street. The shutters were back at their usual range of half-opened positions. "It is not important," he said to her. "I could stay here."

Awdrey stood and helped Joan with the bowls. "We cannot live in this house as if it is a cage. That is what they want. Thomas will be here, Nick too. Walsingham's guardians are over the street. Besides, if we choose to stay here all the time, all day and every day, what sort of life are we leading?"

"Very well, I will go. I will stay there for an hour and then return. You will know then to expect me."

He went upstairs to fetch a pistol. When he came down Awdrey was not in the hall but Annie was hesitantly balancing a glass on a plate which she was carrying back to the kitchen. "Annie, no, that will break," he snapped, striding over to her and taking the glass. He saw the disappointed look on her face and felt guilty. "It is good of you to try to help," he said, handing the fragile object back to her. "Carry it down to your mother, holding on to it carefully."

He watched her go, then went down the front stairs, took his cloak off a peg, and made his way out into the street.

The Belle Savage Inn on Ludgate Hill was one of the largest inns in the city. It had three stories of galleries looking down into the central square innyard. The bedchambers, all of which were lavishly furnished, led off the galleries. In summer, plays were performed in the gravel-covered courtyard, and men would pay a penny to stand and watch, or two pence to look down from the galleries. But in winter few people cared to stand in the cold. Instead the space was used for more active pursuits: in particular the sword school of Giacomo Girolamo.

Girolamo thought of himself as an artist and dressed accordingly in a flamboyant style, with long baggy Venetian breeches. His ruff just peeped out of the top of his embroidered doublet; his cuffs were always neatly decorated with lace. His short hair, trimmed mustache, and short beard were typically Italian and complemented his olive-colored skin and brown eyes. He seldom drew a sword but he was full of wisdom and advice for how others should do so; and when he did need to demonstrate his own skills, like an artist he would make every effort to show off just why he was the master, self-consciously stepping up to the mark with a skin-tinglingly close pass with the point of his blade.

"Ah, Mr. Clarenceux," said Girolamo, seeing his respected pupil entering the courtyard. "I have for you today an excellent challenge."

"Greetings, Signor Girolamo," replied Clarenceux. "Who is my challenger?"

"A rare man in this city, sir. A master of swordsmanship who learned his art in Italy, like me. He studied for four years with the great Camillo Agrippa from Milano, the greatest swordsman of them all. He is not yet ready. So, if you please, in the meanwhile, would you like to practice with me a little?"

Clarenceux bowed and acknowledged the honor. He took off his cloak and flung it onto a table beneath a gallery on one side of the yard. Drawing his sword, he assumed the low ward against the master, who raised his sword into the position of the high ward. At first most politely, they made a play for each other's weaknesses. Clarenceux was an instinctive swordsman; until recently, he had not had any formal lessons. When his sword was too far from his body, Girolamo would seize on the chance to expose a weakness and dart with his blade into the opening. This Clarenceux had learned to guard against—but his warding was unorthodox. Girolamo, on the other hand, was smooth and efficient. He would let his sword hand pass a long way from his body, as if he did not know the rule and was treating his opponent to a free hit. Yet as soon as Clarenceux went for the opening, Girolamo's sword would be there.

"You see the secret, Mr. Clarenceux? It is not just where the sword hand is; it is a matter of the point too. Remember the principle of distances. The way to control the fight is for you to maintain a shorter distance between the point of your sword and your opponent's head or chest than he does between his sword and your head or chest. You are looking at my sword hand—which is good—but you need to bear in mind the point even more, and how close it is to your heart. It is not my hand that will hurt you but the point." Girolamo looked up and raised an arm, stopping the swordplay. "Your adversary is here. I will introduce you."

John Greystoke was leaning over the first-floor gallery. He caught Clarenceux's eye and walked along to the staircase and down into the yard. As always, his loose shirts were very white—whiter even than his hair. "*Buongiorno, Giacomo,*" he said with a nod to the master. "*Va bene?*"

"*Tutto bene. Grazie per avermelo chiesto, Signor Grestocche,*" replied the master.

"So, you speak some Italian," said Clarenceux. "But do you know how to fight?"

Greystoke seemed too casual. "I asked to change the day I come, especially so I could meet you socially, Mr. Clarenceux."

"I never thought I would fight my enemies socially."

Greystoke unsheathed the sword at his side. "I am your protector, not your enemy. You surely have the wit to tell the difference."

Clarenceux raised his sword as Greystoke approached and walked around him, relaxed, with his sword loose in his hand. He kept his weapon raised and the point in front of him, following Greystoke's movements. "Forgive me, Mr. Greystoke. I suffer from a terrible affliction. When people want me to believe something so much, I have a natural tendency to question it."

Girolamo stood back, watching quietly as the two men circled each other. He admired Clarenceux's first thrust, which was expertly performed, but he knew Greystoke would be ready. A swordsman like Greystoke fought as much with his feet as with his weapon. Clarenceux's second blow was similar to his first; an inexperienced fighter would have been thrown off-guard but Greystoke was able to read the movement and step away quickly without losing his balance, this time replying with a strike to Clarenceux's shoulder that would have wounded the herald had Greystoke meant to inflict damage. Clarenceux cursed himself, furious to have given an advantage to his opponent so quickly—and all from concentrating too hard on making his first blow look correct. *You need to fight as if this is real, not swordplay*, he told himself, watching Greystoke make a thrust of his own. Clarenceux twisted away from the point and retaliated instinctively, forcing Greystoke to dart away and regain his balance and composure.

"You fight like a man who has been set upon in a dark alley," Greystoke said, keeping his eye on Clarenceux's movements.

"I learned to fight with the duke of Suffolk's men at Boulogne. You look too young ever to have seen action—am I right?"

"In Italy we don't wait for noblemen to lead us into battle. I have fought a number of duels—" But he broke off as Clarenceux feinted to his left. Girolamo moved, watching the men intently. Greystoke replied with a stab to Clarenceux's leg, to which Clarenceux reacted by beating his opponent's blade away in an amateurish fashion.

"That was a tennis stroke, not the work of a swordsman, Mr. Clarenceux," tutted Girolamo. "You left yourself wholly open; your sword was across your body—you even let it swing behind you. You cannot defend yourself if your blade is behind you."

Clarenceux swore quietly. *If this were a proper fight, I would have grabbed my cloak by now. I would be fighting with everything available.* He backed toward the table where his cloak lay. His swordsmanship had ended the lives of several men over the years, but those had always been bloody, desperate affairs, in which he and his adversary had known they were fighting for their lives. This was more like dancing than fighting.

That very thought triggered something in Clarenceux's mind. Suddenly, he attacked, striking Greystoke's defensively poised sword to one side and going for his throat. Greystoke was caught off-guard, for he had noticed the cloak and had expected Clarenceux to continue withdrawing toward it. Instantly he was struggling to regain the initiative as Clarenceux's blade flashed across his face, ripped open his doublet, and rattled against his own blade. Forced back, he moved in a tactical retreat, ending Clarenceux's advantage and regaining his poise.

"Signor Grestocche is speaking the truth," commented Girolamo. "You fight like a man in an alley. But the more dangerous man—you fight intensely and suddenly, like the attacker."

Clarenceux again went on the attack. But Greystoke was so nimble on his feet that Clarenceux could not see how he would catch him off-guard. He needed the weapons of deceit and deception to win a fight.

"Remember, Mr. Clarenceux, not every part of the arm is as strong as every other. Your opponent may risk a blow when you are being unwise in attempting it, through weakness. Maybe he prefers to attack you after you have mistakenly attacked him."

Clarenceux silently cursed the Italian for distracting him, darting at Greystoke's body only to see him twirl away and counterattack with a high blade across his vision. An instant later he felt the tap of a hit against his arm.

The bout went on for a further twenty minutes in much the same form. Clarenceux scored a hit here and there, where wit and natural contrariness allowed him to surprise Greystoke, but Greystoke scored three times as many. Eventually Clarenceux held up his hand, panting, and said, "Enough. I can see you are a master swordsman. You not only know how to speak like an Italian, you can fight like one too."

"Thank you, Mr. Clarenceux. And if I may return a compliment, I certainly would not like to meet you in a dark alley. May I offer you a drink in the hall? They do have some excellent double beer."

Clarenceux breathed deeply and looked at the white-haired younger man. "Why are you spying on me?"

"You are a suspicious man, Mr. Clarenceux. I have told you already: Walsingham has given me instructions to do what I can to make sure you and your family are safe. That drink?"

Clarenceux walked over to the table and picked up his cloak. "Another time, perhaps. I told my wife I would be home within the hour."

"Then let me walk with you."

28

Friday, January 3

Father Buckman sat at a table in the upstairs chamber of the tavern with two candles burning before him. He listened to the laughter coming from below. Then, adjusting his spectacles, he dipped his quill into the ink and wrote the number of the folio of the book open in front of him. He counted the number of lines down the margin to the word that began with the letter he wished to write and wrote the number. It was a laborious code but it had the compensation, he believed, of being secure.

There was the sound of creaking on the stairs and he saw the landlord's head appear through the opening of the stairwell. The priest nodded. He extinguished one candle, and having withdrawn the other one from its candleholder, he carried it across to the top of the stairs; there he fixed it into a bracket attached to a beam. He walked back into the shadows and hid behind two large chests, one stacked on top of the other.

"Come up," he called.

A woman in her midtwenties appeared, her fingers hesitantly touching the wall. Buckman studied her. She was dark-haired and long-legged, with a chin that jutted out slightly as she moved. Very plain in her face and not intelligent, he observed, but strong physically. He could see that she had passed the age at which the future seems like a blossom unfolding; people were picking at the petals of her flower, and she could do nothing to stop them.

"Stand there, in the light, where I can see you. Your name?"

She was obviously frightened. "Jane Carr."

"What was your crime?"

"I committed no crime, sir. The mistress said I'd taken forty pounds of lamb and suet, stolen it away—but I never did."

"Nevertheless, you were found guilty. So that becomes your crime, whether or not it is on your conscience. Your innocence you can plead before the Lord when you're given your release. How old is your daughter?"

Jane looked down at her feet. "She is by seven, Father."

"Tell me her name."

"Agnes, Father."

He paused, looking at the woman. How well Lady Percy understood her own sex. The slightest weakness—and she could make slaves of women. "Personally I deplore Lady Percy's threats," he said, "but I have not the slightest doubt of her sincerity. She will hang Agnes from a gallows if you do not follow our instructions."

In the candlelight, he saw Jane nod.

"Good. Now, look to your right. There is a table there. It has something on it."

She saw the small table in the shadows and reached forward to lift a cloth folded on its surface. Underneath was a small pistol. It was about eleven inches long and had a wooden handle. She picked it up and carefully held it.

"Do you know how to use it?"

She shook her head.

"Joan Hellier will show you, at the house in Fleet Street. Make sure you take the key and the powder with you too. She will also show you how to enter Clarenceux's house without being detected. You will have only the one shot. Make it count. After you have pulled the trigger, do not wait. Run as fast as you can to the cockpit in Shoe Lane. There will be a man there with a horse. From Clarenceux's house it is but a short distance to that horse. Nothing more will be expected of you. You do not even need to come back here; Joan will tell me of the success of your mission and I will write straight away to her ladyship."

Jane closed her eyes. "I am scared."

"You have nothing to be frightened of. You have already been sentenced to hang, and you have your daughter's life to save. Do this and you will both be set free and sent as far away from your troubles as need be. Lady Percy may have cold methods, but she does have full coffers as well. She rewards loyalty generously."

"But if I am captured, then both Agnes and I will die."

"Agnes will not die if you do your duty. You have my word that I will not let any harm come to her—as long as you carry out this godly task." In the darkness, Buckman crossed himself and blinked. "This is just one of many stages in our planning. It must be carried out cleanly and on time as arranged, after church. We need you to do this for us. Remember, you have nothing to lose and everything to gain."

29

Saturday, January 4

Clarenceux opened the box on the elm table and took out three pistols, their handles polished walnut and their steel barrels and wheel-lock mechanisms shining. He laid each one down gravely, alongside the two daggers and two swords already there. He looked at Awdrey and Thomas. "We will keep all three of these loaded—one in here, one in my study, and one in our bedchamber. We cannot wait until someone is at our door before reaching for the powder flask."

He lifted one and rotated the dog, pushing it to the firing position, then returned it to the safe position. He handed it to Awdrey, who handled it carefully, examining it from all directions. She held it in front of her, in two hands, and stared along the octagonal barrel, pointing it at the portrait of herself. She stopped aiming and looked at Clarenceux. She said nothing but then gazed down at the gun cradled in her hands. "How strange it is that an instrument of such destruction should not be the problem but the solution."

Clarenceux's thoughts returned to Rebecca. Her head had been quietly buried in the churchyard yesterday. Now the very thought of that melancholy moment, and the smell of her decomposing remains, made him feel weak again. He ran a hand over his face and blinked away the incipient tears. "Whoever they are, and wherever they are, they are using time to their advantage. Making us sweat and fear, breaking us down. We must also use the time well—to make ourselves stronger." He looked out of the window and saw the shutters on the house opposite half-open again, as normal.

"Do we trust Mr. Greystoke?" asked Awdrey, behind him. "Should we trust any of Walsingham's men?"

"It was Walsingham's men who tore this house to pieces before," Thomas said.

"We may have no choice," replied Clarenceux.

They heard Annie and Mildred coming down the stairs. Thomas went back to his duties, crossing the hall as the girls ran in, laughing. Clarenceux smiled weakly at Awdrey. "Small mercies," he whispered.

All day Clarenceux felt as if his chest were twisted, listening for a knock at the door, or a shutter at the back to be forced open. He repeatedly looked at the house opposite, as if by watching his watchers he could discern something about the future. When Annie asked him to listen to her reading, he at first briskly dismissed her, then realizing it was his tension talking, not his real self, he sat down with her by an open shutter at the back of the house as she read to him from her horn book, his attention constantly drifting across the rooftops to see ways of approach and escape.

After dark, they ate supper by the light of three candles in near silence. Joan had bought the ingredients for a salad, which they ate with some beef that she had stewed earlier in the afternoon. Only

Annie and Mildred talked freely, prattling on about dolls, toys, and favorite colors until it was time for them to go to bed.

Later that night, while Clarenceux was in his study, Awdrey came up the stairs carrying two pewter goblets of wine. He smiled at her candlelit face and watched her set one goblet down on the table.

"Thank you, but I will not," he said.

Awdrey drained her own goblet, set it down, and lifted his. She looked at the fireplace, where half-burned logs were blackened, with flames licking around their edges. Then she looked at him. "For a moment, downstairs, I had a vision of being alone. I imagined being in this house, after you were dead, knowing you were never coming back." She took a gulp of wine.

"I am not dead. Not yet."

"But they will kill you, as they killed Rebecca." She looked away, clutching the pewter goblet.

Clarenceux pulled the seat on which he was sitting away from the table and leaned forward, with his elbows resting on his knees. "As I see it, we have four options. We could wait here all together, until whatever is going to happen happens. But that would be like rabbits waiting for the ferret to come. Alternatively, I could wait here alone and you could go into hiding with the girls. But I do not believe you and they could move from here without being followed or traced later. If that happened, you would be vulnerable. The third option is that we all go into hiding. But how long could we live like that, as fugitives? The fourth is the only one that makes sense to me. I take myself very publicly on my visitation of Oxfordshire. Everyone will know where I am—and they can come after me with all they have, while you remain here, watched over by Thomas and Nick, Walsingham's spies, and Cecil's guards."

Awdrey drank. "I want us all to go. Together. We could go to my sister's house to the west of Exeter, on the edge of the moor. You remember how inaccessible that place is. No one would find us."

"I do not wish to go there and wait for someone to try."

"But we could be safe there."

Clarenceux straightened himself on his bench. "Do you really think you could be happy, hiding out in Devon?"

She sighed. "I do not know. All I know is that we cannot keep living like this."

Clarenceux recalled the thought he had had when riding across London—that he could end the family's woes by destroying himself. He caught Awdrey's eye and gestured for the wine goblet in her hand. She passed it to him.

"I have hidden the document in Oxfordshire," he said. "We must find those who pursue us and lure them to it, and then destroy everything—them, it, and all our woes. Everything at once."

Awdrey looked at him with astonishment. There being no second seat in the room, she knelt down beside him and placed her hand on his leg. "Is that possible? To lure our pursuers in such a way—when we do not even know who they are?"

Clarenceux put his hand on top of hers. "We know them by what they seek. These moths are not after just any flame. For them only one will do. That is what must guide us. That is what we must use to trap them."

30

~

Sunday, January 5

Clarenceux awoke, washed himself, dressed, and felt his way down the stairs. He moved through the dark hall. Thomas was already up; he had opened the shutters inside the glass windows at the front of the house. A little dawn light was seeping into the street. Clarenceux went to them and looked out; there was a small light in the open window of the house opposite.

"It will be cold in there," he muttered, hearing Thomas in the room behind him.

"Walsingham's men are made of strong stuff," agreed Thomas. "That house isn't a home—it is like a dark lantern, always looking out."

Clarenceux was about to turn away when he noticed something passing in front of the glimmering light. "It is beginning to snow," he remarked. He turned to the darkness of the hall, listening to the sound of Thomas dragging away the blankets and mattress on which he had slept. "Light the fire and candles; let us get ready for church." He was about to turn away again when a voice drew him back to the window. He heard the unbolting of a door and its opening. Although he could not see him, Clarenceux realized there was a man entering the opposite house from the street. His method of monitoring who came and who went was no longer possible—not if they were changing men in the dark.

By the time he was down at the kitchen, where Joan was feeding the tiny flames on the embers with brushwood, he could hear the sounds of his family in the rooms above. The girls were running about. The one good thing about the terrible situation they were in was that his daughters did not let the taut atmosphere distract from their playing.

"Today, Joan," he said, looking at her stooped back, "we will all go to church. No one stays behind."

She turned and looked at him, seeing his face in the darkness barely illuminated by the light of the fire. "Sir, but will not the house be vulnerable to thieves? You always say that—"

"Joan, you know that thieves are now the least of our worries."

She stood up. "I do, sir. Though I wish it were not so."

An hour later, as dawn was breaking, the family ate their breakfast of bread and butter in the hall together. Clarenceux took a black velvet cap which he intended to wear and tried it on, looking in the mirror in the hall. It did not suit him, so he left it on the elm table. Moving closer to the window, once again he looked out, feeling compelled to watch the men on the other side of the street. Now, in the morning light, two of them were waiting outside— Greystoke and Tom Green—their feet trampling the thin layer of snow into the mud.

Once outside, with his breath billowing in the cold air, Clarenceux ignored Greystoke and Green and stayed by Awdrey's side as she steered their daughters down the street. Thomas, Nick, and Joan all followed, Thomas casting suspicious glances at the men. Bells rang out across the city, and now those of St. Bride's started to ring too.

Greystoke, dressed in his respectable doublet and long cloak, walked over to him. "Your wife was reluctant to let me accompany her last Sunday, Mr. Clarenceux. Perhaps she will be more tolerant of my presence now you are here?"

"We are going the same way," replied Clarenceux stiffly. "I am accompanying my wife and household. Let us leave it at that."

Clarenceux expected Greystoke to answer but he did not. Instead the man simply tagged along behind the family. They walked through the muddy street, half-white with snow, with the cold air in their nostrils and the bells ringing louder.

Clarenceux felt guilty, entering church with a pistol hidden inside his doublet. It was almost worse that it was concealed; he knew that God was watching and he knew that He could see the guilt in his heart. But Clarenceux knew that he had to be prepared, and prayed for forgiveness. If God could see his transgression, he reasoned, then He could see that it was not out of disrespect but a desire to protect his family and himself. He glanced at Greystoke, sitting not far away. The other guard, Tom, was standing uncomfortably at the back. He had no doubt that they too were armed.

There came the time in the service to sing Psalm 52. *Why boast of thyself in mischief, O mighty man? The goodness of God endures continually. Thy tongue devises mischiefs, like a sharp razor, working deceitfully. Thou love evil more than good and lying rather than to speak righteousness. Selah. Thou love all devouring words, O thou deceitful tongue. God shall likewise destroy thee forever, He shall take thee away, and pluck thee out of thy dwelling place, and root thee out of the land of the living.* As Clarenceux sang the words he took a strange comfort in the fact that God could have enemies, and that King David could sing with beatific confidence about Him destroying them forever. For those few moments, he felt a sense of grace, as if he did have a powerful ally in his conscience-driven search for peace.

As the service drew to a close, Clarenceux saw Awdrey looking at him. He sensed her nervousness as people started departing from the church. Her fingers fluttered slightly as she rearranged Mildred's hair, which had become tangled. Greystoke and Tom Green were watching him. *What do they know that I do not?*

Clarenceux wanted to do something rash, something unexpected. He wondered about taking the family to eat their dinner at one of the London inns and not head home. But he could not simply do erratic things every time he felt vulnerable. He started to walk out of the church, putting his hand on Annie's head, ostensibly guiding her between the people moving toward the door but in truth finding reassurance in the physical contact.

Most of the snow on the ground had been trampled but everywhere else it lingered, glistening in the sunshine that now had broken through the clouds. They walked back to the house with no more than a few words. Mildred had difficulty keeping up, so Clarenceux bent down and lifted her, carrying her with his right arm. He fumbled in his pocket with his left hand and passed the key to Awdrey. While she unlocked the door, he watched Greystoke and Tom Green walking up the street behind them.

"Daddy, who are those men?" asked Mildred.

"It doesn't matter," he replied, setting her down and leading her by the hand over the threshold. He started to take off her coat inside the door.

Greystoke was coming toward him. But just as Clarenceux, still with his hands on Mildred's coat, saw the man and wondered what he wanted, he heard Awdrey scream. He turned to see both her and Joan open-mouthed, staring up the stairs. There, in an old red kirtle and brown jacket, stood a woman with unkempt black hair. She was staring at them with eyes wide, holding a pistol in each hand. The one in her left was pointed at him, the other at Awdrey and Annie. He recognized the gun in her right hand as his own—and he knew it was loaded.

Springing forward with an almighty cry of "No!" he forced himself toward her, looking up at the barrel of the pistol, wishing he could move faster. He reached for the pistol inside his own doublet, but knew he was too late; the next instant the flash of the woman's gun seared his eyes and he felt the heat and dust of the shot hit his face. An immense noise silenced his hearing. Hitting the wall with his shoulder, he drew his own pistol and aimed hastily at the woman. But in that instant of aiming, to his great shock, he saw the flash of flame from the other gun. There was a second explosion. He saw his daughter Annie hit by the bullet in the shoulder and blood seeping— rushing through her dress. With Annie falling, and Awdrey scream- ing, and the woman turning her head, Clarenceux pulled the trigger of his own gun. He hit her on the left of her abdomen, heard her scream, then saw her drop both pistols and crawl up the stairs toward the hall. Breathless, Clarenceux watched Awdrey desperately soaking up Annie's blood.

Gritting his teeth, Clarenceux followed the woman. He saw her stumble through the door at the back of the hall—and there she hesitated. Someone was running up the back staircase. A moment later, she went up to the second floor from the back landing, pursued by Greystoke, who had a sword in his hand. Nick was behind him. Clarenceux followed as closely as he could. He heard a shutter bang open and Greystoke and Nick shouting, and a scream. Then there was silence.

When Clarenceux reached his bedchamber he saw the body half out the window, with blood running down the wall. He crossed himself, walked over to the woman, checked she was dead, and crossed himself again. Greystoke was standing, silently looking at her.

"Did you have to kill her?"

"She had a gun. Look in your mirror; your face is half-blackened and bleeding. I did not want anything left to chance."

Clarenceux said nothing.

"I meant to protect you and your family. You could say thank you for that."

"Thank you," said Clarenceux, and went back down the stairs.

Annie was on the floor, cradled by Awdrey, who was sitting with her back to the wall. A blanket covered in blood lay across her. Thomas appeared in the open door with the physician from across the street, Mr. Knott, who started to examine the girl. Her eyes were open and full of tears. Looking over Mr. Knott's shoulder, Clarenceux could see that she was breathing with difficulty. The bullet had struck her shoulder; there was pink tissue visible. Blood was in her clothes, in her hair, and across her face. The sight seized Clarenceux and held him, grabbing his head and forcing him to confront reality. *What am I doing to my family?*

There was a creak; Thomas was closing the door, wary of further attackers but Mr. Knott held up a hand and stopped him. "No, I need the light," he said. Picking up a pair of scissors, he cut away a part of Annie's dress.

"Is the woman dead?" Awdrey whispered, looking at Clarenceux. He nodded.

Mr. Knott stopped examining Annie and looked up. "We need to put her on a table or a bed with lots of light—I cannot see what I am doing here."

Clarenceux saw the red blood still seeping from the wound, Annie's frightened eyes, her red lips, her bloody mouth. *Oh Lord God, spare my daughter! Spare her, spare her!* He bent down, placed an arm beneath her back, and lifted her, at which she uttered an involuntary cry. She cried again as he carried her swiftly up the stairs to the first floor, laying her on the elm table in the window there, her lower legs dangling off the edge.

Mr. Knott began to inspect the wound again. He touched something with his finger and Annie cried out. Awdrey caressed the girl's brown hair. Clarenceux held Annie's hand.

"The bullet has gone deep," said Mr. Knott. "It needs to be removed as quickly as possible, so you must send for a surgeon. Call for Mr. Read on Ludgate Hill; he is efficient and nearby. If he is not at home, go to John Hunter, at the top of Water Lane. The longer we leave it, the greater the chance that the wound will be poisoned. I think there is some bleeding internally too. The breaking of blood vessels causes the blood to drip through the body inside as well as out. There is nothing we can do to stop that. She is in God's hands."

Annie moaned. Tears ran from Clarenceux's eyes as he looked at his daughter, smeared with blood, and clasped both her hands to his face and kissed them. "Should we not wash her, clean away the blood?"

"Mr. Clarenceux, we must remove the bullet. There is going to be more blood yet. And water has its own risks, its impurities. Send for a surgeon now, without more ado."

No one sat down to eat that day. Thomas and Greystoke removed the dead body from the upper chamber and cleaned the wall. Greystoke went to see the chaplain, Mr. Bowring, and Thomas the parish constable. When the constable came to view the corpse, there was not much to add to Clarenceux's description of events. The coroner arrived, made a cursory inspection, and left within a quarter of an hour. Joan looked after Mildred in the girl's own bedchamber. Awdrey stayed by Annie's side. John Hunter arrived. After half an hour of careful cutting and struggling with various instruments, as Annie screamed with the pain, drunk on the wine she had been given to quash its edge, he managed to remove the bullet. As the afternoon dragged into evening, and Annie slept, Clarenceux carried her up to her bed and laid her there, where he and Awdrey attended her.

They were still there late that night, watching her by candlelight. It was a small room with little but a chest and Annie's narrow bed. Awdrey sat on the bed, Clarenceux on a stool. Mildred was asleep in her own room. Joan and Thomas were in the hall by the fire with Nick. Greystoke had stayed with them until dusk.

Awdrey pulled back the covers slightly to view the wound. "It looks as if the bleeding has stopped."

"The outer bleeding," said Clarenceux. "Mr. Knott said she could be bleeding inside. And that could go on for days. And there is the danger of poisoning."

"Why would anyone do this to a girl?"

"The same reason as they killed Rebecca Machyn," muttered Clarenceux. He rubbed his hand over his face and closed his eyes. "But there was something strange. That woman fired one of *my* guns—a gun she must have found in the house. She could not have known it was here beforehand. She searched the house, found it, and used it. But the other gun was not mine. And it was not loaded."

"It was," replied Awdrey, stroking her daughter's hand. "I saw the flame shoot out of the muzzle, and your face was covered in soot and bleeding in several places."

"There was gunpowder, certainly—I felt the hot dust, like a sudden very hot wind. But not even a blind woman would have missed me at that range. I do not think there was a bullet in it. Just gunpowder."

"Why?"

"To put us in fear. The woman herself was terrified, that was why she used the second gun. If she had *known* one was loaded and the other not, she would have used the loaded one and then used the unloaded one to make her escape."

He bent forward, speaking low. "Greystoke said that Lady Percy has sent an army of women against us. This woman was one of them. She was given a gun and told to shoot me—but whoever gave it to her fooled her. She was meant to scare us, not kill anyone. It was accidental that she found one of my own pistols—that was not in the plan. If she had killed me, Lady Percy would have had no chance of finding the document."

"Greystoke was on the scene quickly."

"He was." Clarenceux watched Awdrey move the blanket again, to see if the wound had indeed stopped bleeding. After a long minute's silence he said, "It is clear he expected an attack. He was waiting outside before we left the house and he was there when we came home. Did you notice how quickly he found his way up the back stairs?"

"Now you come to mention it, yes."

"I thought that curious. As far as I know, he has not been in this house before."

31

Monday, January 6

Clarenceux stayed up until very late before stumbling into his bed-chamber. Awdrey was sleeping on the floor of Annie's room, so he was alone in the bed. Barely able to comprehend the day's events, he lay down and reflected on the killing of the woman. That forced him to focus on what he now deemed most important: who was John Greystoke—and whose side was he on?

He awoke feeling cold, but the daylight around the shutter told him that he had slept long. He was immediately shaken back to the events of the previous day. Hearing a cry from the adjacent chamber, he leaped out of bed. Awdrey was on her knees cradling Annie, crying. For a moment Clarenceux thought their daughter was dead, but then he saw that Annie too was crying, and moving her hand feebly.

"Get her some food, William."

At the foot of the stairs he saw Nick. "We need bread," he stammered. "Annie likes capon and milk. We need to feed her, to give her strength." He fumbled in his pocket and pulled out a gold angel. "Buy lots of white bread and capon."

Clarenceux then sank down on the back stairs and put his head in his hands. Feeling powerless and anxious, he prayed for Annie. He was still in this state when there came a loud hammering at the front door. Stirring himself, he walked along the corridor as Thomas went down by the front staircase. Clarenceux stood in the dark corridor, listening to the exchange of words.

"Right heartily I greet you. May I speak with the householder?"

"About what business?" answered Thomas.

"About his forthcoming visitation," replied the messenger, a young clean-shaven clerk.

Clarenceux moved forward to stand behind Thomas. "What is it?"

"Mr. Garter sends his greetings, Mr. Clarenceux, and asks that you deliver a reply to this letter by me."

Clarenceux accepted the letter, breaking the seal. He opened it and started to read:

To Mr. William Harley, Clarenceux King of Arms, from Sir Gilbert Dethick, Garter King of Arms, greetings. It has not escaped our attention that you are overdue in making your visitation of the county of Oxfordshire, as agreed in our earlier conversations. On account of it being the Christmas season, we have forborne to press this matter, but now that Epiphany is upon us, it is required of you to set a date for the speedy expedition of your duty. You will please us by making known to the bearer of this letter the date you intend to commence, or, if it be a question of unavoidable delay, the date by when you will have begun the visitation...

Clarenceux stopped reading and thrust the letter back toward the bearer. "Domesday," he said. "I will have set out by Domesday. And if that is not good enough an answer, tell Mr. Garter to take his letter to the privy and wipe his arse with it."

The messenger looked aghast. "Mr. Clarenceux, I will tell Mr. Garter no such thing."

"And if he doesn't like *that* response, tell him he has a choice between his arse and mine," snapped Clarenceux. "I have no time for this. My daughter is—" He stopped himself and glanced up at the windows of the house across the street. "Just go. I apologize for my profanity. I am tired and I am worried for the safety of my family. It is not something I can explain now."

He turned wearily from the door, waving away the messenger and climbing the stairs to the hall. Thomas closed the door.

"Thomas."

"Yes, sir?"

"I want you to go to Mr. Cecil's house and ask to speak to Sir William. They will not allow you within, but ask when you might come and give him a message from me. I need to know whether Walsingham really did send Greystoke to guard me or whether the man is just presenting a bold front. If he did send him, I would like to know why Walsingham trusts him so much. I do not trust Walsingham himself to tell me these things—but he will not lie to Sir William. And ask Sir William one final thing. If Sir William trusts Walsingham and Walsingham trusts Greystoke, can Sir William guarantee his loyalty?"

32

Sarah Cowie was laying on one of the three mattresses in the candlelit chamber when Joan Hellier entered. "What went wrong?" she asked, looking up, her dark hair loose across her face.

Joan shrugged. "It doesn't matter now, does it?"

Sarah sat up.

"Of course it matters. Jane was sent to that house with a specific plan and now she is dead. One of us will be next; what will our mission be? To give our lives for him as well?"

"Not for him. For our daughters." Joan walked across the room to a flagon standing on a small table and poured the beer into a tankard. She swallowed half of it and handed the tankard to Sarah.

"Who is Father Buckman?" asked Sarah before she drank.

"I am not supposed to tell you."

"It is well and good that he sends women like Jane to get killed, but you may not mention him?" She passed the tankard back to Joan.

"Maurice Buckman is a priest. No one ever sees his face. You go to the Black Swan in the parish of St. Dionis Backchurch and ask the landlord if he sells a beer called Old Faithful. If the priest is not there, he says he is out of that brew at the moment, but he can ask the brewer to make some more in the near future. If he is in, the landlord takes you to the back of the tavern, pretending to show you the cask, then sends you upstairs. You have to talk to the priest in darkness, or near darkness."

Sarah's thoughts returned to Jane. The mattress where the dead woman had slept the previous night was neatly arranged. Beside the bed was a leather bag, a folded smock on top. "She should not have had to die. She was innocent."

"I suspect that her innocence was why the priest picked her out. Not you, not me—her. In God's name, if this all comes to an end, and I am alive, I am going to make sure Lady Percy gives her Agnes a good start in life. She deserves that at least." Joan drained the tankard. "That double beer's good stuff."

Sarah got up, took the tankard from her, and refilled it from the flagon. "It's been harder for Jane and me. We weren't used to the life. Jane was caught in a household where her lady decided to get rid of her; her mistress accused her of theft and then paid the constable to rig the jury. She did not know how to act. I'm not much better. I admit I stole. Five pewter plates, worth two shillings and six pence; a salt cellar worth a shilling; and a candlestick worth eight pence— that's what I took. I ran the risk, and I got caught and was sentenced to hang. But it wasn't something I was doing all the time. Jane and me, we weren't to know whom to say yes to and whom no. Most of the time we weren't given much choice."

"My heart bleeds for you," Joan said, watching Sarah drink. She walked to the far side of the room, opening the shutter and breathing the cold air of the night. "But we all need to be harder than that. We cannot afford to feel pity or sorrow, or regret."

"I cannot remove the image from my mind of us killing that woman at Lady Percy's house. I remember all three of us scrabbling with her, to get her on the ground, and you lifting her skirt to have something to strangle her with. And then the sight of her legs kicking, the hairs on her legs, and her red petticoat, her grubby linen socks in those old shoes, just kicking, kicking as you held the hem around her neck."

Joan closed the shutter. "It was something we had to do. Now we have got another task, equally unpleasant. When it is over we can run away and pretend it never happened. And won't that forgetting be blissful. God's wounds—you haven't had to cut off a woman's head." She took the tankard that Sarah offered and swigged the beer. "When you slice through the throat and see the phlegm that you know is just like the phlegm that you are swallowing, and when the blood oozes slowly out of the tubes, it doesn't just turn your stomach; it turns your soul. But then you've got to drive that knife through the bones of the neck and cut it all, just cut everything, with the woman's eyes staring into infinity, as if she can see God and you cannot. You cannot do it without desperation. You have to make it seem as if it's nothing."

"It sounds like butchery."

"No. Butchery is much more refined."

33

Clarenceux looked at Annie as she lay in her bed. If there was too much bleeding internally, Mr. Knott had said, she would be in a worse state by now. But poisoning could happen at any time. Rapid breath, quick pulse, very high or low temperatures, and fever were the signs that the body was unable to cope with the intrusion of the bullet and that the humors were out of balance. If that happened, she should not be bled by a surgeon. She had already lost too much blood for the normal prophylactic of bloodletting to work.

Small feet came running up the stairs. Mildred was standing just outside the door in her night rail, peeping into the candlelit room.

"You should be in bed, daughter of mine."

"Is Annie going to be better tomorrow?" asked Mildred.

"Not tomorrow but maybe in a few days. Do you want to come in and say good night to her? She is still awake."

Mildred came in with her straw doll and gently kissed Annie's arm. She then returned to her own bedchamber. A few noises came up the stairs from the kitchen and the hall. Clarenceux looked at his daughter's face on the white sheet, her milky blue eyes, and he felt as if nothing mattered now but his family's safety, their wholeness. *If I could give up the document to Lady Percy to save Annie, I would do so.*

He picked up the New Testament that was lying on the floor and leafed through it to the point at which he had stopped reading earlier in the day. The heavy black Latin text reprimanded him for his weakness; the sternness of the lettering told him that using the Bible in this way was hiding. At a time like this, he should not be reading just for his own benefit. He whispered to Annie, "I will be back shortly." Five minutes later he was back at her side with a large tome, which he opened near the end and leafed through. "'This is the book of the generation of *Jesu Christe*, the son of David, the son of Abraham,'" he began. "'Jacob begat Joseph, the husband of Mary, of whom was borne Jesus—even He that is called Christ…'"

Late into the night, Clarenceux read from the gospels, long after Annie had fallen asleep and Awdrey had taken her leave of him to sleep in their bed. She listened to his voice in the next room and was lulled by the reliability and security of his words and his faith.

34

Tuesday, January 7

Cecil walked through the garden of Cecil House with Walsingham in the early morning mist. All around them were plants frozen in frost, with icy tendrils and leaves like frozen glass.

"Were you aware that the woman that Clarenceux was so close to has been killed?" Cecil asked.

Walsingham felt the cold, and his gloved hands were holding each other for warmth. "Yes, of course. She was called Rebecca Machyn. His mistress, I believe."

"How do you know about her death?"

"My watchers told me."

"Ah yes. Your spies," said Cecil, looking across the low hedges of the garden, laid in squares. "Would one of them happen to be a Mr. Greystoke, a gentleman with white hair, from the north?"

"John Greystoke, from Cumberland."

"Have you known him long?"

"Ten years. When I was in Padua, he was one of the English émigrés there. He is a fervent, passionate man: an expert swordsman and a fine shot with a gun. He is also a scholar—Dante is his great love."

"You have no doubts about him, none at all?"

Walsingham paused. "What are you driving at, Sir William?"

Cecil stopped by a wall-climbing rose bush, its leaves frozen white against the brown brick. "Mr. Clarenceux has great difficulty accepting that you might have sent a man to watch over him. For reasons of security he has asked me to check that you have done so; he also asks that I give him my word that the gentleman in question, John Greystoke, can be trusted. I am hopeful that I can give him that reassurance."

"Damn Clarenceux! Why does he not just hand over that document and be done with it. It would make all our lives easier."

Sir William looked askance at Walsingham. "Would you, in his shoes?"

"Of course. It is the dutiful thing to do."

"Don't pretend he is a fool, Francis. He is an intelligent man, and his family is in jeopardy. Moreover, his mind is concentrated on the situation in a way we cannot match." Cecil paused. "You know about his daughter?"

"What about her?"

"She was shot. In Clarenceux's own house, on Sunday. By a woman."

Walsingham shook his head. "Greystoke has yet to report it to me. He has probably taken further safeguards. I am sure he will today."

"When he does, see whether he reveals who killed the woman. I would like to know whether he volunteers that information."

35

Clarenceux was sleeping when Sir Gilbert Dethick called. He had spent the night attending to Annie, reading to her from the Bible, tending her when she cried out in pain, which she often did, and mopping her brow when she was hot. Awdrey had taken over from him at first light and Clarenceux had crept off to sleep. Now, as the city bells chimed ten and Sir Gilbert Dethick, Garter King of Arms, knocked on his door, he was snoring in his bedchamber.

Thomas did not know Dethick well. He did know who he was, however, and that Clarenceux trusted him even less than he trusted Francis Walsingham, and liked him even less than that man too. Their verbal fights were famous. Clarenceux would inevitably rise to the bait, with wall-shaking eloquence, and would throw down some impossible gauntlet to the superior herald that, while it left a profound impression, also made him seem both a maverick and unreliable in the eyes of those watching. Part of the problem was that Clarenceux refused to like Dethick on principle. Dethick's grandfather had been a German armorer and Dethick had lied about his birth to gain English denization, even changing his name from Derrick to Dethick to claim a false ancestry. Clarenceux objected to the highest heraldic office in the kingdom being awarded to such a man. It did not help that Dethick's father had married a Dutchwoman and Dethick himself had also married a foreigner. It was not their foreignness that Clarenceux objected to so much as their willingness to do anything to advance themselves. It was as if there was no principle to which they would remain firm, no single truth to which they were loyal.

Clarenceux was honest enough to admit that he also resented the foreigner being given several important diplomatic missions to Germany and Holland instead of him; that did not make him feel any warmer to the man. It did not help either that Sir Gilbert Dethick was particularly good-looking. Although nineteen years older than Clarenceux, he looked more handsome even now, in his late sixties. With his mustache preened, "devilish" was not an inappropriate term to describe his looks.

"I wish to speak with Mr. Clarenceux," announced Dethick from his horse, sheathing the sword with which he had struck Clarenceux's door.

"He is not well, Sir Gilbert," said Thomas with a bow. "But I shall go and inquire if he is well enough to wait on you."

Thomas met Awdrey on the stairs and explained that Dethick had arrived. "Like the fly that settles on an open wound," she whispered, heading down to the door while Thomas went to rouse Clarenceux.

When shaken awake, Clarenceux blinked and tried to go back to sleep. He heard Dethick's name and ignored it. Only when he thought of his daughter did he awake. "How is Annie?" he asked, getting out of bed.

"She is unchanged, Mr. Clarenceux."

He put on his breeches and rinsed his face. "You know, Thomas, over the last few years I have been chased along the top of London Wall in the snow, been attacked in the street, fought a duel in a cavern, been dragged through the sea behind a pirate ship, climbed through Sir William's latrine, and fought a naval battle against impossible odds. And now I would rather do any of those things again than have to speak to Dethick."

"I am sure he holds you in equally high affection, sir."

Clarenceux smiled. He drew a clean shirt from his clothes chest and put it over his head. "Well, let us see."

Clarenceux stepped out from his front door and looked at Dethick astride his horse, wearing his sword openly, which he was permitted to do as a knighted gentleman. Across the street, Greystoke was leaning against the front door of the house in his usual white shirt, with a sword in his belt—worn openly despite the law. Above there was a man watching from the first-floor window.

"Sir Gilbert, greetings. How might I assist you?"

Dethick tugged at the reins as his horse shied away from Clarenceux. "You can help by doing what you have promised to do, what you have been asked to do, and what you are obliged to do on behalf of her majesty. You cannot simply put off the visitation until it is convenient to you. You have a duty to perform."

There were few people in the street, and no one who looked as if they were eavesdropping except Greystoke. "A woman broke into this house on Sunday," Clarenceux said. "She had two guns: one loaded, the other unloaded. The unloaded one she fired at me. The loaded one she fired at my daughter, who is now lying in bed, suffering from the wound. If the guns had been reversed, to whom would you be addressing your comments? Because it certainly would not be me. The College would have no Clarenceux."

"Do not tempt me, Clarenceux. You know you need to do this work. Tell me when—that is all we need to discuss."

Clarenceux shook his head. "In all sincerity, I will set out when the bullet wound in my daughter's shoulder has healed—and not before. Is that clear enough?"

Dethick did not answer. He looked down disdainfully on the upstart herald while his horse jittered in a circle and, without a word, rode off down to Fleet Bridge.

"Tell me," called Greystoke from across the street, "are all the heralds like you? I would hate to be your employer."

Clarenceux walked across to him. "Garter herald is not my employer," he said, looking down the street and watching Dethick cross the bridge and ride up the hill through Ludgate. "He is responsible for the administration of the College of Arms but he has no right to dictate to me." He looked Greystoke in the eye. "I want to talk to you. I want you to come with me."

A short while later, when he was properly dressed, Clarenceux led Greystoke up Shoe Lane to St. Andrew's Church, where they turned right to Holborn Bridge. There the road divided around a single rickety house: the left-hand lane went around the city to the north and the right between the merchants' houses straight to Newgate. They took the right turn, passing long lines of timber-fronted houses. All the way, he questioned Greystoke and Greystoke answered without hesitation. He explained where and how he had met Walsingham—at the house of Signor Giuseppe Buzzaccarini in Padua, in the company of the earl of Devon. They had both been twenty-three. Walsingham had been eager to know more about Italian government. From Padua they had traveled to Venice together in the company of the earl of Bedford. Walsingham was fascinated by the machinations of the Venetian noblemen and their elaborate safeguards against plots. They had been guests at the doge's palazzo together, and Walsingham had supported Greystoke when he had been forced to fight a duel with the husband of a woman who had fallen for his readiness to whisper lines from Dante in her ear.

All the while they were moving toward the great church now called Christ Church—once the home of the London Greyfriars. At the gate, Greystoke was surprised to find that the church itself was the building to which Clarenceux was leading him. He obligingly removed his sword and left it leaning against the wall behind the door. It was no warmer within than it had been outside: the huge echoing space only grew warmer when the parishioners crowded in on Sundays and feast days. They spoke in low voices. But Clarenceux walked on until he came to a particular arch in the nave.

Greystoke pointed up at the stained-glass window above them, which included a number of coats of arms. "You are testing me, Mr. Clarenceux."

"I am."

"The answer to the question is that the Greystoke arms therein were in memory of my great-uncle, another John Greystoke. He was buried in the north aisle. Obviously the tomb has now gone."

"Does that not make you yearn for the return of the old religion?"

Greystoke shook his head. "If we have learned anything from the events of our own time, it is that England has started to change again. Every five hundred years it experiences a revolution. You can see it in the chronicles of Britain. Two thousand five hundred years ago, Brutus came to these shores. Five hundred years after that, Gorboduc's sons pulled the kingdom apart in a civil war. Five hundred years on, the Romans invaded. Move on another five hundred years, the Saxons invaded. Five hundred years after that, the Normans invaded. That was exactly five hundred years ago. Now, England is torn over a matter of faith. It is like an invasion from within, tearing ourselves apart—as in the days of Gorboduc. There will be war, if we do not guard against it."

"Your mother's family was Dacre, was it not?" replied Clarenceux. "*Argent three escalopes gules*, yes?"

Greystoke pointed to the Dacre coat of arms in the window further along the nave. "There. *Gules, three escalopes* argent. You see, Mr. Clarenceux, I am what I say I am. I am John Greystoke and I have been sent by Francis Walsingham to protect you. Ask him yourself."

"I already have," replied Clarenceux stiffly, moving back to the door. "But I don't trust him any more than I trust you."

36

Wednesday, January 8

Awdrey knew that her husband was not in his right frame of mind the moment she pushed open the door to his study. All day they had taken it in turns to look after Annie, whose wound was causing the little girl fear as well as surges of great pain. They were both fraught, both tired and frightened. Then there had been a knock at the door and a message had arrived. Thomas had taken it and passed it to Clarenceux, who had read it and gone alone up to his study, without a word. Now he sat at the table in there, looking preoccupied.

"What is it?" she asked, placing her hands on his shoulders.

He held up the note that he had received from Sir William Cecil. "Walsingham did send Greystoke. They have known each other for the last ten years, having met in Italy and traveled to Venice together. Greystoke is a Dante scholar and an exponent with the pistol as well as the sword. All good reasons for Walsingham to send him, you might think. But at the bottom Sir William has written six words in small letters: '*Hominum credere nolite timere bonum est.*'"

"What does that mean?"

Clarenceux closed his eyes. "I don't know where to begin. It is deliberately ambiguous—a paraphrase of a message that appears in a chronicle. In 1327 the captors of Edward II were discussing what to do with the king after they had forced him to abdicate. According to one chronicle, a message was sent to his custodian that read: '*Edwardum occidere nolite timere bonum est.*' You might read that as 'Do not kill Edward; it is good to be afraid.' However, it could equally well mean 'Do not fear to kill the king; it is a good deed.' Sir William's message can similarly be interpreted in two, opposite ways: 'Do not fear to trust the man; he is good' and 'Do not trust the man; it is good to be afraid.'"

Awdrey looked at the small piece of paper. "Will he protect us? If he has doubts about Greystoke?"

"No." Clarenceux put his head in his hands. "That is the reason for the ambiguity. He cannot be sure. He has repeated to me what Walsingham has told him, but with that Latin he has indicated that he cannot give the guarantee I sought."

Awdrey walked across the room. "It felt like a siege before, but this…this is even worse. Let us go, just go—down to Devon, anywhere! Let us not stay here any longer."

"That is not possible, Awdrey. Annie cannot travel. Besides, if we run away from this trouble, it will follow us. If we start running, we will have even less protection than we do now."

"But what do we have now? We are being watched by someone whom even Sir William cannot trust! William, you seem determined to isolate us. Let us run—while we still can."

Clarenceux brought his hand down hard on the table. "No! Lady Percy has obviously never forgiven me. I think she has found it easier to blame me, and to hate me, than to do anything about her despair."

"You! You, you, you—I think you actually like being the center of attention, the only one who knows where this document is. While it is your little secret, you will never want for friends—but we will never lack enemies."

"It is not like that."

"We are all in danger now, William. We, your wife, your daughters. Annie is probably dying and what do you plan to do? What are we going to do?"

Clarenceux spoke in as calm a tone as he could. "I am not going to damage things further by running. Where could we go? Unless we were to disappear somewhere that no one would ever suspect, what chance would we have? How many people knew Rebecca was hiding in Portchester? Very few indeed—but they found her. If we went to Devon, how long would it be before someone slips a few shillings to an agricultural worker or laborer to find out where we—the strangers—are hiding? How long could we stay in hiding? Who will risk us being on their property? At moments like this, there is a temptation to trade the danger you know for an unknown one, in the hope that the unknown danger is less. But doing so is to choose ignorance, and there is no refuge in ignorance—not from this, not from anything."

Awdrey seemed emptied of her rage. "Then what do we do?"

"We think. We think through everything. This was not a hastily thought-out robbery. Whoever planned it knows they face a great problem in trying to persuade me to give up the document. They know that they have got to terrorize me into doing so, and they know that the only way they can do that is to threaten you and our daughters. Nothing else will really make any difference. And if I am dead, then their cause is lost. If it comes to the worst, I can put a bullet in my head and the matter is over forever. So it is—"

"Don't say such things!" cried Awdrey. "Don't even think that."

"It is true, Awdrey," he said, looking her in the eye. "You do not need to admit it or agree with me, but it is true. And I feel it is reassuring. But, in the name of God, it is not what I want. Last night, as I was watching Annie, and listening to you blessing Mildred, when Joan was putting her to bed, I realized that if I ended my life I would never see our daughters grow, never see them marry, never see them have children of their own. And it overwhelmed me with grief. But that grief is premature. We cannot afford to let such things overwhelm us. You are vulnerable. They are not going to try to kill me—it was no accident that the gun pointed at me last Sunday did not contain a bullet. They want to terrorize me, but they need me alive."

"You are talking about yourself again."

"No—*us*. If we stay together they will have to bring overwhelming force against us at the same time. They will not do that. They have to take advantage of our being separated. Therefore, I will not leave your side. If we have to go anywhere, we go together—but that will not be until Annie is better. We will send Thomas and Joan to buy food and to pass messages. I do have to go to Skinners Hall and the Exchange, and to see Tom Griffiths about the rents of the tenements; but if we have to part I will accompany you somewhere safe. Cecil House is the obvious place."

"What about everything else—your sword-fighting practice, for example?"

"We can forget that. The important point is that we do not open up any weaknesses. We don't allow them to come between us, not when you are here or undefended. And when they make their move on us—which they will—we will have a strategy of our own."

Awdrey took a step closer to him. She put her hand up against his cheek. "Please tell me you were not serious when you said you might kill yourself. It is not something I can bear. It would not make everything good and safe for us—it would destroy me too. Tell me you won't mention it again."

Clarenceux took her hand and kissed it. "I will not mention it again," he said, looking her in the eye.

37

~

Thursday, January 9

Greystoke called that morning at the front door to inquire whether Clarenceux was going to the Belle Savage. When Clarenceux told him, carefully, that he had decided not to leave his family, especially while Annie was still suffering from the wound, Greystoke suggested they practice together in the yard. This they did, for an hour, and once again Greystoke proved the more expert swordsman. Nevertheless, Clarenceux acquitted himself well. He also knew that there were objects around that he could have employed to his advantage had it been a real fight—the stable door, a pair of barrels inside the gate, a spade. He intentionally did not use them. There was no point in telling Greystoke how he really fought. If ever they drew blades against each other in anger, it was better that he should know Greystoke's methods—and that Greystoke should know none of his.

"You fight well for a man of your age," said Greystoke as they went into the buttery with a tankard each to pour themselves some beer.

"You do not know how old I am."

Greystoke supped his beer. "You are forty-eight. Walsingham told me."

"Walsingham seems to have told you a great many things. Is there anything he did not teach you?"

"Dante. He never speaks a word of Dante."

"'*Nessun maggior dolore che ricordarsi del tempo felice nella miseria*,'" said Clarenceux.

Greystoke raised his tankard. "Very good, Mr. Clarenceux. But that is one of the more famous lines. Can you continue the quotation?"

"Alas, no. But you are the expert."

"'*E ciò sa 'l tuo dottore. Ma s'a conoscer la prima radice del nostro amor tu bai cotanto affetto, dirò come colui che piange e dice.*'"

"You will have to translate that for me—my Italian is not so fluent."

"It is Francesca's line. After Dante, in the company of Virgil, has spoken to her, asking her how she knew she was in love, she replies with the famous line that you know: 'There is no greater sorrow than to be reminded of a happy time in one's misery.' The rest means 'and that thy teacher knows. But, if you desire so keenly to recognize the first root of love in us, I will do even as he who weeps and speaks.'"

"Bravo," Clarenceux said. "Some people know Dante, and some people know their Bible. You, I imagine, are one of the few who knows both."

"I pride myself on my Dante, it is true," admitted Greystoke, "but one can never know enough of the Bible to be proud."

Clarenceux poured slowly, making sure he didn't spill a drop.

38

Friday, January 10

Maurice Buckman waited while Joan Hellier ascended the stairs into the upper chamber of the Black Swan. He put on his spectacles and watched her from the shadow. "You are late," he said, as soon as she appeared in the light of the candle.

"I am sorry, Father," replied Joan. "I was making sure I was not followed."

"That is good but it does not excuse lateness."

Joan bowed. "As I said, Father, I am sorry."

"Clarenceux's daughter—is there any news of her?"

"Sarah Cowie and Ann Thwaite have both been watching the house. Neither of them has seen anything to indicate any change."

"It is good that the girl is still alive. The more we hurt his family and yet leave them living, the more we can impress upon him our seriousness."

Joan stared into the darkness. "Why was there no bullet in Jane's gun?"

"It was important that she not kill Clarenceux, merely make him believe he was under attack. It was unfortunate that she obtained another gun—we were lucky she did not use that one on Clarenceux."

"You *wanted* Greystoke to kill Jane? You sent an innocent woman to her death!"

"Her life was already forfeit. She was already dead in the eyes of the law. I needed someone to attack Clarenceux, so Greystoke could show his loyalty by killing her. Would you rather I had chosen you?"

"No, but I regret her death. She was innocent—even of the crime for which she had been condemned."

"We are all innocent. We all have good honest reasons for doing what we do. Even Clarenceux can justify his actions, if only to himself. But we are not concerned with understanding and forgiving—that is God's business."

Joan bit her lip. There was no point in saying anything else. She was just a mercenary in this war.

39

Sunday, January 12

Clarenceux had been awake for over an hour, yet it was still dark. Something had awoken him, some noise. He lay in bed, hearing Awdrey in the next room. Every moment of every day for the last week he had feared the shriek of despair if they were to find that Annie had died. Every time he saw Annie lying still he feared she would pass away from them. However much he told himself it was normal for a man to watch half his children die, he could not accept it. He and Awdrey had not lost a child—he had come to think of them as extraordinarily fortunate. He told himself that, by expecting the worst, it would never happen—like a watched pot does not boil. But he doubted his thoughts. He doubted everything.

As he lay there, he remembered being tortured some years before. All his life he had been quick, agile, and strong, and now it was hard to reconcile himself to the fact that he was in pain much of the time and so much slower than he had been. Younger men like Greystoke had all the confidence now and, moreover, they had good reason to be confident, watching older men wither and weaken. But it was troubling that he was losing his strength when his family most needed him.

He heard the door open. Awdrey came into the room, trying to be quiet. As she got into bed, the ropes beneath the mattress tautened and shifted.

"How is she?" he asked.

"Asleep. I think she's improving."

"It's been a week now."

"I know."

"Either we all go to church today or none of us do."

"I don't want to go," said Awdrey immediately. "We all went last week."

They were quiet for a while. Awdrey put her arm around Clarenceux, and he responded by putting an arm around her.

She whispered across his chest, "Every day I say to myself, it could happen anytime. One of our beautiful girls could be taken from us. This hour might be my last hour of tranquility."

"This state is not one I would call tranquil."

"No, but it could be worse. Every moment is a threat, and every moment that the threat is not realized is one of tranquility. I feel like a candle flame, not knowing which way the breeze will come, nor whether it will be a burst of air that will extinguish me."

He held her close.

"And you, William, what do you feel?"

"I worry. For you, for Annie, for Mildred. I feel weak, stuck in this house, as if it is our castle. How I have prided myself on looking out through wide glass windows, and yet I would now rebuild the front of my house with stone and a drawbridge, if I could."

"It is a treasure, this silence, in the great vessel of the night."

Shortly afterward they rose and went about the day. The morning was bright with springlike sunlight streaming in the open shutters at the back of the house. The decision not to go to church greatly relieved both of them, and Mildred played on the floor of Annie's chamber. Thomas built up the fire in the hall, and Clarenceux went down to inspect his horses with Nick. He had eaten some bread and sage butter for breakfast and was wishing he could simply go for a ride when Awdrey appeared in the yard.

"Where is Joan?" she asked.

"Joan? Why, is she not…" Clarenceux felt the ground slip from under him. He went to the back door and through, along the corridor to the front door and tried the handle. It was locked. Joan did not have a key. "Joan!" he shouted. "Joan!" He turned back to face the way he had come; he had certainly been the one who had unbolted the back door that morning. Surely she had to be still inside? Alarmed, he started to search the house. There was no sign of her in the disused and empty shop at the front, nor in the buttery behind that. He fetched a light and searched behind the barrels in the windowless room. There was no indication of her having got up to light the fire in the kitchen, as was her duty, nor her entering the pantry. Upstairs, Thomas was arranging the hall for the Sunday lunch; he had not seen Joan either. Clarenceux went up the stairs to his study; she was not there. He went downstairs and strode across the hall to the rear staircase. "Joan!" he shouted, fearing the worst. "Joan!" There was no sign of her on the back stairs, nor in the parlor nor in the guest chamber. Forcing himself up the stairs and calling again, shouting for her, he looked in his own chamber and in those of his daughters.

Lying on her bed, Annie looked pale and terrified. Mildred simply looked confused. "Why are you shouting?" she asked. "Is Joan still asleep?"

Clarenceux said nothing. There were now only the attics, the back attic being where Joan usually slept. It was reached by a ladder on the upper landing, outside their bedchamber. Clarenceux searched for a light; he lit a candle from the hall fire, which Thomas had rekindled, and ascended the ladder. As his gaze rose above the level of the attic floor, the candlelight illuminated a naked foot not far from his face. The girl was motionless, her smock and a petticoat rucked up around her knees. He braced himself, to reach forward and feel her bare lower leg. It was like holding a cold joint of meat.

He took another step up into the attic, lifting the candle to look around the dark space. There was no sign of anyone, just here and there a crack of daylight entering where one of the shingles did not sit squarely on those below. He looked down at Joan's corpse; there was bruising around her neck. Not far away was the straw mattress that she slept on; the canvas sheets were thrown back.

But the doors were locked. Joan's killer must still be in the house.

Clarenceux descended the ladder halfway and stopped, unable to believe that anyone would do this in his house. He had had his suspicions about Nick—but he could not believe that Nick would do such a thing. It had to be someone else—but who? Someone that Nick had let out of the house, locking the door behind him.

Clarenceux descended the ladder and stairs quickly, going down to the buttery, where Thomas was moving a barrel. "Joan's dead. In the attic. The doors were all locked last night, am I correct?"

"By the saints, dead?"

"The front and back doors," insisted Clarenceux. "Am I right in saying they were locked?"

Thomas nodded. "You know they were, sir."

"You're absolutely sure?" said Clarenceux in a voice that was more of a shout than a question. "No doubt at all?"

Thomas shook his head. "None at all."

Clarenceux stormed out into the yard. Nick was there in the doorway to the stable. Awdrey saw her husband march out of the house and make straight for Nick, who backed away into the stable as he drew near. "You're the one who is responsible," he shouted. "The doors were locked, on the inside. Either you killed her or you let the murderer out!" He was jabbing his finger at Nick. Rage suddenly took hold of him and he grabbed the boy's jerkin with his left hand and struck him hard in the face with his right. Nick tried to break away but Clarenceux held on. "Who killed her? Who?" He repeated "Who?" in between each blow. After four or five blows he flung Nick against the wall. Only when Thomas and Awdrey between them managed to prevent his blows did he stop. He spluttered and glared at Nick, who was bleeding from a cut below one eye and from both nostrils. "Why did you do it?" he panted. "Why? I do not believe you killed her yourself, but you had to have let the killer out."

Nick dabbed at his wounds glaring at Clarenceux. "I did nothing! I let no one in or out. I had nothing to do with it."

"You will hang for this."

"In God's name, Mr. Clarenceux!" shouted Nick, distraught. "God's my witness, I never did it, nor did I let no one out of the house. I swear it."

"William," implored Awdrey, putting herself in front of him. "Do not rush to conclusions. There may be an explanation."

"I am not rushing to conclusions," snapped Clarenceux. "Someone in my house committed or abetted a murder—Joan's murder. I do not believe it was Thomas or you, and our daughters are not capable. There is only one alternative…"

"Sir, be calm, be rational," pleaded Thomas.

"Damn you, I am calm, I am rational. There is no other explanation for why she is dead and the doors locked. Unless *you* know something."

Thomas did not reply. He looked into Clarenceux's eyes, questioning him. "Nick," he said coldly, not taking his eyes off Clarenceux, "I think it would be best if you were to leave Mr. Clarenceux's house now."

The boy stumbled forward. "Where will I go?"

"Go to your friends on the other side of the road," sneered Clarenceux. "Go anywhere, just get out of my house. The constables will come for you wherever you are."

"William," protested Awdrey.

"*Get out!*" roared Clarenceux at Nick, ignoring her.

Nick left the yard, banging the gate shut behind him.

And then came the huge emptiness upon Clarenceux, the hollow moment, with Thomas and Awdrey both looking at him in shock. And he saw Mildred too in the doorway to the house, staring at him as if he was going to shout at her too. And the cascade of events tumbled through him—the fear of the soldiers changing guard, the murder of Rebecca Machyn, the shooting of Annie and the killing of her assailant, and now the killing of Joan. He felt unutterably sad, frightened, and sick. He leaned against a wall, breathing deeply.

"Someone was in our house last night," he said.

"There is a possibility he still is," ventured Thomas. "It is possible that you have treated Nick most unfairly."

"No. I have just searched the whole house."

Thomas bowed perfunctorily and turned away. "I have tasks to attend to."

Clarenceux said bitterly, "I cannot even look after my family, not even my servants when they are under my own roof."

"I am going back to Cecil House," Awdrey declared. "I will send to Sir William and Lady Cecil and ask them if I can stay indefinitely. For the sake of the children."

Clarenceux looked at her and then looked away.

"I have said this before, William, but you must bring this to an end. We cannot live like this." She waited for him to say something but the emotion that he was fighting showed on his face. He had too many inner struggles to speak warmly to her. "I will go and look at Joan now," she added. "I need to say good-bye to her. She was a good servant."

For the next hour Clarenceux said very little. He went to see Annie, preparing himself for the fact that Awdrey was going to take the girls away again. He asked his daughter how she was and accepted her one-word answers sadly. He wished she would say more to him and let him share her suffering, but how could she? He read a little to her from the New Testament, and saw her turning uncomfortably, and stopped to help her. He went to the kitchen to fetch her some bread and butter. When she had eaten and was asleep again, he simply looked at her, treasuring memories as they came back to him, one by one, from the day of her birth to when she had declared she loved him more than warm milk and Mildred had shouted that she loved him more than God.

He did not notice Mildred standing in the doorway, looking at him curiously. "Daddy, why are you crying?"

Clarenceux smiled and lifted Mildred in his arms and kissed her, and felt tears welling in his eyes again. "For all the good things,

Mildred. I am crying with joy for all the days we have been happy together, and for the joy of life. It is so valuable, and you and Annie are so precious." He held her, pressing her cheek against his. Awdrey came up the stairs and went into their chamber with some clean linen. He set Mildred down again and looked at Annie, whose eyes were open. "Is there anything else you need now?"

Annie shook her head. Clarenceux spoke to Mildred. "Wait with your sister. Let me know if she wants anything."

He walked out of the room and down the stairs to the hall, emotionally and physically exhausted. He wanted to ride away, yet knew he could not. Looking in the mirror he saw the lines around his eyes, his hair awry. The cold neutrality of the mirror in showing him in this soul-disheveled state left him feeling even lower. He wondered if this was what the atheists felt when they looked at the world, that it was all exactly as it appeared, and not overseen by God Who understood and took pity on those oppressed and distracted by their suffering. *Is there any compassion for Man in nature if there is no God?* he wondered.

He went down the stairs to the yard and out across to the stable, where he patted the horses, thinking about how he had shouted at Nick and trying to convince himself that what he had done was necessary: he had nothing to be ashamed of.

"Mr. Clarenceux, sir," called Thomas from the back door. "Mr. Greystoke wishes to see you."

Clarenceux walked through to the front of the house and spoke to him on the doorstep. After Cecil's cryptic note he had no intention of allowing the man into the house.

"You are not going to attend church then," said Greystoke. "That is most unlike you, Mr. Clarenceux."

"After last week, it would not be appropriate. The family feels too vulnerable. I suggest you go alone," he had replied, beginning to close the door.

"Are things all right with you, Mr. Clarenceux?"

"Do you think this general situation is—" But at that moment there was a scream from upstairs. "William!"

It was Awdrey's voice, and there was a note of fear in it that Clarenceux had never heard before. "Stay here," he commanded. As the mind moves into slow motion, he turned and saw the wooden steps of the staircase passing under him, as he forced himself up, hearing his footsteps as if from afar. He entered the hall to turn to his right and saw everything as it should be—except for one hideous sight. A blond woman in a filthy gray dress was standing behind Awdrey with her left hand under her chin and her right holding a knife at her throat.

"I'll kill her—stay back!" shouted the woman, whose face was wide-eyed and terrified. Her voice carried a northern accent. She backed away toward the stairs, dragging Awdrey with her. But she heard Thomas running up the stairs behind her and stopped. When he appeared and took stock of the situation, she gestured with her head for Thomas to move into the front part of the room to stand alongside Clarenceux.

The woman's hair was a tangled mess, her hands were dirty and she had broken teeth. The skirts of her dress were stained down the front, and her fingers blistered. She did not look or smell as if she had washed for a long while. She had lost all self-respect. And she was shaking.

"You know why I am here. Give me the document that Lady Percy wants. Give it to me or I will cut her throat."

Clarenceux stared at the woman. "It was you," he muttered. "You who killed Joan."

"William, please!" urged Awdrey.

"Give it to me!" the woman shrieked, fear and anger combining to make her appear like a crazed Maenad from the ancient world.

"You are out of your mind," said Clarenceux, approaching a step further, causing the woman to back away and dig the knife blade further into Awdrey's neck. A trickle of blood ran down where the edge was cutting the surface. "I have lived with the curse of that marriage agreement for a long time now. I have told some people I have destroyed it. I have told other people that I will use it. The truth is that it is not in this house. It is not in this city. It is not even in this county. If you want me to give it to you, you will have to wait."

"Where is it? Tell me, and you can have your wife alive. Otherwise, it will be two bodies you need to bury."

"It is in Oxford," said Clarenceux. "Hidden under the floor of a room in St. John's College." He paused and stepped closer, and the woman backed away another step. Awdrey was white-eyed with fear, rigid, barely daring to breathe with the blade hurting her. She started gasping.

"Do you see your stupidity?" shouted Clarenceux, feeling angry and desperate at once. "Do you think I would be such a fool as to keep something as precious as that vellum in this house?"

"Please!" shouted Awdrey, her head back, squirming. "It's true!"

Suddenly there was a knocking sound behind Clarenceux and he wheeled around to look—but there was nothing. The room was empty. Turning back, he saw blood bursting everywhere, all over Awdrey. Instantly he rushed forward, but then Awdrey lifted her hands to her face and screamed. The knife had fallen from the woman's grasp. The blood was hers, not Awdrey's. Greystoke had been so quick; he had stabbed her through the neck. Awdrey gasped and reached blindly for

Clarenceux. He held her as she sobbed. Greystoke wiped his blade on the woman's dress and turned the body over.

A moment later, Clarenceux saw Mildred enter the room. The young girl looked with curiosity at the dead woman, her blood running across the floorboards. "Thomas," said Clarenceux. The old servant stepped forward and ushered the girl out of the hall.

"How many more of them are there?" Clarenceux asked Greystoke, holding Awdrey as she sobbed, pressing her face to his chest.

Greystoke shook his head. "That I do not know."

"I don't care!" cried Awdrey, lifting her face. "I don't *want* to know. I just want to go away from here."

Clarenceux held her tight, but quietly he was thinking. Greystoke had thrown something across the room to distract the woman before he thrust. He noted the deftness, the sleight of hand, the silence of his approach, and the accuracy. The swordsman was more than just a show fighter.

40

Monday, January 13

Clarenceux found himself alone in the bed, still clothed, with his sword in his hand. Lying there, he remembered that there were two corpses in the house: victim and murderer, lying side by side in the empty shop downstairs. Although the previous day his household had numbered seven, today it was just him and Thomas. Awdrey was safer where she was, where Cecil's many servants could help look after her and, if necessary, call for a physician for Annie. They were only a few hundred yards away, yet this house was now so cold and empty. It had lost its purpose.

He turned in his bed and lay on his side, remembering the shock of finding Joan. He recalled the sight of the woman with the knife. *How wrong I was about Nick. How hateful I must have seemed, how unjust. And I did not listen to Awdrey—she urged caution, and she was right, for it was that woman all along.*

He threw off the blankets and felt his way downstairs, too full of self-recrimination to care about the cold. "Thomas," he called as he felt for the latch and opened the door to the hall. "Thomas, are you awake?"

"I am now."

"That woman yesterday—how did she get into this house?"

Thomas stirred in the darkness. "I do not know. I suppose she was always hiding, in one of the attics."

"No, I searched thoroughly yesterday. They have found a way in, through a wall or a window. They could be back inside even now."

"The doors are certainly locked, Mr. Clarenceux. And to the west there is only the alley. They would be seen coming in the front, and behind there is the yard. To the east is Mr. Webb's house—and you know he would not entertain such people."

"They have found a way in and it has to be from Mr. Webb's direction," repeated Clarenceux, marching to the front windows and opening the shutters. He could see a couple of lights in the house opposite and the shadowy line of the roofs. "Both these women who have attacked us have attempted poorly thought-out acts. Futile attempts. Yet they have found their way into the house without being seen."

"The first one came in through the back window, we know that. We found the catch lifted."

"She did not unfasten it herself; it was opened from the inside. Lady Percy has sent an army of women after me—it is beginning to look as if someone is placing them in here on her behalf. Perhaps Greystoke himself: I don't think it a coincidence that he has killed both of them."

"But Greystoke was sent by Walsingham."

"Perhaps. Or perhaps Walsingham sent another man called Greystoke and this one has taken his place."

There was the sound of wind through the rafters. Somewhere down the street a shutter banged open. "They could be listening to us now," he said.

"Mr. Clarenceux, we have to go to the constable today."

"We also need to see to the horses. We are without a stable boy." Clarenceux went to the door leading up to his study and paused. "I am so sorry for what I said to Nick. It was wrong. And you were right. I should not have rushed to judgment."

"It was understandable, given the circumstances," replied Thomas.

Then there was no sound but for the wind in the rafters. Both men listened.

"We need to see to the horses," Clarenceux said in a louder voice. He went back to where Thomas was and took his arm. "We will talk outside," he whispered.

41

It's dangerous to stay here," said Sarah Cowie as she saw Joan Hellier in their second-floor chamber. "Greystoke will kill us all, one by one."

"We're not that stupid," muttered Joan, kneeling on Jane Carr's bed and looking through her possessions. She took a comb and the dead woman's money for herself.

"But is the plan working?"

Joan went across to Ann Thwaite's bag, left by the door of the room, and started to rummage through it. "The beauty of this plan is that it cannot fail. Every attempt is just another stage in the plan. Eventually it will be successful."

"What do you mean?"

Joan let an old smock fall from her hands and kicked it away across the floor. She sighed and looked at Sarah. "You've seen a bull baiting. First one dog goes in and it gets thrown, then the next, and it gets thrown too. Some dogs get killed. The older and wiser ones hold back. They know that sooner or later, one of the young ones will catch the bull by surprise, or two dogs will distract the bull, and they will grab it by the neck and worry it to death. Although the bull fights, and catches it with its horn and kills it, the master of the ring sends in another couple of dogs. If they are brave and determined, the bull is as good as dead. It is only a matter of time."

"We are the dogs, you mean."

"It is better to be the dogs than to be the bull."

42

The constable and the coroner, together with their assistants and clerks, assembled at Clarenceux's house that same afternoon. The coroner, whose inquest had consisted of a cursory examination of the corpse and the premises a week earlier, now spent hours going over the details. It was too much of a coincidence, he deemed, that three women should have been killed in the same house within a week. He insisted on taking statements from all the people involved, so Greystoke had to be summoned from across the road. Clarenceux refused to send for Awdrey; the coroner accordingly decided he would go to Cecil House to interview her. The party—with the constables and clerks, Thomas and Clarenceux—made their way to the imposing house by the Aldwych and waited in the great hall while the coroner spoke to Awdrey.

When the officials had completed their work, Clarenceux went up to see his wife and daughters alone.

"Sir William is not at home?" he asked.

"He is with the queen," Awdrey replied.

"When you see him, find out why he sent that Latin message. For my part, I mean to search harder, and that means taking the risk of spending more time with Greystoke."

Late that afternoon, Clarenceux and Thomas saddled up the horses to exercise them. They rode out along the Strand past the palace and the royal menagerie, feeling the cold wind of January on their faces. There was no warmth in the weak sun. Being a Sunday, there were no washerwomen walking back into the city with their baskets of linen, as there would have been on any other dry day. Carters and travelers were hastening along the road to make sure they reached the city by nightfall. The two men ate a small supper of bread, beef, and cheese at a tavern in the village of Knightsbridge. It was dark when they left, for the new moon was only three days old. They rode slowly, with owls hooting in the trees on either side of the road, past the latecomers hastening to the city's suburbs—shadowy carts and riders in the night, black figures shifting in a dark world.

Clarenceux knew that someone had been in the house during their absence as soon as he entered. He went to place his riding cloak on the peg nearest to the door, and there was already another garment on it. Feeling it, he recognized it as Awdrey's safeguard, which had previously been placed on the adjacent peg. "We need a light," he said to Thomas. "Go and ask Mr. Greystoke if he will oblige us."

"Mr. Greystoke?"

"We need to lure him in. He will make mistakes—but if we are not there with him when he does, we will not spot them."

43

That Sunday set a pattern for Clarenceux and Thomas for the next two weeks. Clarenceux rode every day to Cecil House to see Awdrey and his daughters. Awdrey looked tired and worried, and he felt dispirited, as if he was failing her. Thomas and Clarenceux mucked out the horses themselves and exercised them in a new direction each day. Several times they searched the house for a secret entrance but did not find one; eventually they gave up looking. They ate at a different tavern every dinnertime. They also met with Greystoke each day, under the pretext of Clarenceux wanting to practice his swordsmanship. On both Thursdays all three men attended Girolamo's swordsmanship school at the Belle Savage—although Thomas simply watched.

Clarenceux noted the comings and goings of the men at Greystoke's house, asking him about each of the men living there with him: who they were, what their backgrounds were, why they had sought employment with Walsingham. Every time Greystoke replied with confidence and assurance, mocking him for being so suspicious. Which only made Clarenceux more so.

He looked forward to the riding most, when no one knew where he was. Each night when the time came to go home, he felt as if he were forcing himself back into a vice, and that Lady Percy was giving it an extra turn. He had to be there, to play the victim, so his enemies would come to him. The place that had once been a home now seemed oppressive—the most dangerous place he could be.

He knew he was being watched—and not just by Greystoke. Thomas knew it too. Occasionally something would appear slightly out of place. In his study Clarenceux positioned documents so that the corner of a charter would be just tucked under the edge of a book, or his horn ruler would be left with its lower edge on the seventh line from the bottom of a page. From this he knew that what he was reading was also being checked, in case he was using a book-based code. This was doubly worrying: whoever was looking at his papers could read—it was therefore very unlikely to be a woman being manipulated by Lady Percy but someone with an education. Whoever it was, he or she was not entering by way of the rear window. Clarenceux wedged small pieces of dried bread in between the shutters—crumbs that would fall out if the windows were opened. They remained in place.

For the three women in the house two doors to the east of Clarenceux's, the situation was as taut. Joan Hellier informed Maurice Buckman that only Clarenceux and Thomas were now living in the house. Buckman instructed Joan and the other women to listen to all conversations and to take every opportunity to enter the house when Clarenceux and Thomas were away. They used the knowledge that he would exercise his horses for at least an hour every day to time their maneuvers. They too felt trapped. Spying on Clarenceux and Thomas meant an agonizing and tense period for one of the women each day. She had to lie still in the front attic, above the hall, for a whole day, until one of the other women gave the all-clear signal.

This task was shared by Helen Oudry and Joan Hellier. Sarah Cowie was the only one of the three who could read, so it fell to her to check Clarenceux's study. One of the few compensations was the chance to refill their wine and beer flasks and flagons from the barrels in Clarenceux's buttery whenever they crept into the house.

Over the two weeks, the women learned little. But what they did hear was of great importance. They knew where Awdrey was. They discovered when the house would be empty and where Clarenceux went with Thomas. They found out just how much Clarenceux did not trust John Greystoke. Most importantly, they heard Clarenceux himself telling Thomas in a low voice that the document was in Oxfordshire. And this was the message they took back to Father Buckman.

44

Sunday, January 26

Before church, Clarenceux noticed it was beginning to rain, so he waited until the last moment before donning his long cloak and leaving the house with Thomas. He stepped outside and greeted Greystoke with a perfunctory nod; Greystoke was waiting in a similar long garment. Clarenceux continued on his way, holding his hat firmly on his head as the rain came down harder, splashing into the mud of the street. The bells rang out above them, somber-sounding in the rain. Already there were puddles forming as the three men joined the queue and entered the church.

Greystoke seemed to be in an equally somber mood. Thomas was just tense. Clarenceux listened to the sermon, thinking of his wife and daughters and remembering the moment two weeks earlier when Annie had been shot. What hold could anyone have over a woman to make her do such a thing as shoot a child? It did not seem sensible to him that a religious motive underlay their actions. If religious self-sacrifice were the key, why did the woman not attack him in public? He hardly listened to the sermon, preoccupied with imagining the next threat that might assail him.

After the service Clarenceux and Thomas headed to a tavern, the Mermaid in Cheapside, for their dinner. Clarenceux invited Greystoke to join them, as usual. The tavern, however, was busy. All seven tables were full. There was a fiddle player near the fire and two children dancing, a dog nosing from table to table, but the lack of space meant they could not stay. Thomas suggested the Bell in Gracechurch Street, where he used to be on good terms with the innkeeper's wife and was always treated well. Clarenceux had not been there but was persuaded to try it, and Greystoke made no alternative suggestion.

The Bell Inn was not what Thomas remembered. If it was still an inn, it was in name only, as few people would have been likely to stay there. The hall had a large fireplace on one side but was still open to the roof beams. The rushes on the floor were old and, as one trod, the broken shells of mussels cracked underfoot. The walls were whitewashed, to make the most of the light, but here and there were smears where beer had been thrown or spilled. A number of jugs and flasks hung from hooks in the walls; others lay on the floor, in the lee of a barrel or bench. The men were raucous and drinking beer, not wine. The only women to be seen were the landlord's wife and another serving woman. There were just two long tables, and most of the spaces were full, but there was room on one bench for the three of them, albeit in the darkest place, furthest from the window. The aroma of meat in the air made Clarenceux's mouth water. One glance at Greystoke, who looked uncomfortable, told Clarenceux that this would be the ideal place for them to eat.

He saw a platter of carved meat carried by the landlord down to the men making the most noise by the window, beckoned the fellow over, and asked for a similar platter for the three of them, as well as three pottles of double beer. As they waited, Clarenceux turned back to the rowdy group, who seemed no less noisy for the food they had been given. That was when he noticed the boy who was with them.

He was about fourteen years of age, thin, and just above average height, with curly hair, a narrow face, and high cheekbones. There were scars on his face. He had a curiously graceful way of moving, being extraordinarily lithe. He was smiling—laughing even—but he was also nervous—Clarenceux could tell by the small hand movements to his face. He could not hear what the boy was saying, but suddenly all the rowdy men fell quiet as the boy placed something on the table. At the same time he held up what at first seemed to be a piece of paper—but Clarenceux heard the immediate roar of approval and realized it was a playing card. The boy was smiling again, and men were patting him on the back; he picked up a coin from the table.

As their platter of meat and the tankards were delivered, Clarenceux heard someone standing behind him talking about the boy, whose name he heard as Fyndern: "He sleeps in a shed by St. Katherine's wharf…his parents both died in the great plague of sixty-three…bless his soul, his luck with the cards is his only good fortune." Clarenceux drew his knife but offered the first pick of the meat to his companions. Thomas declined, ashamed to eat before his master, until Clarenceux insisted. Greystoke then also accepted and picked the piece of beef nearest him.

"Some people have a hard way in the world," said Clarenceux, nodding in the boy's direction before he put the meat in his mouth.

"I don't think so," replied Greystoke. "Look at the size of the bet."

Clarenceux saw that, where before there had been one coin, a penny, now there were two, and one was much larger than the other. The latter looked like a shilling—a working man's wages for three days. He put down his knife. He wanted to eat but could not drag his gaze away from the boy. No one was saying anything now or even moving; there was silence throughout the tavern. The boy was just lifting his hand up and down. Then, slowly, he turned and held two cards up above his head and flicked them across the table. One landed on the table, face up; the other fell to the ground. Two men scrambled for it and held it up. A cheer went around and the boy bowed.

"Whatever he's doing, he's good at it," said Greystoke.

"Too good," replied Thomas. "Look at the scars on his face. You don't get hurt like that for making mistakes."

The noise of two dozen men chattering resumed. Clarenceux took another piece of beef. "Mr. Greystoke, do you have any idea how the women who attacked me might have entered my house?"

"No. None at all."

A thick slice of bread was placed in front of each of them by the landlord, and Clarenceux signaled his thanks with a raised hand. "But both times you were on hand to attack my assailant, as if you knew she was going to be there. On both occasions you were armed, even when we had come straight from church."

Greystoke seemed put out. "Would you rather I had not attacked them?"

"No, but I do wonder…"

"But why are you surprised that I go armed? Walsingham gave me instructions to watch out for you and your family. How could I do that if I weren't armed?"

"Are you carrying a sword now?"

"Yes. Are you?"

Clarenceux swallowed. "Yes."

"Well then." Greystoke broke his bread and dipped it in the sauce.

He bit off a piece and chewed, looking Clarenceux in the eye. "Both women were dangerous. On neither occasion were you in a position to defend yourself, and my orders from Walsingham are to protect you and your family. The second time, when Ann Thwaite had your wife by the neck—"

"Ann Thwaite? You know her name?"

"I heard what the coroner said," said Greystoke, continuing to eat. "That was the second time. The first—you were too slow on the stairs, with that hip of yours. You claim you'd come good in a real fight, but I reckon your hip would be your undoing. I've watched you long enough; I know it is one of your weaknesses."

"You say that as if it is some kind of threat."

Greystoke lifted his tankard. "On the contrary. It is my business to look out for your weak spots. A good shepherd knows where the wolf is most likely to break into the fold."

Clarenceux took the third-to-last piece of meat. "Thomas, you are being very quiet. What do you think?"

The old man lifted his tankard too, saying, "Would that I had been as agile as Mr. Greystoke here."

There was a shout again from the men watching the boy with his cards.

Clarenceux looked at Greystoke. "I have probably not been grateful enough, Mr. Greystoke, and for that I apologize. But you must know that Mr. Walsingham and I have not always been friends. He has accused me of treason on more than one occasion. He has even wrecked my house before, destroying almost every possession. But that is why I am very curious about what information you have given him concerning me. You have been feeding him information, have you not?"

Greystoke nodded. "I have sent messages concerning both attacks."

Clarenceux drummed his fingers on the table. "Does he intend to do more to help us? Can he? Can you?"

"You ask many questions, Mr. Clarenceux. We can only do what we can—"

At that moment there was another cheer—but only from some of those present, and it died suddenly in the air. Clarenceux looked at the curly-haired boy, who was no longer smiling. He was backing away from a man with short blond hair who was getting out of his seat. Everyone was silent.

"How did you do that?" shouted the blond man. "Is this witchcraft?"

Clarenceux saw the boy lose all confidence with the utterance of that word. Like a dog that has been beaten too often and recognizes that another beating is imminent, he backed away, reaching for the door. But he backed slightly the wrong way. A moment later the coins had been snatched up and the cards scattered. The blond man was between the boy and the door, and there was no escape. "You pick up my money," he shouted.

"You made the bet and I won it," pleaded the boy. "It's my money now."

Clarenceux glanced at Thomas and saw he was frowning. He turned back in time to see the blond-haired man take a swing at the boy. He missed, but voices spoke up for the man. "Go on, Ned, he's asking for it."

"You can be sure of it," said Ned. "He's not having anything from me but a hiding."

Others started to get up. The boy had nowhere to go.

"This is going to turn bad," Thomas said in a low voice.

A couple of men glanced anxiously in Clarenceux's direction. He and Greystoke were the only gentlemen present, their clothes marking them out as men of influence and authority. If anyone was going to intervene, it had to be one of them. Clarenceux rose to his feet. He took a couple of steps and clapped a man on the shoulder, bent down, and whispered in the ear of the surprised drinker, "What is that man's name?"

"Ned Wilson," replied the man immediately.

Clarenceux patted the man's shoulder and walked over to the corner where Ned Wilson was haranguing the boy. Those cheering in support fell silent and drew back. Suddenly everyone was quiet, watching Clarenceux.

"Why are you menacing this boy, Goodman Wilson? What harm has he done you?"

Wilson's gray eyes were vague with drink. "You saw—surely you saw? He's a lying cheat. Or are you his father? If so, you are the father of a lying cheat."

There was a moment of decision as both men reckoned the other. At the instant that Ned Wilson reckoned in his alcoholic confusion that he had enough support to pile into this gentleman, others pressed forward to hold him back and stop him from being so foolish as to strike someone of status. Clarenceux swept back his long cloak, revealing his sword. Greystoke did the same and stepped forward along with Thomas.

"Do you have a name, boy?" asked Clarenceux, keeping one eye on Wilson.

"Fyndern Catesby, sir."

Clarenceux spoke in a loud voice. "If there is a brawl in an establishment like this, the landlord stands a good chance of losing his license." He paused, looking between the faces, seeing the unspoken dialogue. Clearly fights often broke out in there but no one spoke of them. "I have just enjoyed some good meat and I would not want this place to close. Fyndern Catesby, I suggest you come with me and leave these men to their ale and beef dinner. Your tricks are no longer wanted here." He beckoned the boy forward with his hand, then felt in his pocket for the coins with which to pay the innkeeper. Greystoke and Thomas both followed him out of the building.

"Come with me," Clarenceux said to Fyndern, and he began marching back toward Cheapside. Fyndern's tousled brown hair and brown eyes reminded him of his own appearance as a boy. "Your name is most unusual. Your parents cared what they called you, so I presume they cared for you too. Where do you come from?"

"Essex, sir."

"Fyndern is in Derbyshire."

"My father's family came from there, sir, or so my mother said. She died in the plague three years ago. When she died, her brother took over the farm and told me to leave. So I came here."

"Surely the farm should have been yours?"

"It belonged to my mother's father, sir. He was still alive when my mother died. My uncle was his heir."

Clarenceux stopped and looked at the boy in the clear light of day. He watched him scratch his head: presumably he had lice in his hair as well as in his clothes. His doublet was torn and had mud caked in it. His leather shoes were split along one side.

"What was the trick that that man Wilson could not believe?"

"A true trick, sir."

"A true trick?"

"One where I guess the answer—and I am always right."

"Always? Tell me."

"I would, sir, if I still had my cards."

"Tell me in words."

The boy glanced from Clarenceux to Thomas and Greystoke. "I give the man some cards, normally a dozen: six red, six black. And I say, 'Place them facedown on the table in any order you want, and I will tell you its color.' For each one I get wrong I pay a penny—but if I get them all right, then they pay me a shilling for them all."

"How does it work?"

The boy shrugged. "I guess them right. I feel it in my hands. I don't know how or why, but I just know. That's what worries people."

Clarenceux studied him. "I need a boy who can tend my horses, not play tricks. You say you grew up on a farm. Do you want employment?"

"What's the money?"

"Two and a halfpence a day, plus food and a roof over your head."

"I earned a shilling in there."

"You earned it, lost it, and were on the verge of walking out with nothing but a beating. Do we have an agreement?"

Clarenceux knew what the boy was going to say before he said it. He knew for the same reason that the boy could guess the cards: instinct. Clarenceux had known it himself once upon a time, about the same age. He could tell that the boy recognized a similar spirit in him. Kindred and kindness were the reasons why he would say yes, not because of the money.

"Three pence a day and I'll say yes."

"Two and a halfpence a day to begin with—and the food will be good. You'll eat with me and Thomas."

"Meat?"

"Every day that isn't a fish day."

"Then let us try each other out—I'll see if it feels right."

45

Helen Oudry entered the room and closed the door. She looked at Sarah Cowie, who was waiting there, lying on one of the mattresses. "Is Joan still in the house?"

"She has been in there for over an hour."

"She had better come back soon. Clarenceux has just come home and he seems to have a curly-haired young man with him, a new stable boy."

Sarah drew her knees up in front of her. "Christ be told, I am looking forward to the day when we can leave London." She scratched one of her knees. "All the time I am hungry—hungry and thirsty. I worry about someone finding the body of the woman who owns this house and the constables coming here. I worry about hearing Clarenceux on the stairs when I am in his study trying to read his damned books. I worry about not sleeping and, at the end of it all, being hanged. Or worse, not knowing how my daughters fare—fearing they will be murdered by the countess. Would that I could wipe Father Buckman and her away entirely. It would leave the kingdom a cleaner place."

"It is not for much longer. The place we wanted near Cecil House is paid for. I have just seen Buckman. He wants you and Joan to move there tomorrow."

"And you?" Sarah looked up at the woman whom she realized had become a friend through their days together.

"He wants me to remain, to continue spying on Clarenceux. In case he says anything that affects our plan."

"I'll miss you," said Sarah. "Joan is a difficult woman at the best of times. You at least have preserved your humanity."

"Have I?" said Helen, kneeling down on the mattress. "I look at Joan and see a woman who would cut someone's throat as readily as tell them what to do, thinking only of her Jenifer. The truth is that I wish I could be like her. It would make me feel so much stronger."

"You'll never be like her. She was living the criminal life even before she met the countess. You were caught stealing a sheep; me, three pewter plates, a candlestick, and a salt cellar. Ann, a couple of blankets and a ewer. We three stumbled into crime. She embraced it, willingly."

46

Clarenceux placed a dozen cards on the elm table, facedown. There was just enough light from the window for them not to need a candle. He looked up from where he was sitting. Fyndern was standing a short distance away.

"Ready?"

Fyndern smiled. "The first one to your right is a red card, a diamond. It's a picture card."

Clarenceux turned over the Jack of Diamonds. "Next?"

"A black three. Spade."

Clarenceux turned over the Three of Spades. "Next?"

"Hearts, I don't know the number."

"So you can't always see the card?"

"I never see it. I just ask my hands which of the two it is, red or black, and I feel the answer. My hand with the right answer feels heavier. If it is a red I ask my hands if it is a heart or diamond, and I can tell that. But it's accidental if I suddenly feel it's a picture card or a low card. That's not my asking. I feel threes and fours most."

Clarenceux turned over the Five of Hearts. As he went through the twelve cards, Fyndern guessed all the suits correctly. Clarenceux then shuffled the pack and dealt out another twelve cards. Fyndern never came close to the pack. He guessed every suit correctly again.

Clarenceux sat back, looking at him. "The Lord gives you this gift—but I wonder why. What other things can you divine? The locations of lost things, as wizards do?"

Fyndern shook his head, as if remembering something from long ago, before he acquired the carapace of his scarred features. "I never claim to know anything. If someone asks me, I always say I do not know—in case they accuse me. The penalty for witchcraft is death on a rope."

"Only if you kill people. We have not treated normal wizardry as a crime since the old king died."

"All the same, there are people who fear it and hate it. And if I get known for telling when ships have gone down, I will not be able to pretend later I don't have that knowledge if the law changes again. Or if someone looks to blame someone for a mysterious death."

Clarenceux's eyes widened. "Can you do that? Tell when ships have sunk?"

"Give me the name of a ship."

"The *Davy*."

"She is at the bottom of the sea."

Clarenceux looked at the boy, amazed. But for all his smiles, the lad was nervous. He looked away when Clarenceux held his eye. That showmanship he had displayed in the Bell in Gracechurch Street was a defense mechanism. Even his lithe body suggested a need regularly to wriggle out of tense situations.

"How did you get the cuts on your face?"

"One was from a man in Deptford. Another from a man in Bromley. The short one down the right-hand side was from a woman in Hackney. The ones on my back were from my uncle. Those hurt the most."

Clarenceux picked up a candle and took it across to the fire, lighting it from the flames. "What can you divine about people?"

Fyndern ran his fingers over his face. "I look at people and I realize how little I can sense. If I could feel how good people are, or how malicious, I would not have these scars."

"But if you had to say, what about me? And my companions today?"

Fyndern watched Clarenceux walk back to his seat. "You are a good man and true, or so I believe. The old man is loyal to you like no other. The white-haired man is elusive—slippery as an eel."

"And yet you say that you cannot tell character?"

Fyndern seemed suddenly grave. "It is the good men, the loyal ones, that prove me wrong."

"Then why trust me?"

"Because…why would I trust the bad ones?"

Clarenceux had no answer to that. "It is getting close to suppertime. There is bread and cheese. You can sleep in the stables or in the attic—it is your choice—but I have to warn you that somebody has been breaking into the house."

"A woman?"

"What made you say that?"

"I presumed it must be a man—and that did not feel right." He paused, reading Clarenceux's face. "Is that what you want me to do? Catch her?"

"If you can do that, Fyndern, you are worth more than two and a halfpence per day."

"Mr. Clarenceux, I *am*."

47

~

That night, Fyndern sat for a long time in the back attic pondering his change of fortune. Lifting the lantern to look around, he could see three straw mattresses. One was freshly made up, with a plump flock-filled pillow and cleanish sheets; it also felt less damp. This was the one where the dead woman had slept, he reckoned. The pillow still held the scent of a woman's hair.

He dragged the mattress across to another spot, nearer the hatch; then he sat down and looked into the shadows. There were certain patches of deeper darkness, and he asked himself how he felt about each one. Some felt more ominous than others. Choosing the most threatening space, he arranged the mattress to point with its feet in that direction. Extinguishing the lantern, he lay down, and waited. But before sleep overtook his mind, he told himself: *If I hear a sound, wake me. If there is a movement in the air, wake me.*

Three hours later, he was awake, lying on his side, the air cold against his face. At first he wondered whether he had actually heard a noise or whether he had simply woken naturally, but then a small scraping sound assured him he had awoken for good reason. The sound came from beyond the foot of his mattress, where he had guessed the danger lay. There was a small knock, and a piece of lead dropped on a wooden shingle. Through the space that opened in the roof, low down, about fifteen feet away from him, he could see the vague lightness of starshine and the hunched shape of someone very slowly and carefully climbing through.

Fyndern lay still, watching as the intruder carefully replaced the covering over the gap. Such was the darkness inside that he could not see the woman, and he only knew from a momentary glimpse of the shadow of her head that her neck was slender and her hair tied back. There was no wind to cover the sounds she made. She carefully placed one foot on the floorboard and then, ten seconds later, the next, feeling the way by touching the beams of the low roof.

Outside, somewhere not far away, a cat screeched. A dog barked three times, and then was silent.

Fyndern heard the woman take another step. He felt powerful, knowing that she was ignorant of his presence while he could hear her and knew where she was. He also could sense her fear. He concentrated on the sound of her breaths, her fingers touching the beams, her feet finding a secure floorboard that would not creak—gently increasing the weight on it until she felt confident enough to move. And he began to suspect that her fear was because she too could sense him. She knew something had changed. However motionless he was, however calm his breathing, she knew she was being followed. She was forcing herself to take these steps—in spite of her instincts telling her to turn back, to flee.

Still he waited as she crept toward him. Not until she was within six feet did he whisper to her.

"Who are you?"

She let out a short, involuntary yelp of alarm, immediately placing a hand across her mouth and stepping onto a floorboard that creaked.

A second later she steadied herself, regaining her balance. The voice in the darkness had only asked a question, and it had been young and male: the new stable boy with curly hair. She crouched down, ready to spring away if need be. The darkness hid both of them.

Fyndern listened to her skirts brushing the floor. She had only momentarily panicked. *Was she armed with a knife?* he wondered. He sensed that she was unarmed. What gave her the confidence to continue to approach him?

Helen Oudry knew the voice was close. Carefully moving her hand in an arc before her, she felt the mattress. She felt the straw as her fingers touched some protruding stalks. She knew that the boy would have heard the sound. But he did not speak.

"Why are you here?" she asked in a quiet voice.

"Mr. Clarenceux said I could sleep here."

She reached for him and felt the rough wool of a blanket. He said nothing, so she moved her hand, trying to understand his position.

"You ought to go now," he said, feeling her hand moving over the blanket covering his legs. And as he spoke he heard the tension in his own voice. The whirl of unknown emotions unsteadied him. He could barely speak. It was not the first time he had felt a woman's hand on his body, but the previous two occasions had been moments of trembling expectation. They had had a direction, and that direction was the lust he could see in the woman's eyes. Now he could not even see this woman's face, let alone her eyes. He knew he was betraying Mr. Clarenceux by not raising the alarm. She knew it too. Yet she was lingering, despite being so vulnerable.

How strong is he? she wondered. If he should move now, and press his weight down on her, and shout, Mr. Clarenceux would come running with a sword and a lantern. So would his manservant. She was swimming in the dark deep water of the night where nothing was seen and nothing known, only felt. There were no rules here, only feelings. And feeling now was her only defense.

Barely daring to breathe, she ran her hand up over the blanket to his chest. She felt his hand grip her wrist there, trying to hold it hard.

"Let go," she said gently. "I will not hurt you." She heard him swallow and felt the movement of his chest beneath the blanket.

"You should go," he repeated.

"I will, very soon," she whispered, running her hand down over the rough hemp he was wearing. She could feel the anxiety and physical excitement in the flinching of his muscles as her hand moved lower, toward his groin. She paused, wondering whether the boy was too young to appreciate what she was doing, but then her hand moved farther and she had no doubt.

"Do it," he said. "Do it to me."

Helen realized from his use of the word "it" that this experience was not wholly new to him.

"Do it, or I will shout," he urged her.

She pulled back the blanket and smelled the sweat, dirt, and musk of his body. She kissed his chest, his stomach, his abdomen, and smiled as his body jolted in a spasm at the touch of her lips on his skin. Very slowly, she moved her face up close to his and shifted her leg across his groin, straddling him, and lifting the hem of her skirts out of the way. "Do not move a muscle," she commanded, lowering herself onto him.

He reached up and placed a hand on her clothed breast. She clasped his hand there, pressing it to her.

"If I keep quiet, will you stay until dawn?" he whispered.

"Keep quiet," she replied. "Be silent—completely silent, completely still."

48

Monday, January 27

Clarenceux was flummoxed. He came back down the ladder, into the light. Again he looked in the bedchambers: Fyndern was not there. Not under the beds, not behind the doors. "Fyndern!" he shouted. "Where are you?"

Thomas came up the stairs. "The back door is still bolted, the front door locked. He must have escaped by a window."

Clarenceux shook his head. "And he is not in the attic."

"Perhaps he found the entry used by those women?" asked Thomas.

"Either that or they found him," replied Clarenceux.

Twenty minutes later, Clarenceux was speaking to Thomas by the front door when they heard footsteps in the hall upstairs. Both men fell quiet, waiting to see who would appear on the landing. Clarenceux was just remembering standing in the same place, looking up at the woman who shot his daughter, when Fyndern's head popped around the jamb of the door. "I have found the passage, Mr. Clarenceux."

Both men followed Fyndern through the hall, up the back staircase to the ladder to the attic, and then up into the darkness. The boy seemed to need no lantern. He crouched down and shuffled his way forward as the roof level sunk lower and lower. He turned, and called brightly, "This way, Mr. Clarenceux!" and then crept even further toward the low darkness of the eaves. Then, suddenly, there was bright light as he pushed back the heavy leather hide that covered the hole in the roof.

Clarenceux was astonished. It would never have occurred to him to look in such a dark, inaccessible spot. It was obvious now why he had not seen it: it was just a dark corner, like any other.

"You were right to bring that boy home," muttered Thomas, behind him.

"Are you coming, Mr. Clarenceux?" called Fyndern.

Clarenceux followed Fyndern into the eaves and out through the hole in the roof. He inspected the hide cover. The lower edge was stitched over, forming a fat seam, and several pieces of lead were inserted into that seam, weighing it down so the hide did not flap open and let in water. It had been nailed with small iron nails into the shingles above. The opening allowed access directly from the roof valley between Clarenceux's house and Mr. Webb's house next door. A thick rope hung down over Mr. Webb's roof, allowing Clarenceux to pull himself up and over it; at the top he found a short ladder down the far side. Even if the opening had been discovered, the route would have been invisible if the rope had been tossed back over the intervening ridge of shingles.

In this second roof valley, on the other side of Mr. Webb's house, there was another leather-covered opening, much nearer the street side of the house. Clarenceux followed Fyndern though it, plunging into near-darkness in the attic below. He crouched under the low roof, closed his eyes for a few seconds to help them adjust. There was the usual detritus of an attic—old cots, old chests, and servants' bedding. To his left he saw a ladder in an opening in the floor. Fyndern had obviously already explored this route, for he had no hesitation in going down.

Clarenceux descended after him. The ladder entered directly into a servants' room. At the front was a half-opened shuttered window with a piece of linen covering it, moving with the breeze. It threw light across three beds on the floor. On one of them were some inexpensive personal items: a string of rosary beads, a toothpick, and a wooden comb. There was also a small round wooden pomander—the sort that a self-respecting tradesman's wife would carry. He crossed to the window and glanced out; it faced the north side of the street—a view nearly the same as that from his own study.

"The things there," said Fyndern, pointing at a small pile on the bed, "belonged to the woman who last came into your house."

"How do you know?" asked Clarenceux, wondering how far he should trust Fyndern's senses.

"The bedsheets smell of her. The other ones do not," he said simply.

Clarenceux inspected a series of marks scored vertically on the plaster by the window. "You know her smell? You don't happen to know whether she could read as well, do you?"

Fyndern did not catch the note of sarcasm in his voice. "No. But now you come to ask, I feel that she could not."

"Did you see her face?"

"No. It was dark. I explored this way when it was light and I could find my way. This room was empty when I entered. She got away."

Clarenceux walked around the room, inspecting more of the plaster. It was damaged here and there, but only marked deliberately in that one place, near the window. The marks were in two forms, individual downstrokes and pairs. He turned his attention to the bed.

Pride prevented him at first from smelling the bedsheets—but, having cast a quick glance at Fyndern, he threw pride to one side and knelt down and sniffed them. He noticed a mixture of stale sweat, blood, and other body odors mixed with some sweeter smells. He distinctly noted cloves, perhaps licorice too.

"The house is empty," said Fyndern before Clarenceux had asked the question.

"You must have been very close to her to smell her, and yet she got away?"

"She came near me in the darkness."

"Have you searched the rest of the house?"

"Yes—but only to see who was here."

Clarenceux took a final look at the scene. The women had clearly left in a hurry. Or, to be exact, one woman had left in a hurry. She had not even paused to pick up her personal effects. The others had taken their things beforehand. "I don't think you'll be seeing that woman again."

"I did not see her the first time," replied Fyndern. "But if I smell her again, I will let you know."

49

~

Tuesday, January 28

Sounds of a child's laughter came from a bedchamber at Cecil House. Awdrey sat on the floor, rolling glass beads to Mildred across a sloping board. "Eighteen!" exclaimed Mildred, delighted. "Eighteen," echoed her mother, smiling. Sunlight made the bead sparkle as it rolled. "Nineteen...twenty!"

"Well done," said Awdrey encouragingly. "Now, if you were to roll half of all those beads back to me, how many would you have left?"

"Six!" guessed Mildred.

"No, no, think," said Awdrey. "Divide them into two groups."

There was a knock at the door. One of Cecil's ushers entered with a young maidservant, whom Awdrey recognized as a woman called Elizabeth. He bowed. "Madam, your husband is here to see you. And my mistress craves the companionship of her goddaughter in the chapel."

Awdrey turned to Mildred. "Will you be very good for Lady Cecil, and go with Elizabeth?"

The little girl nodded gravely and got to her feet to join the maid-servant, who held her hand out to her, smiling. The usher withdrew.

Clarenceux stepped slowly into the room. He bowed to her formally, then came closer and kissed her.

"We have found the way by which those women entered the house," he said. "They came through a hole in the back attic. It was covered with a hide."

"How did you find it?"

"With difficulty. How is Annie?"

"Improving. She has been up and about—although she is still not well enough to move from her room. Tell me more about the attic."

"I met a young lad in a tavern. I do not know him at all and yet I have the feeling I know him very well. He has a gift for divining things—so much so that he has clearly enraged several men in his time who have cut his face for using his skills to defeat them in card games. I used to have something of a similar gift, when I was his age. Mine was nothing like as marked as his, but I understand what it is to sense the truth. He found the concealed entrance."

"Does this boy have a name?"

"Fyndern Catesby."

"And? Is there a sign of the women?"

"No. When we investigated their chamber, there were three beds. Two were abandoned. The third woman had recently fled."

Awdrey bent down and started to pick up the glass beads that Mildred had left scattered on the floor, replacing them in a small box.

"I miss you," she said suddenly, without meaning to say what she was thinking.

Clarenceux joined her in bending down to pick up the beads, popping a couple in the box. "Do you remember when we were courting? I would visit your father's house and bow so respect-fully, and quote chapters from the Bible—all the time trying to stop myself from imagining you naked." He paused, rolling a bead between his fingers.

She smiled and playfully punched his arm.

He smiled back, and then said, "I miss you too. But now, after everything that has happened, I yearn for a different form of satisfaction, one far greater than mere happiness."

She put her hand on his arm. "You will find it. I have faith in you. I don't believe anyone will ever be able to stop you doing what you want, or at least what you feel is right."

They spoke together for another half an hour about the children, and the dark clouds of doubt momentarily parted to allow gleams of hope to touch them. They went to see Annie in her chamber overlooking the garden. Briefly Clarenceux saw Lady Cecil, her young son Robert, and his daughter Mildred after they had concluded their chapel attendance. Then it was time for him to go. He embraced little Mildred and playfully flicked a lock of her hair, which made her giggle. Lady Cecil considerately took the children away, leaving him to say good-bye to Awdrey alone.

"I will call again on Thursday," he said, putting his cloak over his shoulders. "Tomorrow I have to confront Dethick and agree with him about this visitation of Oxfordshire. I don't think I can put it off any longer—not without him threatening to summon me to answer to the Earl Marshal. But we shall see." He came close and put a hand to her cheek. "Your skin is so soft." He embraced her and kissed her.

Awdrey watched him walk away into the cold damp air of the courtyard. Now she could see that she truly was his Pole Star. His hopes were guided by her existence. She quietly answered questions for him that he did not even think to ask. She steadied him, comforted him, just through merely being part of his life.

50

Wednesday, January 29

In the morning, Clarenceux called again at the house two doors from his own, where the women had stayed. Still the old woman who lived there had not returned, which he found surprising. She was a widow and her married children lived in the city still, so she was often to be seen walking down to the bridge to visit them. As he stood outside with Thomas and Fyndern, rubbing his hands for warmth, he cursed. She was his only hope of finding out who had made the initial approach to her to allow the women to use her house.

Later, Clarenceux went to see Sir Gilbert Dethick at Derby Place, the home of the College of Arms. Dethick lived here in a suite of rooms that he considered too modest for him, the most senior of all the heralds. Clarenceux entered through the main gate to the quadrangle and sent word that he would meet Dethick in the great hall. There he paced up and down, looking up at the familiar coats of arms of past heralds and the painted panels of past kings. He nodded a brief greeting to the familiar servants as they came and went. Only when he saw one of the lesser heralds, the pursuivants, who would be required to accompany him on his visitation, did he speak at any length.

Sir Gilbert strode into the hall half an hour later, his gray hair and mustache neatened in the mirror before making his appearance.

"Mr. Clarenceux, I am glad to see you. Am I to suppose we have progress? Your visitation will proceed?"

Clarenceux bowed politely. "Mr. Garter, I feel that I owe you an apology. We parted abruptly and that was my fault. I am sorry."

Dethick raised his eyebrows. "What? Where is the old I-don't-give-a-fig Clarenceux? Where is the swaggering man who boasts of being the only herald to have killed a man in hand-to-hand combat? Are you here as his impostor?"

"It is something that must be done. If the clerks can be ready on Tuesday morning, I will set out then. Does that meet with your approval?"

"Approval? You would have met with my approval had you set out two weeks ago. But your coming here and giving me the date goes some way to allay my concern. Let us drink to that."

Half an hour later, Clarenceux was walking along Thames Street. A slight drizzle had begun to fall—yet more rain. He walked down to the Thames and stood on Queenhithe looking at the hundreds of small boats crisscrossing the river. On Three Cranes Wharf, barrels of wine were being loaded for transportation up the river to Berkshire. On the far bank, lines of houses faced the river, with the bear-baiting and bull-baiting rings behind them. To the west there was the great structure of the bridge and, beyond that, the forest of masts of ships in the river awaiting lading or unlading at the sea-going vessels' quays. In one of the upper windows of the houses on the south bank, a woman hauled in her washing on a pole that had been left out too long. Another house nearby had a similar pole out; their laundry was getting slowly soaked again. Barges bobbed about on the gray-brown water, moored in midstream; wherries ferried men in ones and twos from one set of river steps to another, their awnings at the rear raised to protect their passengers from the rain. All life was bustling on. All would continue to bustle on, even if he were no longer here to see it.

He looked to the east, where the line of houses on the south bank stopped and the fields met the river. How long would it be before the trees and bushes there were gone? Paris Garden would no doubt one day be a suburb of the city; the trees around the manor house there would be cut down and burned or used for timbers and planking. So many people were now coming into London seeking their fortunes that the city was bound to expand. And where would it leave people like him? More ambitious men would make their fortunes and erect great houses; more people would claim coats of arms and seek to impress their fellow men. His colleagues would never be out of work. But increasingly the heralds would pander to rich self-made men—lawyers, bankers, statesmen, merchants, and courtiers—and collude with them in their attempts to become distinguished and respectable, with many quarterings on their shields.

It wouldn't be the nobility who built on the south bank of the river: it would be the new merchants whose covetousness was like a stench that pervaded the city. Personally, he had never understood the driving ambition to become so wealthy. He accepted his place in the social hierarchy—and while he understood why people with less money than him felt the need to improve their lot, he could not comprehend why men who were already wealthy desired even greater wealth. But he knew such men would one day change everything. They were discovering new countries, new islands, new animals, and new plants. They were questioning the old wisdom—and they were doing these things in the name of the Protestant faith that the queen espoused.

Two bedraggled seagulls came to land near him, both having spied a piece of bread at the same time. They started fighting over it, lifting their wings and uttering harsh, *guaaark* screeches at each other. A third bird came into land, and a fourth. This last one was larger and went for the others with his beak. When the smaller birds had backed off, the larger one stood there proudly, not eating the crust but daring any other birds to come near and steal it. *We are not so different from them,* mused Clarenceux. *For the sake of a crust, people are flocking here and fighting, and the great merchants find more pleasure in having their wealth than spending it.*

The drizzle was coming down harder. Clarenceux looked up at the cold gray skies and started to head for home. In Carter Lane, a familiar voice hailed him. "Mr. Clarenceux, sir, Mr. Clarenceux!" He looked up to see Fyndern running fast toward him. There were beads of sweat and rain on the boy's face when he reached him, panting.

"Fyndern, how did you find me?"

"Sir, I just guessed…But your wife, sir!"

"What about my wife?"

"Lady Cecil has sent a message asking if she can come home, sir, as your daughter Annie is worse for health."

"But Awdrey is already with Lady Cecil."

"No, sir. Apparently you sent a message by way of Thomas to her at Cecil House. Lady Cecil's man said you asked her to come urgently, saying that you were in great danger and needed to pass a message to them in person before fleeing."

Clarenceux did not ask another question. He started to run. People hurrying to get out of the rain saw him and stepped out of his way. Around corners of houses he ran, understanding now how the plot had always been unfolding around him. As he hastened across Fleet Bridge and up Fleet Street, he knew he had been outmaneuvered. They had spied on him from inside his house and from outside. They had tracked his family's movements and learned exactly what was necessary to separate him and Awdrey and to lure her away from safety.

Clarenceux reached the front door of his house and hammered on it, out of breath. Fyndern came running up immediately behind him. Thomas answered.

"Tell me it is not true, Thomas," gasped Clarenceux. He grabbed hold of his servant's arm. "Tell me it is not true!" But he could see in the old man's eyes that his hope was in vain.

"Mr. Clarenceux, I know not what to say. We knew nothing about this until an hour ago, when Lady Cecil sent for Mistress Harley. The servant—he was one of Sir William's ushers, I recognized him—he said Mildred was with your wife. But Annie is suddenly worse. She is feverish and has a rapid pulse."

"It is possible, is it not," said Clarenceux, trying to calm himself, "that Awdrey has gone to call on someone. Maybe she saw the early signs of this development—the fever and Annie's suffering—and sought the surgeon." But then he looked at Thomas, who was shaking his head. "How can she have gone? Someone in the street must have seen her—between here and Cecil House."

Clarenceux threw himself back out into the cold rain, seizing passersby and demanding of them if they had seen a twenty-seven-year-old blond woman and a four-year-old girl with her, with equally fair hair and blue eyes like her mother. But no one responded with anything other than alarm. He grew even more desperate, yelling at people—at the mute windows to give up what they saw, to the doors to open and reveal their secrets. The rain came down harder, and as Clarenceux moved up the street from passerby to passerby, from coal carrier to water bearer to laborer to blacksmith's boy, he lost himself in despair. Behind him walked Fyndern, taking his lead from Thomas.

From the windows overlooking the street, other people observed him. Tom Green looked down from the house opposite. From another window in the same street, Sarah Cowie watched his progress. From a different window in the same house, Joan Hellier watched him. Through a half-opened shutter on the floor above, Greystoke watched him. They saw him go from stranger to stranger, asking in vain, slowly approaching the great edifice of Cecil House, with its unseeing wide eyes of glass.

Sarah Cowie turned away from the window, her heart beating fast. It was so wrong, what they had done. When they had seen Awdrey leave Cecil House, they had been concerned because her daughter was with her. Only Greystoke had been pleased. "The fledgling as well as the hen," he had muttered. And his men had performed the task with careful precision. The cart had been drawn across in front of her and Cecil's servant, shielding them from the passersby while the man was slaughtered with a knife through his windpipe and loaded into the cart and she was seized and hauled into the nearby house, with a thick rope around her head, in her mouth, preventing her from shouting. Joan had seen to Mildred, lifting her up and carrying her into the house, and then taking her up the stairs. That was when Awdrey stopped struggling. She accepted that she could not leave without being separated from her daughter. Now she was huddled with Mildred under a blanket in a back chamber.

"Greystoke wants her moved tomorrow," said Joan, still looking out the window.

"In Christ's wounds, I hate that man," said Sarah. "It is not the fear of

God he puts into me but the fear of something worse. I just hope that now Mr. Clarenceux will come to his senses and surrender the document."

God he puts into me but the fear of something worse. I just hope that now

Mr. Clarenceux will come to his senses and surrender the document."

Clarenceux pushed past the usher in the corridor and opened the door to the parlour himself. The panelled room was empty. "Where is Sir William?" he demanded. "Where is he?"

"He has been sent for, Mr. Clarenceux. I am sure he will return from Richmond just as soon as—"

"Mr. Clarenceux, may I be of assistance?" said Lady Cecil, approaching.

"How did it happen? Where is she?" jabbered Clarenceux, holding out his hands, gripping the air that held no answers. "I don't know what to do. I cannot think."

"Your panic will help no one. Calm down," said Lady Cecil stiffly. "Now, as my usher tells me, your wife and your younger daughter have gone missing. Your other daughter Annie is feverish. I think it would be productive for you, in your wife's absence, to attend to your sick daughter."

Clarenceux was suddenly sober. "Yes, of course."

Lady Cecil nodded and led him upstairs through the corridors of the house to the chamber at the back. Annie laid on a bed beside the window, a woman beside her, wiping the sweat from her brow. She moved her head from side to side and had a gray pallor. Her hair was wet, her night rail soaked, and her mouth open as she breathed rapidly.

Clarenceux crossed himself when he saw her. Her eyes were shifting focus, seeing him and then not seeing him. She showed no reaction to his presence. "Where is my mam?" she asked. "I need my mam."

The woman nursing her moved aside and Clarenceux bent down

and placed his face next to hers, feeling the heat and smelling the sweat of her fever. "Your mam has had to go away, Annie, my angel," he said. He put his arms around her shoulders. "But you are in good hands; Lady Cecil is looking after you."

"I want Mam," repeated Annie, seeming not to understand her father. Then, blinking, she reached out and touched his beard, but let her hand fall back to the bed.

Clarenceux saw the dressing on her shoulder coming away and the yellowing and blood-smeared gash of the wound beneath. He felt the tears come to his eyes and tried to stop them, but he could not. One by one, they ran down his cheek and through his beard, dripping on his daughter's counterpane. He wiped his face, struggling once more to stop them, but the thought of his wife's absence was too much, and the emptiness and anguish overwhelmed him. Gritting his teeth, he pulled Annie toward him, praying silently at first, and then aloud. "Oh, Annie, my sweet, be well, please be well. We will find her. I will spend all day and night trying to find her. I will pray, I will hope—I will never give up hope—and we will all be together. Oh God, help me, help us."

Sir William Cecil handed Clarenceux a glass of wine and took his seat at the table in the private dining room, next to his wife. "I've sent word to Walsingham, and the captain of the watch on the ward, as well as the watch on the bridge. We will have the houses of known Catholic sympathizers searched."

"And the houses hereabouts?" asked Clarenceux. "They must have been taken between this house and my house, only a few hundred yards away. Search those too."

"I will have those houses searched too, all of them along the route. But if this plan was as well-executed as it seems—so carefully done that they were spying on us both in order to seize their opportunity—they will not linger in the same house but remove Awdrey and Mildred to another place, further away. However, should they try to do so tonight they will find all the alleys as well as the highways patrolled. My men will search all the carts, all the wagons. I am confident that if they try to move her, we will catch them."

"One act of kindness," said Clarenceux bitterly. "I took in one document for a friend—and my life has not been the same since. I have made enemies of people, unwillingly. I have been hounded, persecuted, tortured. Friends and servants have been murdered, my daughter shot and now close to death, and my wife and daughter taken. I feel as if the Lord is trying my faith, as He did Tobit, blinding him and forcing him into poverty to test him, or like Job, who was righteous, perfect, and upright, hard-working and wealthy, with seven thousand sheep and three thousand camels, and the Lord smote his house, his lands, his animals, and everything he possessed…"

"'Naked I came out of my mother's womb and naked I shall return thither: the Lord gave and the Lord taketh away; blessed be the name of the Lord,'" said Lady Cecil, quoting the Book of Job.

"'In all this Job sinned not, nor charged God foolishly,'" added Sir William, picking up on his wife's quotation.

"But why do the righteous suffer?" said Clarenceux. And he too quoted from the Book of Job: "'My days are swifter than a weaver's shuttle, and are spent without hope.'" But as he spoke the words, he knew that it was not what he believed. He could never believe in a lack of hope. Not while there was breath in his body.

"There will be a demand," said Cecil gravely, placing his hands flat on the table. "William, I cannot allow you to keep that document. The stakes are too high."

"They have never been higher. But we have already been over this. Even if I give you the document, that will do nothing to help me or my family. And now it is all I have."

"Giving it to me will stop you being the center of their attention. It will relieve the pressure."

Clarenceux looked at Cecil. However kind his eyes, however intelligent, he could not trust him. Cecil was doing what he had learned to do through many years of political survival. He was raising the drawbridge, to protect himself. Sir William Cecil was personally threatened now, and friendship was always going to be a secondary matter.

Clarenceux looked from Sir William to Lady Cecil. She was stony-faced. Fiercely clever, she was on her husband's side in all things. "If Annie dies," said Clarenceux slowly, "I intend to lead my enemies into the place where that document is hidden. And when they are there, I will destroy the place. I will blow it apart. If I am destroyed, the captors will have no reason to keep my wife and sole surviving daughter. I will never willingly surrender that document to anyone."

"That would be an extreme action," said Lady Cecil.

Clarenceux got up from the table and walked to the window. "You are right. There will be a demand. I will wait until I see that before deciding what I shall do." He bowed to each of them politely. "Take care of Annie, please. I will be back to see her tomorrow."

Greystoke threw his sword down on the table in his chamber and poured himself a goblet of wine, which he drank. Through the window he watched as a shutter closed in Clarenceux's house.

Tom Green entered. "What did Mr. Walsingham say, sir?"

Greystoke turned to face him. "Cecil has mobilized half the city to search for Awdrey Harley. He has also authorized the search of all the houses along Fleet Street. We will move her this evening."

"Not tomorrow, as planned?"

"This evening." He poured more wine into his goblet. "Separate them and take the girl on ahead—Sarah is the more maternal, give her the child. As for Mistress Harley, don't take her through the city. The gate wards have all been primed. Best to take her down Water Lane and then by boat to Limehouse now, before nightfall. It's the long way but we cannot risk her being found. Gag her and have her wear a scarf over the gag. Tie her hands and use a safeguard to cover her arms. She will come quietly enough if you tell her how expendable her daughter is."

"And what about you, sir? Will you be joining us?"

"Tomorrow. I have some more protecting to do first."

The anguish of Clarenceux's soul had called for drink, and he had mollified it with wine. Now his head ached. It was late, but he had no wish to retire. He simply sat at the elm table in the hall with a flagon and a pair of candles burning, and the Old Testament open before him. He had been reading the Book of Job once more, reminding himself of the passages and the sufferings. *Why does the righteous man suffer?* After a while he would lose concentration and his mind would wander. But then, like a blind creature that does not know it is in a cage, it would bump into the reality of his situation. He too was caged, between the absence of his wife and daughters, the killing of his servant, the killing of Rebecca Machyn, and his lack of direction.

It was late—past nine o'clock, when Greystoke called. Thomas answered the door.

On hearing the knocking so long after dark, Clarenceux had suddenly been sharp, hoping for news of Awdrey. He was disappointed to see Greystoke in the light of Thomas's lantern. He was even more disappointed to find that the man had come to offer him sympathy.

"What use are you?" he demanded, after Greystoke had said how sorry he was to hear the news. "Walsingham tells you that my wife has gone. Damn it—why did he send *you* to protect us? Your sword is less use than a blade of grass. First you failed to protect my daughter, then you failed to find how the attackers broke into the house. Now you have failed to protect my wife and younger daughter."

"With respect, Mr. Clarenceux, if you had wanted your family to be safe, you should never have accepted custody of that document. I cannot be everywhere that—"

"Did you see anything?" interrupted Clarenceux. "Were your eyes open? Or were you just too busy defending your own great dignity?"

Greystoke said nothing.

"I have had my doubts about you, ever since you killed that woman who shot at my daughter. Too fast you were. Too quick to kill her. The same thing the second time—you killed her so I could not find out how a deranged woman was able to enter this house unseen."

"You are drunk, Mr. Clarenceux."

"I have lost my wife and my child! This house is empty. I think of them and I cannot imagine life without them. I cannot see their faces without hearing their laughter. 'There is no greater sorrow than to be reminded of a happy time in one's misery.' What do *you* know of that? You know only the words. Allow me to translate them into the feeling, so you can see what your friend Dante really meant."

Greystoke stiffened. Tentatively, his left finger reached for his sword, just to reassure himself of the angle of the hilt.

"Mr. Clarenceux," said Thomas, putting his hand on Clarenceux's arm but not taking his eyes off Greystoke. "It is getting late. It is time to let Mr. Greystoke go home."

But Clarenceux was too drunk to catch the subtle meaning of Thomas's warning. "It is not just the timing of the attacks. You knew the name of one of the women—Ann Thwaite."

Greystoke's hand was now resting openly on the hilt of his sword.

"Mr. Clarenceux," he began, "you are upset that I have spied on you. I understand that. But it was always for your protection. I have failed in my duty, and for that I am deeply sorry. I did what I could. As for the name of the woman who attacked you, as you know, I heard that from the coroner."

Greystoke paused, waiting for an answer that would tell him whether he needed to draw his sword.

No one spoke.

"I will continue to do my duty, as Walsingham bade me," he added.

Still no one spoke. Far away down the street, someone slammed a shutter.

Greystoke stepped back, as if to depart. But he added, "It pains me to think that you are so suspicious of me, and that however much I have tried to help you, I have been held at arm's length. I will not trespass on your time any longer."

He did not bow. He simply walked back across the street.

"He is lying," said Thomas.

"I know," replied Clarenceux.

51

≈

Thursday, January 30

In the morning, Greystoke waited until Clarenceux departed for Cecil House. Seeing that Fyndern was watching from the hall window, he took a wherry along the river rather than walk through the streets. The tide being high, the waterman ferried him with no difficulty beneath the great arches of the bridge to Lyon Quay, and there he waited again. Sure now of his free passage, he made his way along Botolph's Lane and Philpot Lane to the Black Swan.

Buckman greeted him as an old friend, embracing him, a sparkle in his bespectacled eyes. "So you have succeeded in wresting Mistress Harley from her husband, and his daughter too. Most well done." The priest pulled over a bench for Greystoke to sit on in the candlelit garret.

"The constant surveillance paid off," said Greystoke, putting his foot on the bench and leaning with his elbow on his knee. "His wife was tricked by a fake message, delivered by a fake manservant, relayed to her by Cecil's trusting ushers. All we had to do after that was to wait. She is now in the old stone farmhouse in the fields near Islington. There it does not matter how loudly she cries; no one will hear."

Buckman smiled and blinked. "This calls for a celebration, a toast." He reached for a pair of turned wooden cups and poured some wine into each one. "I will send to Lady Percy with the good news tomorrow. In the meantime, here's to our success."

Both men drank.

Greystoke leaned forward, cradling the cup in his hands. "Wooden cups. An unlit garret. No one can say you are a hypocrite, Father, in your hermitage in the city. I like that. Luxuries are for other people."

"What I have is plenty in the eyes of the Lord."

"Has Lady Percy sent more women?"

"Three. Of whom two made the grade."

"And the third?"

Buckman gestured to the two large oak chests. "These old trees can be very useful. Especially when weighed down with stones. People expect them to be carted to the quay, and for them to take two or three men to lift."

Greystoke set his cup on the table beside the burning candlestick. He paused, about to speak.

"Yes?"

"I need to ask you a question, Father. If it is expedient and dutiful in God's sight to kill those who threaten our project, are there aspects which…" He hesitated again. "Are there acts which normally would be abhorrent that are permissible for the greater achievement?"

"You are being evasive," said Buckman. "Just because it is necessary to eradicate the threat of a woman going to the authorities does not automatically justify all other moral crimes."

"But some others?"

"Such as?"

Greystoke ran his fingers through his white hair. Eventually he said, "The woman, Awdrey Harley. She is deeply devoted to her husband. And she very probably knows where he has hidden what we seek. Now, we could use painful devices, but such is her devotion that I think we would have more success if we threatened her virtue: by filling her womb with the seed of another man. The prospect of that might turn her."

"I see." Buckman thought long and hard. He started blinking, then reached forward and refilled his cup and Greystoke's too.

Greystoke felt obliged to justify his suggestion. "I know the Commandment about not committing adultery, and this woman is married. But it would encourage her to speak the truth."

"You are right to point to the Commandment. But you are not married—and I presume it would be you who is taking charge of this responsibility. Are you familiar with Deuteronomy, chapter twenty, verses ten to sixteen? 'When coming to a city of thine enemy, first proclaim peace.' In my understanding, that is what you have done already, seeking Clarenceux's friendship. 'If the city makes war with thee, then thou mayst besiege it. And when the Lord thy God hath delivered it to thee, then thou shalt smite all the males with the edge of the sword and take all the women, the children, and the cattle for thine own.' It seems as though the answer to your question is whether you believe the siege yet to be won. Has the Lord delivered the city to you—or just the woman?"

Greystoke felt a stirring in his body. "The Lord saw fit to deliver her into my hands."

"I would caution you: if you do this act, self-indulgence will imperil you—all of us. Be pure, my son. As you observe in the way I live here."

Greystoke nodded. He lifted his foot off the bench and walked slowly across the garret, thinking. "Clarenceux said that the document is in Oxford, in St. John's College. He may have been lying but, at the time he said it, Ann Thwaite was holding a knife to his wife's throat."

"He has said on another occasion that it is in Oxfordshire," replied Buckman. "Helen Oudry overheard him talking to his manservant. Perhaps he is telling the truth. See if you can wheedle confirmation out of him."

"It is too late," said Greystoke, shaking his head. "He knows."

Buckman blinked and adjusted his spectacles. "How can that be? Who told?"

"No one told. He notices things. He watches us day and night, as we watch him. He is the sort of man whose suspicions linger in his mind; he's a man who likes his suspicions, who nurtures them. He picked up on the fact I knew who one of the women was. But the pretense lasted longer than we thought. It served its purpose."

Buckman was silent for a long time. "This puts a different complexion on things. Do not risk confronting him again. I will wait, and let him sweat for a few days, before I send word to him. In the meantime, do what you must with his wife."

52

Clarenceux bent forward and kissed Annie on the forehead as she lay in the bed. Placing a hand on her cheek, he whispered a prayer for her. He tried to think of her gasps and delirium as diminishing, and rosy-cheeked health blossoming in her. It was a picture of a prayer. Then he made the sign of the cross and gestured to the servant standing in the doorway to lead him to Cecil's study.

"William," said Cecil as he entered, looking up from the pile of papers spread on the table in front of him. "Is there news?"

Clarenceux shook his head. "I was hoping that your searchers would have yielded some."

"Apart from the dead body of the gentleman usher who accompanied Awdrey, nothing. No one knows anything; no one saw anything."

"And Walsingham? What about his men? What use has he been?"

Cecil straightened his back and put his pen down. "Mr. Walsingham is doing all he can to ensure the safety of you and your family."

Clarenceux raised a finger. "That is where you and I have to disagree. His man Greystoke is not trustworthy. You yourself cast aspersions on his integrity."

"I simply reminded you that you should err on the side of caution."

"Sir William, listen to yourself. One of your servants has been murdered. Your wife's godchild has been kidnapped outside your own house, together with her mother. And that is not all. Greystoke was signaling to the women who attacked me…He used a mirror to flash the light into their chamber across the street. Twice he entered my house falsely to demonstrate his loyalty by killing them. He is cold and ruthless and he is against me—I know it. I *know* it. Walsingham sent a man who is working for the Catholic cause against me, to spy on me. Walsingham is being used."

"Damn it, William. Have you quite had your fill? Because I don't want to be interrupted when I say what I have to say."

Clarenceux glared at Cecil.

"I asked Mr. Walsingham why he trusts John Greystoke, as you requested. Mr. Walsingham's reasons were sound. They met years ago in Italy, in Padua, when the English religious émigrés were staying in the Republic of Venice. Mr. Greystoke came back to England when the queen ascended the throne. He has undertaken many missions for Walsingham and proved successful, even when in danger of his life. Most tellingly, it was Mr. Greystoke who told Francis about Maurice Buckman. Does that name mean anything to you? He also goes by the name of John Black. He acts as the go-between from Lady Douglas to Lady Percy. It was Mr. Greystoke also who told Mr. Walsingham about Lady Percy's women. Without Mr. Greystoke, this investigation would be nowhere."

"I do not believe that is the whole story," said Clarenceux, walking across the room, clenching his fist.

Sir William rose to his feet. "Give me one hard fact, one indisputable piece of evidence that I can give to Walsingham to show he trusts the wrong man."

"I do not understand you, Sir William. You yourself warned me against trusting him. Yet you will not question Walsingham's trust. And you ask *me* to give you evidence. Why not ask Walsingham to produce proof that Greystoke is loyal to her majesty?"

"You could have made this much easier by handing over that document to me. Much easier for yourself and your family, and everyone else."

Clarenceux said nothing. It felt as if the whole world was against him, and that Cecil was in league with Walsingham and Greystoke and even this mysterious priest, Father Maurice Buckman, alias John Black. But how could that be? Catholics in league with Protestants? Loyal men in collaboration with avowed traitors? The cold sickness of self-doubt muted his protests and forced him to think of home, and the loss of his wife, and the only people left to him now whom he could trust.

He swallowed. "I will go and bid farewell to my daughter," he said.

53

Friday, January 31

Awdrey and Mildred were given an upstairs room with bare stone walls and a shuttered window that had been barricaded with thick planks on the outside. Only chinks of light entered, falling in golden coins on the bed and the floorboards. An old straw mattress and two blankets were thrown on the bed, as well as two folded linen sheets. Otherwise there was nothing in the room except a pail that served as a chamber pot.

Since arriving here on Wednesday night, Awdrey had done little but lie still beside Mildred and talk to her, wishing the child would cease questioning her and, at the same time, feeling grateful for her incessant prattling. She cried when she thought about Annie, and felt a deep dread of being told of her death. She was angry and sad when she thought about her husband, but when she thought about him hard enough, she was proud. She had no doubt whatsoever that his was a path of integrity and righteousness, and that he would prevail. It just took a lot of effort to see him at this deeper level, fighting for what he believed was right. It required her to put herself and her daughters to one side, and even her husband himself, and consider the paucity of options.

The smell of the bed was not good. The straw reeked of urine and the blankets of sweat. The floorboards were old and rough, and damp in places. Mildred received a splinter in her foot, which was impossible to remove with no tweezers and so little light. There was no fireplace, so the blankets were constantly employed, even though they stank. Bread, cheese, and an old apple had been their only sustenance yesterday, and the water had been rank. The worst aspect of the chamber, however, was the awareness that no one but her enemies knew she was here. She could see gray skies and open fields through the tiny gaps between the shutters and the barricades, and knew they were somewhere near a village north of London—she had gleaned that much from the long journey to get here—but that was all. When the clock in the parish church across the fields had chimed ten o'clock a few minutes earlier, it had sounded as if it was about a mile away.

"Mam, how long must we stay here?" asked Mildred, lying on her side.

Awdrey pulled the blanket up around them. "I don't know; it might be a few days, maybe longer."

"Will anyone come to take us home?"

She could not reply. The thought was too painful. She distracted herself by sinking down into the memories that she knew were safe: the day she realized she knew how to read, her wedding day, the day Annie was born after a long and difficult labor.

"I'm cold," whined Mildred.

Awdrey heard footsteps on the landing outside the door and low voices. She strained to understand them but could barely pick up a word. The bolts of the door were shot open. She shivered and felt even colder, even more alone.

"Have you been given food?" asked Greystoke as he entered.

Awdrey did not even look at him, but Mildred sat up. "Look, Mam. It's that man."

Awdrey opened her eyes. A woman was standing in the doorway behind Greystoke—one of the women who had seized her beside the cart two days earlier. Both figures appeared in silhouette. She let her head rest on the mattress.

"Not as proud as when we first met, are you?" sneered Greystoke. "Do you remember that? When you did not wish to be seen with me in the street?"

Awdrey did not answer.

"Perhaps that old man you call a husband is regretting his carelessness."

She felt a bitter sting, remembering it was her decision to leave Cecil House. The usher had told her the message had come from Thomas—saying that her husband was in great danger and needed to see her before he left London. She had asked for one of the ushers in the hall to accompany her.

"Losing a pretty wife like you would be a mistake."

"Curse you, from your guts to your soul," said Awdrey, unable to lie still and listen to another word. She sat up. "No good is in you. You are nothing but deceit; you have no substance."

Greystoke shrugged. "I have substance, and you will know that soon enough. I will leave you so violated that you can never be a whole wife to your husband again. Every time he touches you, you will remember. Every time you desire him, and reach for him, you will hesitate, fearing that he is mindful of your being filled with another man's seed. I will make you the adulterer."

"In what devil's name do you use such loathsome words? You

repugnant whoreson! My husband told me you love the works of Dante. Well, let me tell you there is a special circle of Hell reserved for men like you—one where Dante and Virgil never dared set foot. It is set aside for men who are selfish, cowardly, cruel, deceiving monsters. There, men like you are forced to drink nothing but the blood of their victims and are made to eat the rancid flesh of the helpless on whom they have turned their backs."

As Awdrey shouted at him, Greystoke walked over to the bed and reached down with his left hand to her neck, feeling her hands grasp his wrist as he dug his thumb deep into the flesh. Mildred started crying. With his right hand, Greystoke held Awdrey's thigh through her dress. "Tomorrow. Despite the stench in here, I will have you. You have until this time tomorrow to save your precious marriage."

"What do you want me to do?" she gasped as he removed his hands. Mildred was still crying, holding on to the top of her dress.

"Tell me where that document is."

Awdrey looked at the woman beside the door. She could see now that her hair was dark, and that she was uncomfortable with Greystoke's insinuations.

"You could bring it all to an end most quickly," Sarah pleaded, over the top of Mildred's cries. "Why don't you? Please!"

Awdrey put an arm around Mildred and pulled her close. She kissed her head, soothing her. "You are wasting your time," she said, not looking at them. "I know nothing more than you do. My husband said it was beneath a floor in St. John's College, Oxford. You know that. And that is all I know."

Greystoke stopped at the door and looked at her. "I am not going to waste time now," he replied coldly. "You heard me. Ten o'clock tomorrow."

54

Clarenceux moved a hair aside on Annie's sweat-streaked face, and wiped her forehead again. She was so weak, so pale and vulnerable. He looked up at the woman who had been nursing her. "By now I had thought that things would have turned one way or the other. That it would not be...not be like this."

He looked down at her again and saw her face so changed: the bright eyes unseeing, the delirium holding her from within. He thought of the people possessed by devils in the Bible and confessed to himself that he had never thought that such things might happen to his family. He had been too complacent. *But if one does not live with a measure of complacency, one cannot live. To pour ashes over our heads every day—that is no way to bring up our children, no way to face life.*

He bit his lip and wiped her face again. Every intake of breath, every movement of her hand on the counterpane gave him an instant of hope—an instant that was quickly dashed. He closed his eyes and felt the weight of his tiredness; all he wanted to do was lie down and go to sleep and wake to find that everything was well again—that Awdrey and Mildred were restored to him and at home, and Annie well again and smiling. *So many people must feel the same way,* he reflected. *I am not alone. When there are so many of us who suffer, how can anyone want to make our lives worse? In what way is that a Christian thing?*

He noted Annie moving her hand. She blinked and opened her mouth, and once again his hopes were raised. But she simply moaned and looked past him, through him—her eyes focused on an eternity that she could see and he could not. He held her hand and kissed it.

"Annie, my beloved Annie," he whispered, "I want you to know that I am here and that all will be well for you, that you have no need to fear. You are innocent, you are good, and the Lord loves the good and the innocent." *Why, then, do the righteous suffer?* Clarenceux fought back the question. "He will protect you and give you strength, Annie, and I will pray for you every day. I pray for you and your mother and sister. Our house is empty of laughter; there is dust on the tables and on the shelves. There are rats in our kitchen eating the crumbs of stale bread that have fallen there; there is a leak in the stable roof. The sheets I sleep in are dirty, as are those in which Thomas sleeps. All will not be right again until you, my sweet, are well once more and we are all together again as a family. Come back to us, Annie; if you can hear me in the depths of your suffering, come back to me. I need you."

Annie moved her hand, unconsciously. She stretched out, her hand shaking, reaching for something. Then the vision in her head was gone and her hand fell on the bed. Clarenceux saw no further movement in her. He watched and he waited; he saw her breathing and her eyelids trembling, the beads of sweat—but that was all. He stood up, crossed himself, then made the sign of the cross on her forehead and left the room, wiping away a tear hurriedly lest anyone should see.

55

Saturday, February 1

The light of dawn was in the sky, with a pink shade, as if bad weather was to come. The next sensation that touched Clarenceux was the awareness of the empty space in the bed beside him—and he knew instantly that the nightmare of his life was ongoing. Normally he would have lingered in bed for a minute or two on such a cold day, but not now. Not with that absence beside him.

Moving across the room, he went to wash himself, but the basin of water was frozen solid. He rubbed his body through his linen shirt, using it as a towel to clean himself. He swiftly removed it and put on a clean one—his last—from the clothes chest. Donning his waistcoat, doublet, hosen and shoes, he went downstairs. Thomas was in the kitchen already, talking to Fyndern. They heard him coming.

"Do you want the fire in the hall built high, Mr. Clarenceux?" Thomas was folding up the blankets of his bed by the hearth.

"No, just enough to keep it alight," he mumbled, standing in the doorway. "Tell me, Thomas, how well can you remember the coroner's inquest on the death of that woman who attacked Awdrey? She was killed two weeks ago tomorrow."

Thomas shrugged. "As well as the next man but probably no better."

"What was her name?"

"Ann Thwaite. Why?"

"How do you know?"

Thomas shrugged. "Greystoke said so at that dinner in the Bell Inn. He said he heard the coroner call her by that name."

"She was not a Londoner. She had a northern accent. How would the coroner have known?"

"Half of London has a strange accent these days—some are French and Dutch but many are from the north. She could have settled here and been known to the coroner from another parish."

"No other parish claimed her. She was buried in St. Bride's."

"No? Then…how can Sir William Cecil not accept that?"

Clarenceux walked the length of the hall, his footsteps sounding loud on the floorboards. Opening the shutters, he peered through the quarrels of glass at the house opposite. All the shutters were closed. Either the cold of the night had been too much for them or Greystoke had changed strategy.

"I want you to stay here with Fyndern," he told Thomas. "I am going to St. Bride's. If Mr. Bowring or Mr. Lynton confirm what I suspect, then we know for certain that Greystoke had knowledge of her and knows about the women from Lady Percy—and no doubt is behind Awdrey and Mildred's abduction. Walsingham will have to arrest him."

Clarenceux went to the church, passing one of the churchwardens on the way, who had already unlocked the building. At the vicarage, Mr.

Bowring was not yet dressed but Clarenceux left a message and went into the church to wait. He walked up to the rood screen, stripped now of its cross, pushed the gate open, and passed through, reflecting on how that simple act would not have been possible only ten years earlier. Perhaps in admitting the common man to this, the holiest part of the church, the Protestants were making a claim for the real equality of souls? He felt torn. On the one hand, everything he cherished in the world was threatened—all the beauty and history, the richness, the pageantry, and the sense of communal living—and on the other, there was a degree of sublime purity in the uncluttered closeness to God to which the new church aspired. But why did one have to choose? Why could not the old stand alongside the new? And why did so many of those who wanted "purity" in themselves not care about it in others? They always spoke about *their* souls, *their* communion with God—as if He had a care only for them.

But now, with the pain of Awdrey's absence touching him particularly, he admitted to himself that he too felt a keenness for God to look out for him in particular. He felt the need to pray in that way. He needed to devote his soul as well as his mind and body to the well-being of his wife and children.

He began to pray, kneeling there on the stone, in front of the high altar. He was still there half an hour later, when Mr. Bowring came up the nave.

"I understand you want to see me." He saw that Clarenceux was on his knees. "Are you praying for the souls of all the women who have died in your house?"

All Clarenceux's suspicions and distrust of the new religion came flooding back. He rose to his feet. "Indeed, Mr. Bowring. I need to ask you a question. About the last of the women."

"The last?"

"I want to know if you were told her name."

"No. She was buried in an unmarked grave. I only did so because no one knew her name."

"You are sure?" asked Clarenceux. "Absolutely sure? The coroner did not tell you?"

Mr. Bowring seemed affronted. "Do you think I would lie about whether I knew the name of a woman I had buried? The coroner simply recorded her as 'woman foreigner.'"

"Then you will say the same to Sir William Cecil? To Francis Walsingham?"

"Why? What is it to—"

"Yes or no?" urged Clarenceux. "Yes or no?"

Mr. Bowring looked him in the eye. "I am an honest man, Mr. Clarenceux."

Clarenceux bowed politely. "So am I, Mr. Bowring. There are precious few of us left. Good day."

Joan Hellier sat at the trestle table in the hall of the stone house. She turned the dagger that was lying on the table in front of her, idly nudging the point with her finger so that it moved around like the shadow of a sundial. She turned it toward the smoke rising from the hearth in the middle of the house. The window was open but the gray skies made it feel more like dusk than morning. Across the fields came the sound of the bells.

"Ten," she said.

Sarah Cowie, who had been sitting on the bench opposite, went to the pile of logs; she picked up two and set them down on the hearth.

"She has been quiet."

"She is praying. I looked in earlier when I took her the morning bread."

They fell silent again.

"Do you think Greystoke will do it?" Sarah asked.

"He's a man, isn't he?" Joan left the dagger alone and rubbed her hands together, trying to warm them.

Sarah held her own hands over the fire. "I wish he wouldn't."

"She won't suffer more than a bruise to her dignity. We've all put up with that at some time or other, some of us more often than not. We all have our crosses to bear."

"It brings back memories…" said Sarah sadly.

Joan suddenly picked up the dagger and stabbed it into the table. "Do *that* to your memories. Has it escaped your mind that we have all been sentenced to hang? And our daughters? If he roughs her about a bit, then it is for good purpose."

Sarah stared at her, holding her gaze but saying nothing. She turned away and looked along the track between the recently ploughed soil of the fields.

"Here he comes."

Greystoke tethered his horse in the stable and entered the house. Both women looked at him but offered no more greeting than that. Joan worked the dagger out of the tabletop. Sarah watched him, her back to the window.

"It's dark in here," he observed, taking his hat off. "Light a candle."

"We have none," said Joan.

"Well, build the fire up, then." Greystoke took his cloak off and dumped it on a bench. "Has the woman spoken?"

"She has been praying all morning," said Sarah.

"She's waiting for you," Joan said.

Greystoke nodded. He unbuckled his belt and handed it and his sword to Joan. "Look after this." He turned to Sarah. "You, come with me. Bolt the door behind me."

The staircase was old and wooden. Six steep steps in the corner of the hall turned and gave access to six steeper steps beyond, ending in a short landing and the door to the upper chamber, where Awdrey was being held. Greystoke gestured to Sarah to unbolt the door. Her heart beating fast, she stepped in front of him and did as she was told. The door swung inward and Greystoke entered, closing the door behind him. Sarah bolted it and listened.

It took Greystoke a long while for his eyes to adjust enough to see the blanket-shrouded figure of the woman in the corner of the room. She was holding her child to her closely and shivering.

"Have you decided to tell me where it is?" he asked.

"God will curse you, John Greystoke," said Awdrey, her voice barely audible. "God will curse you."

"That is all you have to say?"

Mildred pointed to Greystoke. "I don't like that man."

Awdrey pressed Mildred to her breast, hiding her face with her shoulder. "My husband destroyed that document."

"No, Mistress Harley. Oh God! How good it feels to say that, *Mistress* Harley, with you cowering in the corner of the room. No, I know he did not destroy it. He said the other day that it was beneath a floor in St. John's College, in Oxford, and you agreed yesterday. If you tell me which room it is in, which building, then I will let you both go."

"God curse you and kill you! I hate you, hate you!" Awdrey screamed. Mildred began to cry but Awdrey was crying more, and screaming "I hate you!" between sobs.

Greystoke just watched. When her shouts had subsided, he knocked on the door and called to Sarah. "Take the child out of here."

"No!" screamed Awdrey, clinging on to Mildred, who was crying too. Sarah opened the door and came in. She felt her way across the room as Greystoke tugged aside the blanket and grabbed Mildred's arm, trying to pull her away. Awdrey hung on to her tightly, scream-ing the word "No!" repeatedly. With Mildred screaming and Awdrey yelling, Greystoke stepped on Awdrey's leg. He bent down and slapped her hard on the cheek and yanked Mildred's arm, pulling her up and away from Awdrey. Awdrey still did not let go, however, and Greystoke hit down hard with his fist, once, twice, and again, bruising her arms. Mildred was screaming in terror now, and Awdrey howling as she started to lose her grip. Another blow from Greystoke and Sarah had Mildred in her arms. She hurried her out of the room, slammed the door, and shot the bolt.

Sarah sat down with the little girl on the stairs. Outside the rain started coming down hard, battering on the shingles of the roof, splashing in the puddles and mud, striking the walls. Sarah wanted to stop Mildred's tears and make all well with the world for her. She heard Awdrey scream inside the room as Greystoke struck her, and she heard him yelling at her. She fought hard and cursed him at the top of her voice. Sarah only heard snatches of what he replied but it was enough. He told her that he hated her husband, Clarenceux, "with his pompous title and his delusions that he is a worthy swords-man, and his pretending to know Italian." Most of all he hated him for thinking he could see through Greystoke's plan. "He has no idea, *no idea*, what is going on under his very nose!" And she heard the sound of Greystoke dragging Awdrey to the bed, and the rhythmic creaking that told her how Greystoke had taken out his hatred for Clarenceux on Awdrey.

Mildred sobbed, and called, "Mam! I want my Mam!"

Sarah did her best to comfort her, holding her as she would her own daughters, thinking of them. She looked down at Joan, who was sitting at the table in the hall, ignoring everything. Sarah felt a tremendous sadness with the world and the cruelty of the men and women in it—the terrible things they did to one another.

When, after ten minutes, Greystoke knocked to be let out of the room, he had an even colder demeanor than when he had entered. He fastened his breeches and stepped past Sarah. "Let the girl go back to her mother—at least until tomorrow," he said as he went down the stairs.

"What? And you are going to do the same thing again?" asked Sarah, shocked.

Greystoke turned and held up a finger to her. "Don't cross me. If you do, you'll get the same treatment." He looked her in the eye. "It's something that Francis Walsingham taught me. You can torture a man to the point of death and he will refuse to speak. Tell him it all starts again in the morning—and that's what breaks him. I will have her for a whore again in the morning."

He took his hat and cloak, and opened the door. The rain outside was torrential, thrust down from the skies. He paused and waited a long time for it to subside, and not once in that time did he look back. Joan said nothing to him as he lingered in the doorway.

The things Sarah said to him, she said silently.

57

Clarenceux thumped the table in Cecil's study so hard that one of the candles on a candleprick went out, a drinking glass fell over, and a pile of papers slid onto the floor. "Walsingham will not speak to me! Walsingham will not even see me!"

"William, you have no evidence. For all you know, Greystoke could be innocent. Walsingham trusts him entirely—and he does not place that amount of trust in just anyone."

Clarenceux ran his fingers through his hair, unable to believe this was happening to him.

"I have *told* you, Sir William. Greystoke knew the name of one of the women who attacked us. No one else knew it—not even the chaplain who buried her. He lied about how he knew her name; he was forewarned about the threat—that was why he was able to surprise her and kill her. Don't you see? He might have been sent by Walsingham, but he knows these women. He knows they have been sent by Maurice Buckman. He knows that they and Buckman are Lady Percy's agents. He knows so much about them that he must be the one behind Awdrey disappearing."

Cecil walked to the fireplace. He stood with his back to the flames. "I am sorry, William, but this is not enough. He thought he knew one of their names—you do not know if he was telling the truth. It proves nothing—especially if, as you say, Maurice Buckman is giving him information as to who they are and when they will attack. It sounds to me very much as if this Maurice Buckman is giving so much information so freely to Greystoke that he will imperil Lady Percy's mission without us having to lift a finger."

"God's wounds, Sir William! It's not like that. What do I have to do to make you see?"

"Evidence, William. You are a herald; you know how important it is to produce evidence for your coats of arms and ancestral claims. Give me some evidence and I will initiate investigations. But without it, what can I say to Walsingham? That I suspect he is a poor judge of character? I've never met this Greystoke. Walsingham has known him for more than ten years. He trusts him."

Clarenceux buried his head in his hands. "I do not know what more to say. If you won't take my word for it, what else can I do?" He uncovered his face and looked at Cecil. "What else can I do?"

"Go home, get some rest," suggested Cecil. "I will send some of my men to guard your house if you wish. All you can do is wait for the Catholics' demand. When we see who is doing the demanding, and how they expect the delivery to be made, then we can take action."

Clarenceux sighed and walked to the door. Before he got there, however, there was a rushing of feet outside and a woman shouting, "Mr. Clarenceux! Mr. Clarenceux!" Without a moment's delay, Clarenceux opened it and saw the woman who had been looking after Annie that morning.

"Mr. Clarenceux, you must come quickly! Your daughter is calling for you!"

Clarenceux was stunned. "Do you mean...the fever has broken? She will live?"

The woman's face was a picture of sheer delight. She had tears of joy in her eyes, and seeing them, Clarenceux felt the tears well into his own. "She will live?" he repeated hoarsely, moving toward the stairs.

"She will live, Mr. Clarenceux!" shouted the woman, hurrying along behind him.

Clarenceux ran up the stairs as fast as he could. Such great hope was in his heart, such anticipation. He ran to the door, which was open, and went to the bed. Annie was lying on her side with her eyes open, looking very tired. She saw her father rush in and tried to sit up but could not. He put his arms around her and hugged her gently.

"I woke up and you were not here," she said.

"I have been here, Annie. I have been here every day." He pressed his cheek against hers and kissed her, holding her tenderly, aware that a deep prayer had been answered.

"Where is Mam?"

Clarenceux glanced at the woman who had entered the room behind him and at Cecil and two of Cecil's servants who were standing behind him, looking in. Word was spreading through the house that the fever had broken. "She has had to go away for a while," he said. "But she will be back soon, with Mildred."

"Where is she?"

Clarenceux paused, feeling the need to lie out of kindness, not to worry the girl. "She has gone to see your aunt and uncle in Devon."

"Does our waking angel want something to eat?" asked the woman who had been tending her.

Clarenceux wiped his daughter's face and let her lie back in the bed. She was clearly utterly exhausted. "I think she will soon, won't you, Annie, my sweet?"

Weakly, she nodded.

Clarenceux glanced at Cecil, who bowed politely and left the room. He placed a hand against Annie's cheek and bent over and kissed her forehead.

58

Sunday, February 2

Sarah Cowie watched from the window of the isolated house. The church bells had rung for a long time that morning, on account of it being Candlemas. Puddles lay on the lane between the ploughed fields. The sky was a cold gray. Birds called as they flew across and stopped on the raised soil beside the furrows, pecking for worms. A copse of trees a hundred yards from the house swayed with the wind, and that same wind chilled her as she stood by the open shutters.

She dreaded his coming. She hated him because he was just so arrogant and callous. There was no way to hold him to account, nothing she could say or do to reprimand him. Twice now, one of Lady Percy's women had been killed when he had been there—and on neither occasion had he saved them.

The birds took off again and flapped in the breeze, being blown backward for a moment until they dived across to one side and flew down to the ground nearer the trees. Spots of rain started to fall on the soil outside.

"Are you going to stand by that window all morning or are you going to do something useful?" demanded Joan, as she placed a pot on a tripod in the fire. "Their slop bucket needs emptying. He won't want the smell of that if he comes back to do her again."

In that instant, Sarah had the feeling she was in Hell. She found Joan gruesomely animal-like—but uncaring too. Helen was the only one of Lady Percy's women she had warmed to in any way, but she had not seen her for ages. Perhaps she too was now dead. In fact, all things considered, Awdrey Harley and her young daughter were the only people whom she did *not* hate—but they had every right to hate her for what she had done. And in the eyes of the Lord, would it matter that she had been forced to do what she had done by Lady Percy? They all would surely have to atone for their crimes on Judgment Day.

Sarah went across the hall and up the stairs to the door of the chamber. She unbolted it and opened it, and stood there, waiting for her eyes to adjust to the darkness. The foul smell of the bucket rose to her nostrils; and with that she knew that if Greystoke did again what he had said he would do, it was not for lust for the woman but because of his hatred for Clarenceux.

After a few seconds, the chinks of light coming through the barred shutters allowed her to see the figures huddled beneath the blankets on the bed and the bucket in the corner. Awdrey did not stir as Sarah went to take the bucket.

"He killed them, didn't he?" Sarah asked. "Jane and Ann—the women who died in your house."

There was a long silence. Eventually Awdrey just said one word. "Yes."

Sarah swallowed. She picked up the slop bucket and left the room, bolting the door behind her, hating what she was doing, thinking only of her own daughters, praying for them. Walking with the bucket across the yard outside, she noticed the figure riding along the lane. For these last moments she could ignore him, as he slowed his horse to ride around the deep puddles. She emptied the bucket in the pit and went to the ditch nearby to fill it with water to rinse it. She was back indoors before he was.

When he entered a few minutes later, he nodded his greeting to Joan and pointed at Sarah. "Take the girl out."

Sarah could not help herself. The impetuosity that had caused her to steal the pewter plates now made her open her mouth and speak her mind. "Why? Does she remind you of the sinfulness of your deeds?"

Greystoke walked quickly over to Sarah and struck her very hard on the side of the face. Down she fell, and a moment after her shoulder struck the ground, Greystoke dropped on her, forcing his knee into her stomach.

"Keep your manners bright and your mouth closed."

As he spoke, Sarah was choking. When he finished, she was sick. He left her lying there and went up the stairs alone, unbolting the door and stepping inside. Sarah lay where she was, listening. She heard snatches of orders from Greystoke—"let go of the girl," "get out of here"—and looked up to see the young girl standing in the doorway, not knowing whether to leave or stay. Mildred remained there, blinking in the light, as the unmistakable creaking sounds of the bed were to be heard. Sarah looked at Joan where she was sitting at the table; Joan caught her eye and then began to cut onions. As if nothing was going on.

It was over quickly. Greystoke appeared in the doorway of the chamber, pushed past the girl, and came down the stairs. He looked at Sarah, who was now sitting up with her head in her hands.

"Until tomorrow," he said to Joan, as he stepped through the door and left the house.

There was a long silence. They heard him ride away.

"*He* killed them," said Sarah. "Jane and Ann—he did it." She looked at Joan and realized from her lack of shock or even a word that she had known all the time. Joan simply went up to the room, pushed the girl inside, and bolted the door again.

Sarah got to her feet slowly. "He did not even ask her about the document," she said, as Joan descended the stairs. "He just did what he wanted. He just raped her for no reason."

"Stop it," said Joan. "He's a cruel bastard, that's evident. We need a cruel bastard on our side if you and I are ever going to see our daughters again."

Sarah could bear it no longer. She went out of the house, slammed the door behind her, and walked across the ploughed field, stumbling over the furrows, weeping in the cold wind.

59

Clarenceux was one of the first out of the church, anxious to get back and see whether there was any news about his wife. He had left Fyndern and Thomas at home in case of a message. Every moment he was not there, his mind kept flicking back to the possibility that, in his absence, a ransom note might have been delivered. As soon as that happened, he could do something—and Cecil could act too. In the meantime, there was nothing. All he could do was get home as quickly as he could and ignore the sad frowns of the houses looking down on him as he walked where he had once walked every Sunday with her.

"Is there any news?" he asked Thomas on his return.

"No, Mr. Clarenceux. I am afraid not," replied the old man.

Clarenceux entered the hall. Everywhere he looked, he could see dust and disorder. No women to do the cleaning, no lady of the household to direct that it be done. He walked to the table, running his fingers through the dust. "I suppose there is no food in the house?"

"Fyndern attempted to bake bread," replied Thomas, looking toward the back stairs. "He asked me not to tell you. I don't think it went well."

"Good that he tried," replied Clarenceux. "He has both wit and application, that boy."

"Not to mention his other skills."

Clarenceux shrugged. "He won't have those for much longer. When he falls in love, he will lose that fineness of judgment. His sensitivity to the truth will be overwhelmed by his greater emotions, like a man whistling in a thunderstorm."

He gazed at the portrait of his wife hanging beside the door. "In church this morning, I looked at the space where the rood cross used to be. And it struck me that the authorities are not just changing the ways we pray; they are taking away the very things we should pray to. Now I find I am losing the things I want to pray *for*, as well. When I look at Awdrey's image there, I see I am not just losing my way of life; I am losing the reason to be alive. If it weren't for Annie…"

He let his voice trail away and sighed. "I will go to see her this afternoon. Maybe soon she will be well enough to return home."

Thomas was surprised. "Do you think that wise? She would be too vulnerable."

"I need her here, Thomas. I need my family. In church they say 'God so loved the world that He gave his only Son.' If God had truly loved Christ as I love my family, He would have given the world for His son."

"And that includes the document?" ventured Thomas.

Clarenceux nodded. "That includes the document. God knows, I don't want to cause a civil war but I would rather all the forces of the world were unleashed against each other than I lose my family."

60

Monday, February 3

Sarah Cowie did not wait at the window that morning. Instead she stirred the cauldron of pottage that was to provide the dinner for them all, kneeling by the fire. Tears constantly ran down her cheeks and she snivelled, wiping her nose on her sleeve.

"In Jesus's name, stop it!" snapped Joan from the back of the hall, where she was in her shift, washing her dress in a tub of steaming hot water.

"You cold-hearted bitch," muttered Sarah.

"What was that?"

Sarah said nothing, hearing the bell across the fields: the knell of ten o'clock. He would be here soon. When he came, would it be to return Awdrey to her family? Would it be to say Mr. Clarenceux had responded to the ransom note and delivered the document to Buckman? She wiped her sleeve over her face again, sniffed, and gazed down into the cauldron, watching the onions, beans, peas, and oats turn over one another. The peas, hardened from the autumn, were finally softening.

Her mind went back to her own childhood, when she had tended the pot for her mother. That was what she should be doing now—teaching her daughters how to cook, how to sew, in the hope that each girl might get herself a husband. A hard-working man who would provide for her and look after her, and instill in her the fear of other men, and never allow her to get so desperate as to venture to steal from the wealthy, not even when the opportunity seemed there for the taking.

The latch snapped open and Greystoke was there, with Helen Oudry. Sarah was pleased to see Helen and smiled at her. "Good day," she said. But Helen gave her only the most cursory of nods.

"I have found a more reliable keeper," Greystoke said as he entered, shutting the door behind him. He came over to the cauldron. "You're coming back to do the washing for the men at the house in Fleet Street." He took the wooden ladle with which she had been stirring the pottage and scooped out some of the broth, raising it to his lips, blowing on it until it was cool enough. He drank with a slurp and threw the ladle back into the cauldron. "That's piss poor," he said. "Put some meat in it."

"I would if I had some," she replied.

He glared at her but said nothing. He put his hand on his sword, unbuckled it, and threw it to her, and she caught it. "Come and look after the child," he said to her, stomping up the stairs.

In the dark chamber, Awdrey was tense. Every muscle in her body was tautened against the touch of the man, every part of her set to recoil. Mildred was fearful of her mother in such a state and had backed away. It was not what Awdrey wanted, but nor did she soften. Her mind was focused on the man and what was to come. Clutching hold of Mildred had not saved her the first time. Lying there inert and not responding to him had not saved her the second—if anything it had made her more sick with herself. This time she would fight. She would get hurt, she knew, but anything was better than feeling she had to accept this.

When the door opened, Greystoke and the woman stood silhouetted against the light, while their eyes adjusted to the dark, as she knew they would. After a few seconds the woman walked across the room, seized Mildred, and left the room without looking at Awdrey. Mildred protested loudly and started crying as the woman took her outside. Awdrey heard her cries growing weaker and she suddenly panicked. *What if they are taking her away?* She started to get up but Greystoke was there, the door open behind him. This was her chance; her eyes could see better in the darkness than his. She ran for the door, trying to avoid him, but he backed toward it and stopped her.

Downstairs, Sarah stirred the pottage. Awdrey was clearly putting up a struggle like never before. She heard her scream and then she heard Greystoke swearing and shouting—and although at one point it sounded as if Greystoke had managed to get his way, after several loud thumps on the floor, he cried out again—this time in agony. It was an awful, inarticulate sound. A moment later he appeared, clutching his jaw, blood pouring down it. Awdrey had torn his mouth, so that his lip was hanging down on one side. He would need to see a surgeon to stitch it up.

"Call Helen back in," he mumbled to Joan, who was still in her smock. "I want that bitch to regret this. I want her to hear her child scream. I'm going to hold her arm and put it in that cauldron—and let her mother hear the consequences of what she has just done."

"Why has Mr. Clarenceux not responded to the demand?" Sarah cried. "This would all be unnecessary if he had done so."

Greystoke looked at her, mopping his lip. "He has not yet been given a demand. We're making him sweat first."

Sarah was stunned. She stared about her, seeing shapes but recognizing nothing. With tears in her eyes she looked at Greystoke, and at the stairs, and at the door. She had to leave this hellish place, now.

She started walking to the door.

"Where are you going?" shouted Greystoke.

"To do the laundry at the house in Fleet Street," she shouted back. "That was what you told me to do."

61

At Sheffield Manor, Benedict Richardson waited behind the servant with the wine glass and flagon while a second servant opened a door. Lady Percy was sitting in a wooden chair by a fireplace, reading. Her sticks were propped up against her chair. At her feet lay two of her dogs, their paws stretched out on the woven rush matting.

"The wine you called for, my lady," said Richardson, with a bow.

She looked up. "Thank you, Richardson. Put the flask on the table. I'll take a glass now."

"There is news as well, my lady. A man in the kitchen has brought word from Father Buckman. Apparently—"

"He was not followed, was he? Did he take care?"

"My lady, he took the usual precautions. Father Buckman's words were passed to him at an inn in Hertford. If anyone was following Father Buckman's man, they will have followed him straight back to London from Hertford."

"Good. What does Buckman have to say for himself?"

"Mistress Harley is in our custody. So too is one of Clarenceux's daughters. They were taken off the street into a safe house, and then smuggled to Islington."

Lady Percy was delighted. "After all these years," she said, look-ing at him, "it makes my heart glad. Oh, the Lord is smiling upon us, Mr. Richardson. I might never have known the delights of a living husband, but I certainly have known the loneliness of being without one, and that is exactly what Mr. Clarenceux will now taste, in all its bitterness. He will soon cave in—if he has not done so already."

"Indeed, my lady, we are in a commanding position."

Lady Percy picked up her sticks. "Come, this is not an occasion to be sitting down. Help me up, young man, help me up," she said, waving one stick at him as she struggled out of her chair. Richardson helped her up and she took several paces forward. She stopped and lifted one of the sticks. "Clarenceux, you will surrender that docu-ment—if I have to cut off your child's fingers to force you to do so. You will give me the means to destroy the line of that whore, Anne Boleyn!" As she spoke, she hit the wall with her raised stick.

Until that moment, Benedict Richardson had always believed that Lady Percy's cause was a pious one. She wanted to expose Elizabeth as illegitimate so she would be replaced as queen by her Catholic heirs, the royal line of Scotland. But in those words and in that beating of the wall with her stick, he realized he had misunderstood her. To her, the Catholic cause was a means to an end. Lady Percy's chief desire was not to destroy Protestantism; it was to get revenge on Anne Boleyn—the first wife and the one and only love of her hus-band, Lord Percy. Lord Percy had never entered their marriage bed, had never once been kind to her, because of his devotion to Anne. Even after the king took Anne for his own wife, Lord Percy had loved Anne, not her.

Lady Percy saw signs of her dead rival's victory over her everywhere—in Anne's daughter Elizabeth reigning despite her illegitimacy and in her chosen form of worship being denied her by the same queen. It was not enough that Anne Boleyn had been executed; Lady Percy wanted her daughter also destroyed.

"What's the matter with you?" she barked, turning and seeing the expression on his face. "This is a cause for celebration. We have all but won."

"I am just so…surprised," he said.

"Why is that? You were the one who told me." She narrowed her gaze. "Don't tell me you are going soft. I thought you were a man of steel. Clarenceux deserves this."

Richardson recovered his wits. He bowed. "Indeed, my lady. I could not agree more. But if I may intrude upon your happiness for a moment, to remind you of the matter of the daughters of the deceased agents in London; we cannot keep them forever. Would you have me return them to their families? Jane Carr has a sister, she told me before she left, and Ann Thwaite a brother."

"Yes, yes. You are tiresome. Let them go. Let all of them go. I have no further need of them—not now we have Clarenceux's wife and daughter."

Richardson hesitated. "All of them? Even those whose mothers are still alive?"

"Why not?" said the old woman, sitting back in her seat by the fire and placing her sticks beside her. "It's time someone else paid for their keep. It is not as if I was truly going to hang them—not unless their mothers were openly rebellious. I'm not a brutal woman. Pass me that wine, if you please."

Richardson picked up the wine flask. "What about Mary Vardine?"

"Ah, her. No, she is a different case. Keep her."

62

Tuesday, February 4

Clarenceux was in his chamber getting ready to go to see Annie when the knock came. He did not hear it himself but he heard Thomas's shout, "I will see to it, Mr. Clarenceux." He descended the stairs, crossed the landing, and went through the hall—and was just about to go down the front stairs when he heard Thomas answered by a gentleman whom he should have expected.

He looked out and saw Dethick mounted on a huge Neapolitan courser.

Closing his eyes and cursing, he hurried down to the front door. "Sir Gilbert, I am truly—"

"You gave me your word, Clarenceux, that you would set out today. Can I not trust you even to keep your own promises?"

Sir Gilbert seemed to have dressed especially for this occasion. His silver-handled sword flashed in the morning light; his embroidered waistcoat was visible beneath the front of his doublet. He was wearing a wider ruff than usual, starched and pleated. His black breeches were of velvet and his hosen were sewn with patterns of gold leaves. His boots were black leather with a silver buckle.

"Sometimes one's promises are thwarted by events," said Clarenceux. "In this case my daughter has been ill with a fever, and it only broke three days ago. I despaired of her life."

"I despair of you doing your duty," replied Dethick. "I despair of the next time you tell me that you give me your word. If you have not set out by the end of the day, I will make this a case for the Earl Marshal to adjudicate. And that will not be to your benefit, I can assure you."

Dethick kicked his horse's flank and the beast took off a little more sharply than its rider had anticipated. He rolled back in the saddle before he regained his balance.

As Clarenceux watched him go, a woman suddenly ran out of the house opposite. Her long dark hair was hanging loose, and she had a troubled look about her. Her shoes were muddy and falling apart; she wore no jewelry, no ruff—nothing fancy at all. She looked as if she were in her early thirties. Her breasts swayed beneath her dress as she ran—straight toward Clarenceux.

"I must have words with you, sir, it is important," said Sarah Cowie. Her blue-gray eyes had the watery look of someone who has not slept for days.

"And who might you be?" He glanced at the windows of the house opposite. Only one was open.

"I must speak to you privily about your wife and daughter."

"Come in," he said quickly, standing back to allow her access to his house. He looked up and down the street, to make sure she was not being followed.

In the hall he shut both doors, so they were alone. "Be seated," he said, gesturing to the bench by the table, feeling the heavy nervousness in his arms.

"I prefer to stand," she replied, her hands folding over each other repeatedly, like the headless bodies of two worms.

"Well?"

"I do not know how to say this, so I will just say it. Your wife is being treated poorly and I know where. If you will give me the document that Mr. Greystoke so badly wants, I will tell you where they are keeping your wife."

"Awdrey is being maltreated? In what way? Where is she? Is my daughter Mildred with her?"

"They are together, in a darkened room, in a house outside London. That is all I can tell you—unless you give me that document."

Clarenceux could feel his pulse racing. "Do you know what document they seek? Do you know what it is?"

"A marriage agreement," replied Sarah, "between Lord Percy and the queen's mother. I have heard Mr. Greystoke speak about it. And I can read, so do not try to pass off something else on me."

"You can read?" Clarenceux took in the disheveled look and unwashed smell. If this woman had had an education, she had fallen a long way. "How is my wife? Is she well?"

The dark-haired woman looked at him strangely. "Her life is at stake, Mr. Clarenceux. Of course she is not well. She is being poorly treated all the time by John Greystoke."

"Poorly treated?"

"He has taken his pleasure of her body at least twice, if not more times. She is spending all her days and nights in an unlit, unheated room, waiting for the next time he will demand that she—"

"Stop it!" Clarenceux felt as if he had been hit. He reached for the table and sat down on the bench. His failure to protect Awdrey tore him apart and left him unable to think logically.

"He has raped her?"

"The first time, he forced himself on her. The second time, she did not put up a fight. The third time, she resisted. I don't know what happened after that."

The volcano erupted. He got to his feet and advanced upon the woman. Grabbing her around the neck, he shouted, "Tell me where they are! Tell me where—*tell me!*"

Sarah Cowie was terrified but did not struggle. "I cannot," she choked as he loosened his grip enough for her to speak.

"You mean you *will* not. When did you last see them?"

"Yesterday."

He seized her shoulders and threw her against the wall. "Tell me where they are, or I will make you sorry you were ever born."

"You cannot make me regret that any more than I do already, sir. I ran away from the house to tell you. I do not want to think of what he is doing to her."

"You women—he has you all under his control, he can tell you when to appear and then he cuts your throats, as if he can command your lives. What hold does he have on you?"

Clarenceux let go of her and stepped away, covering his face with his hands. "Oh Christ! Oh God help us!" For a long while he stood, just praying. "Why do you and the other women all do so much for Greystoke? What hold does he have on you?"

"Not him—Lady Percy. She has our daughters. And she will hang them in our places if we do not complete the task."

"In your places?"

Sarah sat down on the bench. "All of us have been found guilty of some crime or other. Some of us made one mistake and were told we would pay for it with our lives. I only ever stole once in my life, it is true, I swear it; but that was enough. I was sentenced to hang."

"What did you steal?"

"Five pewter plates, a salt cellar, and a candlestick."

Clarenceux got up and walked across the hall. Thomas was right: he could not risk bringing Annie home to this house. He looked at the portrait of Awdrey and closed his eyes. She was suffering. Through no fault of her own. Through no fault of his—except a willingness, long ago, to help an old friend.

"Did you kill Rebecca Machyn?" he asked.

"No, not me."

He looked at her. "Who then, if not you? Give me a name."

"Joan Hellier. She killed her."

"I presume she is another of Lady Percy's women, with a daughter in jail?"

"Yes. She is guarding your wife for Greystoke now, as we speak, with another woman called Helen Oudry. But Joan is of the real criminal community. Helen and I are not used to the life they lead."

"I do not care about the life you lead," Clarenceux replied. "I do not care about anyone but my wife and my daughters and the safety of those in my household." He paused, thinking. "How does Lady Percy tell you what to do?"

"It is Father Buckman who tells us."

Clarenceux hit the table hard. "Greystoke betrayed Buckman to Walsingham: Sir William Cecil told me. If he is working with Buckman—it doesn't make sense!"

Sarah simply shrugged.

He rested his forehead on the palm of his hand. "Let us imagine that I were to surrender the document," he said carefully. "To whom should I give it? Would you take it to Lady Percy yourself?"

She nodded. "I would not trust Greystoke with it. He is a deeply selfish man."

"It would be your death warrant. You would never get to Sheffield. If Greystoke didn't cut your throat for it on the way, Walsingham would. He has men watching Sheffield Manor. This priest, Buckman—do you know how to find him?"

She rose to her feet. "I will call for the document. You will give it to me. I will pass it on to Father Buckman—it is my risk after that."

Clarenceux looked up at her. "I am not giving the document to you or anyone else. As you know, it is not in this house. You said you can read—there can't be many condemned women who can—which makes me fairly certain you were the one who went through the books and documents on my desk when you were staying in the garret two doors down the road." He saw the startled look on her face. "Yes, I have been there. I have seen the marks on the walls by the window where you took signals from Greystoke." He paused but she did not answer, remaining standing in front of him. "You might be able to tell me where my wife was yesterday—but is she still there today? You have nothing to offer me. And now I am not sure that Greystoke will treat you any better than he is treating my wife for betraying him."

Sarah walked to the door.

"Where are you going?" Clarenceux asked.

"Can you guarantee my safety?"

"No. No more than I could that of my wife."

"I have just told you many things. Greystoke will kill me, as he did the others. I don't want to die. I want to see my daughters, Catherine and Elizabeth."

Clarenceux noted the names: one Catholic, one Protestant. This woman was not part of a religious conspiracy of her own volition, that was clear.

"Take me to Buckman," he said.

"I cannot. I haven't been there, and he would—"

"You 'haven't been there'? Then you know where 'there' is. Tell me."

She shook her head. "Not unless you give me the document."

"We will go to see him together."

Sarah opened the door and went down the stairs. Clarenceux got up from the bench and followed her, slowly. He watched as she wrestled with the handle to the front door and stepped down the stairs. "Tell me, where do I find him? If you have any sense of justice, or injustice, you should tell me."

"You cannot help me."

Clarenceux reached behind the cloak that was hanging on a peg at the foot of the stairs and took hold of the sword that was concealed there. He drew it from its scabbard. "The door is locked." He tapped with the point of the sword on her shoulders, as if knighting her from behind, then rested the flat of the cold blade against her cheek. "I mean you no harm, but I have to know where she is. Or I have to know where to find Buckman. They will never find that document, not in a thousand years. If you want to see your daughters again, you have to do what I say."

Sarah stopped struggling with the door. She knocked the sword blade away and turned to face Clarenceux. "You will find Buckman at the Black Swan in St. Dionis Backchurch. You must ask for a tankard of a beer called Old Faithful. Give him the document and he will tell Greystoke to release Awdrey and the girl. Do it quickly—and bring this to an end, for all our sakes."

Clarenceux put the sword blade back against her neck. "And my wife?"

"I am sorry about your wife."

"Where is she?"

"I cannot tell you. If I do, you will not surrender the document to Father Buckman. It does not matter what happens to me now. Someone is going to kill me. Even if I flee, the constables will take me back and hang me. But if you see Buckman with that document, at least my Catherine and Elizabeth will have a better life."

Clarenceux withdrew the blade. "Tell me your name, and you can go."

She looked him in the eye. "Sarah Cowie."

"You are a strange mix of courage and fear, Sarah Cowie."

"We all are. Are you any different?"

63

Clarenceux did not speak to Fyndern. He did not even speak to Thomas. He did not even look at them. He withdrew into the darkness of himself, seeking the core of his despair.

It was the realization of how he had let this happen to his wife, how naive he had been, that caused his double distress. He did not just weep for her; he cursed himself for not recognizing the danger Greystoke had posed. He was like the unseeing optimist, telling his wife to trust him when truly he did not know what lay in wait. But that was the character of John Greystoke: he was not just cruel, selfish, and calculating; he was deceptive too. The *vipera* that lies in wait, curled in the bosom of one's own heart, getting closer and closer and eventually poisoning the soul from within.

Four hours later, in the cold, early afternoon, with the briefest of explanations to Thomas as to where he was going, Clarenceux left the house. Walking swiftly, he passed along Shoe Lane, across Holborn Bridge, up to St. Giles in the Fields, and then down Drury Lane. There he stopped, looking across the gardens at the back of Cecil House. He breathed the air of the day, wishing that somehow his breathing would cease, extinguishing his problems as easily as a candle flame is extinguished when pinched.

There was still one little ray of light left to him, however, and she was in the house that now lay before him. Behind those glass windows, beneath those stone carvings and pinnacles—despite all that carved pomp and elegance—there was a girl who now was the only other free member of his family. With quickening steps he hurried toward Cecil House.

Annie was in the garden, surrounded by a small court of servants. Little Robert Cecil—a diminutive three years of age to her seven— was playing with a ball made of an inflated leather-covered bladder, throwing it to her or kicking it and letting it bounce. She was going after it, albeit slowly, and throwing it or kicking it back. One lady in a dark-red embroidered kirtle was anxiously following her with a small form for her to sit on, it being only three days since her fever had broken. But Annie did not want to sit and refused all suggestions, even when she fell over. Clarenceux recognized a familiar stubbornness. He also smiled to see that Annie was behaving very responsibly to the young boy, as if she were his older sister.

Gradually all the ladies, gentlemen, ushers, and other servants recognized that Clarenceux had come to be alone with his daughter. They bowed to him and withdrew in ones and twos, taking young Robert with them and leaving Annie alone with her father.

"Will you walk with me a little way, Annie?" he asked, holding out his hand.

She took it. "Where are we going?"

"A short walk. I think that you and I should talk a little."

They came to a seat in a small enclosed part of the garden; Clarenceux sat, listening to the birdsong. Annie nestled close.

"I am going to have to go away soon," he began. "There are men and women who have…well, they have hurt your mother and sister. It falls to me to right the wrongs they have done."

"What have they done to them?"

"They have taken them away and locked them in a room."

Annie looked very solemn, at the ground. "Robert Cecil will be sent away to school when he is five. I am seven. Can I go to school?"

Clarenceux put his arm around her. "Girls don't go to school, Annie. Girls are taught to read by their parents. Or a tutor."

The air in the garden smelled so cold and so sweet. The bright sun on the hedges about them and the sparkling on the bare twigs above highlighted the fleeting moment.

"Will you teach me to read?"

He felt his chest tighten. "I will do all I can." He hugged her gently. There was so much he wanted to say to her, about things she would need to learn in life—about families, about history and the wonders of past centuries, and about the joy of having children and seeing them grow, and understanding the future through them. All of this would have to wait. She would find out in her own time.

"You are sighing a lot," said Annie.

"Am I?" laughed Clarenceux, releasing her.

"Why are you crying?"

"Because I love you," he replied with a lump in his throat. "Because I so dearly love you."

64

Clarenceux led Thomas and Fyndern out of the house and locked the door behind them. He did not look up at the house opposite. He remained silent as he walked across Fleet Bridge and through the darkening streets. At Ludgate he spoke brusquely with the guard about the urgent business he, Thomas, and his stable boy had to see to in the city, and gestured to Thomas's lantern, which was necessary for them to go about the city later, after curfew. Soon the three of them were walking through the city proper, with its overhanging timber houses, frozen mud, and gravel streets. The signs above the doorways were fading in the dusk, and people heading for home were dark forms, huddled inside their cloaks against the cold. Church steeples conspired against the sky.

The three men wove through the streets and alleys, around the north side of the cathedral, through Paternoster Row, where the booksellers had already shut up shop, and up to Cheapside, where the market stalls were being cleared away from the wide street. They went eastward, past people carrying market goods on their backs, on their heads, and in baskets; past Goldsmiths Row, past the water-bearers and the great conduit. At the east end of Cheapside they turned right down Lombard Street beneath the gaunt tower of St. Mary Woolnoth and then, after a short distance, they came to Gracechurch Street. Crossing it and passing the church that gave its name to St. Dionis Backchurch, they turned left into Lime Street and then left again into the alley leading to the Black Swan.

The inn was a substantial old building tucked away behind other houses so that hardly any of it showed on the alley. The hall was still open to the rafters, with a rush-covered earthen floor in front of a large brick fireplace. Flasks and bottles stood in the shadows on high wooden shelves, and several spare candles hung in pairs from the common wick between them, draped over metal hooks in the wall. It was crowded with about seventy or eighty people—hot, smelly, and dimly lit, with the fire burning and six bright pricks of candlelight on tables and another eight set on holders attached to the walls. Laughter and chatter were in the air—and music too. Three men were playing together in the far corner: one with a fiddle, another with a set of pipes, and the third with a tabor. The tabor player was beating out exciting rhythms to which various men and women would dance for a short while before stopping to drink their beer. At the far end of the hall were two doors: one leading to the buttery, or so Clarenceux surmised, and the other leading to the private quarters.

As he searched the faces and people, some sitting on benches, others standing, he struggled to see anyone with an apron. He noted round-faced workers; hearty shopkeepers; builders with naked biceps glistening in the candlelight beneath their jerkins; two clerks or students nearby; and leather- and russet-clad workers of all descriptions, some with hats, some with shirts open. Four young women sat together at a table, as rowdy as their menfolk, but otherwise there were only a few women present, dotted here and there in the throng.

There was barely room enough to move. It seemed a most unlikely establishment in which to find a Catholic priest.

Clarenceux caught sight of a woman carrying tankards, but before he could signal to her there was a chanting sound and clapping. Shouts of "Alice! Alice!" filled the hall. Clarenceux looked about for this Alice—and noted that Fyndern was staring straight across the room to the left-hand of the two doors. His attention was so strongly fixed that Clarenceux found himself bound to follow his gaze. A young dark-haired women stood there, seventeen or eighteen years of age, of slight proportions and a gracious smile. But it was not her face or her hair that was drawing Fyndern's attention: it was what she was wearing. It was like a woman's thin linen smock, except it was black. It fitted her body very closely and showed off her curves. Most shocking of all, it revealed her bare arms. Clarenceux suspected that if he could get close enough, he would see her ankles exposed too. Just to see her moving in that shiny black smock was enticing; when she stopped and placed her hands on her hips, looking sideways with a smile, every man present except Clarenceux inwardly sighed, groaned with desire, or shouted with lust.

She broke her pose and walked toward the musicians, who followed her from the corner to a position in the middle of the long wall of the hall. She raised her hands above her head and turned to the crowd. There was a great cheer: she started clapping rhythmically and the crowd did likewise, following her lead. The tabor player picked up the rhythm and added some flourishes of his own, playing double beats. The fiddle player started up with a fast tune, giving the cue for the piper, who followed suit. With the crowd all clapping, the young woman put her hands on her hips again and held the pose just long enough to increase the excitement.

Her confidence was extraordinary. To stand there as an object of attention, practically alone, and yet smiling and holding that pose, drew not just the eye but the whole mind. Thomas nudged Clarenceux and pointed to Fyndern, who did not even realize they were looking at him. "We've lost him, for sure," he said. Clarenceux nodded, turning to look for the landlord but now unable even to see the woman with the tankards. People had not come here for the beer.

When the young woman began to move, Fyndern was not alone in staring at her hips, which undulated and swayed as if she was a river in which every man would want to swim. The women too were fascinated, struck by the confidence with which the girl danced, catching the eye of the each of her admirers, and emulating the movements of sexual gratification provocatively in front of them all.

Fyndern closed his eyes, just to see if he could believe what was before his eyes—but he opened them again quickly, not wanting to miss a moment. He tried to imagine his cheek close to the thin black cloth over her hips—staring as it shifted back and forth with her rhythmic movements. But then he looked at her shoulders: those too were equally sensual...There were just so many parts of her to look at it; her whole body was a sea plant, its fronts undulating with the waves.

A middle-aged man with a beard and bushy eyebrows moved through the crowd, filling tankards. He was the only other person in the hall besides Clarenceux not staring at the dancing girl. The bushy-eyebrowed man, who was tall but not as tall as Clarenceux, noticed him and waited as Clarenceux pushed his way through the open-mouthed onlookers toward him.

"I am looking for a beer called Old Faithful," Clarenceux said.

There was a huge cheer as the woman presented herself side on to the crowd, put her chin on her shoulder, and started to tweak the skirt of her black smock, swinging her hips as she did so. Clarenceux did not turn away from the man.

"You don't look the type to drink Old Faithful."

Clarenceux drew closer to him. "I will see him. Either you introduce me or I will do so myself." He looked the man in the eye again, and repeated slowly and clearly, "Old Faithful."

The bushy-eyebrowed man turned his expression to the right-hand of the two doors. He pointed and then, slowly, elevated his finger to indicate the room above that door. "Don't cause trouble."

Clarenceux started to push through the crowd. It took him some time to reach the door—people did not want to be disturbed as they watched the dancing. Thomas was behind him; Fyndern was still spellbound. "Wait here," Clarenceux said in Thomas's ear. "Make sure no one follows me." He took a deep breath, lifted the latch, pushed the door open, and went through, closing it behind him.

In opening the door, Clarenceux caught a glimpse of the room beyond. There was a substantial ladder set into the wall to the right. The music from the hall was muffled and he had the impression that there had been another sound, a tinkling noise in the distance. Had it been his imagination? He felt around the doorframe for a string that might have rung a bell but found none, and stepped forward, reaching for the ladder. Gripping both sides, he started to ascend, slowly, hearing the faint music, cheers, and clapping from the adjacent hall. One step, two. After a third step his head struck an oak board, which shifted slightly. It was a wide and heavy cover. When he pushed upward, it resisted on the hinged side. He adjusted where he was pressing and pushed harder, raising it.

He was greeted by a single golden light. There was a smell of burning and recently extinguished candles, sealing wax, the fug of airlessness and body odors. He pushed the hatch all the way open and moved up into the light.

"Stop there," came a nasal, slightly high-pitched man's voice. "Who are you?"

Clarenceux did not stop. He climbed the last steps and looked around the attic chamber. There was one candle on a holder attached to a beam, not far from the hatch. The noise from the hall continued.

"Who are you and what are you doing here? Speak now—I have a pistol aimed at your chest."

"You do not frighten me," said Clarenceux, walking to the candle and lifting it aloft. He saw the slope of the roof, the underside of the shingles. The room covered the space above the buttery and the downstairs chambers, and was more extensive than he had anticipated. In the shadows were various items of furniture—but no people.

"Who would have thought of finding you, a Catholic priest, hiding in a bawdy house such as this?"

The voice continued its same nasal monotone. "Who are you?"

"I am the one you will not shoot, Father Buckman. The man to whom you owe your soul. The man whose wife and daughter you have stolen."

"Clarenceux."

"I am he."

"You owe me a document."

"I owe you nothing. You have hounded me, persecuted me, shot my elder daughter, taken my wife and raped her, taken my other daughter, killed my maidservant, made foul use of my property—and my soul is sick of it, tired and sick."

Cheers rang out from the hall downstairs, clapping and hoots, which gave way to chants. The musicians struck up another tune.

The nasal voice seemed colder. "Then I suggest you do something to cure your sickness. Return the rightful property of Lord Percy to his widow, and your wife and child will be returned."

Clarenceux held the candle aloft and walked toward where Buckman was hiding. "I am not going to let you, or John Greystoke, or anyone else anywhere near that document until I know for certain that my wife and daughter are safe and well. Take them into Oxfordshire." Clarenceux moved to one side. There was a table there with a desk slope upon it. An open inkwell, several folios of used and blank paper, and three leather books were also on the table. The candlelight caught the rim of a small bronze bell fixed to a truss.

"Would you care to suggest a particular place in Oxfordshire?" asked Buckman.

Clarenceux did not answer but began to look around the attic, avoiding hitting his head on the trusses of the roof. When he came to the two chests, one on top of the other, he drew back. Buckman had placed a tabletop on its side next to them, allowing him a hiding place such as a child would make when playing in an attic full of furniture. Clarenceux saw the glint of a glass moving and walked back to the hatch, where he set the candle back in its holder. He then moved into the darkness himself.

"I will only hand the document over to you or to Greystoke in person. A time of reckoning has come."

"If you have a duel in mind, I warn you Greystoke is one of the best swords in the kingdom, and a fine shot too."

Clarenceux maneuvered himself behind the chests and saw Buckman move out of his hiding place, around to the far side. He was weasel-like and thin, not tall but with little hair, bespectacled and dressed in a cassock. He was holding a gun and pointing it at Clarenceux as he backed away toward the hatch.

"Go on, run away, if that's what you are edging over there for," said Clarenceux from Buckman's hiding place. "Go and see Greystoke; tell him to make arrangements to take my wife and daughter to Great Milton in Oxfordshire. That is close to where we will make the exchange."

Buckman was near the candle now. He blinked repeatedly as he backed away, holding the gun, saying nothing. Within reach of the candle, he snuffed out the flame, leaving Clarenceux in darkness, and descended the ladder as quickly as he could. Clarenceux heard the dying strains of the music downstairs: less applause this time, and no shouts. He felt his way across the attic in the darkness and followed Buckman. At the foot of the ladder he felt for the door and found the latch at the same time as Thomas opened it. He looked over his servant's shoulder across the candlelit space of the hall to see Buckman leaving by the main door.

Fyndern was staring alternately at Buckman and at Clarenceux, as if asking what he should do.

"Curse the boy," said Thomas, "he's too slow. I told him to follow the man."

"No," replied Clarenceux. "Let him go. Buckman's armed—no need for Fyndern to risk himself. Besides, Buckman's too sharp to lead us to Awdrey. He will lie low, once he has made sure he has not been followed."

The fiddle player was playing alone now. There was an air of drunkenness and the noise of chatter in the hall. A group of men had gathered around the dancing girl and she was laughing nervously, looking from one to the next.

"Where is the innkeeper?" asked Clarenceux.

Thomas indicated the other door. "Replenishing tankards."

Clarenceux took the nearest wall-fixed candle, despite a few glances and complaints from drinkers nearby, and put his hand on Thomas's shoulder. "Come with me," he said as he headed back toward the stairs and up through the hatch, clutching the small light.

He lit the candle that Buckman had extinguished and took the second light across to the table. The papers were theological notes, nothing in code. He opened the heavy leather cover of the first and largest of the three volumes: it was a Bible in Latin. The second was in Italian, Dante's *Inferno*. The third book he recognized as soon as he glimpsed it: it was Henry Machyn's manuscript chronicle. Someone had stolen it from his house.

"Mr. Clarenceux," said Thomas, who had kicked apart the straw mattress and bedding and was now inspecting the two large chests. They were each about three feet high, four feet wide and two feet deep. He lifted one end of the upper chest with some difficulty, due to the weight of the oak. It was locked.

"Mr. Clarenceux," repeated Thomas.

"Open it," said Clarenceux, looking through the *Inferno* for any indications of a code.

"It is locked."

Clarenceux put the book down. "Go downstairs and find a chisel or something metal. We'll break it."

While Thomas was gone, Clarenceux returned to the table and picked up Henry Machyn's book, with its loose cover. He could see nothing strange about it, no extra notes. He started searching the corners of the attic, looking and feeling into the dark recesses, but it was a vain hope. In truth he knew he would find nothing. Buckman had departed too quickly.

He went back to the chests and dragged the upper one off the lower. It fell to the floorboards with a heavy thump and a rattle of its contents. The lower chest proved to be empty.

When Thomas returned with a pointed metal poker to break the lock of the other chest, it revealed only three canvas shirts, two black cassocks, some candlesticks, a pistol, gunpowder, a pair of old leather shoes, and cheap gloves.

Clarenceux tipped the lid and let it fall under its own weight. "I wonder why the innkeeper has not been up here to see what we are doing."

"Perhaps he wants nothing to do with Father Buckman," suggested Thomas.

"Mr. Clarenceux," called Fyndern tentatively from the stairs.

Clarenceux picked up Henry Machyn's chronicle and the candle and walked toward the hatch. He saw the boy's face in the golden light. "What is it?"

"The girl. Some men have paid the innkeeper so they can take her into the back room. She is in danger."

"Christ's love, Fyndern, she is a whore, a common woman. You don't need your delicate senses to see that."

"No, Mr. Clarenceux, she is not, and they are going to use her. The innkeeper has sold her."

Clarenceux wanted nothing to do with the matter. But the knowledge of what had happened to Awdrey made him feel guilty, and the voice of his conscience whispered in his ear: *You can make a difference—if you choose to do so. But only if you choose.*

Thomas emerged from a corner, his candle guttering, shaking his head. Clarenceux heard the voices from the hall. His own instincts told him not to get involved, so why did he trust this boy's? The truth, he knew, was that the boy reminded him of himself in the happy days of youth, when his parents and brother were alive, and when he never suspected that his future would end in an ever-narrowing, ever-darkening, increasingly lonely alley.

"Mr. Clarenceux!" urged Fyndern. "She is only two years older than I am. You must help her."

"Two years? Was that was a wild guess, intuition, or is she touting for business?"

Fyndern let the heavy hatch door slam shut.

"Thomas," said Clarenceux, looking sideways at his old servant, holding up a book. "This is Henry Machyn's chronicle."

"Why not help the girl?" asked Thomas. "The boy means well."

"Jesus, I will pay for her, if he's that desperate."

There was silence from downstairs now. Clarenceux walked to the hatch door, opened it, and descended, with Thomas following. Opening the door, he saw that only about twenty people remained in the candlelit hall. Fyndern was one of them, anxiously looking toward the closed door of the buttery. Clarenceux said nothing but passed the chronicle to him.

"Try the latch, Thomas," he said.

The latch lifted and stuck open—but the door remained closed. Thomas tried shoving the door; it gave slightly, as if someone was holding it shut.

Clarenceux glanced at Fyndern. "Your instincts had better be correct," he said as he stepped back and suddenly charged into the door, putting all his weight and rage behind his right shoulder.

The man holding it shut had been wholly unprepared for the force with which Clarenceux struck it. He went sprawling as the herald burst into the room, looking in the light of the candles from the naked girl to the shocked faces around. "Get out of here!" he shouted with the full force of his herald's voice. "Get out, get out!"

As the strong smell of stale beer and hops hit him, one robust stubble-faced jerkin-clad man stepped forward. "And who are you to tell us—"

He got no further. Clarenceux swept back the hem of his cloak to reveal his sword, which he drew. The blade flashed close to them all in the buttery. "I am William Harley, Clarenceux King of Arms, herald to Her Majesty Queen Elizabeth by the grace of God Queen of England. Leave this place now or die here—I do not care which you choose. I no longer care about anything."

65

Wednesday, February 5

As soon as Clarenceux was awake he got up and knelt on Awdrey's side of the bed, praying for her. The ewer was empty, the basin filled with dirty water. The shirt in which he had slept was also several days old; he threw it in a corner—only to pick it up again when he remembered that there were no clean ones left in his clothes chest. Having put it on and fastened his breeches, he left the chamber.

On the landing he listened for any sign of the girl, Alice, who had come home with them the previous night. Silence. He went down to the hall. Fyndern's bed had been tidied away and there was no sign of him either. Thomas had stacked his bedding to one side and was lighting the fire in the hearth.

"Where's that boy?" asked Clarenceux. "I'll hold you a shilling that he's wasted no time with that strumpet we brought home yesterday." Thomas brushed the old ash dust off his hands. "He is down in the stable, I believe."

Clarenceux went down the back stairs. The back door was open, and Fyndern had already unbolted the stable door. Clarenceux's suspicious mind took him in that direction. Neither of them were in the stable, however, nor even in the stable loft. Brutus snorted in his stall and Maud took some fresh hay from the supply in her manger. *At least Fyndern saw to the horses first.*

He returned to the house and went into the kitchen, where the smell of bread baking greeted him. Fyndern's curly brown hair was near the floor, and the girl's long dark hair not far from his. There they were, both down on their knees scrubbing. Immediately Clarenceux felt guilty; judging by the extent they had already cleaned, they had started before dawn. A burning candle stood on a table and another in a holder against the fireplace. The fire was alight too.

"Good day, Mr. Clarenceux," said Fyndern, smiling brightly. "Alice is showing me how to bake bread."

The girl rose to her feet and bowed. "Good morrow to you, Mr. Clarenceux," she said, with what seemed to Clarenceux to be a Yorkshire accent. "I am grateful to you for bringing me home."

Clarenceux hesitated. "If you can bake bread and clean you are welcome," he said, ashamed of his earlier thoughts. "Where is your home parish?"

"I was raised in Halifax, in my father's tavern," she replied.

"What brought you to London?" he inquired.

"A man who claimed to be a friend of my mother's. He found me begging after my mother died and promised he would marry me, if I came with him to London. That was last autumn."

"Where is he now?"

She shrugged. "Drunk. Dead. Dead drunk. I neither know nor care. He deceived me."

Clarenceux looked at Fyndern, who was gazing at the girl. Asking her to stay was tempting fate, but the opportunity seemed too good to miss. "Can you wash linen as well?"

"Do you have soap?"

Clarenceux pointed to an earthenware pot on a shelf. "Up there. If you will work, I'll pay wages of a shilling a week, with meals and a bed in the attic."

The offer was half as much again as most women earned in service. Alice bowed once more. "You are very kind." She smiled.

Clarenceux could see that she was even younger than she had first appeared in the inn—as Fyndern had said. He took off his dirty shirt and placed it on the stone drainer to his right. "As soon as you can—I have run short. There are more in the buck basket in my daughter's chamber too. Fyndern will show you where."

Thomas came into the kitchen as Clarenceux, semi-naked, left. If the first sight did not surprise him, the second certainly did: Fyndern on his knees. "There's nothing like a doe to make the heart leap," the old man muttered. Then he said to Alice, "Watch out—he will have you dancing again in that black smock."

In his study Clarenceux looked at the piece of paper on which he had charted the comings and goings of men in the house opposite. The very sight of it taunted him; he screwed it up and threw it into the cold fireplace. *My Etheldreda, my love.* The coldness of the room and the house touched him physically. He had no urge to soften it with warmth; he deserved the cold.

Taking another piece of paper, he started to write a few notes toward his plan for exchanging the document for his wife, but however he arranged things, it seemed awkward. Soon that paper too was in the fireplace.

It all came back to Thame Abbey. He was unable to rid his mind of the strategy that he had first thought of when reading Henry of Abingdon's chronicle. It was the way forward: to take his enemies there, into the refectory with its wooden floor, give them the document, and let them send word for Awdrey and Mildred to be delivered to safety—and then to destroy the place, reducing all of them to ashes, as well as the document. But that secret place in the abbey described in Henry of Abingdon's chronicle—what were the chances that it would outlast the smoke and fire?

It would take courage. The chances were that he would die in the flames. He shut his eyes and tried to imagine what it would be like. Many in the last reign had felt it—and some had even chosen to suffer death in that way. There was the case of John Badby in the reign of Henry the Fourth. He had been put on the pyre, and when he was screaming and his flesh turning black and the fat sizzling in his arms, Prince Henry had ordered the faggots pulled away and had offered him a pension and a pardon if he would renounce his heresy. Badby was just an ordinary craftsman who openly refused to believe in transubstantiation—and yet he would not admit he was wrong. Even when the prince told him they would pile the burning faggots around him again, he refused to accept the pension and the pardon, choosing to be burned to death. That was how courageous some men could be in the heat of the fire. But could *he* do it? Could *he* do anything like it?

He had been thinking about what he had to do, turning it over and over in his mind for more than an hour when he heard steps on the staircase and Alice knocked on the door of the study. She entered bearing a cleaned and folded shirt. She held it out to him. It was warm.

"How did you dry it so fast without making it smell of smoke?" he asked.

"In the oven," she replied. "A trick my mother taught me."

Clarenceux stood up and put on the clean shirt, feeling much the smarter for it. He looked at Alice. "How long were you at the Black Swan?"

"Three or four weeks."

"Then you must have become well acquainted with Maurice Buckman?"

"The priest? He did not often show his face." She noticed the collar of Clarenceux's doublet was not straight, and reached out and corrected it.

"What about John Greystoke? Tall thin man with white hair, in his late twenties or early thirties—usually wears a sword."

"No."

"A dark-haired woman called Sarah Cowie? Ann Thwaite? Joan Hellier?"

The girl's humor diminished with all the questioning. "I know none of those women. I just danced there for money and slept in the hall. May I go now, please?"

The city bells began to ring the hour. It was time for him to see Annie. "I am sorry for all the questions, Alice. I'm just a worried old man who needs to know more than he can remember."

Alice bowed and went to the door.

"Alice, one last question," said Clarenceux.

She turned around, still holding the latch with her right hand. "Yes?"

"What is your surname?"

"Vardine," she replied.

66

~

Thursday, February 6

The market traders in Cheapside were setting up their stalls at first light. As the shutters opened in the windows above, trestles were erected and table boards placed on top, ready for wares. Baskets were unloaded from carts and heaped on the tables—here, wickerwork filled with cabbages, onions, parsnips, and leeks; there, apples, dried plums, cherries, and pears. The winter season limited the fruit to only those things that could be kept for months, but at some stalls more adventurous traders displayed vegetables that had come from further afield. Several had edible carrots brought from the Low Countries; others had marrows. One even had a rarity that very few Londoners recognized, perched in a prominent position on his stall of vegetables: a cauliflower.

John Greystoke pulled his hat low as he shouldered his way past the busy traders through to a back alley. Here, he entered a yard through a gate and went up the steps to the back door of the house. He knocked five times—paused—and then knocked twice more. The door was opened by an old woman in a plain black dress and shawl.

"Is he awake?"

"Yes. Waiting upstairs."

He said nothing more but moved through the darkness inside the house to the stairs and ascended quickly. At the door to the back chamber he knocked five times and then twice…and then lifted the latch.

Maurice Buckman had his back to the window, which silhouetted his round head.

"Someone talked," he said coldly.

"It can only have been Sarah Cowie," replied Greystoke.

"Where is she now?"

"At the house on Fleet Street."

Buckman looked sternly at Greystoke. His expression, together with his spectacles, gave him the aspect of a natural philosopher who experiments on creatures, only in this case the creatures were human. "I suggest that you kill her. Soon. She led Clarenceux straight to the Black Swan. The innkeeper had to use the bell to warn me. But her treachery begs another question: how did she know to send Clarenceux there? Someone else must have talked too."

Greystoke was silent. "It could have been Jane Carr—any of the women who saw you."

"Or it could have been you," said Buckman.

Greystoke laughed. "Father, how long have we known each other—ten years? Do you think that, after all that time, I would betray you?"

Buckman was unmoved. "You have repeatedly made use of the woman, have you not? Clarenceux knows."

"It doesn't matter. The herald will soon be dead."

"You have given yourself over to debauchery. Your sinfulness endangers us all."

Greystoke lifted a hand in protest. "You yourself told me the Book of Deuteronomy permitted it. Anyway, threats have to be carried out or they are meaningless. You know that."

"I also know how near we are to winning—and losing—everything. Clarenceux entered the room from which I have conducted our affairs for the last three months—that is not to be tolerated. We will have to use different codes in future. It will take time to reestablish a secure system based on different texts with our friends in the North and in Scotland."

"I can see that."

Buckman moved away from the window and went to the bed. He lifted the mattress and took out a purse. "Clarenceux wants us to exchange the woman near Great Milton, in Oxfordshire."

"It's a ruse."

"Regardless, we will have to prove his wife and daughter are alive, so you will have to take them." He counted out two gold and four silver coins and handed them to Greystoke. "Travel as man and wife, now that you've started treating her as one. You'll excite less attention with the girl. And take the women to help."

67

Clarenceux and Thomas arrived on horseback at the King's Gate of Whitehall Palace at three in the afternoon. The fine morning had given way to patchy gray skies; a rare shaft of sunlight beat down for a moment, then disappeared behind a cloud. One solitary boy, Ralph Cleaver, was on duty, standing by the gate, warming his fingers under his arms. Clarenceux dismounted, gave the reins to Thomas, and addressed the boy.

"I need to speak to Sir William."

Ralph bowed. "I do not know where he is at this exact moment, sir, but I can escort you to the door, where you will be attended. What is your name?"

"How long have you been here?" asked Clarenceux.

"One week, sir."

"No gloves yet?" Clarenceux asked. But the boy said nothing. "Lead on, if you know the way."

Ten minutes later, he and Cecil were walking alongside the River Thames within the garden of the privy palace. Wherries and skiffs peppered the water. On the far bank, trees reached the waterline, adorning the graceful curve of the river.

"I hear news of what will happen almost hourly," said Cecil, leaning on a brick wall and looking across the river. "As things stand, we expect the royal couple to meet at Kirk o' Field in four days' time. If that holds true, then no doubt we will hear in eleven or twelve days that one has seized the other. After that, it will just be a matter of time before the victim dies mysteriously in captivity."

"Sir William, the Scottish royal family's plots against each other have little to do with me. I expect not to be alive in eleven days." He closed his eyes. Saying the words to Cecil made them true, and irrevocable.

Sir William looked at him. "This is not like you, William, my friend. Are you ill?"

Clarenceux shook his head. A tear escaped and he wiped it away, angry with himself for revealing this emotion. "No." He paused while he regained his composure. "Not long ago, you said that one day I would write the letter that begins 'Dear Awdrey...' Tomorrow I am going to write that letter. I don't know where she is, or even whether she will ever receive it, but I am going to write it. More than that, I am going to do my best, Sir William, my very best, to make good all the suffering I have caused her. Ultimately I was the cause of it all. I did one thing, just one thing—I accepted Henry Machyn's chronicle that night three years ago—and all her anguish follows from that. The time has come to write that letter."

Cecil watched a swan gliding gracefully by. "I wish we had some wine."

"I apologize, Sir William. Sincerely I do. But it has to be done. I deluded myself once that at any time I could end all this by destroying myself and the document publicly. Then I saw that I could do so and take a few of my enemies with me. It was still something for the future, unreal. But having heard that Greystoke has raped Awdrey..." Clarenceux hit the top of the wall. "When I heard that, I knew that what had at first been just a wild fantasy had become the best strategy. If it works, Awdrey will be free and well, and so will our daughters, who need her. And my family will never have to face this terror again."

"Don't be a fool, William. Your daughters need you too. So does Awdrey."

"The only thing they need me for is to get them out of the trap that I—I, mark you—let them fall into. They might need me, but they need their freedom much more—and the safety in which to enjoy it."

The swan elegantly avoided a collision with a wherry, paddling to one side. "Don't think like that. You cannot afford to."

Clarenceux stared across to the trees on the far bank. "You know how you live your life, daily, as if nothing changes, and then suddenly one day you realize that your way of life has become a denial: your life *has* changed. You have to adapt, suddenly. Whether it is because of growing old, or falling ill, or discovering that you have enemies or your wife does not love you, or another woman does love you—you change your life accordingly. And when it happens, you become aware that you cannot pretend anymore. Things that you once put a high value on have become meaningless. Pretense gets in the way of life; only the truth matters. You need to adjust to the new reality, to have a new way of settled living—until change is forced on you again."

Looking down at his hands, he saw his knuckles were scuffed and bleeding—he did not recall how or why.

"I remember when all this started, and the reason I opened the door to Henry Machyn that day. I felt that I should not have to put up with the humiliation of running from the authorities on account of my faith. I thought that I should set an example and be true to myself.

When Henry asked me to look after that document, it was my pride and sense of self-worth that made me accept."

"And now?"

"That pride leaves me cold. It means nothing to me. My soul is a flayed thing, stripped of its skin, which was my hope. I am raw, naked, dying. Like a tree with no bark."

A breeze blew across the river and ruffled Clarenceux's hair. From behind them in the palace there came the routine shout of a captain ordering a hesitant man-at-arms to do something. And then the silence was again broken by nothing but the wind and the lapping of the Thames.

"I am sorry," said Cecil finally. "I am sorry for you and for Awdrey, and for your daughters. And for the people who have suffered over the years—Henry Machyn, and his widow, and others. I might be in a privileged position, and elevated above the detail of what most people would call daily life; nevertheless, the details of people's lives do affect me, and their tragedies touch me no less. In some ways, being powerful and influential at court, I am *dis*empowered. Too many things are kept from me, although I do my very best to learn what is going on."

"Sir William, I came here not to trouble you with regrets and sadness but for a practical thing. I need your help. I am going to hand over the Percy-Boleyn marriage agreement. Not to you but to Greystoke, or Buckman, or whoever has abducted my wife. If something goes wrong with my plan, it is vital that whoever receives that document is not allowed to get away with it. If they escape me, then Walsingham and his men must be on hand to seize them. I will leave written instructions with you in advance, when I know when this will happen. But Walsingham will have only two or three days' notice.

He needs fifty men ready to surround a house in Oxfordshire which I intend to set alight with the document on the inside."

"God's wounds, William. You push me to the limit of my patience. Where will you be when you have betrayed her majesty, not to mention me and all our loyal friends?"

"I will be guarding the document."

"You mean to burn yourself?"

"I will not be the first."

Cecil turned away in frustration. He shook his head. "I always knew you would put your family first, before the kingdom and even before your faith. But I did not imagine you would plan to do it so... dangerously, so foolishly."

"It is the only way—unless you can persuade her majesty to accept the document publicly from me in the Guildhall, with all the assembled dignitaries of the city and the Catholic gentry present. Even then—no. Now they would just kill Awdrey and Mildred if that were to happen."

"I will always support her majesty—even over my family." Cecil stared at Clarenceux. "I wish you were of the same disposition. You can see now, I hope, why I trust Walsingham more than you. His loyalty is as unmovable as my own."

Clarenceux stared back. "Mr. Walsingham also takes risks. You might not see them, but he does. Mark my words, Sir William, your future and the Queen's security depend on my calculation of the risks, not Mr. Walsingham's."

68

It was late afternoon by the time Clarenceux arrived at Cecil House to see Annie. Tempted by the offer of chicken baked in a pie and venison pasties, he stayed longer than he had intended, dining with Annie and the servant looking after her. He relished every second of the meeting, hearing her laugh and watching her run around and smile. The wound in her shoulder was now much healed, and she was sprightly and bouncing again, playing with little Robert Cecil whenever Lady Cecil allowed. Only when she thought of her mother did the sadness overcome her.

As he walked home that evening in the darkness, very slowly, Clarenceux puzzled over Cecil's line about Greystoke. It still made no sense to him. Cecil trusted Walsingham, who trusted Greystoke, who trusted Buckman. How could that be? Where was the wrongly placed trust? Surely it had to be between Walsingham and Greystoke, for even Walsingham would never condone what Greystoke had done.

When he reached his home, he felt in the darkness for the keyhole and unlocked the door. He could hear Fyndern upstairs in the hall, clapping rhythmically and singing. He stopped; the occasional soft footfall could be heard. She was dancing for him. He glanced up; candlelight shone out of the door of the hall and across the landing.

"Good evening, Mr. Clarenceux," said Thomas, who was in the dark corridor at the foot of the stairs.

"This is hardly the time or the place for singing," said Clarenceux.

Thomas bowed his head. "No, sir. But I felt obliged, seeing as you had been so kind to each of them."

"I have my reasons for keeping them, Thomas. It is not just charity."

Clarenceux went up the stairs slowly but not quietly, so they would hear his footsteps on the wood. But neither did. They were still singing and dancing as he walked into the hall, which was filled with light. More than two dozen candles were burning.

Alice saw him and stopped instantly. Fyndern turned around.

"I do expect you to work while you are under my roof—and I would appreciate it if you would not dance or sing while the lady of the house is held captive by our enemies. And I absolutely forbid the use of more candles in a room than there are people. So many burning at once is risky, unnecessary, and a waste of money."

He strode across the room and started pinching out candles where he saw them. Fyndern and Alice, both ashamed, watched him until there were only three alight. One of these Clarenceux took with him and went up the stairs to his study. He filled his pen from the inkwell, pulled a piece of paper toward him, and wrote three names as headers: *Walsingham*, *Greystoke*, and *Buckman*, preparing to think through the possible relationships that bound these men.

After a couple of minutes he got up, opened the door, and bellowed down the stairs. "Fyndern, see Thomas and bring me two pints of wine."

It was going to be a long night.

69

Friday, February 7

Joan Hellier thumped on the door of the chamber with her fist at dawn. "Ready yourself, Mistress Harley. We all leave in a few minutes."

Awdrey was lying on the bed with her arm around Mildred. She sat up. *Could she be going home? Had William managed her release?* She tried to put such thoughts out of her mind but the anticipation of a change gave her hope. She went to the boarded-up shutters and looked through the crack, trying to see out. The vague light of the sky allowed only a dim view of the track and the barn nearby.

The shadowy silhouette of Helen appeared in the open doorway, holding a pile of clothes. "These are clean," she said. "Leave your old ones." She closed and bolted the door.

Awdrey went to the pile and felt them. There was a linen shift. Holding it up and tucking one end under her chin, she felt it was small: for Mildred. Further investigation revealed that a pile of clean clothes for Mildred were stacked on top of a pile for her. She took them to the bed, woke Mildred, and urged her to get dressed.

Ten minutes later, Joan opened the door to the chamber. "It is time to go," she said abruptly.

"Where are we going?"

"You don't need to know."

"Has someone spoken to my husband?" Awdrey asked. "Are we being taken to him?"

"He will receive his instructions tomorrow. After that, it is up to him."

Awdrey was deadened by this news. Nothing good was going to happen today. Her immediate reaction was to wish that he would remain steadfast and not give in to the ransom demand that awaited him. But she thought of Mildred. It was better that he forsake his principles, and betray Sir William, than Mildred be harmed. And what of Annie? Was she even alive? Quietly she took Mildred's hand and led her from the room that had been their cell for the last eight days.

In the hall of the house they gagged Awdrey, tied a scarf around her face, and bound her hands in front of her. When Joan approached Mildred with a length of rope, Helen shook her head and put her arm in front of her protectively. "There's no need," she said.

A coach waited in the cold air. Awdrey saw Greystoke, mounted on a high brown horse, his face masked. Two other men were also mounted and masked, and another man was at the front of the coach. Helen lifted Mildred up and placed her inside; Joan gestured for Awdrey to follow. When all three women and Mildred were inside, Joan locked the door and banged on the roof. The coach started to trundle down the track.

It was a carefully planned move. They had even filled the holes in the clay of the path with gravel.

70

Sarah Cowie carried the buck basket down the stairs to the kitchen of the house in Fleet Street. It was not heavy, simply large and unwieldy. The stones she had set in the bed of the fire were hot enough and the water in the cauldron was also hot, starting to steam. The smoke rose from the fire, mingled with the steam, and rose up the wide chimney. Walking out of the kitchen to the back of the yard, she picked up the washing tub and brought it in, setting it down near the fireplace. As she did so, she had a sudden memory of her mother scolding her as a girl for taking the hot water to the tub rather than the tub to the hot water, and spilling it on her feet. She used to say she had been both scolded and scalded that day.

This was a better place to be than the house in Islington. Here she was just a washerwoman—not a spy, not a killer, not a woman hurting another mother. Here she could just lose herself in her work and think about her daughters and their laughter, their smiles. She said a prayer for them, hoping desperately that they were well, and being fed and looked after. Tears came to her eyes and she wiped them away and crossed herself. The large, wide-mouthed cauldron was bubbling. It was far too heavy for her to lift so she used a wooden jug to decant hot water into the tub. When the tub was half full, the dirty linen went in, piece after piece.

She looked at what was left in the basket. Nine shirts, three pairs of hosen, and two pairs of socks. *Why do so few working men wear socks?* she wondered. *Their feet would smell much the better if they did.* She poured the lye into the tub and stirred the shirts around with a stick, pressing them to one side so they would not be burned. Picking up the tongs from beside the fire, she lifted the first hot stone and placed it into the water of the tub; it immediately bubbled with fury, steam rising. Going across the kitchen, she lifted down the scrubbing board from its hook on the wall and fished out the first shirt.

There was a movement. She looked up to see gray-bearded Jack Laney, one of Greystoke's men, staring at her from the doorway. Behind him was Tom Green. They came into the kitchen, descending the three steps without a word. Simon, a younger man with fair hair and a not unpleasant face, was behind them.

"Good morning," she said nervously.

"Good morning," replied Simon, equally nervous. The other two said nothing. Tom walked slowly around to stand between her and the back door.

"What are you doing?" she asked Tom, seeing the strange look on his face.

"I'm sorry, we have orders," explained Simon.

"What orders?" asked Sarah. "Who from?"

"Let us just get this done," said Tom.

"It is not as if anyone is going to come here," said Jack.

"What are you going to do?" asked Sarah, looking from face to face.

"Hold her down," said Tom.

"No!" screamed Sarah—but as that scream echoed in the kitchen, all three men rushed at her. She kicked as they manhandled her to the floor, and tried to bite Tom's hand, but Simon managed to get his arm around her neck and Jack took her legs out from under her. She continued to scream and fight but Simon squeezed her neck so tightly that her desperate call for help became more of a choked cry.

The scream did not go unheard. In the house next door, Mistress Knott heard it, and it troubled her. However, the Knotts had learned the hard way not to pry into their neighbors' affairs. Fyndern and Alice also heard the screams. They both sensed that something terrible was happening, and Fyndern felt he should do something—but what he could he do, as a boy? Mr. Clarenceux trusted him to stay in the house. Also, he was thankful that it was not Alice screaming. Last night he had had visions of her consumed in flames, her loveliness horrifically scorched. Sarah's scream was also heard by passersby in the street; they too did not wish to impose themselves on a domestic affair of which they knew nothing. After all, it was every man's right to beat his wife, as long as he did not actually kill her; why should they intervene? It would take time to find the constable and report the incident. And then, what would they say? They would have to admit it was none of their business.

71

Clarenceux returned from Cecil House not long before dusk. For the last couple of hours his thoughts had been flitting between the children's games Annie wanted to play and the business of establishing why Walsingham trusted Greystoke. He walked slowly. People were coming out of the city with their carts and packhorses, baskets and sacks. Fleet Street was filled with the smells of his neighbors' cooking.

All the shutters of the house opposite were closed.

Two women heaved baskets of vegetables toward him, returning to their cottages from the city. Four boys of various ages pulled wooden sledges piled with crates of cabbages, the older ones taunting the younger. Clarenceux suddenly had an idea. He stood, watching the boys, smelling the cooking smells. He looked back toward Cecil House and began to hurry in that direction. His hip ached and he slowed to as fast a walk as he could manage. At Cecil House he started to run again despite the pain, and gasped to the usher as he entered the hall. He knew Sir William was not at home but that did not matter. "Sir William's library," he said hurriedly. "Show me up to Sir William's library—now!"

Clarenceux heaved himself up the staircase, pulling himself up with the handrail. The usher followed him. They turned left, and he waited for the usher to open the door. Inside he went straight past the portrait of Sir William to the books. He searched the alphabetical arrangement from the start and found what he wanted. He pulled it off the shelf, opened it and read:

Trattato di
Scientia d'Arme, con un Dia
logo di filosofia di
Camillo Agrippa
Milanese
In Roma per Antonio Blado Stampadore Apostolica
M.D.LIII.
Con priuilegio della Santita di nostro
Signore Papa Guilio III.
Per anni dieci.

He slowly closed the book and replaced it on the shelf.

At least now he knew.

72

Saturday, February 8

Clarenceux awoke with Thomas opening the shutters to his chamber. He had no idea how long he had slept—but it was not as long as he needed. He blinked in the light.

"Sir Gilbert Dethick is here to see you," said Thomas.

Clarenceux assessed his wine-night-befuddled mind, shielded his eyes, and raised himself on one arm. He remembered the promise he had given Dethick—to set out on Tuesday. *Damnation!* But that promise seemed like a small wave sipping at the shore compared to the great, mountain-high wave approaching. That was what forced him to get out of the bed, to grab his doublet and throw it over his shirt, and take his sword. Fyndern was by the door, holding it open. Clarenceux strode past him, with his sheathed sword in his left hand.

"Sir Gilbert," he called to the old man on his horse, "I acknowledge my fault. But there is nothing I can do. My wife has not returned, nor my daughter. Nothing you can say will persuade me that I should neglect them to undertake a visitation."

Sir Gilbert looked coldly at Clarenceux. "A man came to me at the College this morning. He did not give his name. He told me that I was to deliver this message to you. He said: 'Tell Mr. Clarenceux that if he wishes to see his wife and daughter again, he is to bring the document to Oxford and hand it to the gatekeeper of St. John's College, addressed to William Willis, and to do it before noon on the feast of St. Valentine. If he fails, to them shall be done what has been done to the traitor in the house opposite.'" Dethick's horse was skittish, and he pulled on the reins, turning it. "I want none of this, Clarenceux. I have delivered that message, even though I am no one's errand boy. And now I deliver my own. Do what you are obliged to do, without further delay."

Clarenceux looked from Sir Gilbert to the door of the closed house. "This man who spoke to you, what did he look like?"

"Does it matter? He was short, fair-haired, about thirty years of age."

"And he mentioned something done to a traitor in the house opposite?"

"I still expect you to set out on the visitation," said Dethick, "although I pardon you the delay. We may not like each other, Mr. Clarenceux, but I respect that a man's priorities are not always those of his profession."

Clarenceux looked at Fyndern, then at Thomas. He turned back to Dethick. "Mr. Garter, I will set out tomorrow. It seems that my private life as well as my profession demands that I ride into Oxfordshire. I will not take any clerks or pursuivants—not on this journey—just my own servants. However, I would ask one thing of you. Will you accompany me across the road?"

Dethick raised an eyebrow. "Across the road? Into the house?"

"Have you any idea what is in there?"

"Your business is your own business," replied Dethick, and he turned as if to ride on. Fyndern, however, stepped swiftly in front of him and took hold of the bridle.

"Let go, boy!" shouted Dethick "Give me my way!"

"A moment of your time, I beg you, Mr. Garter."

Dethick glanced at the house and, after glaring fiercely at Clarenceux, dismounted.

The door was unlocked. But no sooner did Clarenceux push it open than the stench hit him. It rushed out of the darkness of the house to smother them and stick its soft, swollen fingers down their throats. Boiled and scorched meat was the smell that greeted them—but so overpoweringly that it was far worse than the smell of an unventilated kitchen. Clarenceux gagged, but covering his face with a hand, he proceeded cautiously along the dim corridor inside, aiming for the light of the kitchen at the end.

He stopped at the top of the steps leading down into the kitchen. Dethick stood at his shoulder; Thomas was behind him. A ghastly sight lay before them. A woman's headless body lay in the middle of the room—her upper part front down, prone across an upturned tub, her lower limbs on the floor, still kneeling. Clarenceux recognized the dirty russet-colored dress that Sarah Cowie had worn when she had called at his house. To the left was a large fireplace on which stood a cauldron. It had boiled dry but it still contained what was left of the woman's head.

Clarenceux walked into the room feeling nauseous. Behind him he heard Dethick stumbling out, retching. In the cauldron he saw the loose dark hair stuck to the metal and patches of skull exposed where parts of the flesh had fallen from the bone.

There was much fat and swollen white skin. The jaw had loosened and the lips come away, revealing the roots of the teeth in the skull. The eye sockets were emptied where the eyeballs had burst open. On seeing this, coupled with the smell of the boiled flesh, Clarenceux had to turn away.

In the army, at Boulogne, more than two decades earlier, he had watched a surgeon disembowel and dismember a dead man—and then carefully boil each limb in a large cauldron, so the clean bones could be taken back to England for burial. But that had been done formally and properly, in the open air, and for a solemn reason. It had been an unpleasant exercise, but it had been motivated by honor and respect. This was quite the opposite: a horrific thing intended only to put fear into him, and one that dishonored the murdered woman.

He crossed himself and left the kitchen.

Outside, he blinked in the light. He walked to Fyndern and took the reins of Dethick's horse. "Go and find the constable. Tell him a woman has been murdered in a house in Fleet Street and that her head has been boiled. Her name was Sarah Cowie. Say that the house is in the tenancy of one John Greystoke, a man in the employment of Mr. Francis Walsingham."

"Sir, I will. May I look first?"

"If you feel you must."

Dethick was leaning against the front wall of the building, looking green.

"Sir Gilbert, I will set out on my visitation tomorrow."

Dethick straightened himself. He took the reins of his horse and mounted. He said nothing but pulled on the reins and rode slowly back toward the College.

After they had given evidence to the coroner, Clarenceux and Thomas took the horses for exercise. They rode silently beyond Islington and as far as Stoke Newington, returning by way of the main road to the city. The Tower of London, the cathedral tower, and all the lesser steeples of the city bristled against the horizon as they rode back southward. They passed a flock of sheep on the road, and a man carting chickens into the capital. A timber cart was stuck on the side, its wheel broken by a deep rut. Thomas sensed Clarenceux's anger from his rigid posture and his knuckles as he clutched the reins.

Across the sky was a pale golden light, as if the sun was trying to break through the clouds but was forbidden from shining on the city today. At Kingsland, Clarenceux deliberately rode off the highway toward an enclosure of cows, over some rough land that was the vestige of a common. There he stopped and dismounted, and walked along a narrow path, leading Brutus to a wider area, where the trees surrounded a grassy mound and a small stream ran nearby. He let Brutus nibble at the grass on the mound and stood still, looking at the stream and across the fields.

Neither man spoke. Thomas believed that he knew what his master was thinking, yet at the same time he knew that these thoughts were going further, building higher, digging deeper. The man had been crushed into the darkest corner of his soul—and yet he was still unconquered.

"I am going to bring it to an end, Thomas. There is no other way."

"Sir, forgive me—what do you mean?"

In the distance, the city bells began to ring the hour.

"I am going to destroy all my enemies and the document."

"How, Mr. Clarenceux?"

"After we return home, I want you to go into the city and buy two more horses and a cart. I also want you to go to Mr. Carstens, the Dutch apothecary that Mr. Knott uses, and buy as much gunpowder as he can sell you. A whole keg—two, if he has so much. When you have the gunpowder and the cart, I want you to bore a couple of holes in the bottom of that iron-bound oak chest in the old shop and take it to Thame Abbey. I will give you detailed instructions."

He stared across the fields, listening to the noise of the stream. A shaft of sunlight broke through the clouds and cut its way through the leaves of the trees.

Clarenceux continued, "When the day comes, you will wait at an inn in Thame, the Saracen's Head. I will tell the captors to take Awdrey and Mildred there. You will then send me a date as a code, via Alice. If it is them, choose an even number; but if there is bad news, make the month a winter one. If they are dead, choose the present day's date."

"You don't worry that you are being too hasty?"

"I would sooner bring down the judgment of Hell and all its dark angels *now*, and destroy my enemies *now*, than let them ruin another life. Or allow them the luxury of planning their next move. Do not get me wrong; I have been thinking and planning a long while now. I will hand over the document to the people who have stolen Awdrey from me—and I will do it in person. They will not be able to leave with it until I hear she is safe. But when I do hear…that is when I will destroy the building and everything in it."

"But Mr. Clarenceux—that means you too will be destroyed."

Clarenceux turned to face him. "Think about Awdrey. Think about my daughters. I have no doubt that they will grieve for me— but their lives are at stake. I want my daughters to have a chance of life and that requires me to risk everything, including my own life."

"But Mr. Claren—"

Clarenceux held up a hand. "Thomas, no more. Your part in my plan is going to be vital. It has to be done, so let us do it well."

73

Sunday, February 9

The remains of Sarah Cowie were interred in the morning. The chaplain said a few prayers in the church, heard only by Clarenceux. A woman had cleaned out the cauldron and sewn the remains of the head into a leather budget; she had washed and prepared the headless corpse for its shroud, but she had no wish to attend the funeral. She accepted her money from Clarenceux and left.

After the interment in the cemetery of St. Bride's, Clarenceux spoke to the chaplain. He looked into the grave and crossed himself, aware that the gravediggers were nearby, anxious to fill it in. The chaplain too wanted to go. Clarenceux closed his eyes and fumbled in a pocket. He pulled out some coins.

"You do not know this, Mr. Bowring, but that woman had a secret. She was compromised by a Catholic woman in the north who thought that by forcing women to carry out her acts of terror, she could avoid arousing suspicion. But in using Sarah, that Catholic woman miscalculated. Not every thief is without conscience. And Sarah especially had compassion. Her fall was that she once gave into temptation: she stole some plates and other pewter things worth a total of four shillings and two pence. I would like to atone for that, her original crime, and donate to one of the altars the same sum for the benefit of her soul."

Bowring looked sternly at Clarenceux. "Mr. Clarenceux, we do not maintain altar funds as we used to in the old days. It is against the law. And if she was a thief…"

"But, Mr. Bowring, please—for the benefit of her soul."

"I am quite sure that her soul is in Heaven or Hell as she deserves, Mr. Clarenceux, and there is nothing you can do about it now," he said, turning away.

"Then for the poor," implored Clarenceux, following him, trying to control his anger. "Can you accept it on behalf of her soul for the poor?" He put his left hand firmly on Bowring's shoulder to stop him. When Bowring turned around, Clarenceux held the coins up in his face. "For the poor—or have you forgotten them?"

"Very well," Bowring said coldly. "For the poor." He took the money. "Good day, Mr. Clarenceux. May the souls of all the departed rest in peace." He bowed and walked away across the churchyard.

Clarenceux silently said the words of the Lord's Prayer to himself, then went into the church and sat alone. He thought of Sarah Cowie's fate, and Rebecca Machyn's, and that of his servant Joan, and his wife's plight. Their suffering made him angry again, and helped him fix his mind on what he now had to do.

He would never again attend a service in this church. He looked up at the carved vine–entwined columns; after thirty years, he was going to leave forever. The place he sat in would be occupied by someone else. His place as Clarenceux would be taken by someone else. The idea of dying seemed not an end of himself but so many pieces of his identity falling apart. There would still be someone living in his house, someone sitting in his place in church, someone acting as Clarenceux: it was just that that person would have a different heart. What was in his mind would disperse, and what mattered of his life would be continued through his daughters, even though they did not see what he saw or know what he knew. For a moment it seemed unambiguously clear, how unimportant knowledge was. Knowledge seemed just a means to an end, like his house or his possessions—not an end in itself.

He rose from the pew. After forty-eight years of life, most of it thinking and preparing, he had knowledge in abundance. If it *was* just a means to an end, he was going to put it to good use.

Back at his house, Clarenceux assisted Thomas in boring two holes in the base of the chest that he kept in the closed-up shop. He then helped him move it onto the cart that Thomas had bought. Fyndern had taken a shine to one of the new horses: a pretty young brown-and-white mare. Clarenceux watched him brushing the animal's coat and realized it was a long time since he had seen him with a pack of cards. There had been a change in him, a loss of desperation.

As Thomas and the boy rode away on the cart, Fyndern turned and waved.

74

~

Monday, February 10

Clarenceux awoke to hear movements in his daughter's bed-chamber. For one miraculous moment he believed that she was there, and that everything else—the shooting, the abductions, the killings—had all been a dream. Then he realized that the space where his wife slept was still empty; it was Alice in his daughter's bed, not Annie. It all came back to him. He wept and clenched his fist and beat the mattress, his mind focused on the image of the white-haired Greystoke; the lizardlike, blinking Maurice Buckman; and that old, bitter woman in the north, Lady Percy. He yearned wholeheartedly for their destruction.

He rose, opened the shutters, and went to the ewer. To his surprise it was not empty but full of clean water. He filled the basin and washed his face, neck, hands, and wrists, then his feet, and pulled off his shirt and washed his arms and armpits. There was a clean towel nearby; he dried himself. In the chest, when he looked, was a pile of clean shirts. *She will make someone a fine wife when she grows up,* he thought.

The morning was spent writing letters. Alone in his chamber, he cut a quill to the right shape and neatly made a central cut to draw the ink. The first letter he wrote was to Tom Griffiths, a tenant of his, who was always struggling with money; he forgave him the rent due. Next he wrote to his friend in Chislehurst, Julius Fawcett. In his letter he explained what he had decided to do and expressed his regret that they had not seen more of each other in the last year or so. Julius's friendship had meant much to him: their love of old things and past times had in truth not just been about the past but about a shared love of humanity. He added that he was going to bequeath all the chronicles left in his possession to the College of Arms but hoped that Julius would examine them first and select any that he particularly wanted for his own library.

The next three letters were business-related. He wrote to Sir Richard Wenman promising him the return of his chronicle soon. In a quick note to John Hooker of Exeter, he supplied some details of how he thought Sir Peter Carew might be able to claim the barony of Idrone in Ireland. He wrote also to Sir William Cecil, enclosing instructions for Walsingham. When that was done, he pushed away his chair and sat back, preparing to write to Awdrey.

Hungry, he went down to the kitchen and helped himself to some of Fyndern and Alice's bread. Looking for things to do, he helped Alice tidy the kitchen; he saw to Maud and Brutus in the stables; he even took out the first batch of letters and gave them to a messenger boy at the city gate to dispatch. But then, walking back over Fleet Bridge, the city bells started to ring. That letter had to be written now.

In fact, two last letters had to be written—one to Awdrey and the other to his sister-in-law in Devon. Both were difficult. He started writing one, then the other, and each time found himself overcome by emotion. Having torn them both up, he took another sheet and started again, and within minutes he was either crossing out words that did not express his feelings adequately or rubbing his face with his sleeve. The truth was that, as soon as he thought of Awdrey, he imagined Greystoke having her and felt sick. Only gradually did he push the image of the man away and see her as she was, and also rediscover himself as he had been before he became consumed by hatred for his enemies. Time passed. He wanted to write more—but the city clocks struck again, and it was time to bring the last letter to a close. He kissed the page, folded it, and sealed it with the seal on his desk.

It was done. Looking around his study, he saw the old familiar books in the book presses, some still damaged from Walsingham's searching of his house three years earlier. He got up and took the Old Testament he had read to Annie, kissed it, and said a short prayer for her, placing it flat on the table. He ran his fingers over Henry Machyn's chronicle. *What will they make of that strange document in the future?* he wondered. Finally, he handled his father's sword, remembering the bearded old man and his kindness, and set it down next to the Bible. *The time has come*, he thought. *My time has come.*

At Cecil House that afternoon, Annie wanted to play and talk and tell childish jokes. Clarenceux did not mind. For a few moments he was able to forget what was happening to him and enter into her world. Lady Cecil had given her a cat; it had brown and black stripes and sharp claws that dug into Clarenceux's shoulder when he picked it up. Annie was delighted. She had created a sleeping place for it inside her bed and named it Caxton. He had laughed when she said she had first thought of calling it Pursuivant. "Only a herald's daughter would think of that," he said.

Eventually he had to say it was time for him to go. He embraced her and told her he would not be able to visit again until Friday. But then he hoped to see her and Sir William. He did his very best to sound encouraging—and did not mention that Friday would be the last time they would see each other.

Alice helped him pack for the trip to Oxford. He in return looked through his wife's old clothes chest for a dress that Alice could wear. He selected a practical dark green one with a small amount of lace trimming at the neck and buttons on the sleeves. He found a high-crowned hat, a jupp, and a safeguard for her too, to keep her dry on the journey, and leather boots and linen socks. In clothes befitting a lady, Alice was indeed beautiful—but nothing was going to erase the image in Clarenceux's mind of her dancing in a black smock.

They rode together in silence for fifteen miles, he on Brutus, she on Maud. Dusk forced them to stop for the night at an inn in Uxbridge. Eating together by candlelight at the table in their chamber, he asked her more about her childhood. She told him that her parents were both dead, and her sister, who was younger, was living with an uncle—a violent man who beat her regularly. He terrified the girl so much she would sometimes shake and be incapable of moving, holding her hands over her face as he came close to her. And when he touched her, she went like stone—unable to cry out or even speak.

They drank more wine, but the alcohol drew them further apart. It made them more of what they were. Clarenceux became more serious, brooding on what lay ahead; Alice, more lighthearted, more conversational. She offered to dance for him. He shook his head. She danced anyway, performing the same routine in his wife's dress, barefoot, that he had seen her dance in the tavern. It was very different, seeing her dance privately; he had been astonished by her self-confidence in front of the crowd as much as her eroticism the first time. Without the crowd, her performance, in the light of just two candles, made him feel very uneasy. He turned away. What she was doing was captivating—and for that very reason he did not want to watch. The girl did not understand. She stopped and came over to him; she affectionately called him "a sad, old goat," and ran her fingers through his hair. He poured more wine for each of them.

As the fire in their chamber burned down and just a single candle was left alight, Clarenceux declared it time to sleep. He pulled out the truckle bed and dragged it into the middle of the room. Kneeling at the basin, they washed their hands and faces together, and he washed his mouth out, scrubbing his teeth with his finger. Alice glanced at him furtively, and when he had dried his hands, she came to him and turned her back to him, asking for help to undo the dress. He undid the topmost laces at the back. "More, please," she asked. Unwillingly, he obliged, ignoring her pale skin. Leaving her, he took off his boots, lifted the sheets and blankets, and lay down in the main bed, fully dressed.

Standing in the middle of the room in her smock, she smiled at him and walked very slowly to the bed. She put her hand on the counterpane. "I want to lie with you," she said.

Clarenceux turned over. "And I want to lie with my wife. We cannot all have what we want."

75

Shrove Tuesday, February 11

Alice was bright and friendly the following day, as if nothing had happened. She brought Clarenceux fresh water and joined him for a breakfast of bread and cheese before they left the inn. As they rode, the girl talked cheerfully about Halifax and how it was before the Dutch refugees had arrived, which had led to a rise in the level of hostility in the town. She told Clarenceux of the way they executed thieves there by beheading them with a wooden machine. This contained a wide blade set in a heavy block which descended along grooves in the side of the frame. The blade was raised high and the victim placed underneath, with his hands tied. Everyone from the town—or as many as could get near—took a part in the act of pulling on the rope that removed the peg holding up the blade. The latter descended with a huge rush—so forcefully it could easily sever a bull's head.

Clarenceux said little as they rode, half listening to Alice and half thinking ahead. He liked the sound of her voice, however, and he liked to see her smile; so when the conversation dried up, he asked her another question to encourage her to talk. She chattered on about the tavern where she had grown up, and how she had helped her father from an early age to carry tankards of ale and beer to the men in the hall. She clarified that he was actually her stepfather; she had no recollection of her real father, who had died when she was young.

"What about your sisters and brothers?" asked Clarenceux.

"I have just one sister now," she replied in a matter-of-fact way. "I used to have an older brother but he died when he was two, before I was born. My older sisters also died. Only my younger sister still lives. But she is badly treated by our stepfather, as I told you before."

"Before, you said she was with an uncle who treated her badly. You said he left her unable to move or speak."

"Did I?" She smiled. "I sometimes do say that—to stop people asking questions. If a man is mistreating you, and he should be looking after you, it doesn't really matter if he is your father or your uncle, does it?"

"A father abusing his daughter is quite another thing from an uncle abusing his niece. Both are reprehensible but one is more abhorrent because of a father's duty to his offspring."

"Is that so?" Alice asked with sharpness. Almost immediately she softened her tone. "Yes, I suppose it is. After all, we are taught to honor our fathers and mothers; the Bible says nothing about uncles."

The sun that had shone in the morning disappeared behind billowing white clouds and then layers of gray that stretched away to the horizon and beyond. The people they met on the road were hurrying, with their packhorses and carts.

"What sort of tavern was it?"

"Do you mean did we serve beer or wine? Or do you mean was it the sort of place where the women of the house spent every night flat on their backs with a customer between their thighs?"

"I am sorry I asked."

"But you did ask, and here is my answer. From the age of thirteen I was occasionally offered to men. It was expected of me. If your mother is doing all the hard work in the tavern—all the cleaning, the feeding of the family, making the clothes, serving beer to the customers, and, on top of that, having to make money when necessary from pleasuring men—you've got to help out. And when you start, when you're young, men pay very well, which makes you feel good when you want to help your family."

"How did your clients not get you with child?"

"A sponge, soaked in vinegar. My mother showed me how to cut it correctly, so they don't feel it. It never failed."

"There are a lot of confusing things about your past," said Clarenceux eventually.

"Are there?" replied Alice, looking straight ahead. "You must realize I make most of them up."

The admission astonished Clarenceux. It left him lost for words.

"Most of them?" he asked eventually.

"Some of them. The sponge is true."

"You sound as if you do not regret the years of fornication in the tavern."

Alice laughed. "Years of *fornication*," she repeated, mocking him. "Mr. Clarenceux, my art is that of pleasuring men. And like any art, one gains a large degree of satisfaction in performing it well."

Clarenceux turned to her. "Your art now is that of looking after my household. Cleaning. Going to market. Providing food."

They rode on in silence. The clouds approaching were darker, and the air had turned colder, presaging rain. Sure enough, it began to spit. Rooks holding forth with their harsh *croark-croarks* in the trees nearby flew up all at once.

"I am sorry if I have offended you," she said.

"Offended me? I just don't know whether to believe you," he replied.

"Why do you need to *believe* me? Isn't it enough just to like what I say?"

Clarenceux felt old. He longed to be with his wife, to talk to her, hold her. She understood him. She was conscientious, considerate, and womanly—all the things that this girl was not. He longed to hear Awdrey's voice. He had not been himself without her. He had been changed into a sullen and bad-tempered man, angry and fearful. He had to make an effort to be himself, and to find the generosity in his nature.

"The truth is, you frighten me," said Alice.

It was Clarenceux's turn to be amused. "Frighten you? You are such a force of nature, with such a perfect understanding of this sinful world, that I am surprised you know the meaning of the word."

"Some women will always be the friend and daughters of bad men, and they will understand hard drinking, avaricious, lustful, violent men more than good ones, and they will look at men like you and be afraid. All I can do to get level with you is seek your weaknesses. When women like me find them, we work on them, like cracks in a stone, eventually breaking them open. But you seem to have no weaknesses, Mr. Clarenceux. You are too good a man. Worryingly good."

Clarenceux rode on. "I have my weaknesses, Alice. A whole regiment of them. The Lord knows I do."

They rode into Thame that evening. In the yard of the Saracen's Head, Simeon greeted them and led them through to the hall. He did not even raise an eyebrow at the youth of Clarenceux's companion; only later, when Clarenceux had a moment to explain discreetly, did the innkeeper acknowledge that it did not seem proper for a gentleman to be traveling alone with such a young "maiden."

After nightfall, Fyndern and Thomas arrived. Thomas gave an account of what had been done at Thame so far. It had taken more time than they had anticipated to draw the cart and the chest all the way from London to the abbey—they had only arrived that afternoon. They would set the timber in place tomorrow, but the bolts on the refectory door were firmly in place. The chest itself was situated where Clarenceux had stipulated, and the gunpowder had been arranged as he had directed.

Clarenceux sat on a bench beside the fire in the chamber, cradling a goblet of wine. Thomas was not far away, drinking beer, looking into the glowing embers and the small flames licking around a new log. Fyndern and Alice were downstairs in the hall.

"Do you intend to go through with it?" asked Thomas.

"People in the last reign went to the stake because of what they believed," said Clarenceux. "Who am I, and what am I, if I do not risk the same fate for what I believe *and* for those I love, and for whom I am responsible? I admit I am scared, Thomas; I don't know how I will face it. So I don't think about it. If I die, I will die a free man, and I will have liberated Awdrey. But even if I live, William Harley, Clarenceux King of Arms, will die in that building."

Thomas swallowed. "We will not meet again, even if you live?"

"No."

"Then that is the way it must be," said Thomas.

"You will still serve Awdrey, after I am gone? And my daughters?"

Thomas lifted his beer and drank. "I am surprised you can think otherwise. If you are going to risk your life, the least I can do is continue to serve."

"Alice said a strange thing today. We were riding together and talking about her childhood, and she confessed to me that some of the things she said were made up. When the conversation moved on, I told her that I didn't know whether to believe her or not. To which she replied 'Why do you need to believe me? Isn't it enough just to like what I say?' I have been thinking about that since. Belief is what sets us apart from other animals in Creation—and that goes for truth as well as faith in God. Alice is like the untamed birds that twitter with joy and gladden our hearts, or suddenly shriek in alarm and make us fearful."

"Do you trust her?"

"To a point. In some ways she is very knowing and in others very ignorant and frivolous. Perhaps she is not from Halifax, as she says; perhaps that accent comes from a manor nearer Sheffield. But we do not send children to hang. Lady Percy recruited her women from the jails—women who were all mothers and who all had been sentenced to death. Alice does not count on either score, even if she does come from Yorkshire."

"Fyndern is besotted with her."

"Poor Fyndern. She is after someone bigger, richer, and more powerful than he will ever be. And when she has ensnared her prey, she still will not be satisfied—she has ambitions."

"Most women surrender their ambitions when they fall pregnant," said Thomas.

"She even has a strategy for that."

76

Ash Wednesday, February 12

As Clarenceux and Alice approached Oxford the next morning, the puddles in the roads were covered by a thin layer of ice. On the higher ground, a veil of white frost had been laid. Their breath billowed in the chill air.

Across the common to their left they watched as a boy rounded up the flock of forty sheep in his care; he whistled to his dog to bring them in when they started to dart in the direction of a copse. Ahead, a leather-capped husbandman was driving a pair of cows along the highway. The cows were in no hurry, nor was their driver; Clarenceux and Alice rode past. Further along, they overtook a cart-load of eggs being transported in crates of hay—the driver steadying the horse and veering around anything that might damage his delicate cargo.

Oxford itself appeared, with its college towers and four or five church spires. The large open fields gave way to smaller enclosures, with barns and farmhouses plotted at the ends of muddy lanes, and small cottages nearer the highway. Alice had been full of conversation earlier in the morning, and as they drew close to the city, she spoke with even more vivacity. *This is her true territory*, thought Clarenceux, *a place of people*.

They crossed the bridge and passed Magdalen College. Under the gaze of the tall gatehouses and handsome stone buildings, the girl suddenly fell quiet. Oxford was like no place that she knew, and whereas she had chatted excitedly at the prospect of coming into a new city, she was intimidated by this one. The stone college buildings shut out the stranger, being built around quadrangles with small windows that squinted meanly at the outside world and large windows that gazed approvingly on themselves. Riding through Broad Street, she stared at the walls and windows—she had never seen quite so much glass, not even in London. The students caught her eye too; many young men in academic dress walked toward them along the side of the street and her gaze followed them. *Who could teach the other the most?* Clarenceux wondered.

As they turned into St. Giles, Clarenceux looked ahead: on the right was their destination, the frontage of St. John's College, with its central stone gatehouse rising three stories above a handsome pointed arch. He dismounted and handed the reins to Alice. Without a word, he unbuttoned his doublet and reached inside for the package: *William Willis, St. John's College* was written in large letters on the front.

He said nothing but walked to the gate and called into the shadows of a door to the side. A stooped, broken-toothed man of about sixty shuffled out.

"Eh?" he grunted.

"For William Willis," said Clarenceux, holding out the package.

The old man stared at it, not understanding. He looked at Clarenceux again. "No—there's no one of that name in this college."

"I believe a Mr. Willis will collect this on Friday, the fourteenth. It is very important—make sure it is kept safely." He handed him a coin.

"I will, sir. What did you say your name was?"

"Harley, William Harley."

"I will look after it," said the old man, accepting the package and shuffling back into the gloom.

—⸙◎

Riding away from St. John's College, Clarenceux just looked straight ahead. It was done now. They did not say a word until they had left the town along the same road by which they had arrived.

"What was that package you handed over?" asked Alice, as they passed the boy with the sheep on the common for the second time.

"An invitation to a duel," said Clarenceux. "No—a command to one."

77

Thursday, February 13

The evening of the following day, they arrived back in London. At Thame they had inspected Thomas and Fyndern's work and then left, abandoning the cart and riding back toward London all together. They stayed one night in Chipping Wycombe, where Alice was shocked to realize that Clarenceux expected them to observe the fasting rules of Lent—no meat, not even eggs—and Clarenceux was mildly surprised to discover that Alice expected to be able to flout such rules. Fyndern listened to the debate about the restrictions on eating meat in Lent, and Clarenceux's arguments based on Church law; and when Clarenceux had answered all of Alice's questions, he asked: "Isn't the fasting law made by Parliament, not the Church?" Clarenceux had swiftly changed the subject.

Thursday morning had been so wet they had delayed setting out, watching the rain come sheeting down from the east. After three hours, it started to ease but did not stop; nevertheless, Clarenceux ordered them to ride. There was a schedule to keep to, he reminded them, and they were still thirty miles from London. Within an hour, each one of them was soaked to the skin. The sound of the rain pattering on the ground and on the leaves of trees was depressing enough, but the rumble of thunder in the distance hinted at worse to come. Not until midafternoon did they enter Uxbridge, where Clarenceux bought four more leather riding cloaks before setting out again. They ate at an inn in Knightsbridge. Alice and Fyndern did the talking and Clarenceux silently dipped a piece of bread in his chicken broth, watching them beneath a furrowed brow.

At nine o'clock they arrived back at Clarenceux's house. They led all the horses into the stable, stumbling through puddles as the rain splashed down in the yard. Fyndern, who knew the stables best, settled the horses in the darkness while Thomas lit the fire in the hall, striking a flint against a steel edge and igniting the dried lichen. Clarenceux went to his room to change his clothes, feeling his way up the stairs. Alice similarly felt her way to where she knew there was a towel, and then came back down to the hall, rubbing her hair.

Half an hour later, the misery of the journey was forgotten. The fire was alight and the hall illuminated by four golden candles; the wet cloaks and capes were drying. Clarenceux had offered wine, and Fyndern had brought up a flagon from the buttery filled with a strong French red. The smell of the burning wood and the wine created a rich atmosphere.

"Let us hear music," said Clarenceux, at a quiet moment. "Alice, will you sing to us?"

"I am not a singer, Mr. Clarenceux. I can dance but I will not sing."

"I will sing," said Fyndern. After a nervous smile, he got off the bench and knelt, looking at the fire, and began to sing an old song they all knew in a fine voice—not wavering like that of a boy whose voice is breaking, nor yet like the full-bodied voice of a grown man, but hitting the notes cleanly and sustaining them, giving the depth of purity to the solemn old song.

There were three ravens sat on a tree
Down and down, sing, down and down
And they were black as black may be
With a down;
One of them said to his mate
"Where shall we our breakfast take?"
With a down, down, derry-down down.

Down in yonder green field
Down and down, sing, down and down
There lies a knight slain under his shield
With a down;
His hounds lie at his feet
So well do they their master keep
With a down, down, derry-down down.

His hawks they fly so eagerly by
Down and down, sing, down and down
No other bird dare him come nigh
With a down;
Down there comes a fallow doe
So heavy with young as she may go
With a down, down, derry-down down.

She lifted up his bloody head
Down and down, sing, down and down
And kissed his wounds that were so red
With a down;
She got him up upon her back

And carried him to earthen dark
With a down, down, derry-down down.

She buried him before the prime
Down and down, sing, down and down
But she was dead herself before even-time
With a down;
God send every gentleman
Such hawks, such hounds and such women
With a down, down, derry-down down.
With a down, down, derry-down down.

As the last note died away, there was an awed silence. Eventually Thomas spoke. "You have yet another gift, Fyndern."

"It was exquisite," said Alice.

Fyndern rose from his knees. "Thank you."

Alice put her hand on his shoulder as he sat back on the bench and smiled at him. She almost immediately followed this by leaning across him and giving him a kiss on the cheek.

"There is something magical about you, young man," said Clarenceux. "Long may it last."

Silence fell again. The fire crackled. Thomas lifted a pewter goblet to his lips and sipped. Everyone waited for Clarenceux to speak.

"You all now know that I have in my possession an extremely valuable document. You all know, more or less, how dangerous it is. At Thame, I intend to hand it over to John Greystoke, to buy my wife's freedom. We will ride first thing on Saturday and stay at the Saracen's Head on Sunday night. Thomas will stay at the inn; Fyndern will go on ahead to the abbey that night. Alice, you will ride with me to the abbey on Monday at noon. I will need you to be my messenger."

Thomas gave Clarenceux a searching look. "What if Greystoke does not turn up?"

"He will be there. His life depends on it."

Thomas's already deeply lined forehead was made even more so by a frown. "Mr. Clarenceux, are you sure? *Greystoke's* life?"

"Think. Why does Walsingham trust him so much? It is not because they are old friends. It is not because they met in Padua ten years ago. Walsingham would not give two farthings for that if he had even the slightest doubt of his loyalty—and Walsingham doubts everyone. He trusts him because Greystoke has promised to obtain the document for him. If Greystoke does not do what he promised, Walsingham will have him killed."

"But why is Greystoke working for Walsingham?" asked Fyndern. "I thought he was working for Buckman."

"That's the mistake I made," said Clarenceux. "He is not working for Walsingham—merely pretending to. He is using Walsingham; each one is using the other. But if Walsingham knew the truth, he would have him killed straight away. Greystoke spent four years learning swordsmanship with Camillo Agrippa. Agrippa is from Milan but he resides in Rome. When he published his book in 1553, he had it printed by the pope's own printer. Do you think a man like Agrippa would take on a Protestant pupil? And train him for four years, in Rome? No Protestant would have risked even living in Rome for that long, let alone attending swordsmanship classes with a champion of the Catholic Church— and an Englishman could hardly have avoided detection, even if he could quote Dante in Italian. When Walsingham met Greystoke in Padua, he presumed he was an English Protestant; that was reasonable, for in 1556, every town under the administration of the Republic of Venice was full of English émigrés fleeing from Mary's persecution. But Greystoke was not there as a Protestant émigré; he was there as a Catholic spy, feeding intelligence back to his masters in Rome."

"He serves Buckman then. Is that not what we thought all along?" asked Alice.

"The chain of deceit goes both ways. Buckman is using Greystoke for the same reason Walsingham is—to get close to me. But despite its symmetry, there is no beauty in this architecture of intrigue. All the monsters are feeding off each other. As soon as I hand over that document, the fragile bonds of trust will fall apart. Buckman will expect Greystoke to hand it over to him so he can deliver it to Lady Percy. Walsingham will expect Greystoke to deliver it to him so he can hand it to Sir William Cecil."

"It will be interesting to see who he chooses," said Fyndern.

"He won't choose either of them. He is going to take it to Rome."

"Rome!" Alice exclaimed.

"That is where his true loyalty lies. My mistake for so long was to think that all the Catholics were on the same side and working together. They are not. This isn't a two-way fight; it's a three-way one. Father Buckman and Lady Percy are loyal to Lord Henry Stewart; they look to him to restore Catholicism in England. Greystoke is for Rome and Queen Mary of Scots. The forces of her majesty Queen Elizabeth are the third element. On Monday I am going to burn the document they all seek. Neither of the Catholic sides can allow that to happen. It is like a strategically important bridge that they cannot allow to fall into an enemy's hands and yet cannot afford to see destroyed either. As it happens, all three sides expect Greystoke to obtain the document for them. That is why he will be there."

78

Friday, February 14

It was good to walk along Fleet Street in the cold morning sun, thought Clarenceux. It was good to breathe the fresh air, and to see all the people coming into the city. Fifteen hundred years had passed since the Romans had invaded, and still the city thrived. And before that, it had been the city of King Lud and maybe even of Gorbodoc, whose sons had torn the country in two, fighting between themselves. So much time, so many people passed along this street, taking so much for granted, as he had done for the last thirty years. So many would walk along here in future—sometimes idly, sometimes happily, sadly, quickly, slowly, fearfully, joyfully—and more often than not, without even reflecting on what it meant to be here.

Today he was thinking about what "being here" really meant. Whatever happened on Monday, whether he lived or died in the fire, he would never be able to return to this city, never walk along this street after he left tomorrow morning. He would never be able to stand here again and look about him as he did now. Never be able to reclaim any possession of his, or call at his house, or consult a document or chronicle that had once been in his library or Cecil's library.

Even if he emerged well and healthy from Thame Abbey, not even his closest friends must know he was alive. He would have to surrender his idea of himself and give up his fascinations, accepting that there would be things he would want to know that he could not find out; people whose well-being he would want to be sure of, whom he could not contact. He would not even be able to see his friend Julius Fawcett in Chislehurst, for his house was too close to Scadbury Park, where Walsingham had grown up. Everyone had to believe that he was dead, that the last nail had been hammered into his coffin. No one could be allowed to suspect that he was the one who had hammered it in himself.

Awdrey was the exception. If he could not know her in the world he foresaw, he did not want to live. Two women had governed his emotional life for the last three years: one, Rebecca Machyn, was already dead. To be cut off from Awdrey as well would be the death of him. She confirmed what he was; she allowed him to know himself and she defined his place in the world. If he lived, he would take her away from this city and its dangers and live quietly with her somewhere, perhaps in the countryside, or maybe in a foreign country. As he looked at a well-dressed merchant's wife walking toward the city with two female friends and a basket-carrying servant in her company, he had a picture of Awdrey walking through the Bourse in Antwerp in the same way, looking handsome and confident, with her daughters beside her.

How he prayed for her! If God judged prayers by fervor and regularity, surely He had to listen to Clarenceux's prayers for Awdrey and their daughters.

The bells started to ring, and Clarenceux stepped faster toward Cecil House. His chest felt tight and full of strangeness, as if he had inhaled some exotic incense. But there was no more time to feel. Now was the time to act. He had only one day to put his affairs in order.

—❦—

Cecil welcomed him in his writing room, sitting on a bench by the fire. Although fully dressed, his uncovered foot was out in front of him, propped up on a low stool. The book presses, with their brown, white, and black vellum and leather-bound volumes, provided the paneling of reason and knowledge. The portrait of Cecil was similarly reassuring.

"I apologize for not standing; it is this accursed gout. Have you been to see Annie yet?" asked Cecil after their initial formalities.

"No, I intend to do that next. I hear she is playing with Robert in the garden."

"You should be able to see them from this window."

Clarenceux looked out. Fifty yards from the house Annie enthusiastically threw a ball for Robert. Her aim was not good and her expectation of his catching abilities overoptimistic. She picked the ball up and tried again. Again he failed to catch it and the two of them ran to where it lay in the grass as Robert's governess looked on.

"Thank you for looking after Annie."

"It is the least I can do. But listen. You are upset. Take some time."

"I have, Sir William, I have. On Monday, at noon, I am going to hand the Percy-Boleyn marriage agreement over to John Greystoke, the man who abducted my wife and who has subsequently repeatedly forced himself upon her. He has also deceived Walsingham. But I suspect you know that."

Cecil said nothing.

Clarenceux unbuttoned the top of his doublet and pulled out the two letters he had tucked inside. He held up the first one. "You told me once that I would write a letter to my wife. Here it is. It contains my last wishes—please give it to her if the need arise." He handed it to Cecil and raised the second letter. "This one is the instructions for Walsingham." He handed that one too to Cecil.

"I have half a mind to throw both of these on the fire and tell you to pull yourself together, William."

"Then you would do me a great wrong. Even if you were to surround the place on Monday, you could not guarantee my wife's safety. Nor could you guarantee our safety in future. If you arrested all those who are after us, the Catholic plotters in this country will never accept that that document is lost to them. They will simply deny it. Even if you prove people wrong on something they collectively believe in, they will continue to have faith in it—and collectively they will deny the proof. What hope does a man have? They killed Rebecca Machyn just to teach me a lesson. If you take the document from me, I will be killed—or Awdrey will be, or one of my daughters—as a lesson to you. We've become symbols of a refusal to betray our monarch. As Catholics who are loyal to the crown, we are hated by the Catholics who are militant. The only way to end it is for me to be seen to destroy the document and myself. Consider it an act of purification."

Cecil raised an eyebrow. "And this is the way you hope to save your family?"

"I have provided for my wife and daughters," Clarenceux continued. "They should benefit from almost £300 in cash. I hope that you will reward them on my behalf and watch over them if I am successful in this endeavor and stop the document from falling into Catholic hands."

"But the document *already* is in Catholic hands—yours."

"Sir William, this is our last meeting, so I will be wholly honest with you. I have attended the same church for the last thirty years—I have not changed. I have said the same prayers in my heart and sung the same psalms. I believe that God looks after communities that look after their members, and forbids the eating of meat in Lent and the marriage of priests. I believe that the Mass is meaningful in helping the souls of the departed. And I believe it was wrong of the old king to take away the places of memorial, to destroy abbeys and churches, to desecrate all the old holy places. I look at the blank space in the church where my parents were buried—the cold, plain stonework—and I feel the loss of their memorial like a second loss of them in person. I deplore the burning of roods up and down the country. I weep to think of the altars not just unattended but destroyed, and the holy sculptures smashed. All along I have asked myself, 'What is it that makes a man change his faith? How can a monarch command a man's belief?' There is nothing in the world you can say that will make me lose my belief in the old religion. For me, it is like believing in the beauty of women, or that water runs downhill. These are things beyond all persuasion—as much as trying to make me believe my hip does not ache or that I am not in my forty-ninth year. I could say that I do believe what I do not—but I would be lying. Is the rest of the kingdom lying? Some are—and the rest are forgetting. All across this kingdom, people are closing their eyes to the old religion. They see no votive offerings on altars and so they forget that this is a way we may seek divine intervention in our lives. They forget the names of the dead and the holy places of the past. There are empty stone niches in church walls where jeweled reliquaries used to be set, gleaming in the darkness with the Lord's power. Now the young just see holes.

Do you not remember the great tomb of King Henry, in the abbey? Gold, glimmering in the darkness, with the beauty of centuries of devotion from kings, even emperors. In the church of the Greyfriars, there once were the tombs of the queens—Queen Margaret, Queen Isabella, Queen Joan: they were all destroyed and the effigies sold off for the value of the alabaster. Bare stone flagstones adorn that church now. And yet it was founded by a queen of England, and a most loved queen at that—an ancestress of the present queen. Nothing you can say will make me believe that that was the Lord's will. And yet the queen commands this shift of faith—and people all across the kingdom obey. Are we such cowards, Sir William? Not all of us. I might be in a minority but, in losing my wife and my daughter, and almost losing my other daughter, and in losing my dear friend, Rebecca, I know it must be conscience that moves me. It must be. The world will change because of cowardice and complacency—but I will not. If I must sacrifice myself to secure my family's freedom from tyranny, I will do so gladly, in the eyes of God, and with a bleeding but unbroken heart. And those men that call themselves Catholics—those who would steal the document from me, and who would have me start a war in the name of their faith—are nothing of the sort. They are fickle players in the false religion of politics, and their saints are Lord Henry and Mary of Scotland—just as your saint is Elizabeth—and they do not follow the path of righteousness, nor the will of God, but that of self-interest, tyranny, and hatred."

He went back to the window and rested his forehead against the leaded glass. Cecil remained silent for a long time.

"When do you want me to send this letter to Walsingham?" he asked quietly.

"Today. He will need time to prepare."

Cecil struggled to his feet. Resting his weight on the heel of his foot, he limped over and stood beside Clarenceux looking out the window. Annie and Robert were hiding from one another behind the low bushes in the formal squares of the garden, jumping up and surprising each other.

"It is St. Valentine's Day," said Cecil.

"St. Valentine was a martyr too."

"He gave his life for his faith, not his wife."

"What brings me closer to my wife brings me closer to God."

Cecil looked at Clarenceux, studying the face, the beard, the eyes, and thinning, graying hair. "I admire you. No one will remember me for the fact that I too love my wife. All people will remember is that I served our queen."

Clarenceux turned away and walked to the door. "Your wife herself might remember it, Sir William. And your children. They count too."

Cecil took the reprimand silently. "William."

"Yes?" said Clarenceux, looking back.

"I don't know…This cannot be our final good-bye. At least, I cannot believe it." He shook his head in distress and looked at Clarenceux with shining eyes. "I know we have had our disagreements but…"

There was a long silence. Clarenceux came back across the room and embraced Cecil. "Some things are not even within the gift of the most powerful man in the kingdom."

He walked among the box hedges of the knot garden holding Annie's hand. The hedges turned this way and that, and back on themselves, in a square design. He himself felt similarly intricately contorted. In stark contrast to his mood, Annie had been telling him about the sort of horse she wanted to have when she grew older, and the sort of house she wanted to live in—one with lots of glass, naturally, like Sir William's house, only gabled, like her home. She wanted two embroidered foreparts for every dress, and ruffles and slashed sleeves, as well as a velvet gown and cork-soled shoes.

"And who is going to pay for all these things?" Clarenceux asked.

"*You* are, Father," she replied joyfully, turning to him and smiling up at him with her joke.

Clarenceux squeezed her hand, swallowing back the emotion. "I think you will need to find yourself a rich husband."

"I will have nine children," she said with the supreme confidence of a seven-year-old. "Four boys and five girls, and the girls will all marry knights and lords and earls, and the boys can be admirals and captains."

He stopped and crouched down to look her in the eyes. "Listen, Annie, I am not going to be able to come to see you for a while. But I am sure that Sir William and Lady Cecil will look after you very well. And I hope very much that your mam will soon be back, and she will look after you."

"Will you not be here when Mam comes?"

"I don't know, Annie." This was the moment he was dreading. "I don't know what is going to happen to me."

"Are you going to be executed?"

Clarenceux laughed. "No, my sweet, I am not going to be executed. I am going to…to…" *I can never come back here. I will not see her grow up and become a young woman and marry.* "I will be back before long," he said. He ran his fingers through her hair, and then hugged her.

"Why are you crying?"

"It doesn't matter, Annie. It doesn't matter. Will you promise me something?"

Annie nodded.

"If I don't see you for a long time, I want you to do three things. Be brave, always speak the truth, and be kind to those you love. Can you remember those three things?"

Annie held up her fingers. "Be brave, say the truth, and be kind to Mam."

"And Mildred. She is your sister—you must take care of your sister."

"And Mildred. Where are you going?"

Clarenceux stood up straight and took her hand again. "Thame Abbey. But let us not talk about that now. What are the three things you are going to do for me?"

"Be brave, say the truth, and be kind to Mam *and* Mildred."

After his final good-byes, he walked away from Cecil House. He allowed himself one glance back. Annie was waving to him from the courtyard, with Lady Cecil and a number of attendants. And above them, at a window, was the watching figure of Sir William too, his hand raised.

Clarenceux sat at a table in a dark corner at the back of the Mermaid Tavern on Cheapside. Thomas sat opposite him, his hands folded across each other on the tablecloth. Two tankards of beer were placed before them by the landlord's daughter who smiled at them. "Thank you," Clarenceux said.

Thomas watched her leave. His old face was as lined as ever but his eyes were red. "I cannot believe it. After all these years of service: an end."

"Thomas…" Clarenceux began, but then he sighed and stopped. "What am I to do? The Bible tells us we should forgive our enemies and turn the other cheek. But when I think of forgiveness I think of Awdrey's loveliness, and I see Rebecca, and I smell the stench of the woman's head boiled, and I see the gun pointed at Annie. I cannot turn the other cheek. My family means too much to me."

"Then have him arrested."

"We have been through that. We do not have much time left. The code—a summer month for good news, and a winter one for bad…"

"And then what? With Greystoke there, and the door locked and the building burning? I do not believe you are simply going to throw yourself into the flames. I know you, Mr. Clarenceux. I know you well—better than anyone except Awdrey. You are hiding something."

Clarenceux closed his eyes.

"Look, Mr. Clarenceux, when you said before that if you survived, I could not continue to serve you, I accepted it. But I believed you would fight and not just surrender yourself. You said there was a chance. Just tell me you are not going to kill yourself."

Clarenceux lifted the tankard and supped the beer. Thomas was staring at him, and the man's iron frown bored into his mind.

"Tell me."

"No."

"Tell me—for the sake of the years I have served you, and for the sacrifice of my great-nephew, who died in your service, and for all the problems we have faced."

"On Monday it will be the end for this Clarenceux King of Arms. No more running, no more pain, no more memories, no more heraldry, no more house in Fleet Street, no more making love with Awdrey, no more eating and drinking beer with you."

"You told me that before. But your obligation to the truth makes you a very poor liar. This is not the whole truth."

Clarenceux sighed. "No."

"I will never tell a soul."

Clarenceux was silent for a long time. He drank again and looked around. No one was near. Eventually he said, "Let me tell you a story. One hundred and fifty years ago, in the time of the Lollards, there were a number of these men gathered at a house in London. Several of them were knights and very well connected. On the night in question they heard their host, a rich merchant, speak of the pope as the antichrist—and they heard passages read to them from a heretical book. A servant boy was listening secretly, and it so happened that he knew how to read. The boy also knew that these men were breaking the law. When his master dismissed him for some minor infringement of a house rule, which the boy considered most unfair, he went to the mayor and reported the things he had heard that night. He also produced his master's book, which proved to be scandalous. Three bishops read it, condemned it, and ordered it to be burned. The boy also named those who had heard the book read aloud. The merchant himself was arrested, tried, and burned at the stake. A search was undertaken for the others. Some were caught, but two knights were tipped off just in time and they escaped. They rode toward Oxford. But at Thame they turned off the road and went to the abbey. There they spoke to the almoner, saying they needed sanctuary. The almoner spoke to the abbot and the abbot, suspecting they were heretics, denied them entrance. Desperate, one of the men threatened to reveal a secret hiding place built inside the abbey, which had been constructed a generation or two earlier, to hide the precious objects of the abbey from the king's tax gatherers. Only the abbot and the treasurer knew about it; when one died, the survivor was supposed to tell the new abbot or treasurer and no one else. The abbot was thus appalled that their hiding place was known. In order to keep it secret, therefore, the abbot allowed the men to take shelter on condition that, if they got away, they were never to repeat what they knew. They swore solemn oaths. They hid, and the abbey was searched, but they were not found."

"I am glad to hear it. I am so glad." A smile spread across Thomas's face, and he drank a large measure of his beer.

But Clarenceux shook his head. "It is one thing to tell a story, Thomas. It is quite another to kill Greystoke and then ignite a barrel of gunpowder, burn down a building, and survive. And even if it all goes according to plan, I can never come back to London. I have had my fair share of scrapes over the years. I know I have been lucky. But now, at best, everything changes. That is why I am serious when I say that this is where things really do come to an end for me. By Monday night there will be no more Mr. Clarenceux. There will be no more William Harley. I will be just another of God's nameless creatures scavenging a living at the margins of society. If I survive."

"You will survive, Mr. Clarenceux. You always do."

79

Clarenceux did not speak as he closed the door to his bedchamber for the last time, nor as he walked through the house to his study. He said nothing as he checked the kitchen and the buttery. Only when he came back up to the hall and saw Thomas and Alice did he utter the few words, "Let us go," before leading them down to the front of the house, locking the door, and taking Brutus's reins from Fyndern. His silence continued as they rode toward Thame—he in front, Thomas a short distance behind him, Fyndern and Alice at the back. Every so often he would check to make sure they had not fallen behind; then he would nod and continue.

They reached Chipping Wycombe late in the afternoon and settled at an inn. Still Clarenceux did not speak. He sat in his chamber by himself, staring out of the open window. After it was dark he sat in a wooden chair with a tankard of beer that Thomas brought up for him. He said he was not hungry. Thomas ate in the hall, sitting apart from Fyndern and Alice, leaving them to their conversation and flirtation. It was long after dark when he went back to the chamber to check on his master.

Clarenceux was still sitting in the same chair when Thomas walked in, carrying a candle. He set it down on the table.

"I didn't think it would end like this," said Clarenceux. "I recall my father in his last years, staying alive desperately. There was an occasion when a priest came to his house, and he asked my father to tell him about his life. My father responded by saying where he was born, and what the status of his father was, and where he had grown up and whom he had married. And then he started to talk about when he fell ill. Within four sentences he was describing his sickness. Where and when he first experienced each symptom, how much the symptoms hurt, which seasons and phases of the moon caused the most pain. What things he had had to give up doing and how he was managing despite his incapacities. Each subsequent sentence was more about his illness than him. He had *become* his illness. His body had become the church in which his illness worshipped."

"That is not your fate."

"I feel the same inward-looking desperation."

"You have set yourself upon a path, but how you resolve it is still up to you. You can still turn off that path—you know that; you are still a free man."

"The killings, Thomas—the spying, the fear. The hurt. I remember asking Henry Machyn whether, by taking his chronicle into my house, I was risking any danger to my family. He knew I was—but even he could not have imagined how much. And I remember him asking me why I was a Catholic. That is something that has been much on my mind recently; I suspect that it is about loyalty. The more I think about it, the more it strikes me that loyalty has been the driving force of my life and betrayal my greatest fear. My whole life as an antiquary and herald is about the truth, and loyalty to the truth, whether that be the truth of the past or now. The young can betray each other and they can turn against the past, but we must be loyal—to our wives and to our queen, and also to our God and to ourselves."

"I think the young also have a sense of loyalty. Fyndern would follow Alice to the Gates of Hell, and maybe even a few steps further."

"Love is not loyalty. Fyndern has the makings of a good man—but not if he slavishly follows his desires and allows himself to be manipulated. Alice is a little vixen; she has barely got a loyal bone in her body."

There were many things Thomas wanted to say; among them that Clarenceux was a poor judge of young women for the simple reason that he distanced himself from them; and also that a woman like Alice could be just as devoted as a young man. He had noticed the looks the girl had cast toward Clarenceux. But the latter was clearly not in a mood to be argued with, so Thomas let the matter rest, and returned to the hall.

Much later, Fyndern had tried showing off his card skills to two travelers staying at the inn—but he was tipsy and made so many mistakes they were left distinctly unimpressed. They quickly beat a path to their chamber and left him alone with Thomas and Alice in the hall. Thomas urged him to go to bed but the boy wanted to stay up all night, he said, and drink with his friends.

"Go to bed," commanded Clarenceux suddenly from the doorway, looking across the candlelit hall.

He was standing in his shirt and breeches with bare feet and no doublet, but his sword was at his belt. His hair, longer and more unkempt than it had ever been before, was now half-gray. His untrimmed beard was even more gray than his hair.

"Fyndern, tomorrow you will get little or no rest. You must sleep now."

Fyndern got up from the table, unsure whether to trust his impulse to laugh at Clarenceux or his instinct to obey. He looked at Alice. "Mr. Clarenceux, you must not light that fire at the abbey," he said with a slur to his voice. "You will die in the flames—and Alice will too."

Clarenceux raised his voice. "Fyndern, go to bed *now!*"

The confidence of the beer vanished. Clarenceux stared at him as he bowed to Thomas and Alice and made his way past him, and went up to his chamber.

When he had gone, Clarenceux took a seat.

"Should we not all be going to bed?" asked Alice.

Clarenceux leaned on the table. "Yes," he replied.

Alice said, "Good night," and left.

Thomas looked at Clarenceux's brooding face. "Don't place any faith in what the boy says," he told him. "He has no vision this evening. He made many mistakes with the cards."

80

Sunday, February 16

Even after a full day traveling, when they arrived at the Saracen's Head, Thomas could see that Clarenceux remained guarded. He wore a constant frown, his eyes looking at everything. But he did not speak. A few words of greeting to the stable boys when he left Brutus with them, and to Simeon in the hall, and that was all. There was too much pain and tension in the man; he was not speaking to people because he could not.

"Thomas," he whispered finally as they stood in the hall. "Place my bag in the same room in which you and Alice will sleep. Fyndern and I will not be staying here this night."

An hour later they assembled for supper in one of the chambers. The table board had been set up and was draped with a linen cloth; embroidered cushions were placed on the benches and a great many candles were set around the room. There was a flagon of wine on the table and several pewter platters of baked and smoked fish—herring, eel, and even salmon. A salad of herbs and greenery was set out next to the fish dishes: cod with mustard, pike in galantine sauce, and baked turbot.

Clarenceux stood to welcome Thomas and Fyndern. Alice was

already by his side. "It is Sunday. Let us feast," he declared with a smile. He gestured enthusiastically for them to take their places. Alice rose to her feet; Clarenceux said grace, and they all sat. Thomas was startled at Clarenceux's good humor—how lighthearted and easy he seemed all of a sudden. He spoke to Alice of what food she liked and to Fyndern of how the lad imagined himself as head of a household meeting his future wife's expectations of a rich spread on a Sunday. He talked of his childhood and the meals then, and of the regime at school. He spoke of the long, cold dormitory in which more than a hundred boys slept, each with his chest beside his bed. He spoke too of his university years, and how the scholars of his day would sneak out to enjoy the pleasures of the town, in food, drink, women, and song. In those days it seemed that everything worth pursuing in life was to be found outside the high walls of the college. Had the lecture halls been full of roast meat and wine, music and pretty young women, he would have been far more enthusiastic about his studies. Simeon joined them for part of the meal, leaving the serving of wine and the clearing of platters to his servants.

In this manner, the meal continued for two hours. At the conclusion, fruit fritters were passed around and Simeon produced some fine Cypriot wine. This caused them to debate whether Ancient Greek wine would have tasted as good, and whether things Roman—roads and architecture particularly—were necessarily any better than they were in the modern world.

"After all, we know more than the ancients," reflected Simeon.

"What do we know now that they did not?" asked Fyndern, ever curious.

"Forty-five years ago, a Spanish ship sailed all the way around the world."

Fyndern was confused at first; later, when it had been explained to him that the world is a globe, he was astounded. He had never considered that it had a shape, still less that one could sail off to the east and arrive from the west. "You sail that way," he said, holding out his right hand, "and come back from that way," holding out his left.

"If only the human spirit were shaped like the world," said Clarenceux, savoring the sweetness of the Cypriot wine.

Late that night, Clarenceux donned his cloak and gloves, and joined Fyndern in the inn yard. Simeon was there to open the gate for them and lock it behind them. They set out on foot with no lantern. The stars and first quarter of the new moon offered little light, but Clarenceux reassured Fyndern that this was to their advantage; it meant less light by which they could be seen.

They walked for most of the way along the road toward the abbey—until they heard the voices of men coming toward them. Clarenceux grabbed Fyndern's cloak and pulled him back into the darkness beneath the wall of a barn. As the men approached and were only a few feet away from them, they heard Walsingham's name mentioned.

"We have got to get off the road," whispered Clarenceux, once they were alone again.

They moved around the barn to a hedge running away from the road. The weak moonlight allowed Clarenceux to lead Fyndern, slowly and carefully, across the middle of the field, along the balks between recently ploughed strips of land. They felt a breeze on their faces. At the end of the furlong they followed the balk between the next series of strips, which were parallel to the road.

It was only a mile to the abbey by road but it took Clarenceux and Fyndern most of an hour. Even at the gatehouse there were men posted. The dark shadows of trees loomed just to the north; it was a small wood, planted long ago for the now-vanished monks to have timber on hand for rebuilding their roofs and outbuildings. At the foot of an old elm they waited, listening in the darkness.

"I explored this way last time," whispered Fyndern, steadying himself against the elm. "I followed the stream from the fishponds up to the gatehouse there—it runs along the edge of these woods."

Fyndern now led the way, tracing the stream by listening to its trickling sound and looking for the moon's reflection in its surface. The cold night raised the smell of damp earth; sticks cracked under their weight and the bushes brushed their cloaks, clawing at them. Clarenceux heard the leaves rustling above him; he crossed himself and prayed that the sounds they were making would not carry.

"Shhh." Fyndern had stopped. "Listen." He paused, and slowly stepped to the edge of the stream.

Clarenceux could hear an owl hooting and the stream flowing. An animal rustled in the undergrowth on the bank. In the distance, pinpoints of light indicated that men were moving in and out of the abbey. There were about a dozen of them. There was a barn a hundred yards away, and men were waiting there too.

"Walsingham did not follow my instructions," whispered Clarenceux. "He was meant to come after dawn. I told him. How far is it to the drain?"

Fyndern bit off the broken part of a fingernail and spat it out. "It is in the southeast—it empties into the long fishpond."

"Have you got the tinderbox?"

"Yes—yours and a spare from the inn." Fyndern began to tread carefully through the wood again.

Fifteen minutes later, they came to the southeastern edge, where the trees met the great monastic fishponds which formed the eastern border of the abbey precinct. The ground here was lower, and the dark roofs of the abbey buildings, three hundred yards away, could be clearly seen against the starry sky. A duck, disturbed by their movement, quacked and flapped its wings, splashing the water, as it took flight. Fyndern and Clarenceux both crouched down and looked across the undulating ground, but there was no one to be seen. They proceeded cautiously along the bank of the pond. When they came to a tree they sheltered in its shadow and listened. Soon they were within forty yards of the east end of the church. But Fyndern went on further, until they were ninety yards southeast of the abbey.

"It's near here," whispered Fyndern. He took off his boots and thrust them inside his doublet, then let his feet slip down the bank into the shallows of the pond. He moved carefully, one hand on the bank. He stumbled and stepped into a deeper part and swore, but continued searching for the opening. A minute later they both heard the trickling of water and Fyndern placed his hands on the square stone mouth of the drain.

"This is it."

Clarenceux looked up at the abbey, silhouetted against the stars. "Do you feel brave?"

"No."

"Good—you'd be mad to feel brave at a time like this."

There was a pause. Neither of them said anything.

Fyndern crouched down and looked into the blackness. The drain was about two feet high and although there was only a trickle of water running through it, it was oppressive. Also, it smelled foul. "I hope you are going to tell someone to reward me for this if everything goes according to plan."

"I will tell Thomas."

"How much?"

"That will be up to Awdrey. I will tell Thomas I promised you ten pounds."

Fyndern stood up. "I told you I was worth more than two pence a day." He looked at Clarenceux's crouched outline against the stars above him and swallowed. "We will not meet again, will we?"

"No, we will not meet again, Fyndern. But I am glad I met you."

"And me too, I am grateful," said Fyndern in the darkness. "No one has ever trusted me as much as you, and made me feel worth something—more than just a trickster."

"Prove it now, Fyndern. Do this well and you will help stop a war and thereby save countless lives. Use all your skills and senses. Remember, go under the shaft from the refectory, find your way into the kitchen drain. The door to the undercroft is behind it. You have the key. Don't put the boots back on until you are out of the water; we don't want to leave tracks. And remember, everything now depends on you lighting that flame at the right time. When I send the signal. And when you are sure that the fire is going, get out quickly. Swim the pond if need be."

Fyndern reached forward and grabbed Clarenceux's hand. He shook it vigorously and long. Then he let go, crouched down again, and plunged headlong into the stone tunnel.

Clarenceux waited until he could hear no more sounds from the drain. When it was quiet, he turned and made his way back along the bank, moving quickly. Looking at the monastery, he could make out the curve of the moon reflected in the glass. A single light seemed to be burning in the upper chamber of the abbot's house. But the window of the refectory itself was black.

Thomas, Simeon, and Alice were all waiting for him in the hall, gathered around a large fire. Simeon shut the gate behind Clarenceux, locked it, and showed him into the warm.

"I thought you would have gone to bed," said Clarenceux, as he unbuckled his sword and laid it and the belt on the top of a barrel.

Simeon poured him a tankard of beer.

"How can you expect us to sleep?" asked Alice. "We want to know what is going on. We're worried."

"Well, Fyndern is in," replied Clarenceux, taking the tankard. "But Walsingham is trying to control the scene. There are too many soldiers there already. And I suspect more are on their way." He pulled out a pistol from his doublet and set it beside the sword.

"I don't believe that Greystoke will walk into the abbey," said Thomas, "even if his life is at stake. He cannot trust Walsingham."

Clarenceux supped his beer. "We have gone a long way beyond trust. Nothing is left except the politics of desperation. Walsingham still has to use him. I can refuse to surrender the document to Walsingham but I cannot refuse it to Greystoke because of Awdrey and Mildred. Even if Walsingham intends to arrest Greystoke the moment he has possession of the document, he has to allow him entrance to the abbey."

"But what is Greystoke's plan for getting the document out?" asked Alice.

"I don't know. But he will have worked out something. That is why it is so important that Fyndern lights the fire. Greystoke's plan will go up in smoke with the rest of him."

"What about Father Buckman?" asked Thomas.

"He is just the middle man. Much as I would like him to be there, he is going to leave this to Greystoke. He has nothing to gain from being there in person tomorrow."

"And you?" Alice asked.

Clarenceux did not answer. He supped his beer.

"Everything is ready here, for your wife, as you requested," said Simeon.

"Good," replied Clarenceux. "Now, Alice, I want you to go to bed. Tomorrow is going to be a long and tiring day."

Alice took her leave of them. Simeon stayed for a short while and then he too retired. Clarenceux and Thomas sat by the fire.

"If Fyndern manages to light the fire, you must tell Awdrey to reward him," Clarenceux said. "I have put in my letter to her, which is with Sir William, to pay him; but I said to him tonight that I would give him an extra ten pounds. I have also made provision for you in that letter."

"Don't worry about me," Thomas said. "I trust Mistress Harley not to let me starve. But what about you? How will we know about you?"

"Thomas, you won't. You will have to accept things as they are. A conflagration. A funeral without a body. A new Clarenceux—someone else."

"I will have difficulty accepting that last change."

"You have to. For Awdrey's sake, for the girls'. For my sake too. Whatever happens tomorrow, my one abiding hope is that it is not in vain."

81

Monday, February 17

Clarenceux entered Alice's chamber at nine o'clock that morning. The shutters were wide open and she was sitting on the floor by the bed with her knees drawn up under her chin. She looked worried, and her hair was tousled and dirty. She had not slept, she said, but had lain awake worrying.

"What about?"

"About all the things that could go wrong."

Clarenceux reached out a hand and pulled her to her feet. He looked down into her eyes. "Tell me what you think could go wrong."

"What if they don't hand Awdrey over? What if I am attacked on the way back from seeing her delivered? What if Greystoke's messenger takes the key from me? I need more than your prayers, Mr. Clarenceux."

He put his hand to her face, thinking about each of the things she had suggested. "You *will* have more than my prayers; you will have my pistol. Keep it loaded. It will be reassuring to me tomorrow to know that you have it." She looked up at him with a solemn gratitude. "We will leave at a quarter to twelve."

"Will we ride?"

"You will. I shall walk."

"A mark of penitence?"

"No. I don't want to give them my horse."

~~∰~~

When the time came to leave, Clarenceux saw that Alice was waiting in the hall. He turned to Simeon, shook his hand, and thanked him for his hospitality and his service. He pressed two gold crowns into his hand. Then he looked at Thomas and embraced him. With a lump in his throat he said simply, "Thank you, Thomas."

"Mr. Clarenceux, all these years have been an honor."

"Look after them for me." He nodded to Alice, who was holding Maud's reins, and picked up his long black cloak. Simeon opened the gate for them. With one final look back, and a wave to Thomas, they left.

They said very little to each other on the way. The weather was clear and the birdsong was sweet and bright. A few townsmen and women of Thame were on the highway, traveling toward Wycombe and London; a few yeomen were riding into the town. But soon they were at the gate to the abbey, where a small contingent of men was stationed. Two wore breastplates, the rest were not in any uniform, but all were armed and all watched Clarenceux and Alice silently.

A well-dressed gentleman stopped them. "You are Mr. William Harley, Clarenceux herald?"

"I am."

"And who is she?" he asked, looking up at Alice.

"My messenger," replied Clarenceux. "If she does not proceed, nor do I."

The man accepted this. He gestured in the direction of the abbey. "Mr. Walsingham is in the church."

Clarenceux nodded. He looked south to the sun, northeast to the wood he had traveled through in the night, and then southeast to where the path led to the abbey. Nothing now could change him from his intended course. It felt like his last moment of freedom.

On one side of the track to the abbey was a pile of trunks of trees, cut down and shaved of their branches for sale to timber merchants. Several soldiers in armor were leaning against the timber. As Clarenceux and Alice passed, the soldiers roused themselves and started walking toward them. To the north, men were approaching from the barn. He turned and looked behind; most of the men from the gates were also following them at a distance.

On they went, until the high roof of the church appeared between the trees that had grown up around the abbey since the Dissolution. Soon the whole west front was visible, and the west range beneath the lay brothers' dormitory, with the abbot's house at the southern end. Clarenceux looked at the ragged west front of the church, with the piles of rubble and smashed sculpture near the open door. More men were standing here in small groups: some in half armor, some with guns, and some with pikes, one resting his leg on a piece of sculpture. All of them were looking at Clarenceux and Alice. The breeze wafted through the long grasses on either side of the track. Men shouldered their muskets and started walking to their predetermined positions, ringing the entire abbey. Their silent attention, and the threat of their armor and weapons, contrasted strongly with the birdsong and the sunlit ease of the morning.

The worn gothic stonework of the west front was comforting, despite the loss of its statues and the defaced sculpture at its base. It was at least a house of God, Clarenceux told himself as he passed a soldier waiting beside the door. The soldier's face was stern and determinedly unresponsive to Clarenceux's polite nod of greeting. Alice dismounted, handed the reins to a soldier, and followed him into the church.

Silence and a cold light greeted them, striking the stone and casting shadows across the broken-tiled floor of the building. Men stood between the arches, looking at them. The elegant tracery in the windows remained disdainful of the shabby confrontation. In the empty side chapels, the damaged effigies of deceased gentry and clergy looked with wide open eyes to a distant, more glorious future. A handful of last autumn's leaves blew across the floor, caught by the breeze from the window. Fractured saints in the broken stained glass cried for mercy. But there was no glass in the east window—and in the space where the great altar had once stood was a white-haired man, with a sword at his side.

Clarenceux heard his own footsteps echo through the nave. When he reached the crossing, just before the choir, he heard a clink of metal. Walsingham stepped out from behind a column near the site of the altar and took his place beside Greystoke.

There was something chilling about seeing the two of them next to each other.

Walsingham was dressed in black, as usual, with a black skull cap. Greystoke's white hair and white skin, his white shirt and cream-colored doublet were a striking contrast. He even wore light-colored gloves. A small black-clothed man and a tall white-clothed one—eternity and purity. But how hugely those symbolic colors lied. Clarenceux looked from one man to the other. Greystoke's face was a mess, he saw. His lip had been torn from his jaw; it was swollen, red, and stitched up.

"You have brought the document then?" asked Walsingham.

"You have brought my wife and daughter?"

"They are safe enough, and near enough," mumbled Greystoke, his speech impaired by his injury.

The dead leaves shifted further across the floor.

"I want to see them."

Greystoke shook his head. "Not before you surrender the document."

"Are they here?"

"Show us the document."

Clarenceux turned to Walsingham. "How is this going to look to Sir William? You, in the company of a murderer and a defiler of women, a traitor to the State. Will he not judge you by the company you keep?"

"I think you will find that Sir William will trust me no less at the end of the day. You, on the other hand, did not surrender the document to him. If anyone has burned their bridges with Sir William, it is you, Clarenceux."

At that, Greystoke drew his sword and held it up in his white-gloved hand, turning the blade. "Of course, we could just take the document from you."

"Perhaps. But if you attack me you had better be very sure I have the document on me." Clarenceux looked at Walsingham. Then without another word, he walked to the south side of the church.

"Where are you going?" demanded Walsingham.

Alice began to speak, as Clarenceux had instructed her. "Mr. Clarenceux has made arrangements to ensure that you do not renege on your agreement."

As he walked into the south aisle, he saw a woman with blond hair watching him, along with two armed guards. He went on, into the cloister, and marched past the chapter house and up to the steps into the refectory.

The huge room was empty, just as it had been the first time he had seen it—the trestle table and the rushes on the floor, the glazed windows, the stone lectern where the monks used to read to the community. The sole exception was the iron-bound oak chest from his house in London, in the middle of the room. He bolted the door behind him and went across to the chest; he unlocked the right-hand of the two locks and lifted the lid. The smell of the sulphur in the gunpowder rose to his nostrils. Two pounds of it had been scattered across the base. In the bottom of the chest were the two holes he had bored there. The chest itself was firmly nailed to the floor.

He heard someone try to force the door open. Then he heard furious knocking. "Damn you, Clarenceux!" It was Greystoke. "Open this door or I will blast it open."

Clarenceux went to the window and saw Walsingham's men circling the whole abbey, all the way down to the fishponds. It was time to fetch the document.

Six minutes later, Clarenceux unbolted the door. Greystoke angrily pushed inside, holding his sword. "Where is it?" Clarenceux said nothing but backed away as many more people filed into the refectory. Walsingham followed, then the woman from the south aisle of the church, and Alice and seven or eight men. Greystoke advanced on him with his sword drawn and started berating him again. Clarenceux drew his own blade and summoned up the full power of his voice to command the attention of everyone present.

"Back!" he roared. "Back! As God is my witness, Mr. Walsingham, I have not sought a confrontation with you or with that man. But I will hand the marriage agreement over to no one until I know my wife is safe. Where is Maurice Buckman?"

"It matters not," said Greystoke, his sword at the ready.

"Mr. Walsingham, I do not know why you trust this felon, a killer, but I see that you do. Do you know he is in league with Maurice Buckman? Are you awake that Greystoke himself now has control of my wife? Now, listen to me. I will show this document to you so you may know that it is genuinely the marriage agreement that you have sought for so long—and I will show it to Greystoke too, for I want nothing more to happen to my wife—but I will not let either of you have possession of it until I know that my family is safe."

"You are in no position to make demands, Clarenceux," shouted Greystoke.

Walsingham raised his hand. "Nor are you, Mr. Greystoke. Not when I have a hundred men in and around this abbey."

"Let the others out," said Clarenceux. "Just we and the girl remain."

Walsingham's eyes narrowed, knowing that Clarenceux had a plan. But he knew also that Sir William had at least acquiesced to the plan, for Sir William had personally passed on Clarenceux's directions. He turned to his men and nodded.

"And Joan," added Greystoke. "She must stay too."

Clarenceux's attention turned to the woman. Joan Hellier looked back at him. It took a moment for him to understand how she fitted into the story of his troubles—but when he did, he remembered Sarah Cowie's words—and knew he was looking into the eyes of Rebecca Machyn's killer.

The last of the guards left. Clarenceux went to the door and bolted it shut. He gestured with his sword to the long trestle table as Alice took her position at the door. Walking to the middle of the room, he reached inside his doublet for the document, which he pulled out, in its folded state. He unfolded it, still holding his sword, and laid it flat on the table, pushing it in front of Walsingham and Greystoke. Both men leaned over it. Light from the great windows behind them made the parchment easy to read. Walsingham picked out the black-letter names in the old chancery script, together with the terms of the agreement and the names of the witnesses, including the bishops of Durham and Rochester. Both men were suddenly quiet and reverential in the presence of a document of such importance.

When they had read it, Clarenceux pulled it away, and started to fold it up. But suddenly Greystoke drew his sword and brought it level with Clarenceux's eyes.

"Leave it."

For a long, silent moment Clarenceux stared at the tip of the blade. His eyes shifted to Walsingham. "I am not a fool and neither are you. I am sure you can understand the need for me to secure the document until my family are safe." He moved away from the table, taking the document with him, and went to the chest. He turned back to the two men. "To that end I intend to leave the document in here." In their sight he opened the chest and placed the unfolded parchment inside. He locked the right-hand lock on the chest with the key already in the lock and then took another similar key from a pocket in his doublet and locked the left-hand side. He looked to Alice and handed her one of the keys. "Take this young woman to my wife," he said to Greystoke. "She will have one key with her. The other stays here. When I hear that my wife is safe, then—and only then—you can have the document."

Walsingham looked at Greystoke. "How far away are they?"

Greystoke stared at the table, then raised his head and glared at Clarenceux. "Three miles."

"Take my wife to the Saracen's Head in Thame," said Clarenceux firmly, looking into the man's gray eyes. "Alice will accompany your messenger. When you get there, if all is well, she will be given a code word. When you bring back the key and the code word, then the document will be yours."

Greystoke stared at the chest. He looked at Alice and Joan, then back at the chest. Clarenceux could see him wrestling with the decision—whether to take Awdrey in person to the inn in Thame or to send Joan with Alice. Greystoke had seen Clarenceux lock the chest and give a key to Alice, but still he did not trust him not to remove the document in his absence.

"Joan. Take the wife and the girl to the required place, and then make sure this woman returns, with the key. And then we'll be done with these games."

Clarenceux watched Alice unbolt the door and leave, followed by Joan. He stared at the open door. "They will be gone for more than an hour."

"So," asked Walsingham, "this is your plan, Clarenceux?"

"Mr. Walsingham, with respect, you have no place in this deal. You would be best advised to leave."

"I will do no such thing," replied Walsingham coldly. He sat down on the bench by the table and placed his hands together on the surface.

"And you, Greystoke?"

"I am not moving out of the sight of that chest."

"Very well." Clarenceux moved toward the door. "I cannot stand the thought of spending the next hour and a half in this room with a murderer and a traitor. The room already reeks with the foulness of your breath—and that is nothing compared to the stench of your soul. I will wait outside."

"Clarenceux!" snapped Walsingham. "The key. You will leave the key."

Clarenceux reached into his pocket and pulled out the key, placing it on the top of the chest. "You will still have to wait for the other one."

Outside, thirty armed men were gathered in the shaded cloister and around the door. Some were seated on pieces of timber or stonework in the rubble-strewn courtyard at the center of the cloister; others were standing or leaning against the cloister wall.

Walsingham appeared at the door behind Clarenceux. "Captain Johnson, take ten men and follow Mr. Clarenceux wherever he goes. Make sure he comes back here when the women return."

Captain Johnson, a man with large sideburns that covered his cheeks, was wearing a long fawn coat with a leather belt and holding a steel helmet. He bowed to Walsingham and placed the helmet on his head. He signaled to several men, and they all got to their feet or stopped leaning against a wall and stood ready. Clarenceux walked between them and along the shaded cloister. At the end he turned the corner and walked out of the abbey precinct through the door under the lay brothers' dormitory—the route by which he had first entered the abbey with Sir Richard Wenman. He wondered whether anyone from the locality was now riding to Sir Richard to tell him that his abbey had been overrun by Walsingham's men. It did not matter; by the time Sir Richard arrived, their business would be concluded.

He turned left outside the abbey and walked down across the grounds past the abbot's house. There was a worn patch of ground here and he stooped to pick up some stones from the mud. None of the guards questioned him. A short distance away there were some larger, flatter stones; he discarded most of the first handful and replaced them with these. Twenty minutes were spent in this fashion, walking this way and that, picking up flattish stones. When he had twenty or thirty, he proceeded to the pond.

Standing on the bank, the sun bright from the south, he looked across the deep green-black rippling water. The ducks were settled on the surface some distance away. He skimmed the first stone across the surface, bouncing it four or five times. The next stone bounced twice. The next three times. One or two bounced ten or eleven times off the surface but some plummeted straight into the water—including the key to the chest. Captain Johnson's men sat on the ground or watched him idly; no one noticed. When the stones were all gone, he stood for a long time just looking at the green bank and the water, the blue sky, the sun. He thought of Awdrey and Mildred, at last making their journey to safety, and he wished he could see them, embrace them. But this way, they were in no danger.

Captain Johnson's men hurriedly got to their feet as they saw him start to wander back toward the abbey.

He went into the church and walked up to where the altar had once stood. Looking down the nave at the splintered woodwork and broken carving, it felt so wrong that men could wantonly cause such destruction. Captain Johnson's men remained at a respectful distance as, still wearing his sword, Clarenceux knelt on the cold stone chancel step to pray.

One of Captain Johnson's men kicked a piece of wood; the sound echoed away through the nave and aisles. Clarenceux heard the echo. They could smash the images and pull down the rood screen, and even burn the rood itself—but the echoes of their acts continued.

He stood, turned, and projected his deep voice into the body of the church, proclaiming the words to the congregation of air and light: "*Domine, Jesu Christe, qui me creasti, redemisti, et preordinasti ad hoc quod sum, tu scis quid de me facere vis; fac de me secundum voluntatem tuam cum misericordia. Amen.*"

"Mr. Clarenceux," said Captain Johnson, "this building is no longer a holy church. This is not a place for Catholic prayers."

"You think that because it is in Latin it must be Catholic?" replied Clarenceux with a scornful look. "It is a prayer, written by a good but weak-headed king of England. He wrote it in the Tower of London when he was awaiting death, at the hands of other members of the royal family. Do you want to know what it means?"

Captain Johnson looked to his men for support. They were unsure. The symbolism of the church was undimmed.

"It means 'Lord Jesus Christ, Who created me and redeemed me, and preordained me to be what I am, You know what You wish to do with me; do with me in accordance with Your will, with mercy. Amen.' Tell me, Captain Johnson, wherein lies the heresy in that? Wherein lies the disrespect? Do you rather not see the disrespect all about you, in this desecration?"

His voice echoed away. No one answered. He turned back to the empty space that had once been the high altar and went down on his knees once more.

"You are praying to emptiness, Mr. Clarenceux," said one man behind him.

"There is nothing there," jeered another.

A second time Clarenceux rose to speak to them. "If there is nothing here, do you deny the existence of God? For God is everywhere, even where you have torn down His altars. If there is nothing here, does it matter to you that I pray for you, in my Latin prayers—praying that the Holy Spirit will infect your limbs with cancerous sores and make your tongues bleed for your lies? I have seen the plague infest the poor houses in London, and heard whole families screaming with the pain as they die, one by one—the men too frightened to touch their plague-fingered wives, the children crying in bed with the sores pulsating through their whole feverish bodies, and their parents too scared to enter their chambers. Shall I pray for the plague to smite you? If there is nothing here, then you will say, 'Yes, Mr. Clarenceux, do your worst! Pray us to suffer the most miserable deaths! It makes no difference.' But I am far surer that this was, and is, a holy place than you are sure that it is not. For your confidence is founded on ignorance. I am sure that our prayers are listened to, just as you are sure that they fall on deaf ears. I am strengthened by my faith and you are enfeebled by your doubt. I am willing to die for what I believe. Tell me—are you prepared to die for your doubt? Your skepticism is weak—*weak*—and the fervent man will always triumph—not only in the eyes of God, but in the hearts of men and women too."

No one spoke. A dead leaf scratched its way in the breeze across the floor. Clarenceux looked up to the windows; the weather was changing, the sun dimming behind clouds.

"I am going to pray now," he announced, "and I am minded to kill anyone who ridicules this house of God or otherwise disturbs me."

Captain Johnson looked around. Silently he gestured to his men and pointed to the other end of the nave. Clarenceux listened to them withdraw. He remained praying for the next forty minutes, until a man entered the church at the west end and shouted: "They have returned."

He crossed himself. He stood up and slowly returned by way of the south aisle and the door to the refectory. He saw the women walking along the far side of the cloister. The waiting men there jumped to their feet. Alice ran along the cloister when she saw him. Her eyes were alight and she said in an excited voice, "Thomas says, do you remember the thirtieth of June last year? It was like that day."

Clarenceux nodded and looked at the faces around them. He smiled at her. "I remember it well. I remember it so very well." Then, with a sigh and a final glance at the sky, he walked up the steps and into the refectory.

Awdrey wept as she embraced Thomas in a chamber at the Saracen's Head. For a long time they could not speak to one another but could only communicate through their eyes and their tears. Mildred was pleased to see Thomas too and ran to the old servant for a hug.

"Where is William?" Awdrey asked. "And who was that young woman who led us here? She was riding Maud. And she mentioned William."

"She is a whore's daughter and probably a whore herself—but she can clean and tidy a house, and for that we must be grateful."

Awdrey nodded. Thomas noticed how pale she was looking.

"How is Annie?" she asked urgently.

"She is doing well, at Cecil House." Thomas watched her losing strength. Suddenly she staggered and lurched to one side, resting against a wall.

"Mistress Harley!"

She tried to speak but no words came out.

"I will get you some water," he assured her. "Sit down, do not strain yourself."

Thomas hurried across the room and fetched the ewer. There being no cup in the room, he presented her with the ewer and tilted it so she could drink.

"Where is he?" she whispered.

Thomas knew it was his duty to lie. But he also knew that Awdrey would see through him straight away. "He has given me instructions to take you away from here as quickly as possible. They know where you are."

"Thomas, Thomas! Tell me where he is—you are not answering me! I have things I need to tell him." Her hair awry, shockingly pale, her eyes searched his face. Mildred began to cry. "After all this, after everything that has happened to me—tell me now where he is."

Thomas sought his heart for direction. "He is bringing the business to a conclusion. He is destroying the document."

"Where? When can I see him?"

"Mistress Harley..." But Thomas could not say the words. He breathed deeply. "You cannot see him again. None of us can."

Awdrey did not understand. Ever since she had been abducted, she had drawn strength from the knowledge that somewhere in England her husband would be striving to find and rescue her.

"Thomas, please, tell me now—I cannot stand this silence! Tell me where he is—I must see him! Why are you being so evasive? Can you not be honest with me? Please—I am begging you, take me to him."

"No! He is in danger. God knows it is none of my deciding, but he has decided to burn down the building containing Greystoke and the document."

"With himself in it?" Awdrey let out an anguished scream. Mildred's eyes widened in alarm and she began to cry. "Does...does he know about what...what happened to me?" she asked, unable to breathe, reaching out to Thomas, taking hold of the front of his doublet. "Does he know? Is that why? Oh Lord! Let it not be."

Thomas said only, "I need to take you to Oxford, Mistress Harley. You and Mildred must get away from here. We will hire a coach there to take you back to Annie…"

"I want my husband, Thomas. I want to see William." She shivered as she spoke.

"Mistress Harley, you are not well. Eat something and then let us ride to Oxford."

Trembling, she reached for the door. Then the realization hit her: the complete and irrevocable loss of her happiness. She felt faint, her knuckles white on the edge of the door, and to stop herself from passing out, she lay down on the ground. There, breathing heavily, her mind recovered its clarity. And she wept.

Clarenceux closed the door to the refectory and bolted it. Walsingham was standing on the far side of the room, with his back to the east window. Greystoke was sitting on the near end of the bench by the trestle table, with his back to the south-facing windows. Joan Hellier went to stand beside Greystoke. Alice stood beside Clarenceux.

"To whom should I give the key?" she asked.

He did not answer but started to walk across the room, very slowly.

"You have no choice but to give it to me," said Walsingham. "You have seen how many men I have here. None of you can leave this place without my permission."

Greystoke laughed. "Francis, you think like a clock. So regular.

Tick, tick, tick. Steadily all the pieces move to your winding—and not a single second is too small to be overlooked. But the operation of your clock is only as good as the reliability of the pieces. I'm afraid certain cogs have been changed."

Clarenceux reached the corner of the room, not far from Walsingham. There, a few inches off the ground, unnoticed by the others, was a thread looped over a nail in the wall. It hung down between the boards of the floor. Clarenceux bent down, unhooked the thread, felt the weight of the iron bar suspended in the room beneath, and let go.

They all heard the bar hit the stone floor of the undercroft below.

"What was that?" said Walsingham.

"The sound of my gauntlet hitting the ground," said Clarenceux, straightening up. He took off his cloak and let it fall to the floor. With slow steps he walked toward the lectern, looking from Joan to Greystoke; he ascended the three steps to where the monks used to read to their fellows during mealtimes. "Did you think it would be that easy? Did you think—any of you—that I would give up something that valuable in return for merely restoring to me that which is already mine? Did you think I would ever give up the document to a man who so foully abused my wife? And who took my daughter from me? Did you think I would give it to the woman who murdered Rebecca Machyn? I know why you want the document, Joan Hellier—to save your daughter. And I know why you want it too, Mr. Greystoke. For political influence. But both of you have set yourselves on a path that means you and I will always be enemies. That was your choosing, not mine, and I will not give that document to my enemies."

"I am not your enemy, Mr. Clarenceux," protested Walsingham.

Clarenceux ignored him.

"It is over, Clarenceux. I will take the key. You have lost." Greystoke stood up and started to move across the room.

"Joan," said Clarenceux quickly, "if you let that man take the document, you will have failed. He has used his friendship with Father Buckman just as he has used his friendship with Walsingham. He will never deliver the document to Lady Percy, for she is a supporter of Lord Henry Stewart. He is an adherent of the queen of the Scots, and he will take the document to her—or to Rome."

Joan turned to Greystoke, wide-eyed. "Is this true?"

Walsingham looked from Clarenceux to Greystoke and back to Clarenceux. "Have you any evidence for this?"

Clarenceux shook his head. "The truth is the truth, whether or not there is any evidence." He smelled smoke.

Greystoke drew his sword and walked around the end of the table. "A duel is what you want, Clarenceux? Well, that is fine—I am as willing to kill you as I was to rut with your wife."

"Let Mr. Walsingham go first," said Clarenceux.

"No," said Greystoke, taking his position beside the chest. "I think it would be unwise of me to let Mr. Walsingham go now."

"Mr. Greystoke, what do you mean by this?" shouted Walsingham.

Greystoke pointed his sword at him. "You stay where you are. You have nothing to add to this discussion."

Clarenceux stepped down from the lectern and drew his sword. Wisps of smoke rose between the floorboards. Greystoke saw Clarenceux's attention elsewhere and lunged forward immediately. At the last moment Clarenceux parried the blow and stepped to his right, cursing himself for the small mistake. Again Greystoke darted forward; their swords clashed repeatedly as Clarenceux drove back the attempts to stab and cut him. Each time he was giving way to Greystoke.

"I smell smoke," said Walsingham in alarm. "There is fire!"

"I told you that you were no match for me," jeered Greystoke.

Clarenceux swept his sword down and jabbed forward toward Greystoke's thigh but the younger man responded swiftly by turning his defense to an attempt to slash across Clarenceux's face.

"Mr. Walsingham, you know you are honored," declared Clarenceux. "Your friend here was trained by the great Camillo Agrippa, the Catholic swordsman of Rome. Four years, was it not?" he demanded as Greystoke stabbed forward and turned his strokes into a flurry of cuts so fast that Clarenceux had difficulty moving his own blade to defend against them. Again he stepped back and Greystoke attacked, turning an attempt to run Clarenceux through the gut into a swipe across his face, slicing through the cheek. The pain made Clarenceux cry out, and he raised his hand instinctively, feeling the looseness of the flesh. It was a huge cut. Red blood poured across and down from the wide wound. Alice stared in horror.

"Fire!" shouted Walsingham. "Get out of here."

"Not without the document!" said Greystoke, trapping Clarenceux behind the table.

"Then you will die!" shouted back Clarenceux, holding his face with one hand and lifting his sword with the other. Smoke was pouring into the room now through the floorboards. Joan ran to the chest, and then stopped and stared at Alice, who had produced a pistol. Greystoke and Clarenceux did not see it, not taking their eyes off each other. Walsingham did not see it either, as he hurried across the room, choking, and reached up to unbolt the door. But as he yanked it open, Alice pulled the trigger. The report of the gun stunned them all. Walsingham turned and tried to see what had happened, but there was too much smoke in the room.

As the echo died away, Clarenceux looked through the smoke. Greystoke had just been blown flat, a hole torn through his stomach. He wiped his eyes and saw blood flowing across the floor. The man was still alive, just. Still holding the side of his face, Clarenceux glanced at Alice, who lowered the pistol and dropped it.

He stepped over Greystoke's body. "You told me I could not beat you in a fight," he gasped. "But a true fight is more than fencing. And I do not play fair. There is no man on earth I despise more than you." He pointed his sword at Greystoke's right eye. "Go straight to Hell," he said, waiting a second more. Then he plunged the point down and watched the blood seep into the eye socket.

The room was filled with smoke now, the open door only just visible as a shade of light. Clarenceux coughed and sheathed his sword. The noise of the fire in the undercroft was growing louder.

Joan shut the door and bolted it.

Clarenceux heard the bolts and shouted, "What are you doing? Leave this place, both of you while you still have time. You have no need to be martyrs—this is not your war."

"My daughter's life depends on that document," replied Joan. She appeared through the thick smoke, holding another pistol—her own. Clarenceux coughed. He could hear Alice coughing too.

"Open the chest, Alice!" Joan ordered.

"I am trying!" snapped Alice. "But I can only unfasten one lock."

Clarenceux's face was still bleeding and his eyes streaming with smoke-driven tears. He could not stop his coughing. "Alice, get out," he gasped between convulsions of his chest. "Run, now!" He coughed again. "There is a keg of gunpowder underneath the chest, in the undercroft. As soon as the fire reaches it, the room will explode and burn. This is not your fight!"

Alice coughed again, struggling with the key. "No, this *is* my fight. Lady Percy sent me here, along with the other women. She has my mother, Mary Vardine, in her prison. She will let her burn at the stake for killing my stepfather if I do not take her the document—and I would rather burn myself than let her die in that way."

"No! Leave it!" urged Clarenceux. "That is the wrong key. I threw the real one in the fishpond when you were away."

The fire below was roaring now. Clarenceux lunged for the latrine door, to get air to breathe. "Alice!" he yelled looking back. "Leave the chest. You cannot open it."

Joan turned and ran to the center of the room. Spluttering and coughing, she aimed the pistol at the right-hand lock of the chest and fired, smashing it inward. Clarenceux heard the shot and charged back through the smoke. "Leave it!" he commanded as she struggled to open the lid. "Leave it!" he repeated, drawing his sword.

"Curse you, Clarenceux," she spat. "Curse you! Curse you!"

Blind now from the smoke, he slashed desperately through the air. But Alice appeared and grabbed his sword arm. "Joan, do it!" she shouted. He fell to one side and landed on Alice, seeing the orange of the flames through a crack in the floorboards as he went down. Still she held him, trapping his arm. He kicked her and rolled away, then crawled to the chest, feeling it now open and Joan's arm reaching up. With a lunge he thrust toward her body and felt the point puncture her flesh. She screamed in agony, but he cut and stabbed again and again, feeling the point enter her body three times until he heard a scream stop in her throat and her body fall to the floor. Frantic now, he slammed the chest shut, but immediately felt someone trying to open it again. "Give it to me!" Alice's hysterical voice rose above the roar of the fire.

Clarenceux felt Alice's shoulder and grabbed her around the neck. He dragged her kicking and struggling to free herself through the smoke to the door in the wall leading to the old latrine. He pressed her against the wall in the alcove, trapping her there, her cheeks hard against the stone. Still she struggled, even clawing over her shoulder at his wounded face in her attempt to return to the chest.

Suddenly, with an almighty explosion, the gunpowder in the basement caught. Even though they were both protected by the corner of the wall, it smashed them hard against the stone and knocked out their legs from under them. It tore the floor in the center of the room and shattered all the windows. Clarenceux struck his head as he fell. Senseless for a moment, the rising heat burned him awake, scorching his face and leaving him gasping for the cold air that now rushed through the latrine to feed the flames. Part of the tracery in the windows fell out.

Clarenceux felt a semiconscious Alice stir feebly. "Down the shaft—there is water at the bottom," he bellowed at her, hearing his own voice faintly through deafened ears. "Follow the water. Tell Lady Percy what has happened. Tell her the document is no more. Do that for me. Tell her that it is over. It is over."

Choking and gagging, in a state of shock, Alice steadied herself on his arm. Without another word she climbed into the shaft and let herself down, holding on to Clarenceux's hand, trying to slow her fall by grabbling at the stone sides of the shaft. Then she was at the bottom, in darkness, with air rushing toward her and water running away. Numb, she knelt and began to crawl. But within a few yards, when she thought of what Lady Percy would now do to her mother, she put her forehead down into the black water and there, on her knees, she halted—and started to cry.

Walsingham looked at the roaring flames leaping up through the refectory. His face was sweaty and smoke-smeared: despite his diminutive size, he looked fearsome. His men were now gathered in a line from the great pond to the building, passing along any containers that would hold water—buckets, helmets, and cooking pans, even a horse's nosebag. But it was clear that nothing could save the building or anything within it. The two men charged with throwing the water through the windows, who were both standing on a cart, had to come away. Even where he was, forty feet from the wall, he could feel the heat of the flames on his cheek. Within twenty minutes of him leaving the refectory, the roof had caught, the flames leaping up and flowing out through the tracery of the windows. Thick smoke billowed out of all five windows and stretched across the sky.

Captain Johnson approached him. "I don't think we'll be seeing Mr. Clarenceux again. Nor his pretty lass."

"How many of these men are loyal to me, Johnson?" snapped Walsingham. "Before he died, Mr. Greystoke said that 'certain cogs' in my clock had been changed. I would like to know what he meant by that."

"Sir, I am sure that all the men here are—"

"Find the traitors, Mr. Johnson, or I will have you and every tenth man hanged in their place. Instruct Captain Walker to the same effect. Scour the ground. If Greystoke hid or dropped anything here I want it found. Search the sewer system too—it is possible that people are hiding in the old tunnels."

Johnson nodded, bowed, and departed. Walsingham watched him head back into the abbot's house. He looked at the men between him and the pond. They were gathered now in groups, staring at the flames. Pieces of burning ash wafted high on the breeze and gently descended, still glowing.

From his position in the wood, Fyndern watched the thick smoke rising and the flames licking at the roof at the east end of the refectory. He shivered in his wet clothes. A mixture of emotions pulled at him. He felt proud that he had lit the fire as Clarenceux had asked, and that it had burned so well—and yet he was sorry that he would never hear him say thank you. He had come to depend on Mr. Clarenceux's words of trust and encouragement. He was pleased to have escaped through the drain, going down to the fishponds, but his overwhelming concern was for Alice. She had gone back into that building, he was sure. He longed to go into the cloister and search for her, to make sure she had escaped; but if she was not in the fire, Walsingham's men had her by now.

The birds sang in the trees above him. Sitting down in the shade he felt tears come to his eyes. The young woman whose sparkling eyes, beauty, and dancing had so captivated him was lost. And there was no way of knowing. He tried to feel whether she was alive—and he could not. All he could feel was his utter wish that she should be well. All he could hope for was that she should return to Mr. Clarenceux's household to work. And that was all he himself could do now. It was that or go back on the road and make his living from guessing the cards.

The cards! Fyndern felt in his pocket and pulled out his pack of cards. They were soaked and had stuck together. Colors had run; the kings and queens were weeping. He threw them down and looked again at the smoke in the sky, rising faster than ever. He had no choice now; he would have to return to London.

He stood up, picked a long grass, and idly swished it in the air. It was going to be a long walk.

82

Tuesday, February 18

Francis Walsingham lay blinking on an old bed in the abbot's lodging. He had slept for half an hour and had just been awoken. It was still dark, except for a single candle burning nearby. Captain Walker had told him they had found the girl, Clarenceux's messenger. She had been hiding in the drains beneath the abbey, not far from the pond.

"Is she alone?" asked Walsingham.

"My men have been all the way through both drains. There is nobody else."

"Where is she now?"

"Outside, sir."

"The fire?"

"It will not spread."

"I will see her," he said, rising to his feet.

Alice was brought up into the chamber with her hands tied behind her back and two men holding her by the arms. She was bedraggled and shivering. Five other men accompanied them.

"Give her a cloak," said Walsingham as soon as he saw her.

One of the men went looking for a garment.

Walsingham walked to her and looked into her eyes. He appreciated her beauty, her youthfulness, her proud mouth, her precocious sense of her womanhood. "Where is Clarenceux?" he asked.

"He did not come with me. He stayed in the refectory."

"Why would he do that?"

"To protect the document. Until the very end. Destroying it, and his enemies, and himself—that was how he thought he could save his family."

Walsingham looked up into the dark roof beams of the abbot's chamber. The silence seemed to reach him, waiting for him to say something: to have the idea that would resolve the night, the burning and the mystery of Clarenceux's death.

"Who was the woman with Greystoke?" he asked.

"Her name was Joan Hellier. She was sent by Lady Percy to serve Father Buckman."

"How do you know these things?"

"I was working in Mr. Clarenceux's household with Thomas and Fyndern. Mr. Clarenceux prepared us for what we had to do."

Walsingham looked at the guards. "Leave us, all of you," he ordered. When they had left he pointed to a bench. "Sit down." He put his foot on the edge of the bed and rested his arm on his raised knee. "You are going to tell me everything now. Where is Clarenceux and how did he get out? More to the point, where is the document? Who started the fire?"

At first light, Walsingham stood at the top of the steps leading into the refectory, looking down. The fire was still smoldering, intense heat rising, flames dancing along pieces of blackened timber on the huge pile of ashes in the undercroft, smoke still rising in the roofless space. Burned joists jutted out of the wall; there was nothing left of the floor. The wind had picked up and was whirling hot ash around the room, causing him to step back to avoid it coating his clothes and getting in his eyes. On the left, sections of the blackened plaster had fallen away; only the door through to the latrine and the fireplace remained as recognizable features, now meaninglessly high in the middle of the floorless wall. On the right-hand side, two of the windows had lost their tracery and presented broken arches against the sky. The others were stark, skeletal shapes of blackened stone.

"Gather the men to form a chain again," he ordered Captain Walker. "This must all be doused and searched today. I want that chest found, even if all that is left is pieces. The girl says it was laced with gunpowder. But she may be lying."

83

Thursday, February 20

Awdrey sat at the table in Cecil's study. She was red-eyed still from rubbing away the tears, and aching in her soul as well as her body. She stared across at the fire, which had burned down, and closed her eyes. Fire. It would always haunt her, she knew. The thought that across all England her husband did not exist, and there was nowhere she could go to speak to him, and yet men like Walsingham still existed, and Father Buckman, sickened her. The only good things that had happened to her in the last few days were hearing that Greystoke was dead and seeing Annie again. But in herself she felt empty. Part of her was missing.

Sir William and Lady Cecil came into the room and greeted her; Sir William was hobbling with his gout, wearing nothing on his right foot. Despite his slowness, he shut the door carefully behind them.

Lady Cecil put her hand on Awdrey's arm. "I cannot begin to say how much I feel for you. Looking at Annie growing stronger day by day, I longed for when you would be reunited as a family. I am so sorry."

Sir William came closer and held out a piece of paper to Awdrey. It was addressed to her in her husband's handwriting. "He left this with me in case something happened to him. I understand you might want to read it alone. But before I leave it with you, I wonder if you could tell me something. Does the thirtieth of June last year mean anything to you?"

"Yes," she whispered. "It was a very hot day when William and I went for a dinner by the river at Richmond with our girls. We were very happy. I told him I had never been happier in all my life."

Sir William held out the letter. Awdrey took it, her hand shaking. She turned it over, looking at it, seeing her husband's seal intact on the back. Just the sight of her name written in his hand made her want to weep.

Lady Cecil squeezed her hand tightly then left. Sir William also withdrew, closing the door gently behind him.

Awdrey closed her eyes and tilted her head back, not wanting to suffer the emotions she knew she would feel when she opened the letter. She took a deep breath and said a prayer for her husband's soul. Opening her eyes, she looked at the letter and slid her finger beneath the sealed flap.

My dearest wife, my love, my life,

I write this letter in my study, where you have seen me on so many nights, working by the light of a candle. No doubt you have often wished I was not such a bookish man—so wrapped up in old tales, heraldry, ancient chronicles, and charters. But by the time you read this, you will know that I have done a very unbookish thing. I have no way of conveying to you how sorry I am that I have caused you so much worry over these last three years, and so much suffering in recent weeks. I did what I thought was the right thing at the time, when I took possession of that book from Henry Machyn. That one act has wrecked our lives. If, through destroying the document and our mutual enemy, I have managed to restore your good opinion of me, and our daughters' safety and prosperity, then I will have achieved all that I can hope to achieve.

I have not made a formal will—there has not been time. Nevertheless I trust that this letter will serve the same purpose. I pray that you will settle my debts, those upon lease and in shop books. To our faithful and loving servant Thomas I pray that you pay the sum of twenty pounds of good and lawful money. To the boy Fyndern who has lodged with me these last weeks and looked after our horses, I will that you pay him his wages and give him suitable reward for his courage. To the boy Nick, whom I so wrongfully dismissed from my service, if you can find him, I would give the wages owing to him and five pounds. To the girl Alice Vardine who has also lodged with me, I pray that you pay her the wages I owe her at the time of reading this and a fine new dress. Perhaps she might take the position recently occupied by our late servant Joan? That is something I leave to your discretion.

You do not know this but there is a cottage and small farm in the parish of Wargrave, in Berkshire, which is in my freehold. I purchased it for the purpose of hiding the document two years ago. The deeds you will find in my study, in the small chest beside the table. I wish you to go there to see the tenant, John Beard, and to give him five pounds. They are good but poor people, and I wish them to do well.

I pray that you have some two dozen gold rings made for friends in London, that they may remember me. My historical and heraldic manuscripts I wish you to give to the library of the College of Arms but only after Mr. Julius Fawcett has had the chance to look over them and select any items he would like for his own library. To Tom Griffiths, a tenant of mine near Aldersgate, I give and forgive six months' rent.

The chronicle of Henry of Abingdon I wish to be returned to its rightful owner, Sir Richard Wenman, of Caswell in Oxfordshire. My father's sword I bequeath to our daughter Mildred, to be passed to her eldest son; and my Bible in English I bequeath to Annie. I would like my manuscripts and preparatory notes for a visitation of Devon to be given to Mr. John Hooker of Exeter. Finally, the elm table in the hall I bequeath to your sister's husband, Mr. Andrew Holcroft, as a memento of our friendship.

To you, my dearest, beloved wife, I leave everything else.

I urge you to bring up our daughters in the understanding of the True Faith. Teach them that it is better to live peacefully under a Protestant queen in the eyes of the Lord than agitate and live in a state of war, and cause our fellow believers to be persecuted. God knows the truth of faith lies in our hearts, not just in what we profess. I wish them and you peace.

Know that I love you and always have loved you, and I weep to think that I shall not see you again. You have been the greatest joy of my life. You are young and beautiful; you can make a new life for yourself. When you feel the time is right, it is my will that you marry again—a gentleman suitable to take charge of our daughters' upbringing. And when they marry, on their wedding days, kiss each of our daughters for me, and know that in their bodies, my blood mingles with yours still, and, in their kisses, I am kissing you.

Farewell, my love,
William

Awdrey let the paper fall from her fingers. The world was cold, and only shadows moved in it; the only color was gray and the only sound was silence.

84

Friday, February 21

That afternoon, as light was beginning to fade, Cecil passed under the arch of King's Gate at Whitehall Palace and saw the boy there, Ralph Cleaver. The boy bowed low, backing out of Cecil's way. "I see you have gloves, young Ralph," he called.

"Her majesty ordered them for me," replied the boy enthusiastically.

"Excellent," replied Cecil, continuing on his way. "May they last you many years. If you see Mr. Walsingham, tell him I have been expecting him for two hours now."

Walsingham was waiting in the paneled parlor at Cecil House.

"You have a considerable amount of explaining to do," said Cecil sharply when he saw him. "First to me, then to Mistress Harley and, depending on your answers, to the queen. What were you thinking?"

Cecil hobbled across the room, his gouty foot causing him great pain. He poured himself a glass of sack and sat on a turned wooden chair near the fire, pushing his foot out in front of him. He did not offer a drink to Walsingham.

"I am sorry. I knew Greystoke would betray Buckman. I knew he had no love for Lord Henry Stewart—"

"You just did not think he would betray you as well." Cecil knocked back his sweetened wine. "I trusted you. I defended you against Clarenceux."

"I am sorry. He was right. What more can I say?"

Cecil shouted with fury. "You could damn well tell me that he need not have paid for being right with his life! You can tell his widow that she need not have lost her husband, and his daughters their father." He took a deep breath. "The truth I have learned is this: it took a loyal Catholic to stop the damage that a loyal Protestant was about to do."

"I had the queen's best interests in mind."

"You always do. Fortunately for us, the late Clarenceux was similarly high-minded—and he was the better man. Have you caught the priest, Buckman, yet?"

"I have men working on it."

"Oh, God's wounds, Francis! Where is your sharpness, your attention to detail? You have become complacent. Find him, arrest him, and then haul him into the Tower and hang him by his hands every day until we know everything he knows."

Walsingham stood, waiting for Cecil's next onslaught. When it did not come, he said, "I have sent men to search Sheffield Manor for the children that Mistress Harley said are imprisoned there, with instructions to restore them to their families, if they find them."

"That is a start," replied Cecil. "You can also take this as an order from the Privy Council. Lady Percy is never to be allowed out of that house again. Inform her that she is under house arrest for the rest of her life. The income from her estates is to be confiscated. Her nephew Lord Shrewsbury is to be told to limit the amount he gives her to the bare minimum. She is not to meddle in his courts. Only specially designated servants may enter her house, showing a license on each occasion. All her present servants are to be dismissed."

"What shall I do about the girl—the one found in the abbey?"

"Let her go. Clarenceux trusted her. He employed her—she can return to his house."

"She doesn't want to return, she says. She wants to see her mother."

"Well, let her do so, if she has a mother. Help her, for Christ's salvation!"

"And after that—do I still have your confidence?"

"Neither of us can be proud of the parts we have played, Francis. Neither of us. We both did our best and we both failed. But we are true and honest men: we learn from our defeats. At the very least we might know what to watch for next time—and be thankful to Mr. Clarenceux that the Percy-Boleyn marriage agreement is no more."

85

Saturday, February 22

Awdrey was sitting by the fire in the dark hall at home, staring into the flames. Fyndern had retired to the attic for the night, and both Annie and Mildred were long since asleep. Thomas came up the stairs from the kitchen, his slow footsteps creaking on the floorboards. Entering the hall, he looked at Awdrey. "Mistress Harley, may I speak to you about something?"

Awdrey looked up at him. "Of course. You do not need to ask."

Thomas closed the door to the back stairs and pulled a bench over from the table. He sat beside Awdrey looking into the flames.

"I know this is possibly going to add to your distress, but I feel obliged to tell you something about Mr. Clarenceux. He asked me not to tell you, but if he is dead now, my obligation, as I see it, is to you."

"What do you mean by 'if he is dead'?"

Thomas shuffled, uncomfortable. "On St. Valentine's Day he and I were in the tavern on Cheapside by the sign of the Mermaid. It was to be Mr. Clarenceux's last night in London. There were just the two of us, and no one was near. I pressed him on his plan, asking him to promise me that he was not planning to kill himself. And then he said something—but I promised never to tell a soul."

"Tell the flames," whispered Awdrey. "Speak into the fire."

Thomas pulled the bench closer to the hearth. He leaned forward and talked, looking into the glowing red logs and flickering flames. "Mr. Clarenceux told me a story about two knights who had persuaded the abbot of Thame to shelter them from their pursuers. They knew of a secret chamber in the abbey that could not be found even if the building was searched. I believe that Mr. Clarenceux knew how to find that chamber."

Awdrey was quiet. Eventually she said, "What good would it have done? Nothing was left of that refectory but the four walls. Mr. Walsingham has assured us that only the girl was in the tunnels beneath."

"That is true," admitted Thomas. "But Mr. Clarenceux has given you a trail of places to visit, heading to your sister. There is this farm belonging to John Beard in Wargrave, in Berkshire; then he urges you to go to Caswell, in Oxfordshire; then Exeter in Devon; and finally the table has to be delivered to your brother-in-law in Devon. Why did he specify those things? Sir William Cecil and Francis Walsingham, if they had seen that letter, would not have known where your brother-in-law is living. Heaven knows if Mr. Clarenceux survived, but he means you to follow that path…"

"We made just such a journey two years ago," said Awdrey, looking at Thomas. "We stopped at a house in Wargrave; I remember thinking how strange it was that we went there. I will think about this, Thomas. Thank you for telling me."

"Don't thank me," said the old man. "I just whispered it to the fire."

86

~

Thursday, February 27

Awdrey stood at the front window, looking out at Fleet Street as the rain slanted down. The light was a strange orange-pink, and the clouds dark gray, giving the houses on the other side of the street a lurid aspect.

It was late in the morning, when the rain had finally subsided, that they set off with a hired cart and two Flemish horses. The elm table was wrapped in canvas and straw and tied upside down on the cart, and covered with another canvas sheet. The two girls traveled with Thomas on the front of the cart; Awdrey and Fyndern rode on Brutus and Maud.

No sooner had they set off than it became clear that the cart would slow them up enormously. It took them all the first day to reach Brentford, with the wheels of the cart sliding into ruts and puddles, and regularly requiring a shove or a levering out of a ditch. That night they stayed at an inn—which greatly excited Annie and Mildred—before continuing through more changeable weather to Wargrave, which they reached in the late afternoon. The lane to the cottage was mired in sloppy mud and standing water, and the cart rocked heavily as they tried to pull it down the lane. Eventually they gave up and left it under Fyndern's watchful guard in a barn just off the highway. The girls traveled with Awdrey and Thomas on the horses down to the cottage in the valley.

Awdrey looked at the moss-covered thatch and the low eaves of the place, and the pigs rooting in the mud-strewn yard. She chose the driest spot she could find to let Mildred down and then dismounted, by the wall of the house, beside a cart with a broken wheel. The cottage door was open for the light, and she knocked. A tired-looking woman in a brown dress smelling strongly of smoke appeared in the doorway, squinting. She took one look at Awdrey and bowed, averting her gaze. "Oh, Mistress Harley—good day to you. John's away; he'll be back soon, I assure you."

"You know my name?"

"Of course," she replied. "We heard from the vicar's boy that you would come before long. No other gentlefolk come this way."

Awdrey glanced at Thomas.

"Watch that sow, she'll have your arm!" warned Agnes as she saw Mildred in the yard trying to feed a large black pig a handful of mud.

"May we come in?"

Agnes welcomed them both in and gave them a bench to sit on overlooking the fire in the middle of the room. "I can offer you fresh bread," she said, "but we don't have butter. It has been a long time since we have had butter. I have some apples."

"Apples for the children would be much appreciated," said Awdrey, with a smile as the smoke from the hearth wafted in her direction.

"The vicar's boy told us we best be goodly behaved but he didn't say when you'd be coming…" She went outside and called, "Girls, do you want an apple each? Oh, John's here."

Agnes stood back as her husband entered the house. "Mistress Harley has arrived, John."

John Beard bowed to Awdrey. "We are honored."

Awdrey introduced Thomas.

John looked at his wife in the smoky gloom. "We did hear you would be coming and we would have made better provision to entertain you—except we did not know when. Although your husband recently said he did not require the rent, we have been trying to gather as much as we can. I have sold the last of our chickens and—"

"It doesn't matter," said Awdrey suddenly. "I do not want your money."

"But, Mistress Harley, it is *your* money."

Awdrey stood up. As she did so, so did Thomas. "Do you remember the old ways of the church, Goodman Beard? When we used to pray for the souls of the departed? Men used to found chantries so that priests would pray for their ancestors' souls forever."

"Of course, Mistress Harley," replied John, astonished. "But we are told now that we cannot pray for the souls of the deceased. They are either in Heaven or in Hell. Purgatory was never a place for souls except in the beliefs of heretics."

"Well, there are some of us who still put our faith in the old religion, and the old ways. My late husband was one such man. But as you observe, it is no longer permitted for Masses to be said or sung for the deceased. Therefore I would ask you to pray for his soul, silently, every Sunday. If you are willing to swear to do this, I will forgive you all the rent you owe."

John looked at Agnes. Disbelief mixed with joy was evident in their faces. "But your husband," said John, "he was well and strong just a few weeks ago. We shared our broth with him. What happened?"

"There was a fire," she said simply, feeling in her pocket and trying to suppress the emotion rising in her. "William made a will of sorts. He bequeathed this to you."

She handed John a leather purse. He took it and felt the weight of the coins inside. He tipped them into his dirty palm to show Agnes; there were ten gold coins of various sizes, and sixteen silver ones. "Oh, sweet Jesus," whispered Agnes, clutching her husband's arm.

"I will pray with all my heart and soul for his soul and your kindness of heart," said John. "Thank you."

John and Agnes urged Awdrey to accept what little hospitality they could offer for the night, and the couple's good humor and honest conversation won her over. Fyndern was told that the cart was safe; he and Thomas stayed in the barn while Awdrey and the girls slept in the inner chamber of the house.

As feasts went, Awdrey had rarely had a more modest one. But everything tasted all the finer for it being so precious.

—❦—

Having crossed the Thames at Reading, they spent the next three days dragging the cart through the wet roads to Caswell in Oxfordshire. Arriving at the old moated house, they learned that Sir Richard and Lady Isabel were away. However, the chamberlain seemed happy for Awdrey and her family to stay at the house until the master returned the following evening.

"What the devil did your husband do to my abbey!" exclaimed Sir Richard at supper with Awdrey, after she had given him the book. It was just the three of them—Sir Richard and Lady Wenman and Awdrey. Fyndern and Thomas were eating separately, with the servants. "Damn it, the refectory was one part I was meaning to keep. Why could he not burn down the rest of the old ruin?"

Lady Isabel dabbed a napkin to her mouth. "Have a little more sympathy for Mistress Harley, dear heart. I am sure she regrets the loss of her husband more than you regret the loss of your windows."

"I am sorry if I offend you. He was a good man, William. I should very much like him to be dining with us." Sir Richard drank from his cup. "It is altogether a morbid business, this losing one's friends. It is the way of the world. You start out, you and your friends wanting this and that, wanting wealth and power, lands, horses, mistresses, hawks, exotic food—and then you wake up and you have got all the things you wanted, and are alone." He pondered, his knife in his hand, his eyes not looking at the meat in front of him. "I will miss him greatly."

87

Thursday, March 13

It took them a full twelve days to bring the cart as far as Exeter. Near Chippenham they lost a wheel as a tire came loose, and the spokes and rim fell to pieces. Mending that took two days, as a wheelwright had to be brought out to measure the old one, and then he had to return to town to make a replacement. Awdrey and Thomas took the girls on to Bath, to show them the hot thermal springs where physicians recommended ill people bathe for their health, but when they arrived they did not like the smell or the look of the water—or the look of the ailing multitude who were already bathing. Fyndern remained with the cart, which gave him the opportunity to practice his card skills in the inns and make a little money, which he then squandered on entertaining a succession of women of various ages, some of whom fell for his charms and some of whom charged him for theirs. For her part, Awdrey began to worry about the amount of money she was spending.

It was with relief they reached Exeter and found themselves at the house of another friend. John Hooker was deeply grateful for the manuscripts they brought and was both shocked and saddened to hear of Clarenceux's death. He had received a note from him recently that gave him some information about the barony of Idrone. Clarenceux had also said that he hoped he would look after his wife on her forthcoming journey to see her sister. When Hooker expressed his regret and sorrow in the most heart-rending words, Awdrey was again conscious of how fortunate she had been in her marriage.

"But of course," said Fyndern mischievously, "Mr. Clarenceux directed us only to call on the people who would speak well of him—all the people he mentioned in his will. It was not as if he was without enemies."

"It is ironic that in death he has no enemies when in life he had so many," observed Thomas.

The next and final day of their journey was the hardest, going west of Exeter. As Hooker had remarked, "Exeter is the edge of the civilized world. Beyond here you cannot travel by coach unless you are on one of the two principal highways, either to Plymouth or to Launceston. Cross the Tamar and the people don't even speak English. The way you are going, I predict your cart will break a wheel or an axle on the granite-strewn tracks."

It was the perfect place to hide away, thought Awdrey, knowing that if her husband *had* survived the fire, this would be where she would find him.

They proceeded into a mild drizzle for most of the day, and a wind from the west made that drizzle soak through their traveling clothes. Either side of them, the wind tossed the trees—and as they came to the boulder-strewn ford across the fast-flowing River Teign, they decided that Hooker had been right: the cart could go no farther. A miller was persuaded to shelter it and the table in a barn while they proceeded on the horses to find the house where Awdrey's sister and her family lived.

The road reached up a steep-sided gloomy valley, between trees that were ancient and wild. Such woods seemed mysterious and the girls were frightened. Even in the daylight shadows loomed. Few people took this road, and those they passed seemed unwilling to do more than nod acknowledgement and walk on. In many places oaks leaned over the track, their trunks and boughs covered in green lichens and moss. Fallen trunks were completely covered in moss, with last year's bracken and dead leaves around them. The steep rise of the road between the granite boulders was also difficult, but once out of the wood, where the road leveled, the brightness of the place was noticeable. Snowdrops broke the ground here and there, and birds sang continuously above them. The hedgerows were green with grasses and brambles, and punctuated by rabbits' burrows and holes large enough to be badgers' setts. Ivy hung from the trunks of oak trees. For Annie and Mildred it was an adventure: a revisiting of the Garden of Eden—except with drizzle and a cold westerly wind.

Late that afternoon, they arrived at the old granite manor house, set in a sheltered nook of a hill, with mullion windows on the ground floor and two huge granite chimneys rising through the whole build-ing. Awdrey's sister and brother-in-law and their six children and three servants had heard in advance of strangers coming their way, and stood at the front to welcome their visitors. Awdrey saw them as she rode into the yard and searched for William's face. She could not see him. Living on the moor had given her sister a healthy, ruddy complexion, and she smiled as she saw her, but even so, Awdrey looked away, still seeking William. Annie and Mildred wasted no time going off to play with their cousins, but Awdrey dismounted half in a dream, or a daze, and walked forward close to tears, to kiss her sister and brother-in-law.

After the greetings, Mr. and Mistress Holcroft led Awdrey and her servants into the hall. A large fire was blazing away in the immense granite fireplace. Candles burned on both sides, their wax dripping fat down into the rushes. Awdrey took off her wet safeguard and handed it to one of the Holcrofts' servants and warmed her hands. She stared into the flames, swallowing back the disappointment, unable even to look at Thomas.

"We knew you would come soon when we received a letter from your husband," said Mr. Holcroft. "He enclosed one for you too."

He held it out to her. The paper looked yellow in the candlelight. She felt the beating of her heart quicken and her chest tighten. She could not say a word. But, watching her own hand, she saw herself reach out and take the letter and open it. She took a deep breath, said a few words of prayer, and started to read.

My dearest heart,

I hope you never read this. I am only writing it out of fear that something will go wrong with my plan. You will know by now that the letter I left with Sir William Cecil was a message of love—but it was also one of hope. The time it will have taken you to get here should have given me plenty of time to reach this lonely, lovely place in the moor. But if you are reading this, it is a journey I will never make.

I have little time to write and so many things I would like

to say to you. One is that it is perhaps better this way. You would not want to live your life hiding out in the granite clefts of Devon. Nor would you wish to be tied to an old man hiding in such a remote place. You are young, and you can yet make another man happy, for you are the perfect wife. No man could wish for more. Mourn no more than the requisite year, and marry again with my blessing, as I said in my last letter.

For the sake of the reassurance that human memory offers, make a small monument somewhere with my name on it. What you write shall be your choice of words, but if you would do me one final kindness, inscribe my motto on it somewhere: In all our struggles, the last word is hope. For those words have given me much strength over the years, when times have been hard.

Kiss our dear daughters for me. Bless them.

And now, for the last time and forever, good night my sweet Awdrey, my Etheldreda, my love.

Epilogue

Three weeks & four days earlier
Monday, February 17, in the refectory of Thame Abbey

Coughing, and with his eyes stinging as the smoke poured around and into him, Clarenceux felt Alice tighten her grip on his hand. She was as low as she could go, panicking, shouting. He loosened his grip on her wrist and let her fall the rest of the way down the shaft. Then he crossed himself, said, "Go with God," and pulled himself to his feet.

The heat from the fire was terrific, and growing rapidly. He could see nothing except smoke and flame in the room, and could not even tell if the floorboards between him and the fireplace were still able to hold his weight. Tentatively, keeping one foot on the stone floor of the latrine alcove, he stamped on them. They held. The stone itself to which he was clinging was hot now. His eyes and his wounded cheek were stinging terribly, his naked skin burning with the heat. The time had come for him to make his decision. He could either follow Alice down the shaft and live, and face the next attack when it came, or he could take refuge in the monastic hiding place and bring the whole cycle of fear to an end, as he intended.

Stepping onto the floorboards, and trusting God to help him, he crawled into the stone fireplace, his hands and face burning with the extreme heat that rose through the floor. He reached up into the fireplace and found the protruding stone he had discovered when he had first made this climb, when he had come here with Sir Richard Wenman. It was harder with the pain of his wound and the blindness of the smoke, his eyes shut, coughing, and constantly wanting to be sick. But up he went, his fingers grappling for the stones that he could be sure would hold him. As he rose inside the chimney itself, he felt the heat and smoke rushing past him, as he knew it would, reaching for the light and the sky above, which was a mere gray-brown patch at the top of the chimney. He retched and almost lost his grip, pulling his heavy, tired body up toward the wooden door that was set back into the side of the stonework fifteen feet above the base of the fireplace. Up he hauled himself, until his fingers finally reached the sill of the small doorway. Pressing himself back against the narrowing wall of the chimney, he brought his leg up and found a secure foothold, then moving higher, he pushed open the door. It gave way to a small windowless chamber. With a final effort, panting and gagging, he heaved himself half into the chamber, and then drew up his legs, kicking shut the six-inch-thick oak door behind him.

He listened to the roar of the fire, lying in the darkness of the chamber. It was built within the thickness of the double-wall between the refectory and the chapter house, and measured just six feet in length, five feet in height and four feet in breadth. It was only large enough to take two men, but it was secure. Surrounded by a mass of thick stone, it was impossible to see even when looking up the refectory chimney, due to the constant blackness of the soot and the setting back of the door. It was also designed so that the smoke would rush up past the door, allowing the occupants to breathe. As Clarenceux knew, the flames and smoke would rise past the door regardless of whether the fire below was small enough to fit in the hearth or large enough to engulf the entire undercroft. The fire would burn for days—he estimated three—but all he had to do was to lie here and wait. He had some bread in a pocket to help with the hunger.

He coughed again in the darkness and waited, thinking ahead. Walsingham would have to pass on the news that the building had been engulfed by flames and he had been inside at the time. The complete destruction of the building would mean that Awdrey would be told that he was dead, and she would read the letter at Sir William's house. She would recognize the route they had taken two years ago, or Thomas would; and it would take them three weeks from now to cart that table all the way to Devon. By then he would have reached the house and could rip up that last letter. Even though it would be advisable for him to have his face stitched up, he could have that done in Oxford. After three days, he would wait until nightfall, and then let himself down the chimney; bathe and wash his clothes in the great fishpond as best he could; dress himself; and head into Oxford across the fields. He had enough money for new clothes, food, and the surgery bill; he would not need to leave a name. He would dress like a husbandman and sleep rough on his journey to Devon. It would take him seven or eight days.

The roaring of the fire was growing. The speed of the draught and smoke ascending the chimney gave the impression of being at sea in darkness, in the belly of a ship. Clarenceux held the door shut with his foot and looked forward to the darkness and the noise being over.

The first hour gradually passed. His attention turned to his face and how much it stung. He held his cheek to make the wound close up. The events in the refectory returned to him, and he reminded himself how he had stabbed Joan Hellier in blindness—not in order to revenge Rebecca, but to keep the document safe. To preserve the queen. To prevent a war. He was glad it had been that way—Rebecca would not have wanted him to be vengeful. But by the same token, he was glad that he had been able to kill Greystoke, even if the man was already dying from Alice's shot.

The document was no more and his family was safe—those were the main things. Whatever happened now, he had succeeded.

He tried to take a deep breath and struggled to fill his lungs. The air was warming up now. From the great bonfires he had watched on Maydays in the past, he reckoned that the most intense burning would be over within four hours. He would just have to wait for a short while more. But waiting was getting difficult. He squirmed in the darkness, trying to fill his lungs again, and although he managed it, it left him feeling uneasy. He started to turn around in the room, taking his foot off the thick oak door for a moment. A red glow filled the space, which he could see was beginning to let in smoke. Hurriedly he slammed the door shut again with his foot. He felt himself start to panic. The chimney was designed so that the heat would drive the smoke upward; he had nothing to fear from a small amount trickling into the chamber through the gaps in the door. That was nothing. But his fear rose, despite his attempts to reason with himself. He was finding it harder to breathe.

He did not know it, but the outside of the ancient door was beginning to burn. Such was the heat coming up the chimney that the oak, which had dried out thoroughly over the last two centuries, was beginning to smolder. Its antiquity would be the death of him. The tar that blackened the outside of the door was now burning; the outside of the door itself was a sheet of flame. The air rushing up the chimney contained hardly any oxygen; and little by little, sip by sip, the flames were drawing the oxygen out of Clarenceux's hiding place. The chamber that had no difficulty sustaining two men when there was a small hearth fire below now became less and less inhabitable. He felt his lungs tightening; there was no chance of him taking a deep breath. He tried to calm himself and started to pray, silently, so as not to use too much air, but the shortage of oxygen in his lungs made him more desperate with each breath. Eventually, terrified, he turned, keeping the door shut for the moment with his foot, hoping to open it just a little and suck in some of the air that he believed would be rushing up the chimney. He did so—and he saw the front of the door blaze furiously. He slammed it again, tears running down his face, smoke in his eyes and lungs. He could not breathe. He could not leave his place of suffocation.

He began to pray that the fire would die down, that God would help him in this, his hour of greatest need. But an image came to his mind. He had asked the question ever since the days of the old king, Henry VIII, how one man—albeit a king—could command the faith of another. He had wondered no less with the accession of Elizabeth. And now it was being shown to him. He began to understand. Fire needs air to breathe, and when he pinched out a candle he deprived it of air. The Lord Almighty was pinching out the candle of his life. The Church would pass to the next generation, and they would accept the new faith; his generation would be pinched out, one by one, like so many candles of the Catholic Church.

He could not breathe now. His lungs fought to open and to inhale the glorious air of nature, but there was nothing he could do. He could choose to suffocate or he could choose to burn. Many before him had chosen the latter; he could remember the screams. He chose not to move, despite the pain in his lungs. He was like a fish on land, flipping in agony, its gills struggling for the water. It hurt; his lungs were burning within him.

"Calm yourself," he said. "The Lord Almighty will protect and preserve you." As he struggled to breathe, he realized that the voice he had heard was not his own. It was a woman's voice. He was dizzy and felt sick, but the nausea passed, and he heard the woman's voice again. "There is a way out, through the back of the chamber."

So real did her voice seem to him that he opened his stinging eyes and looked into the darkness. The chamber went back farther than he had realized. He moved away from the door, which fell slightly open, flames lighting the way. It was easier to breathe now, on account of a draught of air from the back of the chamber, and he was glad for that. More red light entered, letting him see the shades of a woman's face in the darkness. He began to crawl toward the rear of the chamber, tracing the path of the fresh air. Someone took his hand and lifted it, gently pulling him to his feet. Although the chamber was low he found he could stand quite easily here. Still he could only see vague movements in the darkness of the woman who had spoken, who was leading him away.

Suddenly he stepped into brilliant light—glaring sunshine. The fresh air washed his face; even his wound no longer hurt. He was on the roof of the chapter house, in the afternoon sun. He saw the thick billowing smoke and the men around the building. Further away he could see Awdrey and Mildred with Thomas, setting out on the road to Oxford. He turned to the woman beside him, who was dark-haired and smiling. She was familiar—he had always known her. She was his conscience, his soul, his second self. It seemed strange he had never noticed her before. She had always been with him throughout his entire life.

He did not know what to say, but he did not need to speak. The breeze raised ripples across the surface of the lake, which caught the sunlight. Looking further, he could see the road to London, where he knew his daughter Annie was playing in the garden of the London house with Robert Cecil.

"This is a good way to die," he said eventually.

"Are you ready to let go now?"

"Yes, I am ready." He looked back over the trees of the parkland to where Awdrey was riding with Thomas for Oxford, with Mildred in the saddle with her. "In all our struggles, the last word is hope," he whispered.

"But in the final struggle of all?" she asked.

He smiled. "In the final struggle, the last word is love."

Author's Note

This book is not primarily about the past. Only a few of the events described in it actually happened. Rather it is about loyalty and betrayal—loyalty to, and betrayal of, one's religion, one's kingdom, one's friends, and one's spouse. Any of these loyalties and betrayals is likely to meet with a shrug of the shoulder if set in the modern world, but in the past they were treated much more seriously.

On the day I sat down to write this note, June 3, 2012—the day of the Diamond Jubilee royal pageant on the Thames—I heard an English republican being interviewed on television. He voiced his firm opposition to the continued existence of the monarchy. Such comments in the sixteenth century would have resulted in that man being drawn to the gallows, hanged, cut down while still alive, disemboweled, his guts burned in a fire in front of him, and then his body cut into four parts, each with a limb attached and displayed in his hometown, with his head being placed on a spike on London Bridge. He probably would have been tortured for several days beforehand, to extract the names and whereabouts of fellow antimonarchists. After his death, his wife and family would probably have lost everything they owned as his entire estate was confiscated on account of his treason. And that would have been the *official* reaction, not a psychotic individual's vindictiveness. Women were burned alive for the same crime.

Loyalty to religion has undergone much the same shift. Today public opinion is not outraged if someone changes their faith from Catholic to Protestant or vice versa, or from Christianity to Islam or Judaism. Although in Elizabeth I's reign the number of heretics burned at the stake went down, such executions still took place—as the burning of two Anabaptists in 1575 shows. Catholics were regularly tortured and hanged (especially later in the reign). Again, these were official responses. As for the crime of adultery, there were moral courts at which men and women could be presented even for the merest suspicion for being "lewd" or "naughty" with an unmarried person or someone's spouse.

Loyalty and betrayal simply meant so much more in the sixteenth century than they do today. This is why I set the Clarenceux trilogy in that period.

I do not subscribe to the view that historical fiction has to represent past events accurately. If I wanted to write about the actual past (as far as it can be known from historical evidence), I would write a history book, not a novel. Besides, one cannot write a novel that is truly "historically accurate." The historical record available to us is always incomplete, and often ambiguous, lacking in clarity and open to multiple interpretations. The "facts" (insofar as anything can be factual) are not in themselves coherent enough for us to tell a "true story" at anything more than a superficial level, or in outline. The very best one can achieve is a story that is put together in an intelligent, imaginative, and inspiring way, with integrity—like Renaissance paintings of the Madonna and Child, or the crucifixion, which are all invented and thus false. No painter knew what

Mary or Jesus looked like in the flesh, nor what the weather was like or what the crowd was wearing on the day of the crucifixion: such paintings are symbolic, representative of aspects of Christian culture. But if they were painted intelligently and with integrity, they have purpose. Inaccuracy is neither here nor there when it comes to judging the meaning of imaginative work. Historical fiction is similar in that respect: it may be false but it is symbolic of the past and that symbolism is desirable—in my case to give a suitable backdrop to a story of loyalty and betrayal.

This perspective has brought me into collision with the more traditional historical novelists, most memorably for me in an exchange with Hilary Mantel at the "Novel Approaches" conference at the Institute of Historical Research, London, in November 2011. In her keynote speech Hilary emphasized the importance of being accurate and "authentic." She picked out an example of two historical characters being conflated into one in the television series *The Tudors* to illustrate the depth of inaccurate, inauthentic writing common today. As it happened, I had been invited to write a blog post on this conference for the Society of Authors, and wrote the following reflection on the talk immediately afterward:

> *I could not help but put up my hand first when it came to question time, for I come from a very different point of view. This is because the social landscape of the past is much too interesting to be seen as a backdrop only to what actually did happen. Historians and novelists alike can investigate what didn't happen, whether through "Virtual History" essays or wholly imaginary fictions. And as for simplifying characters, few people ever say that Shakespeare's* Henry IV Part One *is a weak history play*

because it conflates the two Edmund Mortimers into one, so that the Earl of March becomes the husband of Glendower's daughter. Hilary responded that "there is no excuse for ignoring the written record…many heinous crimes are justified because Shakespeare did them. But you are not Shakespeare." Who did that "you" refer to, I wondered: had she aimed it directly at me? I suddenly felt as welcome as Coleridge's man from Porlock. A little later, she charmingly suggested she might have been a little harsh, and that what she had said only really could apply to her own work. She does not make rules for other writers, she said.

I have some sympathy for Hilary's complaint. In an article in the *Guardian*, "The lying art of historical fiction," I had similarly criticized the suggestion in the film *Braveheart* that William Wallace (who was executed in 1305) seduced Princess Isabella (born 1296, queen of England from 1308), and was thereby the father of Edward III (born 1312). That lacked intelligence, as well as integrity. However, the message of my article was that the real test of historical fiction is not how accurate it is but how *good* it is. I stand by the opinion expressed above: "the social landscape of the past is much too interesting to be seen as a backdrop only to what actually did happen." If you follow the example of my *Time Traveler's Guides* and make a journey into whichever kingdom or country in the past interests you, then why not set a story in that country? The sixteenth century was the ideal setting for my trilogy.

There are some aspects of this book that *are* based on historical evidence, however, and it may be useful to draw attention to some of the more interesting ones, as some of the details are surprising or little known.

To begin with, the document that lies at the heart of this story—although it probably never existed—reflects circumstances surrounding the marriage(s) of Anne Boleyn that might well have been true. For further details about this, see my Author's Note to *Sacred Treason*. In that book, the key to the location of the document is hidden in the chronicle of Henry Machyn, a parish clerk and a Merchant Taylor, who wrote an account covering the years 1550–63 (today this is in the British Library: *Cotton MS Vitellius F v*). He was first married to Jone, who bore him several children, including his son and heir John; and later to Dorothy, by whom he had three daughters, all of whom died in infancy. At his death in 1563 he bequeathed his chronicle to his friend, the herald William Harvey, Clarenceux King of Arms, on whom I based my William Harley. I changed the name to emphasize the fictional nature of this character. Likewise I changed the name of Henry Machyn's wife from Dorothy to Rebecca to allow a greater degree of latitude with the facts (and because too many people said the Yellow Brick Road came to mind when they read the name "Dorothy").

Obviously certain other characters in this book are based on real people—Queen Elizabeth; Sir William Cecil; Francis Walsingham; Lady Percy; the earl of Shrewsbury; Sir Gilbert Dethick; Sir Peter Carew; John Hooker; Sir William Drury; Richard Grafton; John Stow; and various Scottish persons, including Lord Henry Stewart (also known as Lord Darnley), Mary Queen of Scots, and Lord Bothwell. I will not insult the reader's intelligence by pretending my characters closely reflect their historical namesakes; they do not. The queen, Sir William Cecil, and Walsingham all carry something of their real selves, but they appear here primarily as signifiers of power—Elizabeth I representing the throne, Sir William Cecil the authority of the queen's Secretary, and Francis Walsingham the connivance of a "spymaster." However, the details concerning the succession and the circumstances of Elizabeth's birth and official illegitimacy are correctly related, as are the details of the plot to kill Lord Henry Stewart (Lord Darnley).

It is in the social detail that I have taken pains to represent past reality—to describe what England looked and smelled like, and, above all, how its people behaved. The hanging scene and the bull-baiting are, as you may expect, heavily imagined, as I have never witnessed either, although some rather unsavory images on the Internet assisted in the recreation of the bull-baiting scene, and I bore in mind Dickens's famous letter to *The Times* when writing the hanging scene. Similarly, the level of violence toward women is extrapolated from what I know of the legal cases of the time. It is important to remember that violence was endemic in Elizabethan England—and so was sexism and belief in the divinity of the social hierarchy. Today we cannot tolerate such sexist and hierarchical attitudes, but they were normal in the sixteenth century, and violence against women was much more commonplace than we could possibly accept today. Anyone who thinks I have overdone this aspect should reflect on a case I noted in my *Time Traveler's Guide to Elizabethan England*. As Joan Somers tended to her mistress's cattle in a field in late 1590, a man called Rice Evans came up to her. He seized her and told her that she could cry out as much as she wanted, for there was no one to hear her. He then raped her violently. Later she realized that she was pregnant. When others noticed, she was summoned to court and prosecuted for the sin of fornication. That is the measure of the degree of sexism inherent in the law. As there were no witnesses, Evans was not prosecuted; instead *she* was the one taken to court to face the consequences and ultimately punished for *his* crime.

In a similar vein, people might wonder about the plight of women in jail. The situation as related here—that women sentenced to death were not hanged if they "pleaded their bellies"—is true. So are the processes alluded to herein; a woman might try to get a jailer, fellow prisoner, or some other man to make her pregnant to put off the day of execution, hoping to slip through the system. Many failed to escape, being hanged not long after their child had been born, taken away and given to a wet nurse. But some were successful in evading the noose. Other aspects of women's roles in society reflected in this book include cleaning—all laundry was performed by women—and the restrictions on women obtaining professional positions. As alluded to by Mr. Wheatsheafen, a woman in the diocese of Exeter did receive a license in surgery in 1568: this was Mary Cornellys of Bodmin, who qualified as a medical practitioner a full three centuries before Elizabeth Garrett Anderson—but exceedingly few women did likewise. And, apart from midwifery and the duty of being a church-warden, that was the only professional or official role permitted to women at the time.

There are a number of characters in this novel who are called John, William, and Thomas. Not only is Clarenceux called William, but Sir William Cecil also appears regularly, and there are passing references to Sir William Drury and William Willis. As for Johns, there are John Beard, John the Egyptian, John Blackwell ("Sir John"), John Greystoke, John Lucas, "John Black," John Parker, John Hunter, John Machyn, John Stow, John Wyclif, John Badby, and John Hooker. Why so many? The last-mentioned five were historical personages. I did think of removing some of the others—but the fact is that more than 50 percent of the entire male population was called John, William, or Thomas, and John was the most popular of the three—so thirteen Johns was about right. In case readers are wondering about a clergyman being called "Sir John," in the early years of Elizabeth's reign, incumbents of parishes still were addressed in this honorific way. As for children's words for their parents: according to the OED, supplemented with further references by my friend Susannah Davis, these were "Mam" and "Dad," and even "Daddy" is to be found in a fifteenth-century poem by John Lydgate.

I ought to admit that I have not always been consistent in using the correct sixteenth-century nomenclature. I have made no attempt to reflect the speech patterns of the period, which many people would find very awkward to read. Moreover, I have been deliberately anachronistic with some terms, such as "nursing." This did not relate to looking after the sick in the sixteenth century; women "attended," "tended," "helped," "kept," and "watched" with the ill, but "nursing" was synonymous with wetnursing. However, explaining such things in a novel—and not using such terms when otherwise I was using normal modern speech—seemed counterproductive and unlikely to enhance the reader's enjoyment.

Certain places are described with verisimilitude—Wynkyn de Worde was actually buried in St. Bride's Church, and its vine-covered columns were a notable feature. The church was indeed lacking a vicar in 1566. Greyfriars Church had lost all its monuments, as described here, including the alabaster tombs of queens, in the 1550s. Portchester Castle was being used as a military hospital. Thame Abbey was a Cistercian house of monks; parts of it survive that indicate the layout was unorthodox. The lake or great fish pond on the east is still there; the church however, has entirely vanished, even though it was about 230 feet long and had a Lady Chapel extending it another forty-five feet. Henry of Abingdon was a real person and he did attend the Council of Constance—but he did not write a chronicle. The Lollard knights are partly based on reality but the story about them taking shelter in Thame Abbey is fiction. The actual hiding place used by Clarenceux exists—but not at Thame. I don't know where it is. I was told about it at an event by a member of the public and promptly forgot about it until thinking through the end of this novel.

The authors Grafton and Stow were actually at loggerheads about the use of Stow's information. In fact, all the sixteenth-century books quoted in this novel are actual texts—including Grafton, Agrippa, and Gratarolus.

I stated in my *Time Traveler's Guide to Elizabethan England* that the cauliflower was introduced to England at a dinner for the Privy Council in 1590, but subsequently I noticed one in Joachim Beuckelaer's painting in the National Gallery, Four Elements: Fruit and Vegetable Market (1569) and another in a work by the same artist dated 1564, so clearly they were available in the Low Countries in the 1560s.

Religion is perhaps the most important and most difficult contemporary detail, and it is a subject I have tried to reflect more accurately than most of the historical novels set in the sixteenth century, which tend to downplay the spiritual values of the age. Some people have expressed surprise that my character behaves as he does, that he has no secret cynical side that allows him to sidestep his religious convictions when it suits him. I find their surprise extraordinary. For a start, atheism as we know it was not really possible in the 1560s. A few people had been accused of being "against God," but as I have written in my Elizabethan *Time Traveler's Guide*, not believing in God was like not believing in trees: the physical and the metaphysical could not be divided. People were deeply involved in the religious quest: the majority of books published in the sixteenth century were of a theological nature. This is out of keeping with the secularism of the twenty-first century; it is difficult for modern people to understand. However, there is a comparison. The religiosity of the sixteenth century was powered by an ardent quest for truth. So too is the atheism of the present day. I am not referring here to the mindless sort of atheism espoused by those who have no concern for anything other than shrugging off religion in the hope of freeing themselves in some way or other from organized religion's limitations. I am referring to those who positively seek the truth, who wish to understand the nature of life on Earth as desperately as a Catholic in the sixteenth century would have sought God's will, and who are not satisfied with explanations that depend on the Old Testament or any other religious text.

When twenty-first-century atheists are challenged as to their lack of belief in God, their faith in God's absence often proves as unshakable as sixteenth-century faith in God's presence: convinced atheists and people following a religious quest are not dissimilar in that respect. In Clarenceux's searching questions about why God makes the righteous suffer, and his skepticism of how one man can order another to change what he believes, I hope I have provided a sixteenth-century struggling spirit who, on the one hand, is true to the religious standards of his time, and on the other, is an adequate metaphor for both the religious searching soul and the inquiring secular mind of today.

(Ian) James Forrester (Mortimer)

Acknowledgments

I did not include an acknowledgement page in either of the first two volumes of this trilogy, *Sacred Treason* and *The Roots of Betrayal*, so I hope readers do not begrudge me using this page to thank a few people for their help bringing the whole trilogy to fruition.

My first acknowledgement of gratitude is to someone I don't know. In the late 1990s an editor at the *Oxford Dictionary of National Biography* sent me a standard commissioning form asking me to write a new entry for the chronicler or "diarist," Henry Machyn (d. 1563). In the course of the research undertaken to fulfill that commission, I discovered much more about Henry Machyn than was previously known (published in full by the *Sixteenth Century Journal* in 2002). In particular, I found that he left his "cronacle" (as he called it) to William Harvey, Clarenceux King of Arms (*d.* 1567). I also discovered a reference to the informal sixteenth-century London association or group of friends who called themselves the Knights of the Round Table, of which Henry was a member. It was that reference which first inspired these novels. Obviously there have been many other inspirations along the way— people and places, personal situations and stories—but the very first spark came from that research. So, a big thank you to whoever it was at *ODNB* who sent me that commission.

My agent, Jim Gill at United Agents, deserves a round of applause for taking the first book, *Sacred Treason*, and finding a publisher when it was still unfinished. I'm very grateful to him for that vote of confidence. Also I am grateful for the foreign rights agents at United Agents, Jane Willis, Zoe Ross, and Jessica Craig, for the encouragement they have given me in selling these books to foreign-language markets.

A very big THANK YOU goes to Martin Fletcher of Headline Review, who commissioned the trilogy and whose enthusiasm for the story in *Sacred Treason* and the two latter novels has been inspirational. I am also very grateful to Martin's colleagues at Headline Review, especially Samantha Eades, not only for helping produce the books but for being so imaginative in finding ways to publicize them. Also to Joan Deitch, who copyedited all three books—and who had to contend with the vagaries of my style. The whole team at Headline has been wonderful.

Thanks to Suzannah Lipscomb for the tour of Hampton Court, and to Susannah Davis for all the references to "Mam" and "Dad." Thanks to my brother, Robert Mortimer, of the London Fire Brigade, for advice about how burning buildings consume oxygen.

I am grateful to a few of my neighbors and friends for helping inspire various characters' appearances and mannerisms in these books, especially the first two. I won't name all the names—but you know who you are. One person I will mention: I am particularly grateful to Andy Gardner, whose conversations in the lanes around Moreton—when he has taken the time to stop his van and chat—have been one of the most pleasing aspects of the process. No doubt Raw Carew will find another ship soon and sail off into the sunset.

I began with an anonymous thank-you and my penultimate one is also to someone I don't know. At an event in Newbury, Berkshire, in 2011, a member of the public came up to me and told me about her house. There was a hiding place in it, a priest hole, and she had lived in the house for many years before she found it. I do not know who she was or where the house is, but the story lodged at the back of my mind. Readers of this book will realize how much I gained from that little detail.

Finally, and most of all, I wish to thank my wife, Sophie. I am grateful for her support and encouragement. She has, at the same time, lifted my spirits and kept my feet on the ground—not a mean feat. I walk all the taller because of her.

Read on for an excerpt from **Sacred Treason,**
now available from Sourcebooks Landmark.

Tuesday, December 7, 1563

It was a cold day for a killing. The Scotsman, Robert Urquhart, rubbed his hands and breathed on them as he waited in Threadneedle Street, in London. Watching the door to Merchant Taylors' Hall, he clutched each finger in turn, trying to keep them supple, his grip strong. He cursed the gray December skies. Only when two men appeared at the top of the steps, walking very slowly and deep in conversation, did he forget the chill in his bones. His victim, William Draper, was the one on the left—the jeweled gold collar gave him away.

He studied Draper. Narrow face, gray hair and beard, about sixty. Not tall but well dressed, in an expensive green velvet doublet with lace ruff and cuffs. Eyes like a fox. He looked selfish, judgemental—even a little bitter. You could see how he had made his money: with an ambition as cold and biting as this weather, and with as little remorse.

Urquhart watched Draper pull his cloak close and wait, standing on the bottom step, above the frozen mud. The man continued talking to his less well dressed companion. The carts and pedestrian traffic of the street passed in front of them, the snorting of the horses and the drivers' breath billowing in the cold morning air.

It could not be done here, Urquhart could see that. Not without risking his own arrest. That would be as bad as failure. Worse—for he knew her ladyship's identity. They would torture that information out of him. Arrest would simply require her ladyship to send another man, to kill him as well as Draper.

He walked to the end of the street and looked back casually. A servant led a chestnut palfrey around the corner from the yard and held it steady, offering the reins to Draper who mounted from the bottom step with surprising agility. Draper offered some final words to his companion from the saddle, then gestured good-bye with a wave of his hand and moved off.

Westward. He was going home.

Urquhart started forward, walking briskly. He felt for the knife in his belt, the dagger in his shirt sleeve, and the rounded butt of the long-barreled German wheel lock pistol inside the left breast of his doublet. He hoped he would not have to use it. The noise would bring all London running.

He followed his victim to his house in Basinghall Street. Four stories high and three bays wide, with armorial glass in the windows. He waited outside for some minutes then drew a deep breath and slowly exhaled, taking a moment to reflect on his mission.

He climbed the few steps to the door and knocked hard. A bald man in knee-length breeches answered.

"God speed you. An urgent message for the master."

The bald man noted the Scottish accent. "Another time, sir, you would be right heartily welcome. Alas, today my master has given instructions that he is not to be disturbed."

"He will see me. Tell him I come with a message from her ladyship. It is she who bids me seek his help."

"Regretfully, sir, I cannot disobey an order—"

"You are very dutiful, and that is to be commended, but I urge you, look to your Catholic conscience, and quickly. Her ladyship's business is a matter of life and death. Tell Mr. Draper I have traveled far to see him in his capacity as *Sir Dagonet*. He will understand."

The bald man paused, weighing up his visitor's appearance and demeanor. He looked at his shoes, dirty with the mud of the street. But the visitor seemed so confident; Mr. Draper might well be angry if he turned away an urgent communication brought by a Scotsman. "Wait here, if you please," he said, stepping backward into the shadows.

After several minutes he reappeared. "Mr. Draper will see you. This way."

Urquhart followed the servant along a dark passageway, through a high hall, and past a pair of large wooden benches piled with bright silk cushions. He noticed a gilt-framed portrait of the master of the house, and another of a stern-looking man in an old-fashioned breast-plate and helmet—Draper's father, perhaps. There was a big tapestry of a town under siege at one end of the hall. Above the fireplace were two brightly painted plaster figures of black women in red skirts, their exotic paganism allowing the plasterer to bare their breasts shamelessly. Here was a whitewashed stone staircase. At the top, a picture of the Virgin. Finally they came to a wide wooden door.

"What is your name, sir?" asked the bald man over his shoulder.

"Thomas Fraser," Urquhart replied.

The servant knocked, lifted the latch, and pushed the door open. Urquhart crossed himself. He loosened his sleeve, felt the hilt of the dagger, and entered boldly.

The room was long, oak-paneled, and warm, and had an elaborate plaster ceiling. Two fireplaces in the far wall were alight, the blazing logs held in place by polished silverheaded firedogs.

The servant turned to his right and bowed. "Mr. Draper, this is the Scotch esquire who has come on behalf of her ladyship. His name is Thomas Fraser."

Draper was sitting behind a table at one end of the room, looking down at a piece of paper. Urquhart saw the same narrow face and gray beard he had seen outside the hall. He stepped forward and bowed respectfully. He heard the door shut behind him and the latch fall.

"You come from her ladyship?" the merchant said softly, looking up. There were tears in his eyes.

Suddenly Urquhart felt nervous, like a boy about to steal silver coins from his master's purse. *Why the tears? Was Draper expecting him?* But there was just one thing to do and the sooner it was done the better.

"Sir," he said, taking another two steps closer, so he was barely six feet from the table. "I come with an instruction from her ladyship." He reached for his dagger.

Suddenly a deep north country voice called out from behind him: "Hold fast! Move no further!"

Urquhart turned. Behind the door as it had opened had been a huge, bearded man dressed in a black doublet and cloak. His hair too was black and curled. In his early thirties, he had obviously seen action on more than one occasion. A livid red mark stretched from above his right eyebrow to his right ear. On his left hip he wore a silver-handled side-sword, and he was holding a pistol.

For one throb of his pulse, Urquhart was motionless. But in that moment he understood what had happened. Her ladyship had been betrayed. He did not know by whom, or how, but it left him in no doubt what he had to do. The instant he saw the scarred man move his pistol hand, he pulled the dagger from his sleeve and hurled it at the man's chest. The next instant he rushed toward him, one hand reaching out to grab the pistol and the other fumbling for the knife at his own belt.

When the gun went off, Urquhart was moving forward. And then, suddenly, he was on his side, the report echoing in his ears.

Only then did he feel the pain. It was as if his scream of agony was a sound formed within the severed nerves of his left thigh. There was a mess of blood and torn flesh. He could see splintered bone. As the sliced nerves and the sight of the shreds of bloody meat combined into a realization of one single, hideous truth, he gasped and raised his head, dizzy with the shock. The rip his dagger had made in the black cloak and shirt revealed a glint of a breastplate. The man was drawing his side-sword.

"You are too late," the north country voice declared. "Our messenger from Scotland came in the night. Mr. Walsingham knows."

Urquhart screamed again as the pain surged. He thumped the floor, unable to master the feeling. But it was not the wound that mattered—it was the failure. That was worse than the physical hurt. It did not matter that he was a dead man. What mattered was that his victim was still alive.

Eyes blurred with tears of shame, he thrust his hand inside his doublet for his own pistol. The scarred man was too close. But he forced his trembling hands to respond and drew back the wheel of the lock. Gasping, he twisted around, aimed at Draper's head, and pulled the trigger.

The noise of the gun was the last thing he heard. An instant later the blade of the side-sword flashed through his throat and lodged in the back of his neck, in the bone. And then he was suffocating and tumbling in a frothing sea of his own blood.

It was not an easy death to behold.

Read on for an excerpt from The Roots of Betrayal,
now available from Sourcebooks Landmark.

Saturday, April 29, 1564

William Harley, officially known by his heraldic title of Clarenceux King of Arms, was naked. He was lying in his bed in his house in the parish of St. Bride, just outside the city walls of London. Leaning up on one arm, he ran his fingers down the skin of his wife's back, golden in the candlelight. He drew them back again, slowly, up to her shoulders, moving her blond hair aside so he could see her more fully. *She is so precious, so beautiful*, he thought. *My Saxon Princess. My Aethelfritha, my Etheldreda, my Awdrey.*

He withdrew his hand as the candle in the alcove above him spluttered. He looked at the curve of the side of her breast, pressed into the bed. The feeling of their union was still with him. The ecstasy had not just been one thrill; it had been many simultaneous pleasures—all of which had merged into one euphoria that had overwhelmed him, leaving him aglow.

She turned her head and smiled up at him again, lovingly. She was twenty-five years of age now. He felt lucky and grateful. Not only for the pleasure but also for the knowledge of just how great his pleasure could be. He leaned over and kissed her.

The candle in the alcove above the bed went out.

He lay down and let his thoughts drift in the darkness. Six months ago he had almost destroyed his own happiness, disconcerted and attracted by another woman. Rebecca Machyn. He shuddered as he remembered how he and Rebecca had been pursued, terrified together. She had seen him at his lowest, and he her. They had supported each other and, in a way, he had fallen in love with her. But he had never had doubts about his loyalty to his wife. That was what troubled him. Two women and two forms of love. It was not something that most God-fearing men and women ever spoke about.

What did he feel for Rebecca now? In the darkness, he sought his true feelings. There was a part of him that still loved her. His feelings for his wife were an inward thing: a matter of the heart. He loved Awdrey because of what he knew about her and what they had built together, what they shared. His affection for Rebecca Machyn was the opposite: an outward thing. She showed him what he did not know, the doubts, the wonder, and the fear that he knew existed in the world.

That outward-looking, questioning part of his nature worried him. The reason he had spent so much time with Rebecca was his possession of a secret document, and that document was still here, in this house. Awdrey did not know. That in itself felt like a betrayal. The document was so dangerous that men had died because of it. When Rebecca's husband, Henry Machyn, had given it to him the previous year, the man had declared that the fate of two queens depended on its safekeeping. And when Clarenceux had discovered its true nature—a marriage agreement between Lord Percy and Anne Boleyn, which proved that Queen Elizabeth was illegitimate and had no right to the throne—he had understood why it was so sensitive.

Only when Sir William Cecil, the queen's Principal Secretary, had asked him to keep it safely did his life start to return to normal. But never did he feel safe. Not for one moment.

He knew, later that morning, he would go up to his study at the front of the house and check that the document was still where he had hidden it. It was a ritual. More than a ritual: it was an obsession. Sometimes he would check it three or four times in one day. The knowledge that he possessed the means to demonstrate that the Protestant queen was illegitimate and that the rightful queen should be one of her cousins—either the Protestant Lady Katherine Grey, sister of the beheaded Lady Jane Grey; or Mary, the Catholic queen of Scotland—was not something he could ever forget. His fear of what would happen if he should lose the marriage agreement beat in his heart like his love for Rebecca Machyn. Both were dark and dangerous. The ecstasy of his lovemaking with his wife was so blissful and so pure by comparison—and yet he could not ignore the dark side within himself.

He felt Awdrey turn over and cuddle up beside him, nestling under his arm. He was a tall man and she of average height, so his arm around her felt protective. She ran her hand over his side, where he had been scarred in a sword fight five months earlier.

"How is it now?"

"Fine."

"I don't want you to exert yourself too much."

"If it had torn just now, it would have been worth it."

He remembered the day when he had suffered the wound—at Summerhill, the house of his old friend Julius Fawcett, near Chislehurst. He wondered how Julius was now. "What would you say to the idea of going down to Summerhill next week?"

"I promised I would take the girls to see Lady Cecil. She wants them to play with her little boy, Robert."

Clarenceux lay silent. Sir William Cecil's wife was godmother to their younger daughter, Mildred. The idea of Annie and Mildred playing with Robert was a little optimistic. Robert Cecil was three, their daughter Annie was six, and Mildred just one. It was Awdrey's polite way of saying that she would not refuse the invitation. Lady Cecil, being one of the cleverest women in England, was something of a heroine to her. Both women had been pregnant together and, although that child of Lady's Cecil's had died, she was expecting again, which made her call more frequently on Awdrey. The relationship was not without its benefits to him too. It was immensely valuable to have a family connection through Lady Cecil to Sir William, the queen's Principle Secretary and one of the two most powerful men in the country, the other being Robert Dudley, the queen's favorite.

Awdrey moved her hand over his chest, feeling the hair. "You could go by yourself."

He was meant to be planning his next visitation. Soon he would have to ride out and record all the genealogies in one of the counties, visiting all the great houses with his pursuivants, clerks, and official companions. The purpose was to check the veracity of all claims to coats of arms and heraldic insignia, and to make sure that those with dubious or nonexistent claims were exposed as false claimants. He had completed a visitation of Suffolk three years earlier and one of Norfolk the previous year. He had finished his notes on the visitation of Devon, and had discussed the gentry of that county at length with his friend and fellow antiquary John Hooker. But he could put off actually going to Devon until June, and so could delay the planning for another week and enjoy the late spring in Kent with his old friend.

"I may well do that," he replied.

Awdrey touched his face. He felt her hand move over his beard and cheek. Her finger traced his lips, then slipped down over his chest, to his midriff.

"How tired are you?" she asked.

About the Author

~

James Forrester is the pen name (the middle names) of the historian Dr. Ian Mortimer. Fellow of the Royal Historical Society and winner of its Alexander Prize for his work on social history, he is the author of four highly acclaimed medieval biographies and the *Sunday Times* bestseller *The Time Traveler's Guide to Medieval England* and *The Time Traveler's Guide to Elizabethan England*. He lives with his wife and three children on the edge of Dartmoor.